Praise for *Absent*

"A searing look at family dynamics and how tragedy and misunderstanding can echo for decades. Sherri Vanderveen reveals the secret—and the soul—of *Absent* with insight and precision."
—Kate Jacobs, *New York Times* bestselling author

"As a reading experience ... the only recent novel even remotely comparable is Mary Swan's Giller-nominated *The Boys in the Trees* ... While *Absent* does not aspire to that book's gothic grandeur, it is the more powerful of the two works, brave and resonant and, ultimately, transcendent."
—*National Post*

"Honest to the core, Sherri Vanderveen's *Absent* is a moving, heart-changing journey through memories and family secrets. This is a tale you won't soon forget."   —Ami McKay, author of *The Birth House*

"The idea of a person being able to flee one life and then invent another is fascinating ... What is charming about *Absent* is its focus on ordinary people; these are regular folks trying to find their way through the brambles of life."   —*The Globe and Mail*

"Vanderveen's talent lies not only in interweaving the characters' complex storylines, but in the precise details she includes ... Vanderveen has the ability to take broken characters and imbue them with hope ... Vanderveen's fractured family is liable to remind readers of their own families. That is the mark of a strong writer and a memorable story."   —*Quill & Quire*

"Besides the understated, impactful elegance of [Vanderveen's] prose .... *Absent* is a fascinating tale of people making do, of crafting as best they can, a life for themselves ... with what they have been left."
—*The Hamilton Spectator*

"Ineffable force and narrative grace ... characterize *Absent* ... Impressive ... There is nothing gentle or flowery about [Vanderveen's] prose. Rather, she allows the narrative, the world of the novel, to accrete fine detail by fine detail ... Owing to it's construction and Vanderveen's almost transparent skill, one is left with a sense of the author's respect for the reader." —*Ottawa Citizen*

"Fascinating and deeply touching ... an intriguing, compelling story about the disintegration of a family and its struggle to heal."
—*Winnipeg Free Press*

"Powerful ... Vanderveen refuses to write herself an easy way out ... The novel shifts gracefully, seemingly effortlessly among ... four characters building understanding and empathy for all of them while simultaneously revealing the flaws in their self-images and views of the world ... Vanderveen resists the predictable and the clichéd to the novel's last word." —*Times Colonist* (Victoria)

"*Absent* is a sensitive and compelling exploration of how one family navigates the emotional black holes of a loved one's disappearance, from the perspectives of the person leaving and those who are left."
—*Scene Magazine*

Praise for *Belle Falls*

"Some of Vanderveen's flashes go straight to the heart of the world's promise and inadequacy ... Beneath Belle's confessional, there's a subtler core of honesty in the book that is all Vanderveen's. When we at last learn what happened in that musty trailer between a despairing old woman and an innocent boy, the scene walks a transgressive knife edge with assurance." —*The Globe and Mail*

"Vanderveen writes with a clear, workmanlike prose that rarely draws attention to itself. While the subject matter lends itself to histrionics and sentimentality, Vanderveen resists the temptation. Instead, she allows Dearing's story to unfold naturally, with an organic pacing leading to a genuine and moving conclusion. It all makes for a powerful work and a most impressive debut." —*Quill & Quire*

"Sensitively written." —*Canadian Literature*

"Vanderveen makes some gutsy choices ... What really works in this novel is Vanderveen's meticulous eye for detail."
—*Winnipeg Free Press*

"[Belle Dearing is] a compelling character, both frustrating and fascinating to the reader." —*The Hamilton Spectator*

ALSO BY SHERRI VANDERVEEN

Belle Falls

PENGUIN CANADA

ABSENT

SHERRI VANDERVEEN was born in Hamilton, Ontario. Her short works of fiction have appeared in several Canadian literary journals. She lives in Toronto with her husband and two children.

For Charles

ABSENT

SHERRI VANDERVEEN

PENGUIN
CANADA

PENGUIN CANADA

Published by the Penguin Group

Penguin Group (Canada), 90 Eglinton Avenue East, Suite 700, Toronto, Ontario, Canada M4P 2Y3
(a division of Pearson Canada Inc.)

Penguin Group (USA) Inc., 375 Hudson Street, New York, New York 10014, U.S.A.
Penguin Books Ltd, 80 Strand, London WC2R 0RL, England
Penguin Ireland, 25 St Stephen's Green, Dublin 2, Ireland (a division of Penguin Books Ltd)
Penguin Group (Australia), 250 Camberwell Road, Camberwell, Victoria 3124, Australia
(a division of Pearson Australia Group Pty Ltd)
Penguin Books India Pvt Ltd, 11 Community Centre, Panchsheel Park, New Delhi – 110 017, India
Penguin Group (NZ), 67 Apollo Drive, Rosedale, North Shore 0632, New Zealand
(a division of Pearson New Zealand Ltd)
Penguin Books (South Africa) (Pty) Ltd, 24 Sturdee Avenue, Rosebank, Johannesburg 2196, South Africa

Penguin Books Ltd, Registered Offices: 80 Strand, London WC2R 0RL, England

First published in Penguin Canada paperback by Penguin Group (Canada),
a division of Pearson Canada Inc., 2009
Published in this edition, 2010

1 2 3 4 5 6 7 8 9 10 (WEB)

Copyright © Sherri Vanderveen, 2009

All rights reserved. Without limiting the rights under copyright reserved above, no part of this publication may be reproduced, stored in or introduced into a retrieval system, or transmitted in any form or by any means (electronic, mechanical, photocopying, recording or otherwise), without the prior written permission of both the copyright owner and the above publisher of this book.

Publisher's note: This book is a work of fiction. Names, characters, places and incidents either are the product of the author's imagination or are used fictitiously, and any resemblance to actual persons living or dead, events, or locales is entirely coincidental.

Manufactured in Canada.

LIBRARY AND ARCHIVES CANADA CATALOGUING IN PUBLICATION

Vanderveen, Sherri
Absent / Sherri Vanderveen.

ISBN 978-0-14-316985-7

I. Title.

PS8643.A6886A63 2010   C813'.6   C2009-906997-0

Except in the United States of America, this book is sold subject to the condition that it shall not, by way of trade or otherwise, be lent, re-sold, hired out, or otherwise circulated without the publisher's prior consent in any form of binding or cover other than that in which it is published and without a similar condition including this condition being imposed on the subsequent purchaser.

Visit the Penguin Group (Canada) website at **www.penguin.ca**

Special and corporate bulk purchase rates available; please see
www.penguin.ca/corporatesales or call 1-800-810-3104, ext. 2477 or 2474

One

WHAT OTTO WILL REMEMBER most about this momentous day, this day of non-coincidences—the small child with the braid, the teenager by the river—is the way the ground seems to bend under his feet, the blades of grass fat and lush after weeks of steady rain. People come at lunch to picnic or sunbathe on blankets or read in the shade, while children play in the park bordered by the river and dotted with clusters of hardy trees. Here the heat doesn't fester and clog the lungs the way it does back east; here the air is glacier fresh, cooled by nearby mountains. Otto sits on a wooden bench roughened by too many winters, his hands held loosely in his lap. He has come, as he often does, to relieve the office strain from his neck and shoulders, his eyes blinking to rid themselves of fluorescent glare.

His feet sweat in his faux-leather shoes, the ones that dig into his ankle bones; he wears them anyway, because brown goes better with beige than black, or at least that's what he has been told, and these are the only brown shoes he owns. He leans down, strips his feet bare, and lets his toes burrow into the cool grass beneath the bench. Before he can enjoy this freedom, another man approaches and sits next to him, nodding slightly in greeting. Otto is dismayed to see this man's shirt, pressed and unwrinkled, while his own is creased at the elbows, and his underarms feel damp. The man carries a pinstriped suit jacket, which he folds lengthwise and places carefully on the bench. The jacket acts as a sort of barrier between them, a warning that assumes conversation will not be necessary, although they both smile pleasantly enough at each other.

When he catches sight of Otto's bare feet, his nostrils flare. He sighs, gathers up his jacket, and moves away, looking back once over his shoulder reproachfully. Otto glances down at his toes, pale and grotesque, bulbous and linty, his nails long overdue for a trim, his heels cracked and dry. He quickly stuffs the offensive appendages back into his socks and shoes, embarrassed by their nakedness and his apparent inadequacy.

Before he sees the child, he hears her name.

Ruby.

Unimportant details register: blond braid, a striped T-shirt, shorts flaring too big around skinny thighs. Her mother calls her name again, beckoning to a blanket unfurled on the grass and held down by Tupperware containers and a juice box. The little girl runs, uninhibited, the braid jumping in rhythm against her back, her arms and legs kissed by the sun, a smear of lotion across her nose. None of this jars him, but the way she falls into her mother's arms—all-encompassing, small mouth open against the woman's neck—does.

A thirty-year gap swallows him whole, sends him tumbling back. Usually the memories only come at night in the silence of his apartment, muffled by carpet and the heavy curtains covering his window. He closes his eyes, but a single scene presses forward insistently: another young girl with a bowl cut and ragged bangs that drip into her eyes, wrists straight but relaxed, fingertips poised above the keys of a piano in a still, silent room, brown drapes closed against the sunlight. (Afterwards, there was no piano, there were no brown drapes. Only charcoal fingerprints and the smell of burned hair. Or so he imagines.)

A shriek, laughter, and the sun beats down on his head. The bench is once again just a bench, weathered and waiting. He stands and nearly buckles, his knees rubbery and suddenly too soft to bear the weight of bones and flesh.

Sometimes the reminders of his old life come in flashes, unexpected and jarring. Earlier today, when he passed an electronics store on his way to the park, a video camera caught him in mid-stride and broadcast his figure on a bank of televisions in the storefront window. There he was: hair thinning on the sides, receding in the front to form a gentle crescent moon, moustache streaked with white and in need of a trim, a starched short-sleeved dress shirt, his beige pleated pants. How different his photograph today, twenty-eight years later. Gone are the long sideburns and black-rimmed glasses, the youthful curve of his cheeks and the way his hair curled on the back of his neck. Gone, too, the newspaper headline—"MAN WANTED IN SUSPECTED ARSON"—though not forgotten. No, never.

Leaving mother and daughter, he heads towards the bridge and stops halfway across, pressing his arms hard against the railing, leaving pink impressions on his skin. Below him, the swollen river churns up silt and surges forward, angry after two weeks of hard rain. To the left on the path by the river, a young woman perches on a rock, her arms wrapped around her bare knees, a crumpled tissue in her hand. From here the tissue seems pristine in its whiteness, a beacon of innocence, first love, and a broken heart.

A jogger brushes by, feet slapping against the walkway, jiggling flesh in shorts and a tight T-shirt, a tiny earphone dislodged and falling from an ear to dangle before the jogger grinds it back in place. Otto remembers when there were no CDs or Walkmans, remembers when earphones were bulky cinnamon buns perched on the sides of his head. He remembers (the acrid smoke in his nose, the way the drapes caught fire and how he ran) listening to rock music in the living room of his mother's house with those earphones plugged into the stereo so she wouldn't hear and complain.

Beyond the bridge, the city rises up in a cluster of mid-sized high-rises and glass-clad office buildings. He touches his moustache, his fingers probing for errant hairs that tickle his upper lip. The river paths are mostly deserted under the bright sun, still too dangerous for pedestrians after the recent flooding; already one kid has drowned, his bloated body found tangled against the riverbank far from his home. The once-pure air—the clean arctic scent of the river—has been tainted by the smell of mud and soaked cardboard. Odd pieces of debris rush beneath the bridge, tangled among broken tree branches: there's one flip-flop, a rusted can, an empty, partially crushed milk carton, and someone's T-shirt.

He watches the girl on the rock, the small scene captured in a square frame from above. She straightens her legs, flicks her head so that her hair flies behind her shoulders. His wife was just like her: same long, pale throat, same mocha hair with streaks of red and a slight wave. She too might have cried like this over him, he thinks. Why not? Though more likely she was glad to be rid of him, no matter what the circumstances. If he tries hard enough, he can rewind the film back to their first meeting in the lunchroom of the insurance company back east, can see his stained and crumpled brown bag and her lavender cloth sack embroidered with the word *Lunch*, her translucent skin, the faint blush high on her cheeks, and the glossy shine resting in the curve of her flipped hair. Days of promise, a small apartment above a clothing shop only blocks from the office, the whisper of smooth legs encased in stockings shifting and crossing under restaurant tables, the lingering hint of perfume on his shirt collars.

His eyes have begun to water, damn them. He now works for an engineering firm, far removed in distance and years from those early days. In his office on the fourteenth floor, the bright fluorescent lights above his cubicle have become more glaring, and his two computer screens give him headaches. That old sense of impending failure has begun to creep in again. They have just hired some thirty-something from the east who makes more money, drives a snazzier car, and lives in a condominium with leather and chrome furniture.

His mother is long gone, but still her voice rises from the darkness when he tosses and turns and worries about work, the increasingly sophisticated computer technology they use now, the young men who understand easily and never make any mistakes, as he does. *Should have stayed in the filing room*, her voice always says. *Who are you trying to fool?* Even as he rose through the ranks, made it to the drafting board tracing layouts, and worked long hours to become a senior designer, her voice persisted, sharp and disdainful. And now, just as she would have predicted, his skills are slipping, as if he has reached his peak, stumbled, and started to slide backward. But damn it, he's sixty-two, after all. He's not expected to stay on top of things forever, is he? *All downhill from here, boy.*

Just this morning, he had settled into his padded black chair, the four walls of his purple cubicle familiar and not yet claustrophobic. He heard the low buzz of morning gossip as colleagues arrived, photocopiers whirring as they warmed up, papers rustled and shifted from one pile to the next, fingertips tapping against keyboards, soft footsteps muted against pale grey carpeting. Otto liked to arrive before everyone else, when he could stand outside an office and pretend that was *his* desk, *his* potted ficus, *his* window overlooking the busy downtown street. He imagined himself reclining in one of those high-backed leather chairs, his family pictures framed and displayed on a gleaming walnut desk. But these offices that occupied the outer rim of the floor were reserved for upper management, jowly men wearing company rings set with diamonds, men well fed on steak-and-lobster dinners.

Otto sipped his coffee and eyed the messy piles on his desk: plot plans, isometrics, layouts, equipment drawings, line lists, process flow diagrams, piping and instrumentation diagrams, and schedules. He selected the most urgent, then looked up as Gary Owens, his boss, rapped two knuckles on the steel bracing of the cubicle.

"Morning, Otto."

"Good morning." Otto sat up straight, expectant, and waited as Gary raised his mug ("Belco Inc." lettered on both sides—of course he would only use a company mug; Otto's bore a picture of a man wearing a suit and tie, his trousers dropped to the ground to reveal red-and-white polka-dotted boxers, a lecherous grin on his face, and the slogan "Mr. Stud"), and smacked his lips.

"I just want you to hear it from me," Gary said, clearing his throat, then coughing. "Darrin's going to be the lead on the India project."

"But ..." *But I'm supposed to be lead; you promised. Darrin's thirty years younger than me; he just started with the company two months ago.* You couldn't say that to a man like Gary, no. Otto swallowed, his lips formed into a semblance of a relaxed smile as disappointment slid down the back of his throat.

"Great opportunity for Darrin," he said instead, and was rewarded by Gary's nod of approval and forceful hand clapping him on the back.

"Next one's yours, Otto," he said. "I promise." Otto rolled his chair back to the edge of the cubicle, angled his head slightly to watch as Gary strode up the aisle. Darrin. There he was, intercepting Gary, his face grinning and head bobbing. Young pup, still wet behind the ears, but he carried that unmistakable aura of possibility and confidence. A go-getter. Otto was never like that. And he sighed, pushed himself back into his cubicle, letting his chair coast, and hit his desk with a gentle nudge, the computer screens blinking to life.

ON THE BRIDGE, Otto rubs his watery eyes. The girl looks up into his stare and mouths a word: *pervert*. She stands, tugs down jean shorts that have ridden high on her leg, and then turns to watch the surge of water and debris. There's a single moment, a flash of recognition when she turns her face to his, and this, the second encounter, is more than simple coincidence, one that steals the breath from his chest and leaves him empty, a sucking wound: Ruby.

Otto lets go of the railing as if burned. His legs move automatically, picking up the pace until they're running, taking him away from the girl, away from the sudden vertigo. At the end of the bridge by the traffic lights, a commuter train rumbles past, bells clanging, blank faces pressed against the windows looking out at him in idle curiosity.

THE DINGY WHITE PAINT of the apartment complex has begun to peel off in sections, uncovering splotches of red brick that look like bloodstains. The lobby smells of disinfectant and mouldy carpeting, and the phone inside the front doors is smeared with fingerprints.

"Afternoon, Ray. Day off today?"

Without turning from his mailbox, Otto places the gravelly voice: Desmond Riff, seventy-nine, retired oil man, alone, old. All of Otto's neighbours fall into the last two categories. He forces a smile.

"Something like that," he says.

Desmond smiles, his skin creasing into well-worn lines, a map of history. Otto holds the door for him, watches him shuffle forward, knowing by heart the complaints he will hear described in the elevator (rheumatoid arthritis, acid reflux). He contemplates taking the stairs, but Otto's no spring chicken himself, and eight floors will more than wind him.

As the elevator groans upward, Otto holds his breath against the stink of enclosed mustiness, slightly sour.

"Anything interesting?" Desmond gestures to the small stack of letters in Otto's hand.

"Mostly bills."

No one writes to him—who would? Bills, offers for credit cards. Once, years and years ago, a white envelope, mysterious and plain, that revealed a detailed dating questionnaire. He filled out his answers while eating his dinner in front of the television that night.

> Why do you date?
> What is your favourite thing to do on a date?
> Do you think moral standards are important in dating?
> Describe your upbringing and ethnic or cultural background.

He had made up his own history when he first came to the city, and how imaginative: a golden-haired mother who died when he was born, a doting father who raised him alone and then died of a heart attack when Otto was twenty-eight, a college education in architecture, and a steady stream of girlfriends, none serious enough for marriage. (It still surprises him how easy it was to shed his skin. He thought it would be harder to disappear like that, but he was wrong. One hand on a Bible in front of a judge, and his new identity sprang from a government envelope, a birth certificate. *Ray Parker*.)

He sealed the questionnaire and placed it in a kitchen drawer. Nearly a year later, he mailed it. He was thirty-seven when he met Corinne, and quite the catch, if you ignored (or didn't know about) the abandoned first wife and children, and the mother suffocated (or burned to death) on the third floor of her house.

How independent Corinne seemed, with her apartment on the main floor of a house that opened up into a small backyard. She took such pains to make it her home, setting trailing plants on the windowsill in the living room, hanging pictures of family (her parents in the city, both grey-haired and lined; a brother, two years older at thirty-five, who lived a few hours away and managed a restaurant with his wife; two nieces, seven and nine, wide gap-toothed grins and white-blond hair) and real oil paintings she had bought from her favourite gallery downtown.

On their third date she showed him her place self-consciously, watching as he took it all in, waiting for his first comment that would set the tone of the evening. *It's perfect*, he said. And it was. She led him to the backyard, where they sat on wooden Muskoka chairs, sipped wine from heavy glasses, and watched the sun set. And then she took his hand in hers, lips stained with red-wine bruises. At nearly every moment, he expected her to recognize him despite the contact lenses, the new moustache. But the pictures the newspapers had published were old by then, forgotten.

On the fourth floor, Desmond leaves the elevator, nodding and smiling as he ambles down the dimly lit corridor. When the doors close once more, Otto lets his shoulders relax. He's no longer such an oddity here. When he first moved in, he was the youngest, the ablest. The other men would greet him, their faces puzzled and curious, but Otto kept to himself, his secrets buried inside, avoiding invitations to poker nights, lawn bowling.

He took the apartment at first sight as punishment, a one-bedroom with olive green carpeting. In his room, he has a bed, an old scratched dresser, and paintings of sailboats on the wall. A long counter with a stove and fridge pushed up against one wall makes up the kitchen; on the opposite side of the room is the living area, with a television on a wooden stand and a brown couch that pulls out to become another bed. The bathroom is possibly the best room, with a claw-footed bathtub, and black and white tiles covering the floor. When he first arrived, he set potted plants on the windowsills in a half-hearted attempt to create some cheer, but they soon shrivelled and died from inattention and lack of sunlight.

He dated Corinne for a year. It was fall when she first asked, on a particularly sunny day. The chill had come early that year; by September, they wore scarves and thick sweaters. They ate lunch together on a bench by the river. She took small bites of her sandwich, stopping to dab her lips with her napkin after each bite, so daintily that he had to smile and was gripped by an urgency he had never before felt.

He took her hand.

"Let's get married," he said, ignoring the panicked voice that rose within him: *No, you can't!*

"I have to ask you something," she said. "We've never really talked about what we want for us, for the future. I want a family, Ray. Do you?"

"Of course." He didn't think about what she meant, not then. But that night, alone, he realized that *family* meant *children*, and that, of course, was unthinkable.

A few days later, he walked to her place in the rain, no umbrella for shelter, letting the drops drip down his neck, making the collar of his shirt wet. When she opened her door, he simply stood, hands at his sides. Did he love her? He did; he remembers he did.

"I'm not Ray Parker," Otto said. He could go no further, the rest of the story caught in his swelling throat. That pale, trusting face now looked confused. She had just washed her hair; it coiled into perfect curls that brushed down her cheek and under her jaw.

At his feet, a puddle formed around the soles of his shoes. Corinne's lips moved, but her words filled with water. He shook his head to clear his ears. Blackness crept from the outward corners of his eyes, tunnelling forward, and Corinne disappeared, leaving Otto with only physical sensations: the pulsing against his temples, the heat spreading up his neck and across his face. For a moment, a wave of dizziness caught him off guard. He blinked, shook his head again, and Corinne reappeared, concerned.

"You're dripping," she said. "Are you sick?"

She moved as if to place a palm on his forehead, but he stopped her.

"I'm telling you something important," he said. "My real name is Otto Sinclair."

"Okay," she said, but her lips twisted. She thought it was a joke. "Still, you'd better come in and change."

"Corinne, please."

"Ray."

He stared at her for a moment. He loved everything about her, the way she lived with such order, the filing cabinet in her office with folders properly labelled by subject and date, colour-coded tabs all facing the same way. She worked in a back room of the house, her bookcase and desk side by side, the small filing cabinet near the back door. The bookcase here had order and reason, unlike the larger case in her bedroom, which spilled over with paperback novels and oversized hardcover books on everything from gardening to Arctic exploration, their spines upside down, some books piled on top of others. In her office, though, such disorder was not permitted. The top shelf was reserved for coffee cans holding pens, pencils, and highlighters; supplies took up the middle shelves (blank paper, a stapler, envelopes and stamps, a box of paper clips); reference books and magazines were lined up on the bottom two shelves.

Once he worked at her place on a Sunday afternoon while she was at lunch with a friend, took out some pens and a highlighter, and left sheets of paper scattered across her desk when he finished. She came in through the front door, chatting and energetic, and froze when she reached the door to the back room, just stopped and stared at the mess he had left behind. He could almost see the enthusiasm drain from her face. She shot him a look of deep unhappiness, betrayal almost, and he realized how important, how necessary, her one place of order had been.

He could never tell her the truth.

"I'm sorry," he said instead. "It would never work out between us." She looked up at him, her face so blank and empty that he could have cried.

OTTO SURVEYS THE PICTURE that hangs above the living room sofa for a long moment. *What a wonderful way to remember your grandchildren*, the woman in the framing store had said. He didn't bother to correct her. Now he dismantles the frame and slides out the crumpled page, his only reminder of the past. He holds it gingerly on his lap, tracing the textured surface, and surveys his room, simple and spare, nearly untouched by his presence for almost twenty-eight years. *Why did I run?*

To leave without warning or explanation is one of the worst things you can do to a child. His chest aches; he has become his father, his absence a tear in the fabric of their lives. Those first years he thought of them always, the pain as sharp in the mornings as at night, but now, time has created the illusion of forgetting.

Ruby.

Gavin.

Lenore.

In his dreams he sees them in silhouette, his wife and two children, their faces indistinct and eclipsed by shadow. He can never replace the lost years or undo the damage, but this he owes them all: the truth, the chance to fill in the gaps of loss. It's time to go back.

Two

WHEN BARRETT COMES DOWNSTAIRS on the morning of his last day alive, Lenore is already in the kitchen, wiping a cloth down the counter as she waits for the coffee to brew.

"Good morning," he says, and she turns.

"You slept late."

"I'm feeling lazy today." He still wears his blue-and-white striped pyjamas, his brown leather slippers.

She smiles, comes towards him for a kiss. "Always were," she says in his ear, and he laughs, holding her close for a moment, his hand on the small of her back, his cheek against hers. As he sits down at the table, he feels the first warning pressure in the centre of his chest, but he shifts and the sensation disappears. *This old body of mine.*

They eat breakfast in reassuring silence. Lenore rises once to turn on the radio, tuning in to a classical station. He thought retirement would bring boredom, a sort of loss or emptiness, but he enjoys these long, slow days.

"What are you thinking about?" Lenore asks.

"Nothing," he says. No difficult cases, no impending lectures, no demands on his time. How different life was more than thirty years ago when he first sat in that conference room, flushed with excitement to realize the potential that lay before him: to change lives by peeling back and reconstructing small faces, to combine surgical skill with a new kind of artistry! He compiled a book of his best work, published and presented papers, travelled all over the world as parents pressed gratitude into his hands. He found it vaguely ironic that he put children back together while he himself fell to pieces in those frenetic early years of his career.

Lenore rests her arms on the table, smiling slightly. A well-loved, familiar face. He has watched the lines deepen around her eyes and mouth, watched her hair lose its glossy shine and fade into grey and white. He knows the muscles responsible for the workings of emotion in that face, has learned to gauge her every shift in expression. It seems remarkable, her constant presence in his life. He still can't justify what he did or how he did it for so long. *Things were complicated*, he used to think he would say, if anyone asked. *Le coeur a ses raisons, que la raison ne connaît point*. Now he realizes it's impossible to explain, save one simple truth: it is possible to love two people at once, despite all best intentions.

He had loved his wife. When they first married, he traced an imaginary trajectory of their life together: home, children, retirement, peace. A framed photograph of an elderly couple holding hands on a bench in the park. He failed to consider disease. For twenty years, a bewildering array of symptoms that came and went, a tide of numbness and tingling creeping along her limbs and then receding, leaving behind a tangled mess of fear, hopelessness. And in the middle of it all, Lenore in the hospital after her son's birth, Lenore years later in his office, applying for a job, her face opening in surprise when he recognized her.

Only once did Rena give any sign that she knew. Late one night—Wednesday, Lenore's night—he came home to find her shaking in the darkened living room. He guided her to the washroom, helped her undress for a bath. Her head seemed too big for her neck and the rest of her body, blue veins pressing outward against the skin on her temples, her face paled by fatigue. She'd had terrible dreams of overwhelming darkness, she told him, a shroud placed over her head. *Don't be silly*, he said. She let him wash her hair, sighing under his touch, and reached up with a wet hand, her grip on his wrist sure and strong.

Don't leave me.

He could still taste Lenore's perfume. Rena held on, her eyes unblinking. Yes, she knew then. His chest tightened, and he leaned forward, pressed his lips against her collarbone, water seeping up his shirtsleeves.

I'll never leave.

After her death, the uncertainty of his future lay before him, the guilt of duplicity heavy on his shoulders. He avoided Lenore, Wednesdays sinking blandly into the middle of the week. When he finally returned to her apartment, he felt too big for the space, unwieldy and awkward. He forced himself through the motions, raising his fork to his mouth, the sound of his teeth and mouth loud in the gaps of their stilted conversation.

"You disappeared for a while," Lenore would later say. "The real you."

And then one day, Lenore's daughter caught him unaware as he stared at himself in the mirror, wondering when it was that he had become old. Her face behind his, she'd smiled, linked her arms behind her back, and sort of swayed. At twenty-four or twenty-five, Ruby still straddled the line between child and woman, her hair pulled back at the sides with two barrettes. *Roo-Bee.* The way she looked at him then—with such casual affection—made him aware of his permanence in their lives. How foolish he would be to walk away from this family after all these years.

A BUMBLEBEE BUMPS gently against the kitchen window, then crawls along the ledge before flying up into the leaves of ivy that cling to the west side of the house.

"The kids are coming for dinner tonight," Lenore says. "And Melanie, of course."

"If she and Gavin aren't fighting again."

"Naturally."

Barrett nods, drinks the last of his coffee, then sets his mug back on the table. "I think I'll work in the studio for a while."

"Is it finished?"

"Almost." He thinks of the small figurines and furnishings, the sense of near completion, and his hands twitch. "Let's get out of the city," he says. "Go up to the cottage tomorrow. The kids can come up on the weekend."

"Yes, I'd love that."

He bought the cottage a year after Rena died. Lenore was still in her apartment back then, Gavin in university, and Ruby in her bachelor pad downtown.

"I bought this for you," he had said when he took Lenore up for the first time. "For us."

They sat on the deck as the sun set over the lake, barbecued burgers and drank wine, went fishing in the canoe. He pulled up on a tiny island, perched on the rocks in bare feet, watched Lenore swim with broad, sure strokes. She emerged dripping, squeezed her hair to wring out the water, then wrapped a towel around her waist and joined him.

"Heaven," she said, tilting her head to let the sun warm her pale throat. His hand drifted to the back of her neck, his fingers in her wet hair. Lenore turned to him there on the rocks and touched his arm, her skin still cool from her swim in the lake.

"I could stay here forever," she said.

Barrett rose, his foot slipping as he did, scraping against the side of a rock. Blood trickled down his ankle.

"Let's go back to the cottage," he said.

Water lapped at the sides of the canoe as they paddled. He stretched out his leg, stopped to dip it once, twice in the lake, washing it clean. Back inside, Lenore took him into the bathroom, knelt in front of him with a cotton ball and hydrogen peroxide.

"I'm sure you'll live," she teased. He stopped her hand and bent his head for a kiss.

In the back bedroom, they pushed the two single beds together. A moth fluttered near the bulb in a lamp, batting its papery wings repeatedly against the shade. Lenore opened a paperback, the pillows bunched behind her neck, but he pulled it away and threw it to the floor before she could read more than a page. When he brought her back from the cottage that summer day, he locked the door of her apartment behind her for the last time and moved her into his sprawling house in the west end.

AFTER DINNER, after the kids have gone home, Barrett returns to his studio and looks down at the diorama, nearly finished now. In fact, it is finished, but he has spent so long on this one that it's difficult to see it abandoned. He dismantled the others once finished, happy to have created them, but he thinks he'll find a special place to display the wedding scene. He moves the figurines about once more before reaching into a box on the shelf and taking down some glue. Here, Ruby walking down the aisle with Barrett, her arm tucked in his, Lenore waiting in the front row. And Gavin with some future wife, someone more suited to him. He has watched them grow up, not nearly as closely as he would have liked, but he hopes they will understand.

"I don't want to replace their father," he said to Lenore. "I think he'll come back someday."

"Why do you think that?"

"How can you leave your children for good? You always said he was a good father."

"He was."

"So he'll be back one day, then."

Lenore laughed and shook her head, then paused, considering. "Maybe," she said.

No, he could never replace Otto, but he likes to think that he has provided enough stability and strength to be remembered.

He studies Lenore's bedroom. He has turned back the covers, placed her glasses and an open book on her night table, waiting for the end of the wedding when she will crawl into bed, pull the covers up to her neck, and turn on her side, legs folded. Barrett had always slept in his own room for fear of crowding her, but now he realizes what's missing, and his forehead smoothes. He works for an hour or more, fastening the pyjamas—the same stripes, blue on white, that he wore this morning—and the brown leather slippers. He washes his hands at the sink, wipes them on an old rag, and carefully lays the pyjamas on Lenore's bed, his slippers peeking out from beneath the bedskirt. He stands back to survey his work and smiles.

Three

THE CHILDREN COME to the visitation but don't stay for the funeral, many of them scarred, others with faces that appear slightly off-kilter, though Ruby can't say why, exactly. They come with sad smiles, children who have grown into teenagers, even adults, and they all remember Barrett and the way he altered their lives.

"Your father was an amazing man." A woman takes Ruby's hands, her palms damp. Beside her stands a small child, five or six and shy; her eye sockets have been moved, her face reconstructed.

"Yes," Ruby says, but her smile is thin. *He wasn't my father. He was my mother's companion.* A more sedate way of saying *lover,* but those two words—mother and lover—in the same sentence still make her neck unnaturally stiff, though she has had twenty-eight years to get used to them. *(And really, Ruby, you know it's been more than that, more than twenty-eight years.)* She quells a surge of resentment.

At the front of the room near the open coffin, Lenore fiddles with flowers, stopping to press her nose into each arrangement. Ruby hangs back, not sure what to do with her hands, how to offer sympathy. For all three days of visitation, she has managed to avoid the coffin and Barrett's face in death, grey-green skin pinked with blush and cover-up against white satin. Instead, she stands near the back, a long, slim pencil, only the collar of her light blue blouse under her buttoned blazer breaking the code of black.

But now Lenore beckons, the muscles of her face slack and weary. "You should say your goodbyes," she says. "We're about ready to start." Dark half-moons bruise the fragile skin beneath her mother's eyes. How easy it has been to forget what Barrett meant to her, after all these years. Lenore clears her throat, waiting. Ruby focuses on her hands resting on the edge of the coffin, the nails bitten down to the quick, the way her knuckles look suddenly old, claw-like. Near the entrance to the room, mourners bend down to peer more closely at the mounted picture display of Lloyd Barrett's life. Ruby and Gavin struggled with that display, wondering whether or not to include a picture of Barrett's wife, Rena; in the end, Lenore said it was only right, that Rena and Barrett were together for many years until her death. *It'll look odd if we don't put her in there somewhere*, she said. So now there it was, the old wedding photograph from the sixties, Barrett dashing and toothy, Rena with her dark beehive and short white dress, both their faces unlined and new. And other photos: Barrett with his medical degree, then in the clinic, wearing his jeans and sneakers and a buttoned-up shirt, a stethoscope around his neck. He kept a box full of buttons on his desk, and another with rainbow-coloured jelly beans.

And now look at him. Ruby blinks, her fingertips slick with sweat. Her mother presses down on her shoulder, squeezes.

"Thank you," she murmurs. Ruby turns with a sympathetic smile, but Lenore isn't looking at her; she has moved forward to touch Barrett's shoulder, tears falling onto his face.

BARRETT WASN'T RELIGIOUS, but some people (Lenore) take comfort in the thought of a God and a heaven with fluffy floating clouds and halos when someone dies. Ruby shifts on her hard-backed chair in the front row, Lenore between her children, grasping their hands. Ruby is grateful for the air conditioning, but even so, her armpits are sticky from perspiration, and the backs of her knees sweat beneath sheer black nylon. Now when she removes her blazer, she will have to press her arms against her sides to hide the dark wet circles standing out against the pale blue fabric of her blouse. Gavin hasn't even worn a blazer, damn him; he is dressed in a black button-down shirt and grey slacks. At least he shaved today, getting rid of that ridiculous goatee thing he had been attempting to grow ever since he lost his last job. Though he would say he didn't lose the job.

The Brothers Grimm (as Gavin calls them) have moved the flowers into this room, and the stench climbs up her nose and slides down the back of her throat. Instead of the coffin, Barrett's smiling portrait—the one Lenore used for the obituary—graces the front of the room on a narrow table. It's hard not to imagine the coffin and Barrett moving at this moment into some kind of fiery hell. (Ruby hasn't a clue what cremation entails, though she knows well enough that you still pay for the coffin, and it gets burned along with the body. When you scatter the ashes later, it's not just bone, flesh, and guts incinerated, but also gleaming polished wood, brass, and satin.)

A rustle in the back, and Aunt Helen arrives at last with Cousin George, both blushing and sweating as they slide into their chairs behind Lenore.

"Sorry we're late," Aunt Helen mutters. "Traffic was a bitch." Ruby raises a tissue, ostensibly to blow her nose, but in actual fact to cover a smirk. Good old Aunt Helen, still the same at seventy-one: tight perm in Natural Medium Golden Blonde (Nice 'n Easy 104), smoking lines pulling her mouth in like a drawstring purse, thin shoulders, and dirty mouth. No wonder her husband checked out early (though no, that wasn't nice at all; Uncle Sal died of cancer back in the eighties).

The service begins. The minister—young, the pink flush on his cheeks rendering him cherubic despite his sombre, dark beard—clears his throat at the lectern.

"Lloyd Barrett was a man of few words but many kindnesses," he says, ducking his head to check his notes.

He didn't know Barrett, of course, but sat with Lenore for hours over the last few days, getting things right. The crowd behind and to the right of Ruby murmurs appreciatively. They are divided: on the right, Barrett's friends from before, the ones who were friends with his wife, loyal to the last; on the left, Lenore's friends and others she has come to know well over the last eight years—colleagues, families who have stayed in touch, Barrett's old friends who have accepted Lenore. Ruby can easily tell which ones are which because the ones who dislike Lenore and all that she stands for refused to approach during visitation, choosing instead to study the photographs, smell the flowers, and place their palms flat on the top of the coffin, eyes damp. Even after all this time, it bothers Lenore, Ruby can see by the way her shoulders stiffen and her nose reddens, the way she lifts her chin as if she doesn't care, her hand fluttering to her throat. Ruby takes her thin hand and squeezes, running her fingers over her mother's knobby knuckles, feeling a thick vein just under the surface of the skin.

The minister chronicles Barrett's life, pausing now and then to check his notes and clear his throat. Lenore leans against Ruby, her shoulders frail. The room fills with assorted sniffles and coughs; someone openly sobs at the back of the room.

"After Rena's death in 1998, Lloyd met Lenore and her two children, and they welcomed him into the family," the minister says. The crowd on the right shifts. And no, that wasn't quite the way it happened, but what would he say, really?

Ruby focuses on Barrett's portrait—the forced smile that doesn't quite make it to his eyes, the raised chin that lends him a sense of overbearing confidence. Handsome, distinguished but aloof, a full head of carefully combed white hair. This is the other Barrett, the professional man. Most days he still wore his jeans, most days his hair stood up in tufts, uncombed or wilfully disobedient. Ruby squints, trying to summon the tears that she feels should fill her eyes, but nothing comes. It's not as if she didn't appreciate Barrett and all he did for them, but she certainly never loved him, not the way she would love her real father if he were still around. Or maybe she did love him, or could have, but the barrier went up too long ago, and now it's too difficult to strip away. Many kindnesses? Sure, sure.

"How's your boyfriend?" Cousin George has rolled up his sleeves and leans back against the cream-coloured sofa in Barrett's—correction, now Lenore's—living room. George lives about an hour north of the city with Aunt Helen and her aging cocker spaniel. George, a bachelor still at thirty-six, has never moved out of his mother's house. He runs the water store his father opened a few years before his death. *Someone has to take care of Ma*, he says. Sometimes, when they were younger, Gavin made sneaky references to how, exactly, Cousin George took care of Aunt Helen, but never in Lenore's presence, and never more than hinting (and Ruby would squeal with disgust and hit him on the shoulder, laughing).

Ruby looks around the room, remembering how it was back then in the small apartment only blocks away. She must have passed this house a number of times on the way down to the river for their Sunday picnics, but Lenore never said a word, never pointed it out to them or said, *That's where he lives with his wife.* Back when they were younger, sorting through the ashes of the fire and settling into new routines and patterns. Now they are no longer a tight unit of three; even after Barrett's death, the family remains fractured and flung in all directions: Lenore in Barrett's house in the west end, Ruby in her bachelor apartment deep in the city, and Gavin and his young wife, Melanie, in their new subdivision in the suburbs.

"Her imaginary boyfriend, you mean?" Gavin asks.

Poor George looks confused, his brow furrowing as his eyes shift from Gavin to Ruby.

"Weren't you dating an accountant?"

"Yes," Ruby says. "That's him. He's not imaginary." Ruby ignores Gavin's snort, wonders how long they have to stay. She checks her watch. She wants to get home before dinner, the thought of searching for bits of conversation over a pork roast and asparagus unbearable.

"How's the store, George?" she asks.

His face smoothes, the worried frown between his eyes relaxing. "Good, business is good," he says. "I'm thinking of buying another."

"Everyone needs water, I suppose."

George nods. "True enough." He turns to Gavin. "What are you doing these days?"

Gavin leans forward and rests his elbows on his knees, wearing the look that Ruby has come to know well over the years, the one that signifies deep thought and reflection. All put on for show, of course.

"Well, George, my last job just didn't satisfy me," he says. "Wasn't challenging enough." George nods as if he understands, but Ruby doubts it. George has worked all his life in the water business. He didn't waste years in university, first in science, then the arts, flailing around as Gavin did for something, anything, that would hold his interest. *(Like you, Ruby? No, never mind.)*

"Here we are, then." Aunt Helen and Melanie trail Lenore into the living room, each carrying a platter. "In case anyone's still hungry."

"I thought you were lying down upstairs," Ruby says.

"I tried." Lenore arranges the platters on the coffee table, pushing them this way and that to make it all fit, the crustless white-bread sandwiches left over from the reception (egg salad, cucumber and cream cheese, tuna fish), sliced vegetables, crackers and cheese, and a small bowl of spinach dip. She settles herself in Barrett's favourite club chair—brown leather, faded armrests—and seems swallowed by its width, her small frame too thin, too childlike for such a chair.

"I tried to sleep," she says again. "But I just kept thinking and decided it would be better to keep busy."

"That's the best plan," Aunt Helen says. "And you shouldn't be alone right now." She looks at Ruby pointedly, but Lenore laughs.

"I've been alone many times," she says. "You don't have to stay. I'm going to take a sleeping pill, have a nice bath, and then go to bed."

"We're taking Mom up to the cottage this weekend," Ruby tells Aunt Helen. "We're going to scatter Barrett's ashes over the lake."

They stay for another hour, staring at the plate of sandwiches and talking about nothing, skirting around the subject of Barrett, the big house, and what is to be done with the rest of Lenore's life. Ruby watches her mother's face, noting the shadowed half-moons under her eyes, and the way her hands tremble slightly and grip the sides of the chair, her fingernails leaving small indentations in the leather.

RUBY CIRCLES THE BLOCK three times before she finds a parking spot. She's in a foul mood; it has taken her more than half an hour to get home in rush hour. She waits for a moment inside the car, taking deep breaths and looking in her rear-view and side mirrors. Someone followed her home from Lenore's, a man with long hair in an orange-and-white VW camper van, but there is no sign of him now. She exhales. *Paranoid!* Her nerves are raw, worn, that's all. She opens the door and slides her legs out. Her car—a seven-year-old used Neon—lost its air conditioning long ago, and Ruby never bothered to get it fixed.

She climbs the steps to the small porch of the three-storey, pink brick house, slides her key into the lock, and steps inside, tension draining. She has lived for eight years in this six-hundred-square foot bachelor apartment, and she wouldn't give it up for the world. *Location, location, location!* A tree-lined street that curves away from the university and the busy city centre, a mix of students crammed into sorority and fraternity houses and wealthy families in cavernous homes.

Ruby slides open the pocket doors that hide her bedroom from the rest of the apartment, peels off her nylons and long skirt, unbuttons her blouse, and throws the sweaty heap into her hamper. She is always surprised by how easy it is to slip into that other person, as if her blouses, blazers, and dress pants (*slacks* her mother calls them, but you don't say that anymore unless you want your younger colleagues—the ones with slanted bangs and dark nail polish—to burst out laughing and roll their eyes) have some secret power or protective armour. At work she keeps mental lists of other people's likes and dislikes, databases of their food allergies, wives, and children. There she can force a smile into her voice over the telephone and smooth ruffled feathers, can herd three hundred guests to breakfast, lunch, across town for a fancy dinner, and maybe a show by Cirque du Soleil. But then, at home, the armour comes off and she falls apart. She throws on old sweats from high school, a T-shirt, two barrettes holding back each side of her hair, makes love to a vibrator she has named Frank, and dreams of a boyfriend (also named Frank to limit the confusion) whom she has described in vivid detail to her family.

Frank. Ruby made him an accountant because that would make him dependable, hard-working, solid. He attends a lot of conferences, this Frank, and works long hours, often through weekends and holidays. She pretends to take off sometimes and disappears into her apartment, calls her mother later with tales of weekend jaunts to other cities or spas tucked away in the country. Yes, Frank treats her well. He pampers her with romantic dinners, rubs her back, and makes her chicken soup when she's sick. He's not married and is, in fact, the best, most real boyfriend she has ever had.

In the bathroom, she splashes water on her face. In their old apartment where they lived for so many years, Ruby had a mirror in her bedroom, the frame painted brown and nailed into the wall too high. She judged her height as she grew by how much of herself she could see in the glass. She used to think she was gawky but cute, spirited and quirky—Ramona Quimby, only older. But in all the family photographs, she is hiding behind broader shoulders or pressing herself against objects, as if pulling in and away from the piercing, directed focus of the camera lens.

The plain fact of the matter is this: she has grown tired of expectations. Only one person has ever appreciated her chicken legs, her cheekbones dotted with freckles, her bowl-cut hair, and bangs that dip into her eyes. Or no, not quite true. Lots have admired; only one has been coveted in return.

You'll find someone soon, Angela always says. Dear Angela, if only she knew. What was it now, four, five years? And two summers ago, the wedding, the satin dresses in taupe (*elegant,* Angela said, *not bridesmaidy at all,* but really, where would you wear a satin bridesmaid dress again?), the pale pink ribbons on the programs, and Duncan in black and taupe, his eyes damp and curiously beaten when he looked at Ruby. God, Duncan, why? *You taste like cinnamon*—remember when you said that? Their son, six months old, trussed up in a ridiculous tuxedo, his bow tie soaked with drool as he beamed and chewed on his fingers in the front row.

Ruby pushes aside two books on the shelf above the computer desk, pulls out a thin notebook, and finds the list hidden on a page in the middle. Number one, the first: Mr. Todd. Number two: a professor in the history department, on the desk after office hours, the door locked. Adam's apple at her chin, slender hips. Number three: a businessman in the doctor's office, waiting his turn, expensive leather briefcase, Armani ties. In her apartment, he hung his suit—shirt, jacket, pants—in her closet, if only for half an hour. Once he used her iron. On and on, a selection of details noted in each case: the tanned, hot skin of a neck, starched white shirt cuffs, buffed fingernails, one a roofer with muscled forearms and sweat-soaked bandana. All of them unavailable, married. Some lasted longer than others. None of them came close enough to leave marks.

And the last entry: "guilty, twisted sheets and throbbing skin and fucked-up sickness in my stomach afterwards." February 20, 2004, a little over a year before the wedding. *Stop! Don't think about it.* Angela bought her the notebook on one of her trips to Japan. "This is my brain," it says on the cover. On the inside, a simple question: "Do you want to play?" How they had laughed back then, laughed and laughed over the absurdities of the language and the way it could be distorted.

They came to Barrett's funeral.

"Ruby, we're so sorry." Angela's red hair hung in perfect ringlets, as usual. Duncan wore a tie, the hapless househusband. His lips brushed hers. Did Angela notice?

"We can't stay," she said. "I hope you don't mind. The nanny has an appointment."

"No, no."

"I'd stay if I thought you were broken up about it."

"You know I'm not."

"It's just that I don't do funerals well."

Duncan rolled his eyes. "No one does funerals well, Angela," he muttered.

"I'm flying out tonight on business," Angela said. "I'll send Duncan round tomorrow to check on you."

"Oh, you don't have to."

"I want to," Duncan said, but he didn't look at her, of course. Her stomach clenched. She hugged them goodbye, breathing in Angela's perfume, imagined Duncan's cheek pressed against hers a little too long.

She flips forward to a blank page, labels it neatly with the date. "Life like nothing," she writes. She closes the diary (*journal*, you call it a journal when you're over the age of fifteen) and retrieves the newspaper, a pair of scissors. On the front page, a glaring headline: "FATHER HERO: SAVES TOT BEFORE PERISHING IN FIRE." She clips quickly, fingers stained with newsprint. She doesn't read the article itself, not yet, but carries it to her desk in the living room. Taking down a plain white box from the highest shelf, she removes the lid and places the article on top of others, all similar. Heroic fathers, reunions, fathers who disappeared but then were found. She clips all year, hides them in the box until it's time. On the anniversary of the fire, she sits down on the floor, reading, letting the articles drop one by one, a scattering of leaves around her crossed legs.

Back to the newspaper, now the obituaries. She finds Barrett's and pauses, her breath catching to see it there in black and white. Swallowing, her hand swiping at her eyes, she cuts carefully, files it away with the rest. She replaces the lid, returns the box to its shelf, and retreats into the cool space of her bedroom.

SOMEONE KNOCKS at her front door insistently. Ruby blinks, glances at the clock to find that two hours have passed. Lost hours. She must have fallen asleep. She throws on a T-shirt, a pair of yoga pants, and slides her pocket doors open, running her tongue over her teeth and wondering if her breath smells. As she always does, she peers through the curtains before opening the door. Duncan. *You taste like cinnamon.*

"Hi," he says, swallowing once, twice.

Across the street, she sees the van again, orange and white. The man is behind the wheel, hair strangely lopsided, sunglasses in the dark, staring at Ruby.

Four

From the deck, the lake shimmers blue and deep, the sunlight hitting each slow ripple and dancing along the surface. Up close, it's more green than blue and layered, the sandy bottom kicking up brown silt. Lenore sits in a Muskoka chair, studying the way her skin sags around her kneecaps, as if loosened from its moorings.

"You can always tell a woman's true age by her knees," she says. Beside her, Ruby has kicked off her flip-flops and leaned back, neck and shoulders white and glaring under the sun.

"And her hands," Ruby says.

"And her neck."

They laugh softly. Ruby has just broken up with her boyfriend—what was his name? Fred? No, *Frank*—but doesn't want to talk about it. *Something happened* was all she said before slipping on those dark sunglasses. Lenore never met him, not after two years of dating, and she had given up, suspecting that the boyfriend was married or worse.

"She doesn't have a boyfriend," Gavin told Lenore repeatedly. "She's just saying she does so that we'll stop asking about who she's dating."

"Why would she do something like that?"

"I don't know. Maybe she's gay."

"Oh, Gavin, don't say that."

And then he shrugged. "You never know these days," he said.

Not that that would be the end of the world, of course. Lenore is not that ancient, not that behind the times. She knows there are lots of gay sons and daughters, but she is certain Ruby is not one of them. There were other boys, after all, a string of men, but nothing seemed to last, never anyone serious enough to bring home to Lenore. A relief when this Frank came along.

And now look at her. She is truly heartbroken, her eyes bloodshot and hanging heavy with dark circles. Migraine, she said when she arrived at the house back in the city, looking so terrible that Lenore offered to drive, though she hated Barrett's big car, and the traffic coming up through the snarled city intimidated her. Ruby slept the whole way, only waking when they hit cottage country.

"I'm sorry, Mom," she says now, her eyes still closed. "I wanted to be more energetic for you."

"I don't need energy right now," Lenore says. "Quiet is just fine with me."

Gavin and Melanie are due soon, in any case, should have been here by now, and then all peace will be gone for the rest of the weekend. Lenore wishes for an instant that it was just a girls' weekend, just the two of them, then feels terrible. It's not that Gavin is difficult, but that wife of his is something else, always whining about this or that, or pouting or crying when things don't go her way.

A little Barbie doll, Ruby had laughed after their first meeting, not in front of Gavin, mind you. But neither of them thought it would last; they thought it was a fling, the older man (*older* was relative; at the time, Gavin was twenty-nine, Melanie twenty-two) and the little girl with the shiny blond hair, those big blue eyes, and little puckered mouth. Lenore can't blame him for being attracted to Melanie, but to marry her? The wedding was such a grand affair, too—showy, with bright pink roses, bridesmaids in pink chiffon, the Catholic church service followed by the reception at that golf club, Melanie's dress busily decorated in lace and satin, puffed out by layers of tulle. She wore a tiara, as if she were a princess. In the church, Ruby, Lenore, and Barrett sat in the front row on the right, all wondering what the hell had happened and why so quickly.

"She's the marrying kind," Ruby had said. "Probably planned her wedding when she was eight years old and now just wants to have babies and take care of the house." Yes, probably. But where was Gavin—in his black shirts and Doc Martens, the old albums he used to line up in alphabetical order—in that big new house in the suburbs?

Lenore shakes her head, pushes her sunglasses back, and slides open the screen door. "Drink?"

"Yes, please."

How she loves this cottage, a real cottage with screen doors and shabby sofas, not a mansion perched on a lake like those belonging to so many of their friends. Or rather, to so many of Barrett's friends. He bought it the first summer after Rena died, just a simple place, a retreat for all of them, but mostly for him. No one but Lenore knows how he suffered in those years.

She grips the edge of the kitchen counter to brace herself against the flood of grief that sweeps over her. *Oh, Barrett.* Ice clinks in two tall glasses. She carries them out to the deck, drops of condensation pooling in the crescents between thumb and forefinger.

"Long Island iced tea," she says.

Ruby takes an appreciative sip. "Hot today."

Lenore drinks, eyes swollen with suspended tears.

"What time is Gavin coming?" Ruby asks.

"He should have been here by now."

"Is he bringing Barbie?"

"As far as I know." Lenore smiles, but adds, "You shouldn't call her that."

Gavin and Melanie don't arrive until nearly supper. Lenore has already made a green-bean salad, pulled hamburgers from the freezer, sliced potatoes and wrapped them in tinfoil with slices of onion and sea salt and the tiniest dab of butter. Ruby watches, making vague gestures to help, but she can't cook at all.

"You better hope you find a man who's good in the kitchen," Lenore has said to her on more than one occasion, but Ruby always rolls her eyes and mutters under her breath, and then laughs to take off the edge.

"I think they're here," Ruby says. Lenore hears the tires on the gravel, an engine idling for a long few minutes before a car door slams.

"Gavin." Lenore kisses him on the cheek as he leans forward. She isn't sure where his height came from. Otto wasn't that tall, was he? In her wedding photo, which is somewhere in the paper box in the trunk of the car right now, his head reaches the top of her ears. The years have unfolded too quickly; in her dreams, the children are often much younger and smaller, their smiles brighter.

Gavin looks tired and a little chubby. Lenore noticed it at the funeral for the first time, this paunchiness that adds a layer of years to his face.

"Where's Melanie?" Ruby has poured herself another glass of the potent cocktail from the pitcher in the fridge.

"She's in the car. I'm sure she'll get tired of sulking and come in."

Lenore feels Ruby looking at her but busies herself with Gavin's bag.

"No, I'll take it in, Mom."

"Same room as usual," she says, gently touching his arm as he brushes past. "Something's wrong," she whispers to Ruby, but another car door slams and here's Melanie, a pale cream weekend bag slung over her shoulder.

Lenore used to be concerned about these frequent fights, but now knows that talking about it will only makes things worse, so she doesn't mention Melanie's puffy red eyes, or the way her chest draws in and out in shuddering waves.

"A drink is what you need," Ruby says, her voice high and chipper. *I do believe she's getting drunk.*

"That's what we all need," Lenore says and smiles. "Let's go onto the deck."

They settle into chairs, bare feet tapping on the wooden boards, three women with drinks in hand saying little, but letting the breeze from the lake calm them. Little by little, Melanie's shoulders lose their tension. You have to be careful with her; she could break if you say the wrong thing or use a sharp tone of voice.

"It's so beautiful here," she sighs.

This lake can heal anyone, Lenore thinks. The best medicine. Cottage sounds: bare feet on the deck, waves slapping against the sides of the dock, laughter carried over water, the loons at night. The air so clean, so unlike the big city with that layer of grey pollution hanging over your head. You just have to breathe deeply, and all the stress disappears or goes into hiding, at least temporarily.

Gavin comes out to light the barbecue dressed in the clothes he keeps in a drawer up here—baggy green shorts with the ripped hem, faded Violent Femmes T-shirt that clings to his burgeoning belly—kisses Melanie on the cheek, and all is forgiven.

After dinner, Ruby and Melanie wash the dishes, and Gavin watches the sunset with Lenore.

"Sorry we were late," he says.

"Everything all right?"

"Just the usual." Except Lenore doesn't know what the usual is and doesn't really want to know. She's not the interfering type of mother.

"So, tomorrow?" Gavin asks.

"Yes. I thought we could scatter them by the island."

She has taken Barrett's ashes out of the car and placed the urn in her bedroom. She'll talk to him one last time tonight, and then let the wind carry him into the lake. Gavin reaches over to grab her hand, holds briefly.

Lenore would like to sit on the deck with Barrett after everyone else has gone to bed, but the mosquitoes are too bad, so she retreats into her wood-panelled bedroom, the single bedside lamp lit, soft shadows in the corners. In the room next to her, Ruby shifts and the double bed creaks on its springs. The comforter smells slightly musty, but that's the way she likes it up here. Back home in the city, in the big house, sheet corners are starched and pulled taut, the towels are thick and luxurious and replaced every year with a new set. Here, beach towels are thrown on the dock and then used for the occasional shower, washed once at the end of a stay and then folded inside cupboards for the next visit; here, manicures chip, makeup dissolves, calluses grow on pampered feet, and no one cares.

Barrett sits comfortably on the bedside table beneath the lamp.

"You silly fool," Lenore whispers.

He had complained about his chest a few times in the last month, but had not wanted to bother his doctor. "I'm sure it's the heat," he said.

"But what if it's not?"

"You worry too much." He touched her cheek, smiled. The children didn't see, couldn't know the tender way he held her at night before climbing into his own bed. When they looked at Barrett, they only saw the past and the years of being tucked away, hidden. But that was Lenore's choice, the only proper thing to do, what with Rena's illness. They all made mistakes, but dignity was always important.

Lenore turns off the light. There's more to say to Barrett, but she will say it tomorrow in front of the kids, and then it will be done. She lets her arms drift down to her sides and the tears come at last, sliding over her cheeks and soaking the pillow. She cries quietly, because the walls here are too thin. No need to worry Ruby. Down the hall, the bathroom door clicks open and shut, and she can hear the voices of Gavin and Melanie, low and bundled together. They're not fighting anymore.

Her tears leave her drained but relieved. The funeral was too awful, all those polite faces, their few friends who really understood on one side of the room, friends from Barrett's other life (his life with Rena) on the opposite side. She didn't want to fight anymore, had no energy to repel their hostile glances or arched eyebrows. And so she shook hands and let her cheeks be kissed, passive and compliant, her eyes filming over and ears closing as they filed past, one after another. *You'll never have to see these people again.*

But funerals are always like that, aren't they? Her mother died when she was eighteen, so long ago she barely remembers it, and her father followed ten years after that, but still those same impressions remain: the dreadful scent of flowers, too much black and heaviness, sodden handkerchiefs or shredded tissues crumpled in hands. Then, as now, she just wanted to get through the funeral and the grieving, fast-forward through the days until life felt normal again.

THEY SET OUT JUST AFTER ten o'clock, when they have all eaten and had coffee and shaken the last bit of the night's alcohol from their system. Ruby is a strong paddler and takes the lead in Lenore's canoe, while Gavin and Melanie follow. Their lake is quiet; no motorboats or mechanical noises ruin the peace of the morning, though there are some swimmers and others in canoes or fishing from small boats. They wave as they pass.

Lenore cradles Barrett between her feet. When they reach the rocky island, they disembark and pull the canoes up onto a small patch of mud. Barrett had always liked the island. He would perch on one of the rocks to watch the cottage, sitting so still that the loons would swim right up to him. *My thinking spot,* he said.

Lenore climbs out onto a rock, a breeze pushing small waves forward to splash against the shore. Ruby passes her the urn, then stands back with the others, respectful and silent. Melanie has already started to cry, dabs at her eyes. Lenore looks out over the lake, the cottage, feels the hush, an edge of the boulder digging into a bare foot. There are so many things they don't know. That first time she met Barrett in his clinic when she was at the end of her rope, the hope she felt that brought her up and out of the darkness. And they don't know—they have seen only one side.

She has a whole speech planned, but now can't say any of it. The lines she wrote last night after dinner—*let the wind and water take you where they may*—sound hopelessly clichéd. She doesn't want that, and in any case, he has already read the words, if he exists anywhere anymore. Instead, she closes her eyes and opens the urn.

"I love you," she says, and scatters the remains. Grey-brown flakes catch in the wind and swirl before falling into the water. She now sees her mistake: the waves push and push, pressing the ashes up against the rocks instead of out into the lake. But maybe it's better that way; he will always be here.

Gavin takes her hand, helps her down, his eyes damp. And Ruby too—she is wiping tears, smearing them across her cheek. Lenore doesn't look at Melanie, doesn't need to: she can hear the gulping sobs as the younger woman makes a spectacle of herself again. She doesn't fit in, this hysterical, weak little kitten of a girl. No one in Lenore's family falls apart like that, not outwardly. Gavin, looking suitably grim, shoots his wife a hard look, harder than necessary. Melanie inhales, sniffs, and falls silent.

RUBY WEARS a blue-and-red striped bikini and a straw hat and leans against the deck railing, her towel slung over her shoulder. Gavin and Melanie are small figures on the dock, moving about, laughing. Gavin slides into the water and lies on his back to kick at Melanie, who shrieks and jumps back.

"Going to join them?" Lenore asks. She has had a nap and feels rested and hungry. She has smeared a thick slice of French bread with peanut butter and raspberry jam and poured herself a glass of milk. A child's lunch.

"Mmm." Ruby doesn't turn but hunches forward more. Freckles dot the pale skin along her shoulder blades.

"I'm sorry about your boyfriend," Lenore says. "If you want to talk about it, you know you can."

"What?" Ruby turns, puzzled, before the creases smooth and she laughs. "No, it's not that." Her towel slips down, lands on the deck; as she bends forward to pick it up, the bones of her spine poke up, symmetrical knobs under her skin.

"Ruby, you're too skinny."

"I've always been skinny."

"True."

Ruby sits down next to her, puddles her towel around her feet, and rests her forearms on rounded knees. The freckles come out more in the sun. She sighs, long and drawn out, two barrettes holding her hair in place on each side of her face making her look younger than she is.

"Can I tell you something in secret? Something you can't tell anyone? Not even Gavin. Especially Gavin."

"Of course."

Ruby breathes fast, looks away from Lenore, then just blurts it out in a rush, as if she is afraid she will lose her nerve. "I'm in love with someone I can't have. I've been in love with him for years and years." She searches her mother's face for a reaction, an expression of disappointment or judgment.

Lenore stills her mouth, her chest tightening. Poor Ruby. Her misery is all too familiar. "Why can't you have him?"

"It's complicated."

"Is he married?"

A quick shake of the head, too quick. Ruby drops her face into her hands. "Yes." Her voice is muffled.

"Oh, Ruby." Lenore sits back against her chair, exhaling slowly. "I don't know what to tell you."

"I think he loves me too," Ruby says. She looks up, cheeks blotchy, dark circles under her eyes. "What am I going to do?"

"I don't know," Lenore says. "I do know that it's easier to step away than to get involved. Much easier."

Ruby falls silent and studies her toes while Lenore finishes her sandwich, her tongue scraping peanut butter from the roof of her mouth, and washes it down with the last of her milk.

"When did you know about Barrett?" The question is not entirely unexpected, but it still startles Lenore. This is uncharted territory for them; her kids have never wanted to know the details.

"It was complicated too," she says. "I first met him in the hospital after Gavin was born. He was there because of Rena, you know. He wandered up to the nursery, stood by the glass window looking in at all the babies when I first saw him." And how dignified he had looked then, even in his crumpled shirt and unshaven cheeks. "He had such a look of rapture on his face, that I had to ask him, 'Which one is yours?' He would have been thirty-five or thirty-six back then, and so different. Tall and thin, handsome, you know. He always had this aura about him that made people look at him and want to talk to him."

"Charisma."

"Yes, charisma. He drew people to him. And when he turned to look at me, he had tears in his eyes. 'I don't have any children,' he said. 'I wish they were all mine.' He pressed his hands against the glass, I remember that, and then turned and walked down the hall, slowly, slumped in a way. I don't know why, but I put my hand up against the fingerprints he left on the glass."

"And that's when you knew?"

"I didn't see him again for three years, and that's when I knew."

"And you were still married to my dad."

"Yes." Lenore doesn't make excuses, doesn't say, *things were terrible between us*, though it was true. "But I don't know what would have happened if Otto hadn't left." And, of course, he had more than just left, he had tried to burn the whole house down, but she doesn't need to say that, nor does she admit to her lie. She does know what would have happened.

A scream rises from the dock. "Fuck you!" The words echo and repeat across the lake. Melanie storms up the stairs, stops when she sees Ruby and Lenore, her face working, twisting, before she runs into the cottage. Gavin follows slowly, still dripping from the lake, the hair on his legs slicked down like a thin layer of fur. He says nothing, disappears inside. Ruby puts her hand to her mouth and starts to laugh, and then tries to squelch the sound by drawing her shoulders forward, wrapping her arms around her legs.

"Unbelievable," she says when she stops laughing. She touches Lenore's hand. "That was a sad story, about Barrett in the hospital. I'm glad you told me."

"I am too."

Gavin reappears, dressed in shorts and a T-shirt and sporty sandals. He stands awkwardly for a moment, his mouth opening and closing.

"Your wife?" Ruby asks.

"Sitting in the car with her bags packed. Waiting for me."

Ruby begins to giggle again, can't stop herself, even as he glares. "Oh, Gavin, I'm so sorry."

"Laugh all you want," he says. "It's my life, isn't it?"

"Well, you put up with it," Ruby says.

"You know nothing about it, so why don't you just shut up?"

"Come on," Lenore says. "Let's not do this today."

Gavin and Ruby hang their heads, ashamed.

"Sorry," Ruby says.

"I think I have to leave now." Gavin checks his watch. "It's nearly supper anyway. By the time we get back it'll be pretty late, with the traffic, and Melanie has to work tomorrow."

"Mom and I are leaving soon too," Ruby says, but Lenore shakes her head.

"I think you should go with Gavin," she says.

"Mom?"

"I'd like to stay for a bit. I've got some things to do."

"What things? No, Mom, don't make me go home with them. You should have told me. I could have brought my car up too."

"Don't be so selfish, Ruby. Mom wants to stay. She's just scattered Barrett's ashes, for God's sake."

Ruby glares at him. "You won't take me all the way home. I know you. You'll drop me off at the bus station, and it'll be ages before I get into the city."

"I'll drive you to Mom's. You can get your car there."

"I think I've heard that one before, and then wouldn't you know, I'm stuck in the middle of nowhere trying to get home late at night."

"I don't live in the middle of nowhere."

"You might as well."

"Gavin, promise me you'll take her right to the house," Lenore says.

He smiles. "I promise."

Ruby sighs. "All right." She heads to her room to pack.

"Gavin." Lenore pats the chair beside her, and he sits. "I don't know what's going on with you and Melanie, and you know I don't meddle, but I hope you get it sorted out." What she really thinks is that Melanie's behaviour has been inexcusable this weekend, of all weekends. *Doesn't the girl have any sense at all?*

"If I know her, she's going to feel terrible about it tomorrow, Mom. We're going through something right now."

Something. Lenore wonders if this something has anything to do with Gavin's lack of employment, and he must read it in her expression, because he glowers.

"Don't worry. I have a job interview next week with a sign company."

"A sign company?"

"They make signs. You know, for the outside of buildings? Name signs."

"Well, Gavin, you know you could always work for Cousin George."

"Yes, I know. And as much fun as I imagine that would be, I'm not sure I'm a great fit for that job. Anyway, Melanie and I—it has nothing to do with jobs."

"If you say so." She lifts up her cheek for a kiss.

"Are you sure you're going to be all right?" he asks.

"Yes. I'll call you."

He leaves her then, and she can hear Ruby complaining as she follows him through the cottage. "I'm already starving, so we better stop at Weber's for a hamburger, and please take me right to Mom's house, don't drop me off at that bus station. Are you listening, Gavin?"

THE DISHES ARE DONE, drying in the rack, the counter wiped down, the lamps in the living room spreading an orange glow throughout the cottage. Lenore lies on the sofa, one arm over her head, the other resting on her chest, feeling it rise and fall. Outside something moves, rustles in the bushes, deep in the darkness. Hopefully not a bear, looking for garbage; they have seen them here occasionally, more frequently in the last few years as the bears have become more accustomed to their human neighbours, and more aware of where the unlocked bins are stashed.

She had wondered if she would feel nervous up here alone, but the silence after the last few days comforts her. She closes her eyes and imagines Barrett curving his hand around hers. Now that he is gone, it's time to rearrange her past, and she hopes he would understand. The box from the trunk of the car sits beside the sofa, lid tossed on its side, papers and photographs jumbled in a heap. But Lenore knows where everything is because she has been either sorting through or adding to it since Otto left in 1979. At the very bottom are the newspaper clippings, including Elsa's obituary, hastily written by Lenore in those first few muddled days.

> Sinclair, Elsa (nee Bischoff)—Tragically, on August 3, at the age of 54. Survived by son Otto, daughter-in-law Lenore, and two grandchildren. Private funeral arrangements have been made.

Of course, there was no funeral at all. Lenore wanted nothing to do with the woman's remains and let the funeral home settle her deep within the earth, quietly, in a plot Elsa had chosen next to her long-dead husband.

Lenore still remembers clipping the obituary and the other articles from the paper, the skin of her face pulling tightly from the corners of her eyes, in a curiously blank state of mind. But her hands shook. The box was nearly empty then, but big, as if she knew that it would fill over the years with journals and papers, some lined and handwritten, others typed at furious speed on the Smith Corona or printed in Courier on her dot-matrix printer. Evolution of the printed word, she thinks. The children know of the box, though neither of them has been able to look inside. She is not even sure they would want to. They have never spoken about Otto or what happened, not since they were younger. *Daddy went away*, she had explained to Gavin, who clutched at her sleeves and didn't understand, but gradually stopped asking for him. Ruby just looked at her with a certain knowing expression—sad, resigned—that should have been impossible in an almost-eight-year-old child. Poor Ruby. Otto lit the fire four days before her birthday.

Lenore pokes the box with her bare foot, and then rises to fill a glass with wine. It's time to organize, piece it together, but she is drained. Tomorrow is soon enough. She will stay for a week, then return to the city to face the lawyers and whatever mess Barrett has left behind, though knowing him, she's sure there won't be much. The wine warms her throat. For a moment, she imagines picking up the box and carrying it down the steps of the deck and over to the firepit, imagines hearing the scrape of the match. But that would be cowardly, and not much different from what he had done, in the end.

Five

OTTO DRIVES SLOWLY through the city. It has changed since he was last here in the seventies. It has grown up, become more sophisticated. Eye contact with strangers is fleeting, smiles minimal. The city has become busier, the people on the sidewalks more determined. Downtown, businessmen and women scurry, even in this heat, their footsteps heavy with purpose. Tourists wearing walking shorts, socks with sneakers, and broad-brimmed hats aim cameras at the skyline or pose in front of statues. One group disembarks from a bus, bright orange caps on their heads, and huddles around a man with a clipboard and a sheaf of maps. It would be easy to disappear in this city now, Otto thinks. Easy to pass through, invisible.

Here is the complex where he and Lenore lived when they first married, the one-bedroom apartment where they slept squished together on Otto's twin bed. The street is much more crowded than before, the four-storey building flanked by a grocery store, a shoe shop, and the dark enclave of an adult video store. There's a vacancy sign taped to one of the apartment windows. Otto takes down the number and calls from a pay phone, nearly chokes when the woman on the other end tells him the rent. "What did you expect, with this location?" the woman asks haughtily. Otto thanks her for her time and moves on.

He heads uptown, watching the homes get larger, grander, the streets quieter. Here. Twenty-eight years ago, things weren't quite as posh. Someone has rebuilt, spruced up, installed new windows, painted trim that makes the red brick stand out. A natural stone walkway replaces the white pavement he remembers, and whoever owns the place now has a green thumb—or a gardener. There's no sign of the fire, no smoky edges or darkness clinging to the third floor. He almost expects to see his mother's ghost, severe and disapproving, reflected in the window.

When Otto was six, he had a collection of elephants on a shelf in his room. It began with a case of the chicken pox. His father brought him a stuffed elephant, pulled it from his coat jacket with a broad smile, touching Otto's fevered forehead with the back of his hand. In the quiet room, the curtains closed, Otto nestled the animal under his chin and tickled his face with the trunk until he fell asleep. His parents took him to a zoo later that year, where the elephants moved slowly, their ears fluttering as they passed one another. And there, a baby elephant, his trunk delicately wrapped around his mother's tail, his baby elephant eyes blinking in trust. Otto wanted to take him home with him, cried and clung to the fence when it was time to leave.

"Don't you want to see the monkeys?" his mother asked.

"No!"

When he was eight, he stole an elephant figurine from the five-and-dime, sliding it into the waistband of his shorts when the shopkeeper wasn't looking. The ceramic warmed against his skin as he moved. He kept it under his pillow the first night, rubbing its smooth back with a finger, then placed it carefully next to the stuffed animal. His father collected copies of *National Geographic*, kept them lined up, tightly packed, on a shelf in his den. Sometimes Otto pulled them out, one by one, and flipped through the glossy pages as his father worked. He loved the den: the great oak desk with space beneath for a small boy, the clack of his father's Underwood at night as he typed letters for the city's biggest newspapers, shirt sleeves rolled up, cheeks flushed, his teeth squeaking as he ground them together. *What are you on about now?* his mother would say with a certain amount of exasperation. His father wrote about everything: the state of the roads, a crooked politician, assorted commentary on various articles or opinion pieces. No one ever published his missives, but that didn't matter to Otto or his father. He held his pen the way Otto held his, with his whole fist clamped down, as if writing took all of his strength. In school, the teachers were forever correcting Otto's tense grip, forcing his fingers apart, arranging them awkwardly on fat pencils.

"Daddy does it like this," he complained to his mother.

"You are not your father."

He lay under the desk, watching crumpled balls of paper climb higher in the wastebasket. He touched the sharp crease in his father's slacks, smelled the leather house shoes he wore, and pulled the magazines towards him. And there he saw it: a picture of a man riding an elephant, grinning for the camera as oversized hands rested on skin that looked tough, leathery. And though he found it difficult, sometimes impossible, to read in class, here in the safety of the warm space under his father's desk, he read that a mother elephant was called a cow, that its sensitive trunk had thousands of muscle groups and, most impressively, that elephants could cry, laugh, and grieve.

When Otto was twelve and his father dead only a year, he brought home his report card and stood in front of the shelf in his room, the card in his pocket, the edges of his secret digging into the top of his thigh. The shame of that moment, the sinking sensation of failure, stays with him always. School confused him, colours shifting into nearly indistinguishable hues, the alphabet jumping around, letters transposing themselves. Even in kindergarten, the instructions were complicated: *Twist the tissue paper around the pencil like this, girls and boys, and then dip it in the glue and paste it onto the can. Then put the pipe cleaner through the hole at the top. When you're finished, you'll have a lovely Christmas ornament to take home to your mommy.* Otto would carry home a can smeared with dabs of glue and torn paper that Elsa would take from him dubiously.

What's this?

A present for Christmas.

The report card was now smudged from Otto's sweaty fingers repeatedly rubbing the teacher's slanted, loopy writing, as if to erase the words and grades. When he took his turn reading aloud from the primer, the letters on the page jumbled and blurred, and his tongue swelled until he couldn't speak. He put his hand in his pocket, touched the card yet again. This, despite imprisonment in his room, even during the summer, his school books open on his desk while the afternoon light fled from the sky and his mother stood breathing just beyond his door. She would see his report card and slam her palm on his desk, her voice frantic. *You're just like your father!*

The elephants seemed to mock him from his shelf. They belonged to a different time. He clenched his fists, pounded once on the shelf, then swept everything onto the floor, stamping and stomping again and again. He picked up the stuffed elephant and ripped him until the ears fell away and he realized what he had done. *I'm sorry, I'm sorry!* He cradled the animal in his arms, tried uselessly to stick the ears back on, then crumpled, sobbing.

Otto's skin prickles, and he turns away from the old house, silent, wishing that it had burned to the ground.

"Can I help you?"

A man has emerged from the front door and now comes down the driveway to where Otto sits in his orange-and-white VW van, still staring.

"I used to live here a long time ago," Otto says.

"Oh." The man looks behind him at the house and then, as if it's expected, asks, "Do you want to come inside?"

Otto shakes his head. It's the last thing he wants to do.

"No. No thanks."

Ruby is the only one he can track down at first, the only one with the same name, an address in the city. He finds her easily in the white pages, parks on her street, and waits. Here she comes, all grown up in her blouse and dress pants, pointy shoes with slight heels. She makes him feel old, the way she looks now, but he can still see the child peering out beneath the bangs. And she looks like him, in a way, with the same roundness to the face, the same shape of her eyes. She is tall, like her mother, but her hair is straight, no flip to the ends.

The first night in the city, he parks two streets away from Ruby's apartment and sleeps in the back of the van. He follows her for a few days: to her office west of the city, to the funeral. Outside the funeral home, he shuffles past the three of them, taking comfort in the wig and fake beard, his van parked a few blocks away. How regal Lenore looks, her white hair swept up in a chignon, her face pensive in grief. Ruby touches her mother's shoulder. *Lovely service*, she says. A younger, larger version of Otto stands next to them: Gavin, who was only four when Otto left and is unrecognizable from that little tow-headed boy, his hair now starting to recede at the front, his slightly overgrown belly. Gavin nods. *Barrett would have been pleased.* The young blond woman beside him raises a crumpled tissue to her mouth. Otto nearly stumbles but rights himself in time, keeping his head low. Lloyd Barrett. *Of course.* He supposes he didn't leave her much choice. Gavin says something Otto can't hear, and Lenore turns with a small laugh. He remembers the way her hair fell against the nape of her neck and inched towards her mouth in sleep, remembers the smell of her in the sheets and pillows.

After the funeral, he follows them to a mansion in the west end. She has done well for herself, his wife. He sits behind the wheel, watching. This, then, is his family, not shattered into pieces as he has imagined, but together still, whole, grown up, and solid. His hand touches the hardened, crumpled paper on the passenger seat.

THE HOUSE IN THE WEST END is beautiful, with a wide driveway and one of those ancient oaks on the front lawn that has probably spread its roots under not only this house but across half a block. A house firmly entrenched in history and old money, a house bearing a quiet dignity. On Saturday morning, Lenore loads her suitcase and one of those cardboard book boxes into the trunk of her car. Ruby drives up a short time later, a weekend bag slung over her shoulder, and climbs into the passenger seat, leaving her own car parked near the garage.

Before she leaves, Lenore heads across the street in Otto's direction, her expression determined. Otto lowers his head, pretends to jot down a note as he raises a cellphone to his ear. She is so close that he can hear the soft squeak of her flat shoes on the pavement through the open windows of the van.

"Keep an eye on things for me, would you, Jack?"

Otto shifts his eyes to the right. A man in a broad hat rises slowly from his garden, leans on a shovel.

"Off to the cottage?"

"I'll be gone for a week or so."

"Sure, Lenore. You take care."

Otto nods into his cellphone. On the paper in front of him now, he does scribble a note: "Empty, one week."

As Lenore walks across the street towards her car, Otto starts the van and drives away slowly, nearly humming. He returns later in the middle of the night, when the street has fallen silent. He parks the van blocks away, in a neighbourhood where the parking regulations are not so strict, and walks, taking deep breaths of the summer night. He has forgotten how humid it is in these parts, how the heat of the day can become trapped under awnings and in the pores of the sidewalks.

After a group of young boys has swaggered off down the road and turned into a private lane, he creeps up Lenore's driveway, finds the key under a flowerpot near the side door where he watched the maid place it the day before. There's no alarm, not in this neighbourhood, where everyone trusts everyone else and the streets are signposted as dead ends. At this hour, most of the houses on the street are dark, lifeless. Inside, Otto smells the floral aftermath of the funeral and catches the vases and flowers in the beam of his small flashlight. Climbing the wide staircase, he runs his hand up the banister. *Nice things.*

He doesn't want to sleep in Barrett's bed, and so he is relieved (and yes, somewhat snidely happy) to find that Lenore has her own bedroom here in this house. He could have chosen one of the two guest bedrooms, but something draws him to Lenore's—the scent of her perhaps, a vague memory rising up and wrapping around him like a soft cocoon. He brushes his teeth in the ensuite bathroom, propping up his flashlight on the counter, noting the cream-coloured hand towels hanging perfectly on the golden rods. Lenore's style has changed over the years.

The bedsheets are pulled taut and tucked in around the mattress. He folds down the blankets and lies on the bed fully clothed, his hands cradling the back of his head, surprised by his sense of calm. The smell of lavender rises from freshly laundered sheets. *You shouldn't be here.* He'll stay for a day, maybe two, no more.

HE SPENDS HIS FIRST FEW DAYS poking about the house, peering into rooms, drawers, and cabinets, aware of his intrusiveness but unable to stop himself. He isn't looking for anything in particular, but stumbles across the albums with photographs on a shelf in what must have been Barrett's study. The day before, he discovered a selection of fine Scotch in the dining room, and now he pours himself a drink, settles into the club chair in the dining room, the albums piled on a small table beside him. Here he sees his children as they grew, their gap-toothed smiles and sticky faces lengthening, their features becoming more distinct, less innocent. Graduation, a wedding, Gavin next to the blonde he had seen outside the funeral home. Otto lingers over photographs of Barrett, the substitute husband and father, then throws the album to the floor.

Not until the third album does he understand how Lenore has dealt with his absence. He feels sick as he surveys the altered photos, some cut in half, others in thirds, leaving only a shoulder, a hand, the barest hint of a head. Some pictures missing entirely, two pages at the beginning of the album chronicling their wedding reveal only empty, yellow-edged rectangles, all of it proof of her rage, his betrayal. He returns the albums to the study, rinses his glass in the kitchen sink, and climbs the stairs to her room, moving mechanically. Under the sheets, his sleep fitful, troubled. *You shouldn't be here.*

Ruby and Gavin nearly catch him when they come by on Wednesday afternoon. He has been napping but snaps to attention when he hears the front door open and close. He slides from Lenore's bed and hovers at the doorway, listening for sounds below and praying it's not her, not yet, not now when he is caught unawares like this. Not when he has not had the time (though he has had lots of time) to prepare his speech or go over what he wants to say. His toothbrush is still resting on the sink in Lenore's bathroom, probably still wet from this morning, the pristine towels damp and puddled on the floor from a shower, and her bed is unmade.

Footsteps in the foyer, the sound of keys thrown onto a table. Otto slips into a closet in what must be a guest room. Through the wooden slats of the closet door, Otto sees Gavin walk by the doorway, head down. For half an hour, Otto listens to the jangle of coat hangers and drawers sliding open and closed in the next room before someone else arrives, pauses a few doors away. Inside the closet, Otto holds his breath, surrounded by the stink of his nervous sweat, but Ruby passes by without a word. In the next room, she greets Gavin, says something about boxes. Otto puts his ear to the wall.

"Remember when Dad left?" he hears Ruby say clearly, and he strains to hear more, his eyes widening in the dark. The conversation rises and falls.

"… those nice guys somehow do all those nasty things and then keep going every day, doing all the little things they always used to do …"

He leans forward and presses his hands to his face.

OTTO PACED THE HOSPITAL CORRIDORS, his hands sometimes thrust into his pockets, sometimes twisting in front of him, sometimes reaching out to touch the green walls. The soles of his shoes squeaked against the floor, and the antiseptic smell burrowed into his nose and slid down his throat so that he could taste it. He was twenty-six. To his relief, a door at the end of the corridor opened, and a smiling man approached. He was ushered into her room, a gown hastily thrown over his shoulders, the baby handed to him. Ruby stopped writhing, stared up with buggy alien eyes at her father, a thick patch of hair sticking up on the top of her head. Wrinkled fists curled under her chin. Otto smiled at Lenore, unable to speak or do anything but hold his daughter.

When Lenore became pregnant, they were living in a one-bedroom apartment downtown, not far from their work at the insurance company, which was housed in a shining high-rise with thirty-five floors. They dated secretly for six months before announcing their engagement, sharing secret smiles in the elevator, Lenore clutching her purse demurely in front of her if any other passengers sidled in. She worked until the wedding, after which she quit in a flurry of good wishes, because that's what women often did when they married back then. The other ladies at work (*girls*, they called them *girls*, Otto remembers) threw Lenore a goodbye shower, loaded her up with casserole dishes, oven mitts, aprons, and even (amid much laughter and suggestive elbowing) a tiny rattle, *just in case*.

The wedding was modest, with only family and a few friends, Lenore in a short white dress and veil, tin cans jangling from the back of a friend's car as they drove away. Otto's mother came, dressed in grey instead of black. She might have smiled once or twice, especially after a drunken guest persuaded her to dance and made her drink a full glass of champagne. Otto would even swear later that he saw her take off her shoes, though Lenore always laughed at the thought.

They weren't so young—Otto twenty-four, Lenore twenty-nine—but still the future held such promise. They honeymooned in Mexico, ate lobster and shrimp, snorkelled in the mornings, and made love and napped in the afternoons. Lenore tanned so well; Otto would slide the hotel sheet down, down, until he reached the white outline left by her bikini, would press his cheek against her leg just to feel the heat.

Back home, they settled down in the small apartment. Lenore felt comfortable in the role of housewife, after all those years spent taking care of her father. She cooked simple meals, bought flowers for the table, used real linen napkins and her mother's wedding china. By their second year of marriage, Otto was starting to wonder why she wasn't pregnant yet, but then it happened, suddenly and surely, and she started to bloom and waddle and glow. Pregnancy suited her, filled out her tall frame, and made her more womanly, or at least that's what Otto thought.

There is a photograph somewhere, or used to be—hard evidence of Otto's awkward position, the rigid arms, the baby's head bent sideways into the crook of his arm—but it's just something else he has had to give up, those photographs. But at least he has the memory, and memory can be sharper than photographs at times. That first day in the hospital, he wrapped his arms around Lenore and Ruby *(my girls)* and just breathed in and out, wanting to capture and preserve the moment forever.

OTTO WATCHES FROM LENORE'S window as Ruby and Gavin leave on foot down the street. He presses his nose to the glass, leaving hot prints, his hands shaking with the urge to touch them both.

Handprints on construction paper.
Sticky kisses.
Christmas concerts.
Bruised knees healed by kisses and Band-Aids.
Graduation.
Boyfriends and girlfriends.
Marriage.

He has missed them all.

Back in Lenore's room, he tidies up. The children will be back. He folds the towels in the bathroom, packs away his toothbrush, and wipes down the sink with toilet paper. He makes the bed again, pulling the sheets as smooth as he can, trying to make his corners sharp, wiping his hand over the pillows when he has finished, hoping to erase his scent, the imprint of his visit.

That night, he hides in the basement. It is largely unfinished, with concrete floors, bare drywall, and wires that dangle from the ceiling in places. Boxes and storage containers line the walls in rows of two or three. Three rooms open off the main area. The laundry room and full bathroom are more welcoming, with finished tile floors, modern lighting, and evidence of recent cleaning, but in the furnace room cobwebs cling to the corners, and a thin layer of dust lies on every surface. Behind the rattling furnace and one wall of the bathroom, Otto finds a narrow space that must have held an oil tank at some point. He pokes around the main room until he finds an old sleeping bag, then takes it behind the wall and unfurls it, laying it flat on the cold concrete. It will do.

Six

THE STREETS HERE TURN to cobblestone, twist and dip in curving slopes. The residents have somehow managed to put up signs warning of dead ends to discourage traffic and Sunday gawkers, but the streets keep going, with nary a dead end in sight. Despite herself, Ruby loves it here by the ravine and river, with the quiet scenes of domesticity: women out front raking leaves in slouchy pants, hair pulled up into casual-but-chic knots; children with basketballs or hockey sticks and flushed cheeks. Everyone here decorates for every holiday, their enthusiasm seeping through the cut-out leaves and the elegant white and blue lights adorning the windows. A minuscule community, the private curling and tennis club, sturdy oak trees arching into the sky, branches hovering protectively over the sidewalks and lawns.

Ruby pulls into the driveway of her mother's house and stops the car. Gavin is already here, Melanie's white Volkswagen Cabriolet parked at an angle, the front tires only inches from the corner of the house. Gavin only learned to drive last year, at the insistence of his in-laws; before that, he was a true city boy, getting around by streetcar, subway, and taxi.

"I'm here!" she calls out as she opens the front door.

"Upstairs," he says.

The house smells musty. The windows have been shut and locked since Saturday when everyone went up to the cottage; it's Wednesday afternoon now, and all the summer heat has gathered inside and festered.

"God, Gavin, you could have at least opened some windows around here. Or turned on the air."

She heads up the wide staircase in bare feet, hand lightly whisking the polished banister. The maid comes every Friday. As she passes Lenore's bedroom, she notices that the bed is unmade and frowns, shakes her head. Poor Lenore—it isn't like her at all to leave things unfinished. Gavin is in the master bedroom, Barrett's room. He has opened up the closet and is surveying the suits and shirts, his back to Ruby. When he turns, Ruby nearly flinches.

"You look terrible," she says.

"Well, what do you think? This isn't exactly easy for me." There was a time when Gavin believed Barrett was his real father. Or maybe not believed: *hoped*.

"It's been a rough couple of days," he mumbles. "Anyway, thought you could go through the drawers and I'll do the closet."

"The boxes are in the trunk of my car," Ruby says. "Are you okay?"

"I'm fine."

They sort in silence for a while. Lenore doesn't want to keep any of his clothes. *Send them to charity*, she said. Ruby doesn't like it one bit, her mother staying up at the cottage alone, but what can you do? Her mother is a grown woman, after all, quite capable of taking care of herself. Isn't she? Ruby saw the box in Lenore's trunk, knew what it contained—clippings and photographs and scraps of writing about Otto and what happened so long ago. Lenore kept the obituary, every newspaper article about the fire, the last a brief paragraph that had been relegated to the back pages. No one cared. Even the police lost interest after a while. *There's no proof he started the fire*, they said. *He's just gone.*

"Remember when Dad left?" she says now, surprised even as the words leave her mouth. She can barely remember Otto after all these years, and maybe that hurts more than his leaving. There aren't any whole photographs of him anywhere, only slices of shoulders or sideburns. Lenore keeps thick albums of all their photos on a shelf in Barrett's study. Ruby has flipped through those pages more times than she can count, watching over time as the glue left the pages, and the photographs beneath the clear plastic sheets began to slip and slide and tumble down to the bottom.

There used to be photographs of Otto, lots of them. The spaces he occupied in the albums now are blank, sticky yellow squares, missing pieces of the puzzle. After the fire—did they ever really talk about that? Ruby can't remember, though she must have asked at some point.

Gavin's head pops up. He frowns.

"Otto?" he asks. He has never called him *Dad* or referred to him as his father. "What about him?"

"I don't know. Just thinking out loud, I guess."

Gavin would hardly remember, at least not the details. He was only four when Otto left.

"Sometimes I wonder what he's doing, if he's still alive. All of that kind of stuff."

Gavin shrugs. "Probably married again," he says.

"He couldn't get married, could he? He and Mom never got divorced. She just never heard from him again."

"Maybe she did. Maybe we just don't know."

"I don't think so. Mom's not like that." But then Ruby wonders. They have almost never spoken about Otto or those years right after the fire. Anything was possible.

"He was pretty young," Gavin says. "Around your age. He's probably living with someone, maybe has a couple of kids."

Ruby never thought about it like that. Otto was young, only thirty-four or thirty-five. Of course he would have found someone new, if he were still alive.

"Do you think he ever thinks about us?"

"I don't know how you can't think about something like that, at least every once in a while."

"I wonder about those men who commit those crimes, you know. Murders. And how all their neighbours go around saying stuff like, 'He was such a nice guy, so normal.' But those nice guys somehow do all those nasty things and then keep going every day, doing all the little things they always used to do. How do you do the laundry, knowing that you cut up some girl into little pieces?"

"Or set fire to your house while your mother was upstairs? Leave your wife and kids with nothing?"

The bottom drawer sticks and Ruby has to tug. Boxes of small square handkerchiefs—the kind Barrett always stuffed in his pocket—spill onto the floor, and suddenly Ruby is crying, her nose stuffed up and throat choking her with tightness. Gavin bows his head, ties draped over his hand, his shoulders twitching.

CHRISTMAS 1978. Brightly coloured lights and tinsel were wound around columns and draped across store entrances in the mall. Ruby held on to her mother's hand, fearful of all the people rushing past, the children screaming or crying or stamping their feet, the anxious expressions on their faces. Her mother seemed relaxed, a small smile on her lips. She was wearing the shimmery lipstick, the one she always wore on special occasions, along with her perfume. Ruby was dressed in her Christmas outfit: a maroon velvet jumper and white blouse, black patent-leather shoes over white tights that itched. Gavin was at home with Daddy today, so it was just the two of them. Ruby felt important.

Up ahead, the line for Santa stretched a long way, but Ruby didn't mind waiting. She had printed out her list over and over again, a list in each colour of pencil crayon, memorizing it so that she would remember when the time came. *And what would you like for Christmas, little girl?* She waited patiently, hoping she wouldn't have to go to the bathroom suddenly, like last year. But last year she was a baby, wasn't she? Just six years old, and she started to cry when her mother put her on Santa's lap. Silly Ruby.

This time she smiled, though Santa's eyes looked a little mean, and one corner of his beard slipped down past his lips. His knees were too bony, the belly against her back too soft. But no matter. She smiled brightly, looked to make sure her mother was watching. And as Santa asked her the all-important question, she couldn't answer right away. Her mother wasn't watching her but was talking to some man Ruby had never seen before.

Little girl, what would you like for Christmas this year? An impatient Santa, ready to slide her off his lap. Ruby heard him but couldn't find her words. Her mother leaned into the man, smiling, laughing, and throwing her head back so that he nearly kissed her white throat. A click of the camera, and a woman dressed as an elf, round red circles painted on her cheeks, took her hand and led her down the steps. In the photograph in the cardboard frame, Ruby is looking away from Santa, her brow furrowed in concentration and worry. Her mother slid the photo into her purse without comment.

"This is Dr. Barrett," she said. "My boss."

The man held out his hand. Ruby pulled away, her lip pushing out in a pout. Something was wrong.

"Dr. Barrett's going to have lunch with us today," Ruby's mother said, and now the whole day was ruined.

They sat together in the restaurant, Ruby's chair pulled all the way forward. She remembered to sit up straight, a paper bib tucked into the front of her velvet dress. She didn't like Dr. Barrett, if only because he had dared to intrude on her time with her mother. He was trying to be nice, making jokes, and looking at her directly. Mostly he just talked to her mother. Ruby could tell that the words they said meant nothing and were meant to fool her.

Her mother chattered the whole way home on the streetcar, but after they got off, as their feet crunched up the street towards her grandmother's house, her mother's voice dropped off, and the smile slid down and away.

"Will we tell Daddy that we had lunch with Dr. Barrett?" Ruby asked. Her mother paused for a moment, just a moment, her hand flying up to touch her throat. She smiled.

"Of course we will," she said. Ruby knew she was lying.

She didn't squeal until dinner, all five of them seated around Grandmother's table. She can't imagine now that she did it on purpose. She wasn't old enough to calculate, surely. There must have simply been a pause in the conversation—conversation too stilted and strained, mostly her grandmother speaking to Otto about people no one else knew, Ruby's mother forcing a polite smile.

A lull, and then the heavy silence that seemed to permeate the dark house. (Her mother, when they first arrived the year before, made an effort to bring in lightness, pushing back the drapes thick with dust, and polishing the windows with a rag that turned black in no time. It didn't make any difference; the darkness returned stealthily, a thief in the night.) In that one blank moment, when everyone chewed and swallowed and thought of something else to say, Ruby scraped her fork across her plate.

"We had lunch with a man today," she said. To her credit, her mother did not flinch, but her fork stopped momentarily.

Her father looked up. "Oh?"

Ruby nodded. "After we saw Santa," she said.

It is easy to read more into a vague memory than the event warrants, and it is difficult to know how much is true. Her father flicked his eyes from her mother to Ruby, back to her mother, considering (the lipstick, the perfume, the outfit).

"And who was that, Lenore?"

At the sound of his voice, Ruby was suddenly aware of the enormity of her mistake. It was in the way he said her mother's name, clipped, edgy, and chopped in two—Le-*nore*—rather than a single, curved line tumbling from his mouth in an easy sigh.

Her father swallowed hard. Her mother didn't answer at first but lifted a napkin and blotted her lips, a partial lip outline traced in red staining the paper.

"Dr. Barrett," she says. "We ran into him and he invited us. What could I say?" She blinked, opened her eyes wide, and tilted her head to the side, looking at Ruby's father so intensely that a blush reddened his forehead, slid down his face and neck, and disappeared beneath his shirt collar. "There's nothing wrong with that, is there, Otto?"

He looked away. Grandmother chewed slowly, her eyes small, narrow, and Ruby bit the fleshy inside of her cheek, her tongue poking the lumps and bumps she found there. (Other things she did sometimes at the dinner table to make the time go by faster: looked at her reflection in her spoon, crossing her eyes; surreptitiously tore up the paper napkin hidden on her lap, tearing and tearing it into tiny pieces until she held a pile of confetti she then squished into a ball. These occupations were made more exciting by the fact that they had to be done in secret so that her grandmother didn't see.)

They lived in the basement of her grandmother's house. They moved here last year when Ruby's father lost his job. *It's only temporary*, he said then. Ruby hated it here. Her parents slept on a pullout sofa while she and Gavin were stuffed in the tiny basement bedroom. They could hear her grandmother's footsteps above them at night. She missed the apartment they used to live in and the way her mother's face used to blush to show she was happy. Lenore didn't laugh much anymore; her mouth pulled inward all the time, as if she was biting back words she wished she could say.

RUBY LETS GAVIN CARRY the boxes to the basement alone. It's creepy down there, a huge cold concrete space, unfinished but full of potential. Barrett always intended to make it into a games room or home theatre, but he never did. Only the maids go down now, and only to do the laundry or fetch the buckets, mops, and rubber gloves. Ruby always feels watched in the basement, as if invisible eyes are peering out from the uneven, damp walls.

"That's it, I guess," Gavin says, coming back upstairs. "For now, anyway." But he seems to be in no rush to leave.

"Is something wrong?" Ruby asks.

Gavin looks older suddenly, the flesh soft and sagging in his face. He sighs.

"Let's go for a beer," he says.

The pub is familiar, just around the corner from their old apartment, the one paid for by Barrett for so many years, until Rena died. On the patio, Ruby presses her fingers against a cold half-pint of beer and watches Gavin smoke a cigarette.

"I thought you quit."

"I did," Gavin says. "Melanie left me. She moved back in with her parents."

"Oh, Gavin."

He looks over her shoulder, eyes blank. If he feels remorse, guilt, or even sadness, Ruby can't see it on his face.

"How are you?" she asks. But they have never been the kind of family to analyze or dissect their feelings. They are more likely to make a quick joke, something to cover the hurt and pain.

"I'm sorry, Gavin."

A young couple pauses to read the menu posted on the wall of the pub, their hands linked, loose and tanned. The man tilts his head, says something that makes the woman laugh, then lets go of her hand and places his palm against her lower back. As they turn to leave, Ruby jerks her head sideways, away.

"So what are you going to do?" she asks Gavin. "Move back to the city?" This thought pleases her: once again, the family would be together, whole, in one place.

Gavin takes a swallow of his beer, wipes his lips with the back of his hand (and then, Ruby notices, swipes his hand along his army-green shorts).

"I'll move in with Mom, I guess," he says.

"You can't."

"Why not?"

Do you really want to be a leech for the rest of your life? Only she doesn't say this, no. Instead, she tries to laugh, make a joke. "How are you going to pick up women when you live at home with Mommy?"

Gavin scowls. "That's the last thing I need to worry about," he says.

A sluggish trail of foam slides from a frothy puddle at the bottom of Ruby's glass to her mouth. She feels good right now, a slight buzz from the small amount of alcohol, the late afternoon heat eased by a wind that blows across the lake from the south. Later, she knows, it will be easy—*easier*—for the loneliness to creep in, just when the sun sinks and dusk turns the grass cool against bare feet, when families light barbecues and call out across the street for the children. Ruby will sit on her small porch with her feet resting on the black iron railing, hands on her knees, just watching and waiting for it to happen to her too.

IF SHE CLOSES HER EYES, what does she remember? That first night in the backyard on Garden Street, a picnic table, the clink of empty bottles, and the smell of cigarettes carried on the summer air. Angela had strung patio lanterns across the top of the fence that glowed blue, green, and orange on their skin. Duncan stretched back, his curls a little too long on the sides, swooping down over his half-lowered lids, lazily watching her. So languid, his movements, at ease.

You remind me of someone, he had said, and she named movie stars, women rich with power and fame. He shook his head, a smile (bemused? affectionate?) playing on his mouth. *Maybe in my past life*, he said.

Angela rested her arms on the table, fists curled under her chin, her eyes glassy, adoring, fixed on his face. A comfortable moment—the three of them, the late night, the way lights in neighbouring windows winked on and off. Nights like this—you could stay here forever. Ruby likes to remember this moment because things always change, and the warmth and security would drain from their faces. She kicked off her sandals, dug her toes into the cool grass, heels leaving rounded imprints.

Angela rose for more wine, hooking the empty bottle on her index finger, swinging it back and forth.

"Behave yourselves," she said, winking. "I'll be right back." She tottered slightly, missed the door handle the first time, turned her head to laugh.

Then they were alone. They had been talking about Ruby's father—her real father, not Barrett—and the way he had disappeared. Duncan smiled at her.

"Do you ever wonder what he's doing now? If he ever thinks about you?" he asked.

She did, in fact, wonder, though not often anymore, but the question hit hard. In the first few years after he left, she had wondered all the time. *What did I do, Daddy? Why did you leave me?* Now it was more like a periodic ache, a vague absence.

"I'm sorry," he said. "I shouldn't have asked." He touched her shoulder. "I can't imagine how difficult it's been, Ruby."

Is that when it happened? The way his mouth folded softly around her name, a quiet voice, eyes steady and probing, too intimate, perhaps. Ruby wanted to press her nose into his neck, that space just above his collarbone, and breathe in deeply. *Duncan.*

He lifted his chin as if in response, as if he knew, then looked away, cleared his throat. Silence wrapped around them. A raccoon emerged from the darkness, balanced on the edge of the fence, its toes catching and tangling in the patio lantern wire. Angela returned with the wine, breaking the stillness of the moment. She swung her legs over the picnic bench, and Duncan turned to smile at her. An ache—of loss or melancholy—spread across Ruby's chest.

NO, SCRATCH THAT MEMORY. Another one, please. Ruby was eight, standing in the playground of a new school, alone and lonely. She pressed her back against the brick building, watched a group of girls skipping in front of her.

Girl Guide, Girl Guide, dressed in blue,
These are the actions you must do:
Stand at attention, stand at ease,
Bend your elbows, bend your knees.

Salute to the captain, bow to the Queen,
Turn your back on the dirty submarine.
I can do the heel and toe, I can do the splits.
I can do the hoochy-koochy, just like this.

One of the girls broke free, approached. She wore a white knitted cardigan and brown corduroy skirt. Her knee socks sagged and slouched to her ankles. When she reached Ruby, she knelt down to play with the safety pins and tiny coloured beads adorning the laces of her sneakers, turned up her face to make sure Ruby saw. Friendship beads. This girl was popular. And now she stood, her red curls a tight halo around her face. Even then, at only eight years old, she had the high cheekbones, the aristocratic slant to her nose.

"You have no daddy," she said, small white fangs pressing into her lips as she smiled.

"No." Ruby didn't move away, didn't flinch. Instead, she stared back into those green eyes, stared and poured honesty into her eyes, face blank and impassive, until the other girl's smile slipped.

"I don't have one either," she said. She pulled a bag full of grapes from the pocket of her cardigan, offered it up. "My name is Angela."

Ruby took out a grape, green and smooth, and popped it in her mouth, her cheeks watering from the sudden burst of sweetness.

HI, DUNCAN HAD SAID there on her doorstep on the night of Barrett's funeral, and what did Ruby do? She shut the door in his face without a word and hid away in her room, pulling her pocket doors closed. Duncan knocked once or twice, then disappeared, and she hasn't heard from him since.

No, she hadn't shut the door. She smiled as always and opened the door wide, her heart tearing in a single, jagged motion. Of course she let him in, watched as he hunted in her cupboards for some wine and two small tumblers she bought on a business trip to Sweden. He was so sure of himself, leaning back against the counter and looking at her as he drank.

He brought greasy burgers.

"Stellar combination," she said, smirking. He stuck out his tongue. They ate in the living room, scattering crumbs on her couch, but she didn't mind. When they finished, she rooted around on her bookshelf for Scrabble. She spread the board on the coffee table and sat cross-legged on the floor, letting him take the couch opposite. They had played often, Ruby and Duncan. It was customary, a habit by now.

"Dirty words okay," he said.

"And slang."

"And made-up words, as long as you can defend them."

When she and Gavin were small, they made up an entire coded language, and a new alphabet of symbols to go along with it. They wrote it all down in a notebook and practised their speech whenever they could. The worlds they used to create.

After the fire, Lenore took them to a cottage on the beach. Ruby remembers emerging from the ocean, the way her cold skin mixed with sand as she huddled behind a makeshift cave of lawn chairs and a towel spread between two dunes. The warmth there in that small space, the ability to forget as her hair splashed wetly against her cheeks.

They played seriously for a bit, then became silly.

"*Urgle?*"

"The sound you make when you choke on water."

He nodded, serious, contemplative. His next word: *fuck*. He let his fingers rest on the small squares as his eyes met hers. She looked away first.

"You seem okay," he said.

"Am I not supposed to be?"

"I mean about Barrett."

"Oh." She had forgotten. "I'm sad," she said. "But mostly for my mother."

"Not for you?"

"No. Maybe a little. It's funny, in a way. It seems like we've known him forever, but until Rena died, we only saw him once a week."

"On Wednesdays."

"Wednesdays."

"How did his wife die again?"

"I think it was pneumonia. But she had M.S."

"Do you think they were happy?"

"My mother and Barrett, or Barrett and his wife?"

"Your mother."

Lenore on Wednesday nights: perfume, a new dress or necklace, her hand fluttering up to her throat as she glanced at the clock before he arrived. And the way she exhaled when he rang from the lobby, a sigh of pleasure, anticipation.

"Yes, I think they were very happy," she said.

"I guess that's all that matters, then." Something in his voice made her look at him closely. He leaned back against the couch, face blank, unfocused. She shook her head.

"Is it?" she asked. "I always wonder about his wife, what she knew or heard. She must have known. How could you not know if your husband was cheating on you for fifteen years?"

He wasn't listening, studying the Scrabble board instead. As if he didn't want to hear what she was saying, but maybe that was all in her head when she thought about it later. Maybe he didn't have any kind of intentions at all.

"When are you going back to work?" he asked.

"When we get back from the cottage. We're going up to scatter Barrett's ashes. I could have taken more time, but we have a meeting next weekend, and there's too much to do."

"I have a show next weekend. You'll miss it."

"Yes."

"I have some new songs."

She focused on her tiles. *Are they about me, your songs?* Her letters spelled *regret*, her hand against her cheek wet with tears.

"Ruby?" He rose quickly, the Scrabble board catching on his leg and tipping, scattering letters over the floor.

"Don't." She pushed him away. He stretched out his legs, hung them over the end of the sofa, and moved slowly until his head rested in her lap. Her fingers reached out involuntarily to smooth back his hair and rest comfortably in his wild curls. The way he looked at her then.

"What do you want to do with your life?" he asked.

"What?"

"What do you want to do?"

"I have a job."

"Yes," he says. "But what do you *want* to do?"

She laughed, tapped his face.

"I'm serious, Ruby."

Her hand stilled. "I don't know," she said, suddenly swamped by a sense of sadness. She didn't know, has never known. She shook her head.

"I just want to be happy," she said. He frowned, and his eyes deepened.

"What did you want to be when you were little?" she asked.

"The usual," he said. "Firefighter, astronaut. I knew I wanted to be a musician from the time I was twelve or thirteen."

"I wanted to be adopted by the Six Million Dollar Man or the Incredible Hulk," she said.

"Two very different choices," he said, pretending to be serious.

"I never had any ambition to be *something*." Angela wanted to be many things: airline stewardess, veterinarian, artist, pilot.

"What are we doing?" she asked.

"Hanging out."

"Come on, Duncan." He pulled away, sat up, and slid down the length of the couch to the other end. Her palms missed the feel of his curls.

"I'm leaving Angela," he said.

"What?"

"Not for you, for me." He looked down at his wine, touched a finger to the rim of his glass, then to his lips. "It's not working out."

She sat stupidly silent until he smiled, awkward and uneasy. "Say something. I can't stand the silence."

"I don't know what to say."

A fluke, the first time he came by on a Friday night months and months ago. He called from a pay phone. *I'm in the neighbourhood. Meet me for a drink?* And she had. They drank together for a few hours, and he went on his way, back to the live-in nanny, Angela away in the States for a conference. Then a month later: *Can I come over?* He unearthed the Scrabble board, leaving prints on the dusty cover. They never spoke of Angela or Bram but fell into a rhythm of easy conversation. She could almost imagine they were friends, except for the way her stomach fluttered with nerves, the way her skin reacted when he touched her by accident. She had forgotten such chivalrous kindness: a hand on her lower back in greeting, his cheek pressed against hers, the solicitous questions about her life, her interests, the books she had read, the music she liked. He listened, head slightly angled, his eyes focused, intent.

"Oh, Duncan. What about Bram?" The toddler who looked like Duncan, the infectious grin and eagerness to see the world, the way he placed his hand in his dad's and held on tightly with immeasurable trust.

He dropped his head, stopped breathing for a moment.

"I don't know what else to do," he said. "Ruby, I can't do it anymore. You don't know."

She didn't. She had not spoken to Angela—really spoken—in more than a year. After Bram came along, their lives shifted and separated. What did Ruby know or care of diapers and potty training, Bram's garbled mispronunciations that seemed so funny to Angela? After the last few telephone calls full of stops, starts, and awkward laughter, they just gave up.

"She works upstairs all day and I never talk to her. When she's finished for the day, we eat dinner, and there's nothing. There's just Bram. I can't—Ruby, that's not a marriage. That's just holding on. We haven't slept together in—"

"Stop."

"Yes." He shifted, leaned forward to rest his arms on his knees. When he looked up at her, his skin was pale, pinched. "Why didn't I meet you first?"

"Why did you marry her?"

It was wrong to talk like this, so terribly wrong. And yet she could not stop. She wanted him to say what she wanted to hear. Just to hear it once from him, to know that it meant something.

"I loved her," he said. "I did. But she's not the same person anymore, or maybe I'm not. We've gone in opposite directions." He hadn't shaved in too long; dark stubble shadowed his cheeks, his chin, the cleft below his lips.

He bent his head to kiss her, his hands wrapped around her wrists. She pulled away.

"No. No, Duncan."

"Ruby."

"She's my best friend."

"Not anymore," he said, but he dropped his hands.

"You should go," she said. She couldn't look at him.

At the front door, he touched her once—a brief instant of contact, his palm burning through the thin material of her T-shirt.

"Ruby, you know …" He looked away, didn't finish. She closed the door behind him gently, then leaned, head bent to touch the wood, unspoken words threatening to choke her.

Seven

THE TEMPERATURE HAS CLIMBED to a record-breaking high. It's all anyone can talk about—on the street, on the news. Gavin doesn't care, comfortable in his suburban, air-conditioned home, or driving around in his suburban, air-conditioned car. *Her* car, if you want to be specific. Gavin doesn't. He prefers to pretend. At the end of the month, Melanie will move in and toss him out, and he'll be back with his mother in the city, riding the subway and counting the tokens in his pocket.

He turns up the air conditioning, even though it's still early enough in the morning for the air to have a hint of coolness, and follows the signs towards the hospital. He learned to drive just last year and now turns up a CD loudly, the music, as always, calming his nerves. Melanie has been in some kind of accident, and his father-in-law (soon to be ex-father-in-law) called and asked—no, *demanded*—that Gavin come. Of course Gavin's worried, but he does feel a flash of annoyance, as if Melanie has done it on purpose, this accident. And who knows? Maybe it's just a way to grab his attention. Her father didn't say much on the phone. *She hit a tree*, he said. *I think you should come down here.* That doesn't sound all that serious, does it?

He pulls into emergency parking, but doesn't pay at the machine. Fuck it. It's Melanie's car, anyway; she'll get the parking ticket, if there is one. The heat rising from the black asphalt hits him as he steps from the car. He has never worn sandals before, but Melanie bought him these great spongy brown ones this year. Very sporty and manly, not like those woven, I'm-retired-and-will-now-wear-white-socks-with-sandals kind, the cheap ones you can sometimes find at the dollar stores.

On the fourth floor, he follows the signs to the critical care unit, only mildly nervous, and checks in at the front desk. Mr. Torrent, Melanie's father, is there already, a solid figure outlined against the window, his back to Gavin. And in the bed, her arms by her sides, Melanie.

At first he thinks her face is gone, sliced off in a single blow. Bandages cover her skin, reveal only a bloodied nose and bruised lips. A tube snakes into her mouth.

"Is she …?"

Mr. Torrent turns from the window, his arms crossed in front of his chest. "She's sedated," he says. "She's in a lot of pain."

Clumps of her hair—her pride, combed, and conditioned to perfection every day—stick up in hardened tufts through the bandages. She would be appalled if she could see herself now. Gavin smiles, imagining her mortified rage, the hissy fit that would follow.

"Is something funny?" Mr. Torrent stares, icy eyes, pale lips, his fingers working, working against his shirt collar, tugging and pulling. Gavin shakes his head. The Torrents have never liked him, think he's a bum. Not that he has ever done anything to prove them wrong.

Melanie's mother comes into the room, two coffees in her hands. Her eyes are small in her face, swollen and rimmed with red and pink. She freezes when she sees Gavin. He nods, and she turns away, hands a cup to her husband.

"I didn't know you were coming," she says.

"I called him," Mr. Torrent says. "Of course he'd want to come."

And now they are both staring at him, a wall of anger and dismay. Gavin reads it on both their faces: *she deserves better*. He wants to disappear, tell them they're right. She does deserve better, and he told her that all along.

"I'm so sorry about your father," Mrs. Torrent says, and, for a moment, Gavin wonders what Melanie has told them about Otto.

"Oh, you mean Barrett," he says. "Yes, thanks." He nods, perhaps a little too vigorously, boisterously. Mrs. Torrent purses her lips in disgust.

Around them, machines hum and click, and Melanie's chest rises and falls in mechanical rhythm. Gavin has been in a hospital twice before in his life: once, when his sister had her appendix out, and once more recently, just after Barrett died. The antiseptic smell burns his nose and eyes. He wonders how long he has to stay here pretending, how much is required before he can escape.

"She was driving my car," Mr. Torrent says. "She's not used to it, the size." He drives a Mercedes sedan, heavy and dignified, so unlike Melanie's zippy Volkswagen. "It was late at night, and she took a curve too fast." His voice catches, but his eyes are dry. His wife touches his arm, closing her eyes and uttering a single soft grunt.

"The car's totalled. It wouldn't have been so bad, but there was a tree branch, a limb that had been knocked down in some storm. No one ever cleans up the mess." He pauses, clears his throat a few times. "It went straight through the windshield. The glass ... glass in her face ..." He turns, places his hand against the wall, and abruptly leaves the room.

Mrs. Torrent's face is still, unmoving. Her eyes, Gavin sees, are the same shade of blue as Melanie's—pale, nearly translucent.

"Her face will never be the same," she says. "She hit the steering wheel. They'll have to redo everything."

Gavin tries to swallow, but a rising panic has sucked the moisture from his tongue and the roof of his mouth. He sees now where this is all heading, and the suffocating awareness is too much. He grasps the end of the bed, squeezes. Mrs. Torrent moves towards him slowly, presses her palm against the back of his hand.

"I know things haven't been easy," she says. "I'm glad you came today. Melanie would be glad." Her hand on his is heavy and clammy, a dead weight. He pulls free. Nodding, head bobbing like a simpleton, he backs out of the room, watching Mrs. Torrent's face transformed from pain and grief to confusion.

Outside the room, he exhales. The red exit sign beckons at the end of the long corridor.

"Where are you going?"

Gavin knows he should lie, say he's going for coffee, a snack, *anything*, but he stands mute, lips pressed together. Mr. Torrent's skin is grey, and the flesh seems sunken beneath his eyes, his cheekbones. Gavin focuses on the man's impossibly large ears, the long lobes, the strands of hair protruding from the greasy-looking canals. He has never noticed these ears before and wonders if the man's face is shrinking before his eyes.

"I don't think you understand the situation," Mr. Torrent says. His first name is Bill, but Gavin has never been invited to call him that, never been invited to call him anything, come to think of it—not Dad, or Bill, or (Gavin's favourite) Mr. T.—and Gavin has gone out of his way to not refer to him by name. *Your dad*, he would say to Melanie and, when addressing Bill, *you*. If he had to get Mr. Torrent's attention, Gavin always waited to catch his eye.

But now, Gavin seizes the moment, straightens up. "She left me, Bill," he says. Mr. Torrent moves so quickly that Gavin doesn't have time to react, feels himself pushed hard against the wall, his shirt (and some stray chest hairs) bunched up and held in the other man's fists.

"You little shit," Mr. Torrent says, his face now ruddy, swollen with angry blood, his eyes bulging. He releases Gavin, wipes his palms along his slacks, the sudden anger draining away but still visible in the tightened muscles of his jaw, the way his shoulders rise up under his supersized ears. "You owe her this," he says quietly. "*In sickness and in health*, remember?"

IT WAS JUNE, A CLEAR, perfect day with fluffy clouds and a breeze. Melanie wore a designer knock-off wedding gown with lots of beading on the top and a fluffy skirt. She had planned it for a year, driven Gavin half crazy with the details—what did he care what flowers they had? What was the difference between satin and silk? Weren't they both shiny? He didn't know which style of bridesmaid dress would best flatter both her fatter and skinnier friends.

"Whatever you want," he told her, but that was the wrong thing to say. Her eyes welled up, and she turned away, hurt. It's not that he didn't care, but he warned her right off the bat: he told her he was afraid of commitment, unreliable, lazy. He meant it because it was all true, but she took it to mean he was a challenge, something to fix. She looked up at him with those trusting blue eyes and slowly unhooked her bra. What could he have done?

It worked like this: they met, had sex right there in the club downtown where she had come with a gaggle of similar-looking friends, all dressed in sexy halter tops and jeans that hugged their asses. Gavin had been dragged there by friends determined to get him laid. He hated dance clubs, hated the guys with their slick in-style clothes as they danced ever closer to their target of choice, hated the way they eyed Gavin quickly and then looked away with a smirk, as if he were no competition at all. Gavin, dressed in his black T-shirt, his green shorts that used to be pants until he decided to saw them off at the knee, leaving behind a ragged, trailing hem, and his Doc Martens. And the women—perfumed and glistening, perfectly made up. Those girls were high maintenance. He knew it, everyone knew it. But sexy.

They had sex in a bathroom stall standing up and she cried afterwards, clung to his neck, her eyeliner smeared and mascara running down her cheeks. He said he would call, but didn't mean it, thought she was probably crazy and way too young anyway, but the sex was pretty good, and she was hot. She wrote her number on a tissue in lipstick, pressed it into his hand.

He didn't call her for three weeks, then dug up the tissue and squinted to read the numbers, drunk and unsteady, feeling sorry for himself, twenty-nine years old and living in a bachelor apartment with nothing on the walls but an old Smiths poster. He told himself that at least he wasn't like Cousin George living with Mommy, but his job at the laundromat barely paid the rent and wasn't exactly fulfilling.

The number was long distance, but he called anyway. He almost called collect.

"May I ask who's calling?" Mr. Torrent's voice was indifferent, deep, polite.

"Gavin," he said, wondering if he should add more detail. *I met her in a bar three weeks ago; we had sex in the bathroom.* (Now he would like to travel back in time and do this, just once, just to imagine his strangled face, the veins popping on the side of that big head of his.) The phone clicked, then clicked again as she picked up. She hesitated, agreed to drive into the city on Friday. As soon as she said yes, he felt instant remorse. *What am I doing?*

She showed up at his door on time. Gavin had showered and shaved, scarfed down a quick bowl of soup from one of the Korean places down the street, and brushed his teeth. She smiled. She was wearing a short light blue skirt. Her legs were tanned, her left ankle encircled by a delicate gold chain. He could see a lacy bra through her thin sleeveless blouse. He took her to Coffee Time. He had planned to take her somewhere nicer, somewhere farther downtown, a cute little café with overpriced desserts, but he didn't really want to talk to her at all. She sipped tea (she didn't drink coffee), and told him all about her life in the suburbs: living with Mom and Dad, the English degree she just received in June, her original plan to go to teachers' college like all her friends in the fall.

"What do you do?" she asked, and Gavin realized that he hadn't been listening at all. He had been staring down her top at the hint of cleavage and wishing he could dive under the table and slide that skirt off, bury his face between her thighs. He took her back to the apartment and did just that, listened to her whinnies and delicate cries. When she kissed him hard and told him she couldn't stay overnight, he wasn't too disappointed.

He didn't call her for a month. By the time he did, she was in the city at teachers' college, her father said. Gavin couldn't tell from his voice if he knew who he was, but he left his name and number just the same. She called that night and then arrived at his apartment, a small cake wrapped in cardboard balanced in one hand, wearing jeans and a T-shirt bearing the word *Love* in the centre of her chest.

"I knew you'd call." She was happy, glowing, her blond hair longer and shinier than Gavin remembered. He smeared strawberry jam on her body and licked it off.

Now that she was in the city, they saw each other all the time. Sometimes they went to the movies, but the dates invariably ended with his fingers between her legs, and then they were stuck listening to other people crunch on popcorn as she bucked and gasped over the movie soundtrack.

By December, she had told Gavin she loved him and invited him home to meet her family. He declined, pled family commitments that would take him from the city over the holidays, and then he retreated into his apartment and didn't answer the door or phone for a while. He called her again in February; she hung up on him. He figured that was it and continued on his way, but one night she showed up at his door in a tight black dress and high heels that he convinced her to keep on while he fucked her.

"You're using me," she said afterwards.

"I'm not." She lay on the bed, naked from the waist up, her pantyhose ripped down the middle, the heels of her shoes digging into Gavin's old Star Wars comforter.

"Convince me," she said. It was a variation of a conversation they had for the next four months, and it was always the same, but he started to notice that when she left his apartment, he could still smell her perfume, her hair, could still feel the skin at the back of her neck against his fingertips. She cooked dinner for him and made his lunches for the next day, wrapping his sandwiches in Saran Wrap and making the menu as balanced as possible, always including an apple or carrot sticks.

"You don't eat well," she said, frowning.

"Are you going to start dressing me next?"

"No, but I'll undress you anytime you want," she said, sliding her hand inside his pants.

In June, she took him home to the suburbs to meet her family: her father, who wore a giant Rolex watch, owned a construction company, and looked at Gavin as if expecting him to call him *sir*; and her mother, a faker version of Melanie, with short blond curls, carefully made-up eyes, and a mouth stuck in a false smile. There were no other children in the family. When Melanie took him on a tour of their house by the lake, he nearly threw up at the sight of her pink ruffled bedroom.

"I think you need more stuffed animals," he joked, and she told him not to worry, the rest were in her dorm room in the city.

At dinner he was grilled by her father, and he didn't get any answers right. He didn't have a steady job, he wasn't trying hard enough to impress them (in truth, he didn't care what they thought about him), and his family didn't have money, not the kind they obviously had.

"We've worked hard to make sure that Melanie has whatever she wants in life," her father said, looking at Gavin steadily. "She's a princess, and whoever she marries will have to take care of her the way we always have." Gavin tried not to choke on his veal. Who said anything about marriage?

Melanie drove them home. Gavin had every intention of breaking up with her right then, but she came inside and asked him what he was going to do with a bad girl like her, and he took off her skirt and showed her, and then he convinced himself that breaking up with her would not be the best thing to do. And now it was summer, so he met her friends, who were all boring and looked the same, and she met his, or some of them. She didn't like his friends, he could tell. She thought they were too alternative, weird, and hard. Some of them scared her. Since she was seven years younger than Gavin, his friends, eyeing her breasts, clapped him on the back for having hooked up with such a young chick. He did feel like a stud, and the sex was very good. She wasn't a virgin, not by a long shot, and wouldn't her daddy be surprised to know that?

In July, she had a breakdown and sobbed on his bed one night until he thought about calling for help.

"But what's wrong?" he asked. "Please tell me." Finally she looked up at him, all messed up, and told him that it wasn't going anywhere, that he had destroyed her heart and wrecked her life because now all she would do from now on was think of him and why it all had to end.

"I'm in love with you," she said, sniffing bravely. "But you don't love me, so I'm going to leave. I need to find someone who will love me."

Gavin didn't try to stop her when she left, but when she was gone, he didn't know what to do with himself. He woke in the mornings with eyes open wide, unblinking. The sense of something missing became heavier and harder to bear. One afternoon, brushing his teeth for the first time that day, he smelled her perfume again, so strongly that he staggered and had to grip the edge of the sink with both hands.

"Took you long enough to call," Melanie said, pouting. It had been three months; she had nearly given up.

"You just like me because your father doesn't," Gavin teased.

"You just like me for the sex," she countered. "And because I'm so young and hot."

But it wasn't her youth that drew him, not really, and not her ass or any other body part. It was the way she leaned into his chest as if he was her hero, the only one who could make things all right. He felt those tiny shoulders or the way he could encircle her wrist and then some with his hand. He proposed that November, and they were married in July. Gavin lifted the veil and leaned forward to kiss her, his mother, Barrett, and Ruby sitting incredulously in the front row on the left, Melanie's scowling father and rather frightened-looking mother sitting on the right. And Gavin was sucked into a swirling sticky cobweb, his arms and legs stuck and paralyzed, so that he could do nothing to free himself. A single droplet of sweat trickled down his cheek. Melanie wiped it away, pressed her fingers to her lips, and whispered in his ear, "Don't cry, silly man."

AT HOME, there is a message from his mother, telling him that she will be home in two days, and thanking him for packing up some of Barrett's things with Ruby.

"Good." Said out loud, in the empty house. His mother has always needed solitude. *I need some me time*, she used to say to them when they were young, and she would close the bathroom door, light candles, and soak in the tub for an hour with a good book. *Nothing better*, she would say when she emerged, her cheeks flushed and hair curling. Gavin would drink in the steam, his fingers leaving prints on the bathroom mirror as he brushed his teeth. Ruby is like that too, happy in her hovel of an apartment, barely any friends, and no boyfriends (aside from that ridiculous figment of her imagination). Gavin has never felt the urge for complete isolation, never understood those who did. Even when he lived alone, he always had friends, often crashed in a drunken stupor on someone's couch overnight. He used to be like that: carefree and light, the guy everyone liked, a blast to have around.

He takes a beer and a bag of Doritos and sits at the patio table in the backyard, staring at the wasteland that is his yard in his T-shirt, shorts, and spongy brown sandals. Melanie wants a pool, that was her big plan for the yard, just another *Daddy, buy this for me?* on her list, just like the house, furniture, wedding, and honeymoon. Broken bits of chips litter his chest and belly. He licks salt from his fingers, not caring as orange dust settles on his T-shirt. This is Melanie's life, not Gavin's.

The morning after the wedding, he watched Melanie slide her finger beneath the flap of the envelope, her puzzlement turning to incredulity, her mouth dropping open. *Oh my God, Gavin, my parents bought us a house!* A house Gavin had never seen, in one of those neighbourhoods so new that the sidewalks had yet to be poured. No grass or trees, houses slapped down on torn-up ground in rows of sameness, far from his family and friends in the city.

Near the apartment in which he grew up, forest and green tumbled down to the river. Pebbles and rock, waterfalls, ducks. Sometimes foxes crept down from the wooded ridge. Every Sunday, Lenore packed up the kids and a picnic, and they took their bicycles down to the riverbank, spread out a blanket, and ate crispy potato chips and sandwiches warmed by the sun. *Our day of rest*, Lenore would say. Here, in the suburbs, there are no ravines. You can head south and hit the lake, of course, but it's not the same, not cozy and small, not familiar.

Gavin sighs, rises too quickly so that blood rushes to his head. He sits down again, bows his head, suddenly sickened by the image of Melanie's stained bandages, the quiet of her forced breathing, her parents' grey skin. He feels the weight of his guilt, of all he has done. He should never have married her, should have been honest with her, with himself. And now she's an invalid, and it falls on Gavin's shoulders to take care of her. Mr. Torrent was right: he does owe it to her.

ON SATURDAY, GAVIN STAYS overnight at his mother's house. Something has brought him here, some compulsion to drive through the old neighbourhood again. He parks outside the apartment complex where they used to live, turns off the car, and opens the windows, letting the heat creep in and prickle his skin. He doesn't remember moving here, of course; he would have been what, four or five? This was his only home until Rena died and Lenore moved into Barrett's house, when Gavin was in his twenties. By then, Gavin was in residence at the university, taking philosophy, history, and easy, first-year electives, smoking a lot of pot, and drinking a lot of watered-down pub beer. *What do you want to be when you grow up, little boy?* When he stopped to think about it, he didn't have a clue. His jobs after he finally managed to graduate show his confusion: he worked (always temporarily) in restaurants, car washes, laundromats, and convenience stores. For a while, he sold advertising space for a community newspaper, then worked as an assistant to a film agent. He sold coffee, hanging his arm out the drive-through window, a microphone perched over his ear, and then fitted shoes on smelly feet in a sporting-goods store. One summer, he tried physical labour (planting trees), but he really wasn't suited to the outdoors and complained incessantly about the heat until they fired him.

Melanie, who has psychoanalyzed him many times, claims his problems stem from the fact that he has never had a father figure. Gavin can't remember Otto at all, and all the photographs that might have helped jar his memory are gone from his mother's photo albums. Barrett was a constant, of course; he is the one who set up the family in the apartment and supported them, the one who paid for university, clothes, books, and everything else. But Barrett wasn't around all that much, not in the first few years. He usually came over Wednesday nights for dinner and a movie with Lenore. When the kids were older, they would sometimes go out, but Barrett was married and discreet. He never wanted to hurt his wife, he said.

My wife. Barrett was stiff in the beginning, as if afraid of treading on toes, and perhaps he was, his jokes obviously planned in advance to put them at ease. But then he relaxed. *Hello, little man.* A smile, long fingers in Gavin's curls, his large hand curving to rest on his cheek, hesitation falling away.

Gavin prepares the house for his mother's return, opening the windows to air the place out, then setting the air conditioner on low to lessen the heat and humidity. He could not bring himself to look at Barrett at the funeral home. Lenore said she understood, touched his wrist gently, her eyes damp. His chest emptied out for her. What would she do, who would take care of her?

He walks to the corner and heads down the street, buys a bouquet of flowers for Lenore, then places them (still held together with an elastic band) in a vase of water, which he sets on the kitchen counter. *I'll take care of her now.* The New Gavin: responsible, dependable, solid. Damn Melanie and her bruised, broken face. Damn the Torrents, the empty house with its matching espresso furniture, the framed art from HomeSense, the ceramic tiles in the kitchen that freeze his toes in the winter.

SWEAT DOWN HIS BACK, soaking the sheets. He wakes in the night, sits upright in the guest bedroom. A tidal wave, Gavin caught in the middle, arms up over his head in surrender, gritty salt caught in his teeth. He takes a deep breath, pressing his palms flat by his sides. *Just a dream, Gavin, go back to sleep.* His senses sharpen; he cocks his head. He can still hear water coursing through the pipes in the house, as if someone is taking a shower or has flushed the toilet.

He slips into his shorts. He is nearly blind out in the hallway, but the skylight above the stairs illuminates a path, and his eyes adjust. All is silent. There are five bathrooms in this house. All three on the upper floor are quiet, as is the one on the main floor. No one is in the kitchen, and the tap isn't dripping or leaking anywhere that he can see. *Maybe you imagined it. Maybe it was just part of the dream.*

He flicks the switch at the top of the stairs leading to the basement. Ruby hates it down here, thinks it's creepy, and even Gavin pauses, a bare toe on the wooden stair, before heading down. Basements are always like this, especially partially finished ones in older homes. This house—according to Barrett—was built in the early 1900s. Even so, something feels different, or maybe it's just the lateness of the hour, the silence of the house climbing into his ears until he imagines he hears the scuttling of mice and breathing. His neck prickles, and his muscles run with nervous energy. *Is someone watching me?*

"Hello?" he calls out, mostly to make himself feel better. "Anyone here?"

He can hear the water now. The toilet is running. He sighs, jiggles the handle until the noise abates. Old plumbing. He wonders if Lenore will sell now. A house like this, in this area of town, would easily net over a million bucks. And she doesn't need the space, never did, really.

He sniffs. It smells different down here too. It smells—well, *used*. And there, the sink is wet, but the tap is off. He turns slowly, convinced he will come face to face with an intruder. But there's no one there. Forcing his legs to move, he walks down the hall and flicks the lights on everywhere—in the main room, the laundry and furnace rooms. Empty and still, the boxes piled where they were, nothing out of the ordinary. Still, the feeling of something out of place doesn't disappear, not when he turns off the lights, not when he climbs the stairs and returns to the guest room and climbs into bed, pulling the sheet up to his chin though he's sweating, and not when he closes his eyes.

MELANIE IS SITTING UP, eating a Popsicle in her hospital bed. The bandages are gone; in their place, a criss-crossing of red lines, bruises, and scabs. But overall, she looks fine.

"Your face isn't wrecked," he says. "That's great."

"Is it?"

"Your parents said you'd have to have surgery."

"They tend to exaggerate."

She still has not looked at him. Her hair lies limply along the sides of her face; she pushes it out of the way as if it irritates her.

"Well, I'm glad." He doesn't know if he should sit or stand, how he should fold his hands, or where to rest his arms. Finally, he pulls up a chair—institutional yellow, with padded armrests—and sits by the bed, thinking of what to say next. He expected her silence, at least at first, but he did think she would be happy to see him, that her face would light up with something like relief. He was wrong.

Melanie sighs, looks towards the window where someone has pushed aside the heavy curtains.

"It's hot outside," Gavin says. "They say it's a record. Hasn't been this hot in—"

"Just stop." Her voice is flat, as limp as her hair. She has neglected her Popsicle, and pink syrup has dripped over her fingers, stained the edge of her sheet. Gavin takes a tissue from the box on the bedside table, offers one up. Instead of taking it, she finally looks him in the eye.

"Why are you here?" she asks.

"For you," he says.

"Don't do me any favours." She lifts one eyebrow. "My parents called you?"

Gavin nods. "Of course," he says.

"I told them not to," she says. "In the hospital that first night. I could taste the blood on my teeth and knew they'd call. But then I passed out, or they gave me drugs. I don't remember anything else."

"You stopped breathing," Gavin says. "They had to put a tube in your mouth. I was here a few days ago."

"I don't remember."

"You looked terrible." She still looks terrible, but of course he doesn't say that.

She shrugs. "So what do you want, then?"

"I don't want anything," he says, and then, when she continues to look at him without a word, "I don't know what I want."

"Well, I'm not the one to figure it out for you," she says. "I've already wasted too much time on you. What a joke that was."

"What?"

"The marriage."

Gavin shrinks back, eyes the wall above her bed, where someone—presumably one of her parents—has taped a picture of Melanie in glowing health. She cranes her neck to follow his gaze, snorts.

"My parents," she says. "They thought they'd have to reconstruct my face. They decided to bring in photographs so that the doctors could see what I looked like before. But nothing's even broken, just sore."

"What were you doing out so late?" Gavin asks.

"Like it's any of your business." She takes a tissue then, wipes her hands, places the melting Popsicle in a kidney-shaped dish on the table, and pushes it away from the bed. "I was on a date."

"A date?" Gavin stands, his hands clenching and unclenching. "A date? You'd only just left me, Melanie. Not even a week before, and you were on a date already?"

Melanie bursts into laughter, low and mocking.

"Oh, come on, Gavin. What did you want me to do? Cry into my pillow at home? Put on a face mask and listen to sad music?"

Yes, he did expect that, and why not? Hadn't he been stuck at home, a lazy heaviness in his limbs, watching old, terrible movies all night, every night?

"It's not like we had one fight and I went storming out," she says. "We fought all the time. We didn't get along, and we had nothing in common. We've never had anything good together, except sex."

"That's not true."

"Of course it is. And so what, you're trying to defend the marriage now? Why? Because you want to get back together? Give me a break. You've already admitted you don't know what you want. Well, you know what? I *do* know what I want. I'm only twenty-five, I want a real husband, someone who loves me, who cares. Not someone who sits around unemployed, listening to his damn CDs, getting fat, and complaining about his life with me, about how hard it all is to live like he does. And I want kids, which we all know …" She looks away, her voice crumbling. "Just go, Gavin, please."

"I was only trying to do the right thing," he says, struggling to keep the bitterness out of his voice. "It's not only my fault, you know. There are two people in every marriage."

Her head snaps up, the pale blue of her eyes magnified by tears. "And what should I have done?" she asks. "Forced you to love me?"

THE HEAVINESS IN HIS CHEST stays with him throughout the drive to the city. His mother will be home later tonight, and Ruby has left a message saying she is back from her business trip and will try to make it for dinner. Melanie is right: he is an ass. It's true he wasted her time, but she's young and won't have any trouble bouncing back. Gavin, on the other hand, is thirty-two and homeless, with no job or any prospects whatsoever. His history degree—framed and dusty, hidden away in one of those boxes in Lenore's basement—is useless. He has gotten fat and lazy, and has started smoking again. He drinks too much, sleeps too late, and the only meals he can cook come from a box or can be ordered online or by telephone. *What a catch!*

Imagine wanting to have kids with him, but that's exactly what Melanie wanted. *One baby*, she pleaded, night and day. As if it would save their marriage, turn Gavin into the husband she thought he would become. And over the last few weeks, it was all she talked about. She started taking her temperature every morning and marking it down on some silly chart. Finally, in the car on the way to the cottage, he had had enough. She had been going on and on as usual about how the weekend would be perfect timing, joking about thin walls, and warning Gavin that he wouldn't be able to walk properly at the end of the weekend—all this when he was heading up north to scatter Barrett's ashes.

"That's enough," he barked.

"What?"

"Where are we going, Melanie?"

Little lines puckered in her forehead. "To your cottage?"

"Right. And why are we going up there?"

She looked out the window, silent, but he knew he had found his mark.

"Right." He tightened his fists on the steering wheel. "The only father I've ever known," he said. "Where is your head? Are you thinking properly?" *A little melodramatic, don't you think, Gavin? The only father you've known?*

Melanie pressed herself against the car door, her head bent, neck curving so that her feathery hair fell against her cheek and hid her face.

"So, no, I don't want to try and make a baby this weekend. I don't want a baby right now, period. So please, just stop talking about it."

She stayed quiet for a long time, but didn't cry as he expected. Gavin looked over at some point to see her lower lip pushed out in a pout, the defiant way she crossed her arms in front of her chest, but slumped down in her seat, making herself as small as possible. He channelled the rage that rose unexpectedly into ridicule.

"Look at you," he jeered. "Sitting there pouting like a child. You want a baby? You *are* a baby, a spoiled little baby princess who's mad she isn't getting her own way. Well, fuck that, Melanie."

"Just shut up!" She lashed out, striking him in the shoulder. "I get it, I get it, so shut up already!"

"Spoiled little baby girl. Want a bottle, baby?"

"You suck, Gavin." And then she did start to cry, angry tears, and by then they were pulling up to the cottage. He went inside to greet his mother and Ruby and tried to shake off the tension that had crept up his neck, leaving Melanie by herself. And even when they had both cooled off, when they warmed under the sun with drinks, and Gavin put his hand on her shoulder and squeezed, he knew that something had shifted, that what he had said—and how he had spoken to her—was unforgivable. Not because it was mean, though it was, but because it came from deep within, from someplace true.

Eight

IN BARRETT'S STUDY, Lenore hangs up the phone, an old model with a rotary dial, heavy and black.

"You're not keeping up with technology," Gavin complained, but Barrett just shrugged.

"So?"

"The new phones have so many features. Wouldn't you like to know who's calling *before* you pick up the phone?" Lenore could have told him that he was wasting his time; Barrett rarely picked up the phone, in any case. But she stayed out of the conversation, merely turned her face and smiled.

"Well, that would ruin the whole surprise of a phone call, wouldn't it?"

"Surprise of a …?" Gavin shook his head. "What about an answering machine?" he asked. "What if we need to get in touch with you urgently, and you're not here?"

"If I'm not here, how will an answering machine help you get in touch with me? I still won't be here to take the call."

"Give it up, Gavin," Ruby said. "You know he won't budge."

The truth was, neither Barrett nor Lenore had any need for new technology, not when something old worked just fine. *That's the problem with kids these days,* Barrett said. *Always tossing out the new before it even has a chance to become old.* He claimed he was sick of all the phones and fax machines at work; when he came home, he wanted peace and quiet.

Well, you've got that now, Barrett, don't you? Lenore's chest clenches in a familiar way, but only for a moment. Her grief catches her by surprise, sometimes, when she is least expecting it, but the time away up north has given her a kind of acceptance, as if she too is at peace. She spent a lot of time on the dock, staring down at the lake and listening to the quiet sound of water against the rocks. We've all had a good run, she thinks.

This is all that's left, isn't it? Tying up loose ends, organizing, preparing for the end, cataloguing your successes and failures. She looks at the stack of papers on her desk, a manuscript of sorts. Since she came home, this is all she has been doing, sitting here at the new computer. (How lovely they are, she thinks. So much easier than a typewriter, and friendlier, with those soft clicks, the delete key, the swirling colours of the screen saver when she thinks for too long.)

At the beginning of it all, she added a cover page, with a single line of text, a title: "The Pattern of Life." It has a nice ring to it. She isn't sure yet what to do with the manuscript. For a few days, she thought she might let Ruby or Gavin read it, but now she has rejected that idea. For one thing, it's too hokey, and they would probably be embarrassed. For another, handing over those pages would be akin to giving up, to saying, *that's all there is.* Lenore isn't sure, but she thinks she might have another twenty or even thirty years left in her, and who knows what she might do then? And besides, there's Otto. There's something unsettling in the way his history trails off into a dead end. Without closure, the manuscript will remain incomplete and unresolved.

"Where are you, Otto?" she asks out loud, speaking to the hefty medical books that line the shelves. "Where have you been all these years?"

The study has been decorated in rich dark colours, masculine and soothing. Barrett used to smoke a pipe on occasion, and the scent of the sweet tobacco has caught and held in the thick folds of the taupe drapes. The window overlooks a portion of the backyard. From here, Lenore can see the gazebo and the flowerbeds that sprawl to the edge of the ravine.

She places her hand on the stack of paper. It's not the first time she has wondered about Otto or his whereabouts, but she doesn't usually dwell on it the way she has in the last few days. After the first sweep of anger, she has felt nothing—no disappointment, no rage, certainly no remorse. Sometimes she believes the emotions must lie dormant, in wait for something momentous, a chance encounter on the street, the sudden recognition of the shape of his shoulder brushing her arm. She used to check the mailbox, certain he would write one day, equally sure that he would not risk personal contact. How is one able to disappear without a trace? She is curious, in an offhand, casual way. Does he ever think about his children or wonder what kind of people they became?

Our kids are a mess right now, Otto.

This weekend she will have to tell Gavin that he can't move in with her. It's time, she will say, and she will try to ignore the hurt-puppy droop of his eyes. He's over thirty, a marriage under his belt. At his age—well, best not to think of that. It's time for Mama to kick Baby from the nest, no matter how many feathers he leaves behind on his way down. She has never really had to worry about Gavin the way she has Ruby, even with all his faults: his lack of steady job, his failure to commit. When he told her about Melanie (hanging his head as if ashamed), she had to stop herself from shrugging and saying, *I knew it wouldn't work out*, or, worse, *She just wasn't the right girl for you.* Instead, she smiled sympathetically and placed her hand on his shoulder, squeezing tightly. It's not her place to tell him what to do or how to do it, but independence is underrated in Gavin's head.

She has hidden the box under Barrett's wide desk, and now she pushes it out with her foot. At the cottage, she dumped it all onto the floor and sorted it out by year, so now it's more or less in order. Here is Barrett's obituary, and backwards she goes, down through Rena's death, down, digging deeper until she gets to the envelope of photographs at the very bottom, the pictures that were plucked or sliced from the photo albums in the seventies. She had done it in a fit of rage, all at once when the kids were at school so they couldn't see or know. Ruby would never ask, just as she'd never mentioned Otto since he left, and Gavin would not remember that they used to exist, not until he was older at least, old enough to piece together the meaning of the glue residue on the ridged pages or the angled, hasty dissections.

When she sorted through the contents up at the cottage, the envelope of photographs made her pause. She had not looked at them for years—at least ten, probably more. They could have gone up in flames, a burning pile of memories in a kitchen sink, perhaps, but Lenore restrained herself. When she pulled out the first photograph of Otto on their wedding day, the resemblance to Gavin was uncanny. And he would never know; he had never seen a photograph of his father.

Once, when he was fourteen or fifteen and just hitting his rebellious stride, he had asked—no, *dared*—her to show him a picture. Just one, he'd said. It had come from nowhere, she thought. Just this sudden demand: *Show me a picture*. He had been angry at something Barrett had done or said (or something Barrett hadn't done or said, depending on how you looked at it). *I just want to know if he's my real father*, Gavin said. *Just show me a picture*. Or something like that. They rarely fought in this family. Mostly they held everything inside until their feelings had been diffused, and then made jokes about it, poking fun at one another, entering into a battle of wit and innuendo. On the odd occasion when tempers did flare (and they did, especially when the kids were teenagers), Lenore never raised her voice or fought back; she just walked away and refused to be drawn in. On that day, looking at Gavin's face, the way he clenched his jaw and his fists unconsciously pinched the skin of his arms, pulling the hairs, she ignored what he had said and shook her head, and then left the room before he could say anything else.

Ruby brought up Otto for the first time the other day, out in the gazebo. Lenore has often wondered if Ruby thinks about him in those pockets of time when everyone feels alone, betrayed. Does she imagine what might have happened if Otto had stayed? Ruby was always a quiet child. When she was five, she picked up pieces of glass, buttons, and pretty rocks from the schoolyard, and kept them in a jar like her own box of glittering jewels. She liked to run her fingers over the glass and watch the way the shards sparkled in the sun. She was pale and dreamy-eyed, slow moving as if swimming, pushing through heavy thought, oblivious to the world around her. If you asked her about school, she had to be coaxed into conversation, each word pulled from her mouth. When she did speak, she concentrated on the morbid *(a dead bird outside at recess, all the feathers pulled off and chewed)*, the physical misfortunes *(this girl, she fell off the swings today and knocked out her front tooth, and this boy, he fell down the stairs carrying a UNICEF box and now he has this big purple bruise on his forehead)*, or simply the unfortunate *(this girl, no one likes her because she has these big thick glasses and crossed eyes, and everyone holds their noses when she walks by, and she's always getting things wrong in school, so we laugh)*.

A day or so after the fire, Lenore took Ruby's hand and led her to the couch in the modest bungalow in the west end where they were staying with a friend. She lifted her daughter's chin and looked at her closely, drawing a line down her smooth cheek and under her jaw, hoping to make her smile, even laugh. But Ruby just squirmed away, didn't meet her mother's eyes.

"Ruby, do you want to talk about it?" Bony knees and elbows, a few days away from her eighth birthday. Lenore could tell she would be tall, even back then. That and the colour of Ruby's hair, those were Lenore's, while the rest—her face, eyes, freckles, and the way her small nose tipped up at the end—were her father's.

Ruby pressed her lips together and shook her head.

"Are you sure?" Lenore asked. "I want you to talk to me. You haven't said a word since Daddy left."

This time, Ruby didn't respond at all. She simply looked through Lenore, her eyes blank and unfocused.

"I just want you to know one thing," Lenore said, gathering the girl into her arms and pulling her onto her lap. "You didn't do anything wrong. I didn't do anything wrong. And Gavin didn't do anything wrong. None of us made this happen. Just remember that for me." She released her then, watched her unfold and walk away without looking back.

She knows now that Ruby buried what happened so she could move forward. Children are resilient; even so, her friends advised her to get Ruby into therapy. Lenore resisted, just watched carefully for signs that her daughter was faltering, and there weren't any. Not at first. She appeared to adjust, moved into the three-bedroom apartment without complaint. Lenore helped Ruby decorate her bedroom, painting the walls pink and adding red and white accents: a throw pillow, a hand-woven rug, a lamp with dancing butterflies. A girly bedroom. Ruby seemed pleased to have a door that closed, a room of her own. She did well in her new school, made friends with Angela and a small crowd of girls. The colour returned to her cheeks, as did her smiles and laughter. She and Gavin closed ranks, especially when Barrett came over. When Gavin was seven, he and Ruby created a new language and wrote out an alphabet in a little notebook Lenore bought them, then spent the next month sending secret messages under Lenore's nose.

"We're having pork chops for dinner," Lenore would say, and Gavin would grin, turn to Ruby. *Delum cris pat*, he would say, and Ruby would press her hands to her mouth and snort.

The notebook was lost eventually, and what a shame. How fun it would be to pore over it now with the kids, to remember how it was back then, to make them remember. They are dismissive now of the good years, or so it seems. Dismissive of Barrett and all that he did for them. *It could have turned out so differently*, Lenore wanted to tell them many times. Instead, she has written it down in her—well, her book, if you need to put a label on the stack of papers on Barrett's desk. *It could have turned out badly.*

"My mother will take us in." Otto sat with his hands folded in his lap. He didn't look at Lenore. The kids were in bed, the lamps in the corner throwing soft light. They were in a two-bedroom apartment now, in the same building as before, but it was still a tight squeeze, especially with Gavin, who was two and a rambling ball of energy. Lenore staggered to her feet at the end of each day, amazed to find herself in one piece, while the rest of the apartment had been torn up, pillaged. Ruby was five, much more sedate and in kindergarten. She could not have been like Gavin when she was two, or Lenore would never have wanted another.

"Okay," Lenore said. Otto looked grateful and took her hand, but she wasn't in the mood and pulled it away, scratched at her knee instead. *Okay*, she had said, meaning, *What else can I say?* This wasn't how she expected her marriage to go. She did not want to move in with his mother, who had seemed rather dour on the one occasion Lenore had seen her. But her own mother had died in a streetcar accident when Lenore was eighteen, and her father died of a heart attack just before she met Otto. So what, really, could she say to him? Where else could they go?

She was an old maid when she met Otto at the ripe old age of twenty-eight, and she liked him immediately: the way the corners of his eyes crinkled when he smiled, the boyish lift and hue of his cheeks, the perfectly proportioned hands and feet, his fingernails clean and smooth. There was something about him that made her want to take him to her apartment and feed him home-cooked meals, something slightly scatterbrained and exuberant, but vulnerable. And he was a gentleman: he held doors open and pulled out chairs. Once he held an umbrella over her while the rain fell hard on his head, insisting it was good for his constitution. She had begun to lose hope of ever finding someone for herself. When her father was alive, she was too busy taking care of him to even think of dating, never mind marrying or having a family of her own. And here was Otto, with shining, lovestruck eyes. He doted; he needed her. He was the first man she kissed.

Her father owned a clothing store for men downtown. Nothing fancy: dress pants and shirts, a few ties that never seemed to change over time, a row of shiny shoes displayed along the back wall, their boxes stacked according to size on neat shelves below the display. The store itself was small and dark, sounds muffled in the folds of sweaters and hanging racks of wool coats. Her father had his regular customers, who all seemed to age at the same pace, their heads shrinking, ears growing bigger, and eyes smaller. He prided himself on knowing the names of each and every one of those men, of knowing their family history and the details of their latest health concern. He kept a meticulous record of everyone's measurements and sizes. *Good morning, Mr. Wren*, he would say in greeting, his face spread wide in a smile. *How's your wife and daughter? How about your bad leg, bothering you much these days?* And Mr. Wren would smile in return, grateful to be remembered.

"Customer service is the key," he told his family. "That's why I'll stay in business while other stores fold."

Indeed, his customers were loyal to the last, but other stores moved in around him and flourished, welcomed by a younger generation of buyers who didn't want stuffy shirts and suit jackets, who didn't want anyone knowing their names or history, who only wanted to go about their business uninterrupted.

He could not have made much money, but it was enough—or so it seemed—for a bungalow in a reasonably nice area. They did not have the newest appliances, but they had two bedrooms, a manicured lawn, and a lovely border of flowers around the perimeter of the house. Her mother, too, seemed happy enough, at least in the early years, but by the time she died, the marriage had begun to crumble. It wasn't that her father was a terrible person, but he was different at home, different than he was in the store during the day. At home he would brood and criticize, especially when it became apparent that the store was struggling. Later, Otto's mother would remind her of her father: the same habit of automatic disapproval, the same desire to find as much fault in this world as possible.

Her mother withdrew from him entirely. She became obsessed with order and cleanliness; the skin of her hands was rubbed raw from scrubbing. When he started in on her in the evenings, she listened without a word, her face blank, unresponsive. This inability to fight back—to care enough to say something, *anything*—gnawed at Lenore. That two people who married for love should end up this way frightened her. At her mother's funeral, her father stood by her grave long after the service ended, the prayer book closed. The minister gestured, speaking in low tones, and grasped her father's elbow gently in an effort to lead him back to the church. Still he stood. When he finally looked at Lenore, his mouth gaped open like a bloodless, sunken wound. Rage eclipsed any pity she might have felt. *It's too late for regret*, she wanted to say. Instead, a wail rose from her chest. She let him pull her forward into an awkward embrace.

She resolved to keep her marriage honest, if nothing else. It seemed so simple, back then. *I will never let that happen to me*. But what did she know of marriage or the bricks of silence placed carefully and solidly to keep everything in place? Only later would she see that avoidance was not the same as acceptance, that her mother's distance was not a lack of voice, but her only means of escape, and that Lenore, too, would repeat the pattern in her own way, removing herself from an unpleasant truth.

When Otto lost his job, there wasn't a lot of money set aside; he never worried about finances or planned for unexpected emergencies. Suddenly fired. He snapped his fingers when he told her. *Just like that*. Lenore shared his outrage, at first. How could they, without warning? But as the days passed, she began to wonder. Surely there had been some hint, a sense of impending failure. He must have been slipping for a while—months, maybe a year. She used to work there, after all. She had typed up warning letters before. How many chances did Otto get?

"Did they give you a warning?" she asked, just once. She saw by the way his shoulders rose and tensed before he answered that Otto felt defensive.

"I told you," he said. "There was nothing. They just called me in and told me they were letting me go."

Lenore didn't believe it, and now the money was almost gone, there weren't any job prospects, and they had to leave the apartment or find a way to pay the rent.

"Just for a while," Otto said now. "Until I find a job, and it shouldn't take long. We can live in the basement. There's a kitchen down there. We can sleep in the main room and put the kids in the bedroom."

It was damp in the basement, and the olive green carpeting and fake-wood-panelled walls made the space seem smaller, darker, than it was. Ruby clung, her legs wrapped tightly around her mother's body, her hands like claws, digging into Lenore's back. The kitchen tap dripped, and the tiles behind the sink were peeling from the wall.

"It's degrading," Lenore whispered that night. They slept on the pullout couch, all four of them. The kids were too scared to sleep in the tiny bedroom. There were spiderwebs in the corners of the room, and the mattress smelled mouldy. Thank goodness they brought their own blankets, sheets, and pillows to make everyone more comfortable. They stacked the boxes from their apartment along one side of the wall, but they didn't have much. Elsa Sinclair refused to let them move in any furniture, even temporarily, so they stored their kitchen table, an old battered sofa, and their real beds with Lenore's sister, Helen, and her husband, Sal.

"It's only for a short time," Otto said, trying to pat her arm in reassurance, but she pulled away and heard him sigh.

"Why couldn't we stay upstairs? Why did she put us down here? There are two spare bedrooms up there. And you said she always wanted a bedroom on the third floor."

Otto didn't answer. Ruby turned and pushed her face into Lenore's neck, away from Gavin's small curved body.

LENORE HAD LITTLE CONTACT with Mrs. Sinclair. Otto told her she preferred it that way and handed her a list, the printed letters firm and slanting slightly to the right.

1. No running or stomping or loud noises
2. No television
3. No washroom use after 10 P.M.
4. Silence on Sundays (no guests!)

"No washroom after ten at night?" Lenore asked. "What kind of rule is that?"

"She doesn't want to be woken up." The washroom was on the second floor, next to the old woman's bedroom. Elsa was an operator for the telephone company, had worked there for years and years, ever since her husband's death when Otto was eleven. She worked from eight to four, five days a week. On Friday nights, she went out; she belonged to some sort of club for church ladies. On Saturdays, she cleaned and puttered about the house. Only on Sunday, after Elsa returned from church and spent much of the day supposedly reading the Bible, did the family gather in the main dining room. She did not appear as grim as Otto would have had Lenore believe, but she made no effort to draw out Lenore or the children. She cooked large family dinners, rising often during the meal to refill a plate or glass, to pass out more napkins, or to check on dessert in the oven. She ate quietly, looking away when Lenore caught her eye.

Otto was vague about his mother's history. He thought the Bischoffs originated in some far-flung corner of Germany, though he wasn't sure where, exactly. At some point, Otto's grandparents had anglicized their last name—probably, Lenore surmised, during the war. *Bischoff* became *Bishop*, and *Elsa* became *Elizabeth*. She married

Thomas Sinclair in 1944; Otto was born a year later. Whatever became of Otto's grandparents, he couldn't say, though he thought his grandfather had died before his birth; his grandmother, he told her, either died shortly thereafter or returned to Germany. In any case, he never saw her again.

"Don't you want to know about your grandmother? Other relatives you might have?" Lenore once asked. "Aren't you curious?" But unlike her, he didn't seem to have a need for connections. It was ironic, really: Lenore had no one but Helen and wanted more, while Otto had others but wanted none.

"This is ridiculous," she said. "No washroom after ten? What about the kids? Gavin will be toilet training soon, and Ruby sometimes needs to go. What if they get sick?"

"We'll get a potty for night," Otto said.

"I'm not going to the bathroom in a pot because I might wake her up. Come on, Otto."

He seemed to have an answer for every ridiculous restriction, but Lenore told herself that he was in a difficult—and rather humiliating—position. *It's only temporary.* And so, for a while, she peed in the pot with the rest of them, and took it upstairs to empty every morning. But she made sure to do it after Elsa had gone to work so that she didn't have to pretend she didn't mind.

They stayed healthy throughout the summer, but Ruby brought germs home from school in the fall. Lenore had hoped to be out of the house by then, but since they were still there, she decided to take matters into her own hands, hauled her feverish, hacking children up to the second floor, and installed them in the second bedroom.

"I won't have them throwing up in the kitchen sink," she told Otto. She turned to Elsa with her hands on her hips, daring her to say something, but the other woman frowned, her eyes sympathetic.

"Of course not," she said. She reached out, touched Gavin on the forehead, then pulled back as if burned, her eyes flicking to Otto, compassion sliding into what looked like guilt.

"What was that about?" Lenore asked later, but Otto shrugged.

"How should I know?"

By Christmas, Elsa had settled herself in the third-floor bedroom, presumably so she wouldn't be bothered by these bathroom intrusions, but Lenore and the kids remained in the basement.

When they first moved into Elsa's house, Otto was optimistic. Every morning, he showered and shaved, put on an ironed shirt and a tie, and headed out the door. He told Lenore he bought the day's newspaper and sat in the library, poring over the want ads, circling the ones that looked promising, and then made cold calls, copies of his resumé packed in his briefcase. *Companies are only hiring summer students*, he told Lenore. And later: *The summer is a slow season.* He took a break for two months and played with the kids in the backyard. It was a good summer, especially during the week when Elsa was at work, and they could all pretend to be a family again. They had lunchtime barbecues with hamburgers and watermelons, played in a plastic pool filled with cold water, wore wide-brimmed hats and sucked on Popsicles while the sun beat down, turning them brown.

In the fall, Otto headed out again. No one was hiring. This is what he told Lenore. *Most of the summer students have stayed on*, he said. Lenore suggested that he shift his focus and apply outside his field. He said he already had. He took a few months off, fixed up the third-floor bedroom for his mother, ripped up and replaced the old tiles in the basement. Lenore sewed bright curtains to hang over the sink as if there was a window to cover (there wasn't), and bought throw rugs second-hand. She hung Ruby's art from school on the wall of their bedroom and found a lamp in the shape of a teddy bear. At Christmas, Ruby asked Santa for *our own house, please*, and seemed moderately disappointed to wake up in the same place on Christmas morning. At least the spiderwebs were gone from the corners, and the musty smell had disappeared.

In the New Year, Otto stopped shaving and grew a beard. *Makes me look more mature*, he said, and it did, but it also made him look a little bit like a stranger. He also found a job selling knives from door to door. Otto said he didn't mind, at least not at first, and anyway, it paid the bills. Lenore started hunting for an apartment.

"Why don't we save up for a house?" Otto said. "Stay here awhile longer. What harm would it do? We're already here, and it would just be easier."

So they stayed. Otto rode the bus all day with his briefcase of knives, and Lenore ventured up to the main floor of the house during the day. Elsa kept her photographs arranged neatly on the piano. Here, a framed shot of Otto's father, a film archivist at the university. Otto didn't look much like him, though there was a similarity in the shape of his jaw and eyes. It was hard for Lenore to imagine this man in the photograph, who looked amiable and approachable, marrying Elsa, but maybe she had been different back then. People did change, after all; grief took a terrible toll. On the piano, there was another black-and-white photograph in a heavy silver frame, this one from the wedding, stiffly posed. Elsa looked fresh and unsullied in this photograph, her groom beside her hopeful, expectant. They must have clenched their jaws to keep from smiling.

He killed himself when Otto was just a boy. Took a bottle of pills and washed them down with alcohol. Otto rarely talked about it, and who could blame him? What a heavy burden to carry on your shoulders. It was no wonder he grew up so fast, and even less surprising, perhaps, that Elsa was so grim. She had fallen into her sadness and anger and let the years pile up, one by one, each marked by a new layer of dust in the living room drapes.

Otto lost his sales job in the spring and couldn't explain why, at least not to Lenore, and now he seemed to be shrinking, losing steam.

"Come on, Otto," Lenore said, but he sat on the sofa in the basement, his legs crossed, his foot tapping on the floor. He wore the same white T-shirt for days in a row, stained yellow under the arms, coupled with his flannel pyjama pants and a pair of slippers. Lenore could not stand being in the house with him during the day because she was afraid she would start to nag, and she didn't want to become one of those wives. She took Gavin to the library and the mall, or just out on walks, came home for lunch and cooked a big pot of soup for all three of them. In the afternoon, Gavin and Otto both napped, leaving Lenore alone to wander the house or read the books she brought home from the library. Sometimes she would do housework, but the apartment was small, and Gavin liked to help with the chores, so she used the sleeping time to relax. *Me time*. Time to recharge and think things through.

"Are you depressed?" she asked Otto one night after the kids were in bed, but he turned his back and pretended to sleep, and that's when her patience began to slip and anger crept in.

"You are not the only person living in this situation," she told him. "Please remember that."

She saw the ad in the paper by chance one day. Probably Elsa left it on the stairs for Otto, but he wasn't interested in going through the classifieds with a pencil anymore. *Just let me take a break*, he said to Lenore, and his voice was so close to cracking, so worn and fragile, that she worried and touched the back of his neck. *Please tell me what's wrong, Otto*. He shrugged her off, clutched a bathrobe, and headed upstairs to the washroom.

Lenore set three-year-old Gavin up at the coffee table with the comics and a crayon, then spread out the classifieds on the small Formica table. She was looking at ads for Otto, but came across one for a receptionist in a doctor's office. She didn't pause over the ad, not then, but mulled over the idea for a few days. It could be the perfect solution. Let Otto have the summer with the kids while she brought in some money and let him recharge. She thought he would like that.

"What do you think?" she asked him in bed that night. He didn't answer for a while. She focused on his hands, folded on top of his chest, watching them rise and fall in time with his breathing. He hadn't touched her with those hands in months.

"If that's what you want," he said finally.

"I'll just go for an interview," she said. "We can decide after that."

It took her a few false starts before she found the clinic at the children's hospital. *Plastic Surgery*, the plaque on the door read, with a list of four names below. She sat in the row of chairs that lined one wall. Typical, she thought: outdated magazines on a table beside her, a potted fake rubber tree with dusty leaves in the corner. But there was a basket of toys on the floor, and children's books on a small shelf—marks of distinction in an otherwise commonplace waiting room. A small boy played with the toys, his back to Lenore, his jumpsuit pulled tightly up his back. Chubby arms and legs, much like Gavin, and blond, the hair at the base of his skull flicking upward in curls. She exchanged a smile with his mother, who sat across from her. The woman's cheeks were hollow, and the skin beneath her eyes sagged, as if she was overcome by a great fatigue. A figure opened the door, a man in rumpled slacks, hair that stood up in sections as if he'd yanked and twisted it. The little boy turned when the man called his name. The magazine Lenore held nearly slipped from her fingers. She drew her thumb down the edge of the paper and felt a sting as one of the pages sliced into her flesh. Grateful for the distraction, she brought her thumb to her mouth and tasted blood.

The little boy smiled at the doctor, and his features stretched, grotesque. Bulging eyes showing too much white, set far apart and oversized, prominent forehead, and a lower jaw that thrust forward.

The nurse at the front desk watched her with a frown.

"You'll have to do better than that," she said after the boy disappeared down the hall with his mother. Lenore sat back, magazine closed on her lap, and waited.

After twenty minutes, the small figure emerged again, chewing rapidly and with great gusto.

"Say thank you, William," his mother said.

"Thank you for the jelly bean." *Tank u for da juwy bean.* Lenore smiled: just like Gavin.

The doctor bent to take the child's hand. "You're very welcome," he said. "We'll see you soon."

He waited for mother and child to disappear behind the door before extending his hand to Lenore.

"Mrs. Sinclair?"

"Yes."

"I'm Lloyd Barrett. Come on down." He gestured over his shoulder, and she followed him down the hall to a room on the right. An average-sized room with a desk and chair, a brown, rather shabby sofa against one wall, a small window nearly obscured by a pile of books, and toys on the floor. Beside the desk, a cupboard stood partially open, revealing more toys and books in a jumble.

"We meet the families in here," Dr. Barrett said.

"That boy," Lenore said. "William." She hesitated, unsure of how to phrase her question. *What's wrong with him?* seemed so terribly rude.

"Crouzon syndrome," he said. "Relatively common, I'm sad to say. The skull fuses prematurely, leaving no room for the brain to grow. The pressure distorts the features."

"Can you fix him?"

"We can try. Do you know anything about craniofacial abnormalities, Mrs. Sinclair?"

"Please call me Lenore." She placed her purse on the floor beside the chair and held out her resumé.

"Lenore." He tested her name. He would have been thirty-eight then, the same age as Lenore. His hair was still light brown, rather than speckled with grey, and then entirely white, as it would become by the time he turned sixty, but the skin of his face was weathered, mature. Dr. Barrett looked vaguely familiar, but she couldn't place him, and he seemed to be having the same difficulty.

"I think I've seen you before," he murmured. "But I can't think where." He looked down at her resumé. "Have you been in the hospital before?"

"Only when I had my children," she said.

"Ah, that's it." He sat back, as if pleased with himself and his memory. She shook her head.

"I'm sorry?" But then it came to her: the hospital, his prints fading on the glass of the nursery beneath her hand. His sadness and grief, the way he spoke of his ailing wife. There was a framed picture on his desk, facing him, and Lenore fought the desire to turn it around, to see the woman who surely belonged within that frame.

She smiled at him, but her palms were uncomfortably moist. She crossed her legs, listening to the whisper of nylon, and tried to relax. Barrett nodded slightly and smiled back.

"Let's talk," he said.

IN THE BASEMENT OF THE HOUSE, the smell of sleep. Lenore took off her shoes at the top of the stairs so she wouldn't wake Otto, but he shifted on the sofa bed, turned.

"How did it go?"

"It's mine, if I want it."

He shuffled under the covers and then sighed.

"Do you want to do it?" he asked.

Of course she did. She looked down at her husband, trying to muster sympathy and understanding, but could only come up with pity.

"I start in a week," she said.

"IT'S AN EXCITING TIME for us, the clinic," Dr. Barrett said, showing her down the long hallway, the four exam rooms with tables, equipment. "Treatment rooms." Rooms for removing sutures, releasing wired jaws.

"If you're interested in the job, you'll be making our appointments. Mrs. Fielding—the nurse at the front—she'll take care of the patients, talk to the families. You won't have to do much at first, but it's going to get busy. I'm the only craniofacial surgeon in this hospital. In this city, in fact. And we have big plans. Kids from all over North America will come to me." Said with assurance. She looked for signs of bluster, an inflated ego, but found nothing, only a gangly man, a wide smile, a contagious energy.

"I'm interested," she said.

IN THE KITCHEN, Lenore pulls the paraphernalia from beneath the sink: basin, rubber gloves, sponge. Old habits die hard. She'd never had a hobby as Barrett had, but she's always had this. She removes jars, bottles, containers, and the platter of sandwiches—rank now, damp around the edges—left over from the funeral, and places everything in rows on the countertop. It doesn't always have to be the fridge. Once Lenore spent a morning cleaning the inside of her washing machine, getting into the grooves and hinges with a Q-tip. Everyone always laughs to hear of it, especially when Barrett teased and mimicked her almost-frantic attention to detail. *Really, Lenore*, friends would say. *You do have a maid.* But Lenore doesn't consider it work, and this is what none of them understand. Cleaning with such mindless intensity relaxes her. The repetitive motions and the feel of rubber gloves snug against her fingers are soothing.

She never uses vinegar because that reminds her too much of her father's house after her mother died, when the floors could never be clean enough for him, the faucets always stained with invisible fingerprints or flecks of toothpaste. Her father would work himself into a rage over the smallest hair caught in the drain. Lenore let him rant without saying a word; she knew his anger wasn't for her. He raged against the injustice of life, the improbability of a God, the way the newspaper boy threw the paper so that it caught in the bushes flanking the driveway. And when he was finished, he sank down into the sofa with a drink in his hand, *her* favourite records playing over and over again, and Lenore was free for the day. More than once, she came home to find him asleep, the needle scratching uselessly against the centre of the record.

Lenore has a photograph in one of the albums, a picture of her mother at age nineteen, standing in a garden. The sun must have been bright that day; her mother's hand is raised as if to shield her eyes. She wears a dark print dress with shoulder pads, and her hair (auburn, Lenore remembers) is set in waves and held back on one side with a clip. Lenore has her eyebrows: dark, and thick, and meeting over the bridge of her nose. Lenore plucks, but her mother did not. At least not when she was nineteen. The photograph is slightly out of focus, but it is still her favourite because of the saucy, daring expression on her mother's face.

After her mother died, Lenore lost her father too. Not physically: he still filled a room with his presence, sat at the table and ate the meals that she cooked for him, day in, day out. But emotionally, he disappeared. Helen was twenty-two and married by then, living an hour away with her husband, and the loneliness of the house—the way the walls creaked and settled at night—was too great. At night as she lay on her single bed, the tears would etch paths down her cheeks to wet the pillow, but she never made a sound, always kept it to herself. If she appeared in front of her father with reddened eyes, he looked away. He didn't want to know or hear. He had his own remorse, his own way of dealing with his pain and guilt. *I shouldn't have kept at her the way I did*, he said. *Why did I do that? Always criticizing her.* Here he would hold up his hands, palms to the ceiling, as if to say, *and for what?*

When he drank too much in his chair, he would sometimes reminisce. *I kissed her for the first time in the middle of a café.* He would look straight ahead when he talked, his one hand wrapped around his glass, the other gently grasping the armrest. (After his death, Lenore donated that chair to charity, but not before noticing the way the wool had worn down on the armrests from so many days and nights of gripping and unconscious stroking, the oil from his fingers breaking down the material.) He never seemed to notice Lenore as his audience; his eyes would fill with tears, especially if it was late and he had been drinking for long.

For ten years she took care of him. After he died, she sold the house. The store was close to bankruptcy, and his debts were greater than anticipated. She married Otto and what did she expect?

I'll take care of you for the rest of your life, Barrett once whispered.

On Wednesdays, she used to dress carefully, taking her time with her makeup and hair. She massaged scented lotion into the skin of her neck and shoulders and smiled for her children to show that Barrett's absence during the rest of the week didn't bother her.

"Don't you want more?" her sister wanted to know.

"Please don't, Helen."

He never lied to her. She could hardly make demands by then. She took what she could and accepted her solitude. In time, the silence became a part of her life, and she learned to enjoy the small pleasures of her days: the sleepy smell of Ruby and Gavin in the mornings, bare arms around her neck for bedtime hugs, idle chatter and coffee with friends, the warmth of the radiator on a cold night in winter. Of course that wasn't enough; of course she wanted more.

That August, when they did not yet have the apartment, when they still reeled from Otto's disappearance and their sudden displacement, she sat in the parkette around the corner from the hospital. She sat and wondered why she had done what she had the last time she saw Otto: the cheque on the table, the look on his face. She had caused the fire. Guilt gnawed in the pit of her stomach.

He found her there, as she knew he would, stood in front of her for a long time.

"I read about the fire," he said gently. "I was worried. Why didn't you come to me?"

"I couldn't." She wouldn't look at him, but he must have read her thoughts on her face, because he sat beside her.

"It wasn't your fault," he said. "Surely you don't think—"

"He must have known."

"No."

"Yes, Barrett. I flaunted it, waved the cheque in his face." He sighed, a heavy sound, and she knew that he didn't know what to say.

"What I did ... I made him a failure."

He took her hand. "Where are you staying?"

"With a girlfriend until everything is sorted out, but we can't stay for long. There's just no space." She lifted her head. "What am I going to do? The children—"

"Let me."

"We may have to move in with my sister."

"No," he said. His fingers rubbed the skin on the back of her hand. "Let me."

LENORE SCRUBS THE VEGETABLE BINS at the bottom of the fridge, wiping at her eyes with the back of her arm. It's too hot for this kind of cleaning; she should never have started. She isn't finding the usual pleasure or peace, and her back aches. The house is too silent. Barrett should be here with her now. Damn him and his refusal to go to the doctor when his chest first began to bother him. *Indigestion*, he said.

"You fool," she says out loud and stands, wincing at the way her knees crack and her bare toes slip on the ceramic floor. And now she has risen too quickly: blood rushes to her head, making her dizzy, and she is suddenly furious at her body's weakness and age. She picks up the basin and flings it against the wall, not even flinching as dirty water sprays in all directions. She presses her forehead against the wall, her arms hanging limply by her sides, and soap dripping from the ends of each rubber fingertip.

Nine

ELSA DIDN'T DISLIKE LENORE. She didn't know her well enough for like or dislike. When Otto told her they would marry, she could only sigh and stare at him for a moment.

"Are you sure?" she asked him.

"I'm twenty-four," he said. But he looked away, and his cheeks were mottled pink and white.

"If you say so."

She never expected the marriage to last, knowing Otto as well as she did. She met Lenore for the first time at the wedding, a pretty thing with an easy smile. Elsa was sure she would be able to like her, given the chance, but Otto never introduced them before the wedding. Elsa went alone, her small purse clutched against her chest for security, regretting for a moment that she hadn't bought a new dress, something more cheerful than her best church outfit, a soft shade of grey. Crowds always made her nervous, especially when she was alone. Otto escorted her up the aisle towards the front row, but she tugged sharply on his elbow. When he resisted, she let go, spun about, and settled herself on a chair in the back. He stood in front of her for a moment without saying a word. *Mother, please*, he whispered, casting glances around him to see if other guests had noticed. When she didn't budge, he sighed, muttered something under his breath (something that sounded suspiciously like *fucking typical*), and returned to the altar.

She had never met any of his girlfriends, in fact, though women had flitted in and out of his life with great frequency. Otto had a certain quality that drew women to him—much like his father—but he couldn't keep them around. Or maybe he didn't want to keep them around. Elsa never knew.

"I wish you all the best," she told Lenore at the wedding. It was the right thing to say, and she meant it, too. She tried to keep the warning note out of her voice. *Run away from him. Run, now!* Lenore must have seen something in her eyes or the way Elsa's chin pulled up, puckered and pitted like an orange. She kept smiling, but her mouth tightened.

"Thank you," she said, before slipping her gaze away to the next person in line.

Elsa stood in front of Otto. The breath squeezed from her chest as she leaned forward, kissed him on the cheek.

"Good luck," she murmured, and moved away before she could see his face darken.

A WAIL CAME THROUGH THE FLOOR. Usually she couldn't hear the children; she spent much of her time on the second and third floors of the house. On Saturdays, they were difficult to avoid, even though she tried her best. She woke at six and headed downstairs with her laundry baskets, sorting and filling quickly. At the end of the hallway, she could hear Otto's snores and the soft rustle of sheets that let her know his wife was awake. Back upstairs to dust and vacuum the first floor, stopping only for a cup of black tea, and toast smeared with marmalade, the dry crust scraping the inside of her mouth.

Otto sent the first announcement by mail, a simple square card with their firstborn's photograph and date of birth. Elsa waited by the telephone for the call that would surely come. She longed to touch a tiny fist, to stroke her pink flesh. *Ruby*, they called her, a good, solid name. The arrival of a child called up memories of Otto's birth and those first few rosy years, the fat cheeks and dimpled legs and elbows, sloppy kisses and desperate hugs. Her loneliness threatened to crush her.

The call that didn't come was more damaging than his refusal to introduce the two women before the wedding. She imagined a blond child growing sturdy, bow legs straightening. And then, in the paper, she saw the second birth announcement, and this time, Otto didn't send her a copy by mail. She composed letter after letter, her pen digging into paper in hard strokes, but destroyed them all before they could be mailed. For five years, Elsa had no contact with any of them.

And look now. She wiped down the piano with a soft cloth, moving aside the pictures in their heavy frames, lingering, as always, on Thomas' young face. After his death, she took that photograph and shoved it face-down in a drawer, enraged by his cowardice. Only later did she take it out and place it back on the piano, the only tangible reminder of Thomas, aside from the photos.

His musical ability had taken her by surprise. He played with gusto, foot pumping on the pedal, shaking his head and nodding in tempo, manic energy bursting from his fingertips so that she almost expected to see sparks fly. And then, as suddenly as it began, the music would stop, and he would slide from the bench as if exhausted. She learned to put aside what she was doing when he played, take in the moment and hold it close. This man at the piano—*this* was her husband. Sometimes at night, she still imagined she could hear him playing, as if calling out to her in the darkness.

She pressed down hard, her hand arranged in C major; the simplest of chords reverberated in the quiet room and then faded beneath her tingling fingers. Footsteps sounded on the stairs leading to the basement. Elsa put the photographs back in their places, dropping the dusting cloth in her haste. She stuffed it in the pocket of her robe and climbed the stairs to the second, then third floor, breathing heavily. As she sat down on her bed and surveyed the room, an image rose, unexpected and so serene that she swayed: the oldest child sitting at the piano, her fingers moving lithely on the keys, Elsa standing by her side, nodding in approval. Ruby, she felt sure, would carry Thomas' talent. She closed her eyes and pictured the living room flooded with light. There on the sofa sat Lenore and Otto, their little boy at their feet. Everyone smiling. *Yes, why not?* Music could heal all wounds, her father used to say as they listened, night after night, to the phonograph in the living room, the needle scratching against the old records.

WHEN ELSA PINNED THE FLAG to the window, Otto took it down again and again. He draped it across the back of the sofa after she had gone to work and pinned it back up again before the bus dropped her off down the street before dinner. He was ten or eleven—no, maybe twelve or thirteen, because Thomas was gone by then. Once she caught him with a pin in his hand, the flag drooping awkwardly.

"What are you doing?" she asked.

He froze and peered over his shoulder but said nothing.

"You put that back."

"Why?" The plaintive, whiny sound of his voice made her cringe.

"I put it there for a reason. Put it back."

He obeyed, but not without casting a sullen, disdainful look in her direction.

He called her once six months or a year after the wedding. She contained her pleasure at the sound of his voice. She didn't admit to anyone—certainly not to him—that his silence, their non-relationship cut her deeply.

"Mother," he said, then hesitated. She listened to his breathing, the choked quality of his voice, and panicked.

"What's wrong?" Her hand gripped the receiver. An accident, a death. Or no, maybe an illness—Otto was sick, was that it?

"I was thinking about that flag on the window," he said. "Why did you keep that up there?"

"I don't understand the question."

"After everything that happened," he said.

"What happened?"

"As if you don't remember. I just wanted to be normal."

"Normal? You were normal. That flag had nothing to do with that."

"But it did. You put up that flag to show everyone we were different."

"I put it up because I wasn't ashamed of who I was. To remind me."

"Everyone laughed at us, at me, because of you."

"Who was laughing?"

"Everyone. You and your damn flag, the way you didn't want to associate with anyone, as if they weren't good enough for us."

"What are you talking about?"

"Those boys at the window."

She was still. If they had stood face to face, she would have backed away then, her arms crossed in front of her body for protection.

"That was a long time ago," she said. The rage of that day came back, her horror.

"All those days were a long time ago," he said. "Day after day just piled up, one on top of the other. The little incidents, they all added up."

"You can't still hold on to that—"

"You have no idea what it was like for me. No one wanted anything to do with me after that."

"You're exaggerating."

"Am I? Do you ever wonder why I had no friends in high school? Why I never went out anywhere?"

"Because of that one day?"

"It wasn't just one day, that's what I'm telling you. They wrote on my locker. They left me threatening notes. I came home late almost every day because I had to wait for everyone to leave. Had to be absolutely sure they were gone before I left that school. I was so afraid. I couldn't fight back, I was too small. You have no idea what that does to a kid. You ruined me."

Elsa couldn't speak. Pain struck her throat and radiated down her chest, under the curves of her rib cage. As if, she would later think, she had been stabbed in the gentle hollow at the base of her throat, sending tiny rivulets of blood coursing downward. *My only.*

"Why didn't you tell me?" she finally whispered. "I could have helped you."

His laughter burst forth, maniacal and braying. "Help me?"

"Have you been drinking? Are you taking some kind of drug?"

"You're not *listening* to me! I'm trying to tell you how I feel, what you've done to me."

"What I've done?" Her voice rose. "I've done nothing but my best for you, Otto."

"You're not welcome in my life anymore."

"What?"

"I won't let you put me down anymore. I have a new life now, and I'm happy. Despite you, I've made something of myself. I'm free."

"Don't do this, Otto."

He hung up. In the darkened hallway, one hand pressed flat on the telephone table, she dropped to the floor, the receiver clunking onto the hardwood beside her.

You are not who you think you are, Elsa used to say. *None of us are. By us*, she meant her family: her father, dead and buried; her mother back home in Germany with her sisters. She saw it herself, once, on the streetcar. A young man turned to his companion and said, *It's warm for April.* Only he said it in German. He looked at Elsa, her face glowing with comprehension. *Did you understand what I said?* She nodded once before her mother's hand clamped down on her arm, squeezing, her lips compressed. A woman sitting on her other side stiffened, moved away, and then stood, as if she couldn't bear the sudden stench. Out on the sidewalk, her mother bent down, grasped Elsa's wrists.

"Remember what Papa told you," she said. "It's better that way." She stood again, took her hand, and led her down the street.

Elsa inhaled the sweet scent in her father's shop. When her mother wasn't looking, she dared to break a piece from a fresh baguette displayed in the front window and chewed it slowly, her face turned away so no one would see. The letters on the glass curved in white, a backwards arc: *Bishop's Bakery*.

"Elizabeth!"

She ran to her father, his white apron pristine as always, his cheeks pudgy and red from the heat of the oven. Now, at five, she could wrap her arms around his waist and touch her fingertips together behind his back.

"Are you coming home, Papa?"

"I am."

He had lost his accent long ago; his voice was deep and smooth, with only the barest hint of the sharp corners that belonged to the old language.

They were, in 1930, two families, and it was important to remember which was which: the home family, in which Elsa was merely herself, Elsa Bischoff; and the public family, in which names were changed for reasons she couldn't comprehend. *It's better that way.*

"They were ashamed to be German," she told Otto. The shame couldn't help trickling down to Elsa. In 1943, she worked at a plant near the lake that had been converted to manufacture munitions. She worked on the floor in cotton overalls, her hair covered by a bandana. That fall, a group of old men from the university came to film them. Amid the balding heads, one young man in spectacles, one eye slightly turning towards the left, smiled at her shyly before he left. She played that single smile again and again as she worked, wondering at the sudden heat in her face, the pressure against her rib cage.

On their first date, he took her to a movie about a soldier who falls in love with three women.

"I love Deborah Kerr," she said after the film.

"You remind me of her," he said.

"Really?"

"Really."

She didn't believe him, of course, but his obvious admiration, his earnestness, made her smile back. And later, when he kissed her, she let him press his hands against the small of her back. She climbed the stairs to the room she shared with her mother in the rooming house, settled into their double bed with a sigh, replaying the kiss over and over until she fell asleep.

On their next date, she told him about her father's bakery, the way he had collapsed when she was fourteen, and was dead before his head hit the floor. He took her hand.

"I'm sorry," he said simply. His skin was smooth, his fingers long and tapered. They were, she decided, the hands of an artist, or how she imagined the hands of an artist would feel. He wasn't handsome, exactly. His forehead was a touch too broad, his eyes too close together. And there was the matter of the eye that tended to wander, as if in conversation he were thinking of something else. It was disconcerting to look at him directly sometimes; she could never quite tell which eye she should follow.

"Lazy eye," he told her. "But I assure you I'm not lazy." She would find this to be true later. He never could sit still for long. Even here, in the restaurant, his leg jittered beneath the table, and his shoulders twitched. Later still, after they were married and she moved into his home, he always had to be doing *something*, could never sit for long with a newspaper or curl up with a book. At dinner, his mouth was in constant motion. His hands rearranged salt shakers and napkins and moved his cutlery from one side of his plate to the other.

"My mother can't stand the smell of bread anymore," Elsa said. She had sold the bakery and moved them to the rooming house to save money, although Elsa didn't say this now.

Thomas Sinclair was an orphan. His parents had died some five years earlier in an automobile accident. His father had been a pharmacist, and Thomas lived in their house comfortably enough that he didn't worry about money—a good thing, because he didn't make much at the university.

They sat in a small restaurant, the lights dim, a white napkin spread over her lap. He sat close to her, his arm brushing hers, smelling of soap and some kind of cologne. She imagined him preparing for their date in front of a mirror, brushing his teeth, slicking back his hair, dabbing his neck with scented lotion. That someone could make those preparations for her was overwhelming.

"I need to tell you something," she said. She hesitated, fearful of the concern that washed over his face.

"What is it?"

Still she hesitated. Perhaps she should not have brought it up, not this soon. Or perhaps she should have told him outright, even before the first date. Now she had more invested, had begun to anticipate their dates, and imagine the way his hands felt against her back.

"Never mind."

"No, tell me."

"It's nothing. Forget I said anything."

"Elizabeth." He took her hand, rubbed his thumb against hers. "Tell me." She exhaled, certain he wouldn't mind, but equally certain he would turn out to be one of *those* people.

"I'm German," she said. "I'm not Elizabeth Bishop. I'm Elsa Bischoff. I thought you should know."

She held her breath, waiting for the stiffness that would come over him, make him pull away from her. But he threw back his head and laughed.

"Is that all? Elsa, you had me worried. I thought you were married or had twelve children."

"There are a lot of people who don't like Germans," she said, but the weight of her worry slipped away. She laughed, suddenly giddy with her own absurdity. Of course he didn't mind.

"I'm not one of them," he said. And then: "Never be ashamed of your heritage, Elsa. It's part of who you are."

Was that when she fell in love with him? Perhaps. Or maybe it came when she told him her mother wanted to return to Germany after the war.

"There will be nothing left of Germany when this war is over," Thomas said. "Don't go back." He leaned towards her, gripped her shoulders with both hands fervently. "I won't let you go back, Elsa," he said.

NO ONE KNEW WHY Thomas killed himself, least of all Elsa. She searched endlessly for a note, a message of some kind—under the cushions of the sofa, beneath the bed, in her wooden jewellery box. She sorted through the post, certain he would have at least mailed her a last letter, something for her to hold in the darkest hours of her night, to smell the ink and imagine his hand pressing down in urgency on the lined paper. There was nothing. And when well-meaning neighbours put a sympathetic hand on her arm and asked if there was anything they could do, she could only tighten her jaw and stiffen her neck. There was no time for grief, after all, not with an eleven-year-old boy—a problem child himself—to care for.

In those days, family problems were simply buried in the closets or tucked away neatly so that the ragged ends didn't show. Certainly Thomas had his moments—not depression, no. There were extremes. His inability to sit still, his tenacity over those damn articles and letters he wrote to the newspapers. Elsa could almost see an idea take hold: his eyes would glaze over behind his glasses, and his gaze would become fixed, rigid. The first time it happened, she didn't know what was coming.

"Thomas?"

No response. His index finger caught between two pages of the daily paper, as if frozen in mid-movement.

"Thomas!"

He looked up, his face blank as he stared at her, then blinking to dispel the fog.

"The dogs are everywhere."

"What dogs?"

"Stray dogs. There are hundreds of them in the city, starving. In the garbage bins last night, did you hear it?"

"Thomas ..."

"Digging for food, starving. So skinny, have you seen them? They're everywhere."

"I'm sure it was a raccoon in our garbage last night."

But he wasn't listening. He put down the paper, threw it onto the floor beside his chair. The normal Thomas always folded the newspaper when he finished, placed it back in the magazine rack beside the fireplace. He disappeared into his study and closed his door.

In the future, Elsa would always recognize the signs: the disruption in his orderly pattern, the closed doors. *Another spell.* She did not need to intrude to know how she would find him, his sleeves rolled up, ink on his fingers, scribbling, scribbling away. And the next morning, two or three letters sealed in envelopes, addressed to various papers or organizations.

This first time, letters weren't enough. Otto was four. In the morning, she woke late to find the space next to her in bed cool and undisturbed, and a deep silence in the house. Pulling on her robe and cinching it around her waist in her customary double loop, she shuffled downstairs, still blinking and muddled from sleep. She stopped in the kitchen. Every cupboard was open, bowls pulled onto the floor and counter, eggshells and waxy brown paper still bearing smudges of fresh ground beef from the butcher shop lay on the counter.

In the backyard, Otto roamed naked from the waist down, following his father around the yard. Thomas looked up when she emerged. He smiled and waved at her with a hammer.

"What are you doing?"

"Building a dog hotel," he said. And indeed, a long wooden platform stood on its side. As she watched, he lifted a plank from a pile behind him, settled it perpendicular to the base, and began to hammer, pulling nails from the pocket of his robe. Elsa's stomach churned uneasily even before she noticed the bowls of raw meat. *There's something wrong with him.*

"Why aren't you at work?"

He looked at her in silence.

"Work?"

"Otto, come here," she said. She took the boy's hand and led him towards the house. "Let's get dressed. Your feet! Look how filthy you are."

At the door, she looked back at Thomas to find him once more engrossed. He raised his hammer.

In the afternoon, Thomas came back into the house to shower and change. He kissed her on the cheek with a smile.

"See you after work." Just like that, the urge disappeared.

When he was gone, Elsa cleaned up the yard, collecting scattered nails and splinters of wood in her cupped hand. The meat went into the garbage, and she scoured the bowls and restored order to her kitchen. The half-completed wooden structure stayed at the back of the yard for a week before Thomas dismantled it without a word.

Elsa never broached the subject with him, relieved that whatever it was that had so gripped his mind was now finished or resolved. The next time she saw the newspaper thrown haphazardly on the floor beside his chair, she braced herself, but aside from one evening of closed doors, and a neat stack of letters on the hallway table in the morning, nothing more happened.

SOLITUDE IS A STRANGE CREATURE. Elsa grew accustomed to her routine, the pacing of her days. In the mornings, she read the paper over tea and toast with peach marmalade, and sometimes a hard-boiled egg. After work, she ate a simple meal, alone. She thought of Otto and his family often, but refused to acknowledge the pain those thoughts caused, the way her chest tightened, making it difficult to breathe.

Friday evenings, she met her group of church ladies for cards and idle chat, women mostly her age with families and husbands and grown children. Only Greta was a widow. She lived with her daughter and son-in-law and two dogs and seemed to think that she and Elsa should be the closest of friends because of their similar circumstances. Greta sought her out a few months after Elsa became a regular churchgoer, one widow recognizing another by her sombre dress and the way she moved her lips soundlessly during the hymns. For a few years, Elsa tried: she visited Greta for dinner, took the streetcar downtown for lunch, shared recipes and swapped church gossip. They never spoke of grief or loneliness, though Elsa could sense both just beneath the surface of Greta's cheerful smile.

One afternoon, she arrived for tea at Elsa's. They sat on the front porch on wicker chairs and sipped silently, watching pedestrians—mostly young mothers with children in prams—walk by.

"This is lovely," Greta said to break the silence, fingering the scalloped edges of the cushion beneath her legs. "Did you make it?"

"I don't sew," Elsa said, abashed to see Greta's look of surprise. Domestic chores had always bored her; she cooked, cleaned, and pressed, and could sew on a button or darn a sock, but she never had any desire to move beyond the basic skills. Why bother, when you could buy a housedress from a catalogue or the bargain shops cheaply?

"Oh."

Elsa knew that more was required, that she should take the conversation further by pressing Greta about her obvious skills as a seamstress, should profess shame at her own inabilities as a housewife or mother, but she could not muster the energy. And so they fell into silence again. Elsa let her eyelids droop, drowsy and warm. Beside her, Greta sniffed once and burst into tears.

"Greta, what's wrong?" Elsa half rose from her chair, alarmed, but Greta waved her back, pulling a handkerchief from her pocket and pressing it to her eyes as she sobbed. Elsa waited until her friend's shoulders stopped shaking before she asked again.

"What is it?"

Greta sat back, folding and refolding the delicate handkerchief. When she looked at Elsa, her eyes seemed sunken and small.

"Is this all we have now?" she asked. Elsa thought of her days, marked only by routine and the odd moment of joy: a sale at the Bi-Way, a blue jay perched on a windowsill, the smell of freshly laundered sheets, sun-bleached on the line.

"I don't know," she told Greta. And then: "No," she said. "There's more than this."

Greta said nothing for a long moment. When she spoke, her voice quavered, a thin strand of uncertainty.

"I hope you're right," she said. She sipped her tea and placed her empty cup back in the saucer with a delicate clink. "Jonathan has a job offer out west," she said. "I'll have to go with them." Elsa had never met the son-in-law. She had a vague impression of a beefy, red-faced young man with a crewcut. He worked for the government, somehow. Either Greta had never bothered to explain what he did for a living, or Elsa had never listened.

"You're moving?"

"What else can I do?"

Elsa almost offered to find out if there were openings at the telephone company where she worked, but something held her back. Finding Greta a job would only be the first hurdle. She envisioned poring over the newspaper, circling advertisements for apartments and rooms for rent. Even worse, she would be expected (or no, she would offer, of course she would) to inspect these places in person, the airless rooms, mildew in the corners, and paint peeling from window frames. She would muster up enough enthusiasm for the both of them, ignoring Greta's gloom, brightening the apartment she chose with cut geraniums and mums, bleaching and waxing floors to erase the stain of history.

Greta released a quick sigh and then rose. It seemed to Elsa that her eyes were wide with reproach when she said goodbye. A few months later, she moved out west, following her daughter and son-in-law because she had nowhere else to go. Only later did Elsa wonder if

Greta had hoped to stay in Elsa's home, if she had waited that day for an offer that never came.

ON SATURDAYS, she rose early to complete the daily chores: laundry, sweeping, dusting. In nice weather, she hung her wash in the backyard, beat the knotted rag rugs, and laid them flat on the grass to air in the sunshine. Sundays were devoted to God. Of all the days in the week, Sunday was Elsa's favourite, not for the worship as much as the ease with which the day passed. She had been raised Lutheran, but attended church infrequently throughout her childhood, only finding comfort in the wooden pews and the resounding, firm voice of the pastor after Thomas died. At first she hid near the back with Otto, the weight of the open hymnal on her palms somehow soothing.

She attended every Sunday, moving closer to the pulpit each week, row by row. By the time Otto stopped going with her, she sat only a few rows from the front, dead centre, and she sang loudly, chest surging with a feeling she couldn't quite define when the voices of the choir swelled. The knowledge of her helplessness, of His ultimate power, assuaged her guilt over Thomas' death. Over Otto.

After church, she stopped at her favourite bakery and picked up a box of sugared doughnuts. Back at home by herself, she brewed a pot of tea and ate the doughnuts one by one, her elbows resting on the kitchen table, licking thick powder from her index finger to flip the pages of her women's magazine. After Otto and his family moved in, she hid upstairs in her bedroom with the doughnuts and magazine, unwilling to let any of them see her like that, at her most unguarded.

Yes, Sundays were the days of worship and indulgence. In the early afternoons, she read the Bible for a short while or wrote letters to her mother in Germany. When Thomas died, her mother sent her a German flag by mail. *Please come home*, she wrote. It was tempting. Late at night, Elsa made lists of the pros and cons, but always it came down to Otto and the effort it would take—selling the house, uprooting a son who already had enough difficulties (*strict routine*, the doctor had said). After months of consideration, she wrote back with her decision and hung the flag in the front window of her home as a reminder to herself. *I won't forget*, she promised her mother.

Elsa took a nap in the late afternoon before rising around four to begin dinner preparations. Even before Otto moved back in, Sunday dinners were more lavish and rich than at any other time, with roast beef or a whole chicken, potatoes thick with gravy, and vegetables dotted with butter or cheese. Sated by seven, she took a long bath, leaning her head against the rim of the claw-footed tub. Sometimes she read the rest of her magazine, but usually she let her eyes close.

She took it as a sign that she first felt the lump on a Sunday, His day of rest, shortly before Otto moved in with his wife and children. An accidental discovery, a brush of her hand against skin, slippery with soap. She paused only momentarily, then rose in the bath, water sloshing down the sides of the tub. By the second summer of their stay, after she had moved up to the third floor, the lump had grown and pressed painfully against her now-dimpled flesh. More alarming, she could feel a second, smaller lump under her left arm, and her back had begun to ache.

IN THE SUMMER OF 1977, Elsa came home from work one day to find Otto waiting on her front porch in a suit, his face shiny and red from the heat. He scrambled to his feet when he saw her.

"You took the flag down," he said.

She waited silently, quelling the trembling in her hands by folding her arms in front of her chest.

"You look well," he said.

"I can't say the same of you."

It was true. He was too thin and pale for the season. He shifted from side to side, bouncing a little.

"I was wondering if we could talk."

She led him into the living room, sat down opposite him in the wing chair facing the sofa. He blinked in the dim room. She kept the windows closed during the day, the curtains drawn to keep out the heat, but in the last few days, she had not bothered to air out the house in the evening.

"I need to apologize for the terrible way I spoke to you."

"Yes."

"I'm sorry. I don't know why I said those things."

"Apology accepted."

He licked his lips, looked around. "Not much has changed in here," he said, producing a hopeful smile. Elsa would not budge.

"What do you want, Otto?" She knew him too well, knew that beneath his nervous laughter and the way he lifted a closed fist to cover his mouth when he coughed, he needed help.

"The children are big. Ruby's five, six this August. Gavin's two. And Lenore is well; she's a good mother."

Elsa sighed, her shoulders collapsing forward. "What do you need?" she asked, her voice softer. Otto paused, swallowed once, and looked away.

"I've lost my job," he said. "We don't have any savings."

Elsa pictured her rib cage splitting open, a shaft of sunlight searing through her chest. She rose.

"Tea?" she asked.

"Please."

In the kitchen, she wondered why it was that she felt suddenly so much lighter, her mouth stretching into a smile. She reached above the sink to open a window and set the kettle on the stove.

Ten

RUBY WORKS WEST of the city, in one of those unremarkable square grey buildings with shiny elevator doors. She always takes the stairs up, breathing through her mouth on the third-floor landing, where someone keeps pissing in a corner. They clean it up every time, of course, but the urine sinks into the concrete and the stink remains. By the time she reaches the sixth floor, she's puffing a little and sweating a bit more because the air conditioning in the building has only just kicked in.

The office is dark behind the glass doors, as usual. She is always the first one here, but it's not because she's dedicated: there's less traffic if she leaves before seven-thirty. Digging in her tote bag past a book, her lunch, her wallet, the ugly cardigan she always brings for the late-afternoon fridge-like temperature, and miscellaneous pens, mints, and lipsticks, she unearths her pass card, swipes it in front of the small box on the wall next to the door until the little red light turns green, and pulls open the door. Insight Communications springs to life as she walks down the halls, flicking light switches, pausing to turn on the copy machine in case she needs it soon (she knows she won't; she will spend the next half hour checking her email and reading the news online, only opening folders and looking busy when her co-workers begin to arrive).

Now in her fourth year at Insight, she finally has an office instead of a cubicle and has tried to make it her own with potted plants (always drooping, because her window faces north), a striped mug from home on her desk, her troll pen with its fuzzy pink hair, and one of those squishy stress balls on top of her computer. The rest of the small space is taken up by menus, lists, and folders of printed Excel files. Post-It notes scribbled with names, numbers, and reminders frame her monitor.

Insight organizes medical conferences for pharmaceutical companies hawking their newest and greatest medications. Three hours of lectures, followed by an afternoon of golf or massage, cocktails and dinner at a swank restaurant. The extracurricular activities are always strikingly absent from the glossy, four-colour reports the production department churns out or the pseudo-academic research papers published under the names of prominent specialists on the pharmaceutical companies' payroll.

Ruby loves many parts of her job: the detail, the organization, the colour-coded folders and labels on her desk, the way she can work through her email inbox efficiently, knocking off jobs and taking care of problems one by one. She has a knack for calm in the midst of chaos, can soothe the most ruffled of feathers over the phone. And there are certainly perks. Expensive hotels, suites with shiny bathroom tiles, flat-screen televisions mounted on the wall above Jacuzzi tubs, plush robes hanging on wooden hooks.

She is perfect over the telephone, sitting serenely in her office, but in person, she is a failure, and she wonders how much longer she can continue. By the end of every conference, her face aches from forced smiles, and her patience has worn thin. In person, she finds it difficult to keep the disdain from showing on her face when someone complains about the quality of the bread or asks repeatedly when the chocolate fondue will be ready.

It used to be fun, years ago, when she was still an assistant, and Angela worked as a staff writer before striking out as a freelancer. The photographs posted on the bulletin board above her computer mark the good times. There's a snapshot taken three years ago during one of their first conferences together in Las Vegas: Angela and Ruby, arms linked and drinks in hand, grinning broadly. And pictures from other conferences: here in California, there in Halifax, one in Jamaica—the best trip of all, so far—in that hotel with the private butlers and sweeping terraces.

It is so tempting, sometimes, to tell them what she really thinks, those doctors and wives who fax in expense reports itemizing new leather jackets or shoes, who berate Ruby when the mountain air has the audacity to be too cold, who mostly treat her like nothing simply because they can.

What do I have here? What do I really have?

Oh, stop whining.

At lunch, Ruby takes a phone book down from the shelf in her office, closes the door, and flips through the Yellow Pages as she eats at her desk. She knows there are a lot of people like her, people for whom work is merely a job, not a career, and certainly not a passion. Take Lenore, for example. Or Gavin, though Gavin doesn't really count, because he hasn't held the same job for more than a year at a time. And look at Duncan, part-time bartender, part-time musician. He isn't full of angst and worry, but then he has a hobby, at least, something that takes him away.

"You don't have to love your job," Barrett once said over a Sunday dinner of pork loin and roasted potatoes. "But you should at least like it. That's where you spend most of your time." But, of course, Barrett wouldn't understand; he not only had a career, he also had a passion for the job, the kids, the faces he made whole and normal.

She stops at an ad for skydiving, presses down hard enough to leave black ink on her fingertips.

"You can always come home," Barrett had said. "If you want to figure things out. You're always welcome here." A casual suggestion amid the soft clink and clatter of cutlery on china. He smiled at her as he chewed.

Ruby tears the ad from the phone book and slips it into a pocket of her tote bag.

IN HER APARTMENT, the message light on her answering machine is flashing, but she ignores it for a minute, strips down instead, and wonders what else she could do with her life. She is just like Gavin in so many ways, except he quit pretending a long time ago. She pours herself a glass of wine, hits Play, steeling herself for Duncan's voice. There is a pause, long and full of static, the sound of distant traffic, and then the dial tone.

She stands for a long moment with her finger on the Play button, her mind flashing uneasily on the image of the stringy-haired man in that Volkswagen van she kept seeing in odd places. Was someone following her, tracking her movements? Someone waiting for a slip—an unlocked door, perhaps, or a late-night empty parking lot? She should probably tell someone, maybe Gavin, so that if she winds up dead, they will have some kind of lead.

Oh, stop it, Ruby. She shivers, her arms covered in goosebumps, and moves to her front bay window, parting the blinds carefully to look outside. There is no sign of the van or the man. She shakes her head and turns, catching sight of the calendar above her computer, today's date circled in red. As if she could forget: August 3, a few days away from her birthday. The white box from her highest shelf is waiting for her on her desk. She lifts the stack of articles, testing their weight, then selects the first and begins to read about fathers who care. When she is finished, she shreds the pieces of paper methodically, her fingers tearing, tearing, stained with newsprint. She stares ahead at the wall above her computer, sees nothing. How long has she done this? Years—more than ten, fewer than twenty. She gathers up the strips and carries them to the kitchen sink, bends, lights a match, and steps back as the paper catches. Twenty-eight years today.

"Hi, Mom."

"We missed you last night at dinner. How was the conference?"

"Good. The same. The usual." She laughs, then pauses. She wonders how Lenore feels about the anniversary. Does she celebrate? Or now that Barrett is gone, is she looking back with her own version of regret, a crumpled pile of tissues on her bedside table? Or maybe—possibly—she has forgotten after all these years. But then Lenore laughs.

"I know," she says. "Twenty-eight years today. But we've done all right, haven't we?"

"How are you?" She means: *How are you now that Barrett's gone?* And she means: *You're not crying alone in a dark room, are you?*

"I'm fine," Lenore says. "Aunt Helen is here, actually."

"Oh, good."

"You don't have to worry about me, Ruby."

Ruby carries the receiver to the couch, sits with it cradled by her side, pretending she doesn't notice its silence.

FEBRUARY 20, 2004, one year before the wedding, 9 P.M. The small bar was crowded, bodies pressed up against one another, smoke heavy in the air. Ruby took the subway across town by herself, swaying slightly on the train, her head drooping first down, then side to side. She pulled at the fingers of her gloves, stopping briefly to tease a hole in the thumb.

The ride was so tiring, the rhythm, the whine of the brakes, the other deadened passengers sitting beside and in front of her with blank faces. No one meeting her eyes, or worse, those that stared back, glazed. But today was different: today she felt restless, uneasy.

She didn't take public transit often, so it was possible the poems had been up for a while, but today was the first day she noticed them, posted high on the walls like a border of wallpaper. These were not poems scribbled by some aspiring creative type, or taped up on flyers; these were more official, with fancy type and the logo of an arts program in the lower-right-hand corner. She couldn't read the words from her seat, but she tried, squinting and wondering if she needed glasses. She could just make out certain words and phrases, and sometimes a name or two. She would have liked to get up and read them more closely, but subways scared her a little: all those people, all those eyes, watching.

Brian, her most recent affair, drove a BMW and looked at people who took the subway with either pity or disdain, depending on his mood. *All those freaks.* She had been seeing him quietly for four months now, her longest relationship, if you could call it that. Certainly he was smart and good-looking. He knew how to order and taste wine, wore a suit to work every day, and smelled of cologne when he picked her up for their dates. He sent her flowers every two weeks just for the hell of it, let her pay one out of every three times, and rinsed out the sink after he finished brushing his teeth.

"What does he *do*?" her mother wanted to know.

"He's a consultant for some investment firm," she said. "I don't know." Lenore made an approving sound, her tongue tapping against the back of her teeth. Brian had a house in Leaside, a wife, and two girls under the age of five.

The background aroma of wet wool and slush caught on boots filled the subway car. A pair of teenaged girls wearing too much makeup, and shoes with four-inch-thick soles, left a lingering scent of youth and something darker, something forbidden, as they exited. Across from Ruby, a pair of young lovers groped openly, his hand creeping higher and higher on her thigh. Here, a man with a Jamaican accent, laughing and chattering to himself, and there, a Jesus freak, pamphlets in hand, settling into a seat next to a young man who shrank against the window. Ruby watched them all, her headphones on, scarf twined around her neck, winter hat covering her ears.

"I'm glad you came," Angela said in the bar, squeezing her hand.

"Me too."

"It just gets so boring after a while, especially if I'm here by myself," Angela said. "The same old thing." She had been dating Duncan for two years.

Ruby ordered a drink from the bar, sent it down her throat quickly, the whisky burning and warm. She ordered another.

"How's Brian?"

"Still married."

"Funny." Angela's lips angled downward, the way they always did when she asked about Brian, or James, or Anthony, or any of the others.

"Are you in love with him?"

"I don't know. My heart doesn't pound when I see him, if that's what you mean."

"Is that what you're looking for?"

"I'm not looking for anything."

"Liar." Ruby smiled at her friend, but Angela looked away, drank, lit a cigarette, and finally turned back to Ruby with a sigh.

"You know what I think?" she asked. "I think you're looking for something you're never going to find." She smiled, shrugged. "And besides, all those things you're waiting for? Swept off your feet, heart palpitations? They only happen in books and movies," she said. "That's not real life."

Duncan walked onstage, a guitar slung over one shoulder. He propped his foot on an upended wooden box and posed before the audience, his curly hair forming a halo around his head. The audience laughed, whistled. The spotlight flashed against his tight T-shirt, curved past his sideburns, and rested in his deep brown eyes. He began to play, to sing. Ruby closed her eyes and swayed, the voice lifting her. When she opened them at the end of the set, she felt giddy. The gnawing sensation in her stomach was, for the first time in weeks, gone.

Interesting that such energy can be contained, she wrote in her journal the first night she saw him.

> You can see it caught in the tense lines of your limbs. Legs pressed tightly against the fabric of your pants, the muscles of your thighs bulging with the effort. The buttons of your shirt strain against your chest. Marionette arms. Fingers slick along the strings of your

guitar. Voice rising from below your rib cage, exploding with a sound of pure beauty controlled.

She had paused then, tapping her pen against her teeth in the silence of her apartment. And written something that she hastily ripped from her notebook and buried at the bottom of her garbage can.

I wonder. If you were to remove those pants and discard the shirt, popping the buttons and letting them fall to the floor, if you were to press those thighs against mine, drape your limbs (slick with sweat) over mine, if you were, finally, to abandon all control, what sound would then emerge?

DUNCAN IS STANDING on the porch, slouching a little, glum.
"You didn't come to my show on Saturday," he says.
"I was away, remember? I had a conference."
"Come out for a walk?"
"Now? It's raining."
"Please, Ruby." She pauses, wondering if she should, but he looks so miserable that she can't say no.
The streets are empty and silent, the rain glistening on black pavement under the lights.
"How are you feeling?" Duncan asks.
"I'm all right," she says. "You? Is Angela back yet?"
"She's home." Their footsteps echo on the shiny pavement. Duncan walks with his hands in the pockets of his jeans, hair in his eyes.
"It's done," he says. His nose reddens, and tears slide down his cheeks to mix with the rain. "I told her. It's over."
"I'm sorry, Duncan."
There is a terrible neighbourhood bar around the corner with red-painted walls and odious smells. Ruby and Duncan sit together at a table by the front window.

"It was awful," he said. "I've never seen her so furious. She said she'd do everything she could to keep Bram from me. She can't do that, can she?"

"I don't know." Ruby is helpless, her pint glass cold against her hands, the sleeves of her shirt damp. She shivers, takes a drink.

FEBRUARY 20, 2004, one year before the wedding, 11:59 P.M. Angela was long gone, pleading a sudden headache.

"My father ran away when I was seven," Ruby said. She thought she might have had too much to drink: there appeared to be two of Duncan, and he swayed a little.

"I know," he said.

"Angela told you."

"You told me. We talked about it once."

"He set fire to the house. None of us were there, except for my grandmother. She was upstairs in her room. She lived on the third floor, and we lived in the basement."

"The middle floors no-man's land?"

"I suppose."

The dark front room, piano lessons measured by the thump of a cane. The smell of the woman, the way her skin wrinkled in folds under her chin, a single black hair. She wore flowered housedresses with collars and sturdy brown shoes with stockings too thick to be called nylons. The hatred rose up, sure and solid. She had never really thought much about her grandmother, but now the old woman's image loomed in her mind, and she placed all the blame squarely on her shoulders.

"I think I hate her," she confessed. "When they found her after the fire, she was already dead."

"He killed her?"

"She must have suffocated. I never really asked. We never talked about it, my mom and me."

"It must have been hard," he said. "I can see why she wouldn't want to talk about it, or even think about it."

"I suppose it was hard," she said.

"And what about you?"

"What about me?"

"How were you after the fire?" He placed his hand over hers in sympathy, the warmth increasing until her skin burned.

"I was fine," she said. "At first I saw him everywhere. Kept thinking he'd come home one day, that the whole thing was a joke. I'd see him on a bus with a bag of groceries in his arms. Or in a car—once there was this man who looked just like him. His head was turned to the side, so I only saw his sideburn, the nose, half a mouth. I was convinced it was him. I sort of tugged on my mother's hand to show her."

"And then he turned."

"He turned to look at me, and of course it wasn't him. Wasn't even close. And then, after a while, I stopped looking for him."

The truth was, she couldn't remember anything. She remembered before the fire, when her father and mother and everyone lived at the house, remembered the creaking floors and the strained silences at the dinner table. And she remembered the after part, when they lived in the apartment, when Barrett came to visit every Wednesday. But the in-between was hazy, confused, and she couldn't remember any conversation with her mother about her father or what happened on the day of the fire. Like the photographs in her mother's albums, the memories were just gone, leaving blank holes in their place.

SHE MAKES DUNCAN a mug of tea. He scoops out spoonfuls of sugar and lets the shallow curve of the spoon sink slowly down, watching as the sugar melts. He has had too much to drink.

"I'm fine," he says. "Really." He puts the spoon in the sink and—*what is he doing?*—undresses. First the shirt, pulled smoothly over his head and dropped onto the kitchen tiles. Jeans, boxers. He stands naked save his socks, groggy, his chest a thick forest of black hair. Ruby focuses her eyes on his face, refuses to look where they seem to want to go.

"What are you doing?" she asks.

"I think I should go to bed."

"Here?"

He walks into her bedroom.

"I could make up the couch," she says. He climbs into her bed, pulls the duvet up around his chin. She sighs, grabs the extra sheets and blankets from the hall closet.

"Please come lie with me," Duncan says. She hesitates.

"Please," he says.

At first she's afraid to go near him in the bed, imagines an invisible wall between them. He burrows under the covers and finds her leg, pulls her against him.

"No, no," he mumbles. "No clothes. We're all naked here." His fingers fumble clumsily against the buttons on her pyjamas.

"Duncan," she says. Her top slides off, gets tangled on her arms, then is flung to the floor. He hooks his fingers in her waistband, slides them off too, kicks them to the end of the bed. She doesn't know why she lets this happen. One half of her expects to fight off his groping hands, while the other half is confusedly numb. *Wrong, it's wrong, this is wrong!*

But his intent, tonight, is not sexual. He pulls her flesh against his, turns her around spoon fashion, and clasps his arms around her waist. She is not aware of his tears until she feels them, wet against her shoulder.

IN THE MORNING, she is encircled from behind by the softest skin she has ever felt. The softest skin. The strongest grip. It takes her by surprise, his strength. And now, and now, where to go from here? The urge to stay, to nestle in that warmth, is overwhelming. She lifts his arm, sweaty and heavy, from her waist, and pads quietly to the phone. *Terrible migraine, won't be in today*, she tells her boss.

In the shower, her hands linger on her breasts, smoothing down the water, imagining his hands instead—no, *stop*. She pinches her arms. Towel-turban wrapped around her hair, steam in her wake, she finds him in the living room, a sheet resting on his hips, confused.

"Where are my clothes?" he asks. They lie on a heap on the kitchen floor where he dropped him. He looks away. "I must have been gone," he says. "Sorry."

"It's okay," she says. "Really." She wants it back, that warmth, wants his arms around her in that viselike grip, flesh on flesh, for comfort.

After breakfast (hangover food—eggs, bacon, strong coffee—for which he is inordinately grateful), they sit on the couch in silence.

"So what will you do now?" she asks.

"I've rented an apartment."

"Already?"

"Ruby, have you been listening to me at all? It's not like I woke up last week and decided. I've been thinking about it for a long time. Months, maybe a year."

"Oh."

"What are you doing tonight?"

"Dinner with my mother." She watches as he rises, smiling sadly, lets him kiss her on the cheek.

"I'll call you in a few days," he says. "Once things settle."

"Okay."

HER MOTHER IS IN BARRETT'S study, a new computer set up in front of her.

"What's this?" Ruby asks.

"Do you like it? Gavin helped me with it on Sunday." She pushes back from the desk, raises both arms above her head, and stretches. "I feel like I've been sitting here ever since," she says, laughing, coming forward with a hug.

"How are you?"

"I'm fine, Mom, how are you doing? *What* are you doing?"

"Everyone's got to have a hobby, Ruby." Her mother looks good, tanned from the week up north, certainly more relaxed. She looks *adjusted*.

"A hobby. So you're writing now?"

Lenore shrugs, guides Ruby out of the room.

"Just my way of dealing with the past," she says.

They sit together in the backyard gazebo, staring down into the ravine. Lenore seems aware of Ruby's sense of loss, seems to look at her more deeply, to touch her more frequently and for longer. She hands her daughter a glass of lemonade, kicks off her sandals, and arranges silk throw pillows behind her back in the swing. Ruby doesn't offer any information, afraid of what will come out if she begins speaking about Duncan. Instead, she mulls over Lenore's writing, her ability to take the past and shape it into something recognizable.

"I don't remember any of it," she says. "After Dad left. I must have asked you about it."

"You never did. It struck me as odd. Gavin asked a million questions, always wanted to know when Daddy was coming home, but you …" She shakes her head. "You never said a word, you and your pale face, so solemn and sad and knowing."

"I just went about it," Ruby says.

"You did. And after a while you were all right, I suppose. I tried to talk to you once, a day or so after it all happened. You had this blank look on your face the whole time, as if nothing I said was getting through. You didn't want to hear it. Something kept you from thinking about it."

"I'm thinking about it now," Ruby says.

"That's what happens when we lose someone," Lenore says. "We start thinking about it more closely."

"But I'm not thinking about Barrett," Ruby says. "Why Dad after all these years?"

"Barrett was your other dad."

Ruby turns her face away so that Lenore can't see her expression.

FEBRUARY 20, 2004, one year before the wedding, 1:30 A.M. Later, she would wonder why she offered him a drink at her apartment, and why he accepted, both of them drunk enough already. Was it on purpose? Were both of them seeking something missing? In the cab ride, he sat back against the seat, his long legs folded in the cramped space. He reminded her of a grasshopper.

Then came his confession: "Angela hates my music."

"No she doesn't." Ruby shook her head.

"She doesn't hate my music," he said, "but she hates the fact that I still do it. She wants me to grow up, I think. Get a real job."

Ruby didn't know. In fact, she hadn't spoken to Angela about Duncan in a long time.

"She never minded before," she said, as the cab drove down her street and slowed to a stop in front of the pink brick house.

"She does now," he said, digging into his pocket for his wallet. She studied him, the way his sweater cuffs poked out from beneath his winter coat, slightly frayed, brown, the smooth skin of his wrists, the way he gently smiled at her, reached across, and opened her door for her.

"I think you're just great," she said, enough alcohol in her blood to make it easy to say without blushing. She said it with admiration. "I don't think you should ever stop doing it, if it's what you truly want. If you're passionate about it."

He stared, his eyes changing somehow, turning more liquid.

"Thank you," he said.

Inside her apartment, Ruby filled two glasses, drank until thick red wine coated her lips and mouth. *Your lips are stained*, she told him, laughing. *Yours too*, he said. The mood was so right, so great, and then everything just crashed. Ruby was suddenly crying and couldn't explain why. Maybe it was the way the room felt then, or the way Duncan laughed and smiled as if she was interesting, as if she was worth it. She started crying and couldn't stop, and he took her face in his big hands and kissed her to make her feel better, and somewhere along the line, the kiss changed to something deeper, and the sheets were hot and sticky and wrapped around their legs on the bed, and her nails dug into soft flesh. *You taste like cinnamon.*

She pushed him away before it could go any further, and more tears came when she realized what they had done. Duncan apologetic, stricken, twisting his winter hat in his hands. *Oh God, Ruby, we can't tell Angela.* Nothing happened, she told herself later, nothing more than a kiss.

A month after that night, Angela was pregnant, and her future with Duncan moved forward one space. Something hard clamped down inside Ruby. *That's it then.* But later, there was a song he sang in a hushed club, and he only sang it when Angela wasn't around to hear.

> This we did, and this we hurt
> This bed, white sheets
> I wish that they were mine
> Fabric sliding
> Skin on skin
> Never any notion of right or wrong
> I'll keep these photographs
> Mine forever for always
> In frames behind my eyes
> And always will I wonder
> If you see me at all.

Eleven

ON RUBY'S BIRTHDAY, Otto wakes cramped and stiff from his position behind the wall. The novelty of living in Lenore's basement without her knowledge has worn thin. The sleeping bag bunches in the night, and the concrete bleeds cold dampness. His hips have begun to ache. Now that Lenore is home, it's more difficult to move about during the day, and the sense of impending confrontation looms. *I'll do it this weekend.* He hasn't given much thought to how, exactly, he will make his presence known, though he is certain accidental discovery would be the worst possible scenario. Perhaps he should pack up his belongings, stow them away in the van, and announce himself via the doorbell, perhaps with a birthday present for Ruby in his hands. He is mulling over the details of the plan when the side door leading to the basement opens.

He presses as far back into his space as possible. Heavy footsteps, a feminine voice humming a song he can't quite place. *The maid.* At the entrance to his hiding spot, he can see the edge of the bucket, the long slender handle of a mop. *She's going to see me.* He is such an idiot. Did he move his toothbrush out of the bathroom? He used the toilet in the night but couldn't flush it, couldn't take the chance that Lenore would hear the rush of water through pipes upstairs. For the past few days, he has waited, listening for the creak of floorboards and the sound of the front door closing before moving. Lenore took her breakfast outside in the garden, sometimes stayed out for an hour or more. He watched her once, stood well back from the basement window, and saw her distant figure in the gazebo, her head bent over a newspaper, legs crossed.

Why didn't you think about the maid? How could you be so careless? The footsteps come closer, and he stops breathing, worried that the nervous tickle in his nose will become urgent. *Don't sneeze!*

"Marie? Is that you?"

The footsteps stop, head back towards the stairs.

"Good morning, Lenore."

"Oh, good. I need to talk to you." More footsteps as Lenore descends, and now both women stand only a few feet away.

"Is something wrong?"

"No, no, nothing like that. I just wanted to tell you—well, now with Barrett gone and just me, I don't think you need to come here anymore. I can take care of things myself."

It's the closest he has come to Lenore in twenty-eight years. Her voice beyond the wall—unchanged—wreaks havoc. His heart thuds heavily against his ribs, the sound of rushing blood fills his ears, and he needs to go to the bathroom. Otto shifts uncomfortably, his shirt wet beneath the arms. Without the aid of visualization, he can pretend that she hasn't changed since that first day in the lunchroom at the insurance office, the way she blushed shyly when he said hello and, later, the musky smell of her neck. And now he can't remember why he left, the memory of that last year together slipping away.

Most of the women he dated before Lenore were his age or younger, but each had a maternal affection he enjoyed. They straightened his tie, smoothed his hair, and brushed imaginary lint from the shoulders of his jacket. They clucked over him, fed him homemade casseroles and roasts, and didn't seem to mind that he never took them home to his apartment. When they discovered that he lived with his mother and had no intention of moving out—well, *that* little gem bothered them.

Lenore was the first woman he wanted to protect. Though she was older and taller than Otto, she had an air of fragility, as if her bones were too thin to support her body. And shy, so shy she blushed when he looked at her. On their first date, she confessed she had not been out with many men; later, after they made love for the first time, she admitted she had not been out with any man before.

To Otto's relief, the voices move away down the hallway. He is only half listening now, too focused on creeping cautiously forward on his hands and knees. With one hand steadying the mop, he lifts the bucket and sets it down in front of a set of shelves, away from his hiding spot, his arms shaking from the effort to move slowly. He rolls up the sleeping bag, retreats to the farthest corner behind the wall, and ducks his head so that the women are less likely to hear the sound of his breathing.

The voices return.

"... this weekend, I guess?"

The bucket scrapes across the floor.

"On Sunday," Lenore says. "They're coming for dinner. Thirty-six. She makes me feel old. I don't know where the time ..."

Her voice fades and disappears beneath the clatter of feet climbing up the stairs. Otto exhales. *Sunday.* On Saturday night, he will leave, check into a hotel, and get a restful sleep, one not broken into pieces by cramped spaces, a cold floor, and the persistent scuttling noise made by mice in the walls. He will shower and shave, spruce up a bit. And then, shortly after dinner, he will arrive bearing a small bouquet of roses, white for forgiveness, for hope.

He shifts, feels the urgent push of his bladder. Not wanting to risk the washroom, he looks about for a container. There are rows of paint cans on an upper shelf, but those probably won't do. The bucket is gone, of course. The rest of the furnace room is relatively neat and container-free. Lots of bags here—could he use one of those? He is about to reach for one (*check for holes, Otto, check for holes*) when he sees the plastic watering can, half-hidden by a Rubbermaid bin.

Behind the wall, he lets himself go, sickened by the sudden stench of ammonia that rises and fills the small space. He covers the watering can with a shirt from his knapsack and settles back on his sleeping bag, staring into semi-darkness.

IT IS NOON before the maid leaves. Otto watches though the basement window until he sees Lenore carrying a plate and a tall glass, her spine straight as she walks across the yard to the gazebo. A headache creeps up over the back of his scalp and behind his ears. He settles the wig on his head and grabs the bag containing his wallet and toiletries, always aware that his hiding place could be discovered in his absence.

The side door creaks slightly in the humidity, and the heat hits him with force, his head beginning to itch and sweat beneath the wig. The door has just closed behind him when he hears Lenore humming, and he freezes, pressing his back against the wall, holding his breath. She comes around the side of the house but keeps her head down. *This is it, Otto*. There is a small chance she won't recognize him, not with the wig and the many years that have lined his face, and she would not expect him to suddenly appear, not at her home, in this city.

Lenore heads down the driveway and opens the gate-like doors of the garage. Otto takes slow, small steps sideways, watching her back, ready to stop the instant she begins to turn. She bends over what looks like a dollhouse, arms extended and palms flat on a long wooden table. Otto moves more quickly, lifting his feet high to avoid the scrape of stones or dried leaves. How ridiculous he must look, and how suspicious, should a neighbour happen to glance out a window or pass in front of her house. His feet touch sidewalk and he bends to fiddle with his bag. *Safe now*. When he rises, Lenore has emerged from the garage and stands with a hand shielded above her eyes as she strains to look at him. From this distance, she wouldn't see anything.

Otto raises a hand to wave, then moves off down the street, giddy with relief and the first contact with her in almost thirty years.

IN THE PUB just a few blocks away from the house, Otto orders a chicken pot pie and a beer. He sits inside rather than on the patio, hidden in the coolness at the back of the bar, close to the washroom, the wig stowed safely inside his bag. After he left the house the day before, he hit the YMCA for a swim and a shower, and then checked into a hotel downtown. It is more expensive than he had anticipated, but he appreciates the fine white sheets, thick duvet, and gleaming tiles on the bathroom floor.

He drinks deeply from his pint glass, setting it down empty and ordering another. He doesn't drink much, never has, but today is a momentous day, and he is entitled. Yesterday he waved at Lenore, and tomorrow he will be reunited with his family. Never has he felt more optimistic.

On his way back from the washroom, he finds a pack of playing cards beneath a dartboard and carries them to his table. He begins to lay them out, one by one, and contemplates the neat rows as he eats. When he has finished, he moves his plate to the adjacent empty table, picks up the cards again, shuffling lazily. He orders another beer, forms a triangle with two cards on the table, fiddling until they stand steady. After school, he would sit at the desk in his room, a textbook open in front of him. Homework time. All the other boys were out playing baseball or hockey, but not Otto. *I fooled you, Mother.* He kept the cards in his desk. He would pull them out and build houses, collapsing them with a single finger when he heard her footsteps on the stairs.

There are four triangles in front of him, the simplest of bases, but he is rusty after all these years. He picks up an ace, places it flat across the tips of two triangles, parallel to the table. It used to matter to him how the cards were chosen, as if the numbers and suits in the right order would make for a stronger house, but now he doesn't care.

"I've never seen anyone do that before." The waiter stands off to the side, smiling, inquisitive. He is young, maybe twenty, and has round circles stretching out his earlobes, like a member of an ancient tribe. "Good balancing."

"Balance and friction," Otto says, stacking cards layer by layer until his house is complete. "It's all about support. Watch." He pulls on one of the lowest triangles, and the cards fold in and collapse.

He begins to build again, this time using a more complex grid pattern, a waffle of cards, until the pack is empty.

"Now." Otto slides out a single wall from the base. Nothing happens; the small sturdy structure remains standing, firm. "See? Proper balance, equal friction."

"Right."

"Not as fragile as you'd think."

"No?" With a smile, the waiter sets his empty tray on top of the cards. He doesn't let go entirely, but relaxes his hand so that the weight of the tray crushes the cards, and they flatten against the table.

"Proper balance, unequal friction," he says with a laugh. "Another beer?"

THE DETAILS ALWAYS RUINED HIM: the multiple forms and paperwork, the signatures, the filing. Otto lost telephone numbers, misplaced his pens, forgot to write down important information, so that the follow-up was more difficult, if not impossible. Twice the insurance company warned him, though he didn't tell Lenore this. When they fired him, they did so with expressions of sadness and sighs of disappointment, all things to which he was accustomed.

He put off telling Lenore for a week. He rose in the morning as if it were an ordinary workday, brushing his teeth, shaving, and buttoning up a clean, pressed shirt. He sat on a bench in front of city hall, watching the pigeons flutter and peck at the ground. Sometimes he boarded a streetcar and rode from one end of the city to the other. Without work, the day seemed endless. His sense of ineptitude grew.

On Friday, he waited for his mother on her front porch and tried to swallow the nausea and shame. *Crawling back to Mommy, Otto?*

She didn't seem surprised to see him, though it had been five or six years. She had aged, the flesh of her cheeks pulled down by gravity to rest in thick folds along the sides of her mouth. The house too, had festered: inside, it was damp, dark, and stank of unwashed dishes. When she disappeared into the kitchen to make tea, he pulled apart the heavy drapes and stood back from the cloud of dust that swirled in the afternoon sunlight.

"It will be temporary," he told his mother. He could tell that she would never forgive him for what he had said to her that day on the telephone. The damage was too great.

"We'll stay in the basement; you'll hardly see us." His mother nodded, her face blank, noncommittal. He quelled the resentment that simmered deep within his chest.

He had so wanted to prove her wrong, and it seemed, for a while, that he had been victorious. Long years at the same job, Lenore growing fat and rosy with two pregnancies, their happiness and the sensation of utter freedom. They talked about buying a small house, something with a garden and a yard for the children. How wonderful to be responsible, to plan a future together; how marvellous to erase the shadow of expected failure.

"You should call your mother," Lenore would say. "Doesn't she want to meet the children?"

"No," he said. He didn't want any part of his mother's dour predictions to enter into this new life, didn't want her over for tea or dinner with stories of Otto as a child, the doctor's visit, the school reports. He was a new man, now, reborn. The old Otto was dead and buried.

But at night he heard her voice, felt her hands pressing down as he sat at his desk, those hateful years of books and homework while the sun poured in through the window. She had stolen his childhood.

"It's for your own good," she said.

Piano lessons, classical music instead of what he really wanted, loud music and the chance to be normal: to get his fingernails dirty, his clothes wet from the river, to find water snakes, and make secret caves of mud, sticks, and old leaves. He knew instinctively he could work with his hands, not his mind, but it wasn't good enough for his mother, there in her billowing housedress, so unlike the other mothers on the street in their neat suits and stockings, with their kind smiles and cookies sent to school wrapped in waxed paper. Did she not know how it looked? That flag in the window proclaiming their difference, their—no, *her*—refusal to be one of them, as if she were above that simple, domestic life. And later, the darkness that fell over the house, the strange, musty smell of the rooms.

Once, at fourteen or fifteen, he defied her, came down from his room and turned on the radio to blaring music, sat cross-legged and close, his eyes slits as he waited for her footsteps.

"What do you think you're doing?" She had to shout over the music.

"It's what I want," he said, his back to her. "*This* is what I want." She reached beyond him, turned the knob counter-clockwise until he could hear nothing.

"You don't know what you want. You don't know who you are, what you have in you."

"I know I'm not who you want me to be," he said, finally turning to stare at her. She said nothing in return, her lips clamped down.

He never had enough distance or perspective. He called her one day about six months after the wedding. Did he hope to put the past behind them both? *I have a wife, a steady job, and I've never been happier.* But he started badly, his thoughts too jumbled. She must have made some sound, a clicking of tongue against the roof of her mouth, or maybe a disbelieving cough. His hand tightened around the telephone receiver, his sudden rage surprising and hot. Ugly words spewed from his mouth. When he hung up, his hands shook so much that he had to sit on the edge of his bed and press his arms between his legs.

OTTO IS DRUNK. He has moved to the patio among the young people, girls showing bare midriffs and boys with tattoos and piercings. He sits in a corner and watches them come and go, some holding hands, others laughing too loudly in groups of three or four.

Even now there is no relief from the heat, the air thick and moist. Otto's pants feel damp against his chair. At the table beside him, two young men talk about death and aging while their girlfriends or dates listen, leaning on the table with sun-browned arms.

"If you don't people your world now, you'll have no one when you're old," one of the men says. "And you'll die alone."

"Unless you have a big family," the other says.

"That's what I'm talking about. You build your family, but kids move out, right? And your partner dies, unless you go first. So you have to have others. Friends, lots of friends. Hobbies. Things to keep you occupied."

"There was a study about people who do crosswords and puzzles." A young woman leans forward, curly hair tumbling forward over a shoulder. "You're less at risk of Alzheimer's if you keep your mind active."

"Right. But if you're holed up in your apartment doing crosswords all day, and you have no friends or support system, you're still going to die alone."

"You'll just live a longer, lonely life, totally aware of it."

"So what's worse, do you think? Having Alzheimer's and being completely unaware of what's happening to you, or watching your body break down and knowing what's happening? Watching all your friends and family members die one by one? I'm not sure I'd want to outlive everyone. Better to go first."

The young woman shakes her head. "I don't think people with Alzheimer's are completely unaware. I think they have moments of clarity when they know exactly what's happening to their mind but can't do anything about it. That, to me, would be worse than anything else."

"The helplessness."

"Yes."

The curly-haired woman looks in Otto's direction, catches his stare. She whispers something to one of the men, and he turns, smiles.

"Beautiful night," Otto says. He would never have spoken to them if not for the beer. These people would be the same age as his children, maybe a bit younger.

"Can I ask you something?" he says.

"Sure." They have all turned in his direction now, curious. Otto scrapes his chair closer to their table.

"Hypothetical situation," he says, then clears his throat. "Suppose you had a father who disappeared when you were young. Maybe four, maybe seven. You don't see him for almost thirty years, you have no contact with him and don't know what's happened to him or where he is at all. Suddenly he appears on your doorstep and wants to make amends for leaving you like that. What would you do?'

They are silent, contemplative. The curly-haired woman tilts her head to one side, studying him.

"Disappeared with no warning?"

"Nothing."

"No letters or anything over the years?"

"No."

"I don't know," one of the men says. "Thirty years is a long time. I guess it depends on what our relationship was like before he left."

"That might make it worse, though," the other woman says, the one who has been silent for most of their previous conversation. She is a bit older than the others, blond and rounded, with deep laugh lines around her mouth. "I mean, if I was close to my dad and he left without a word for that long, I think I'd be pretty upset with him. It would take a lot to get over the hurt."

"If I was seven, I'd wonder what the hell I'd done to make him leave."

"And if I was four, I don't know that I'd remember any of it. I wouldn't want anything to do with him reappearing in my life. Why would I?"

Otto presses his lips together. *They'll want nothing to do with me, either of them.* His throat swells with pain.

"Thank you," he says. He moves his chair backwards, his face away from the group, not wanting them to see his grief. How could he have been so foolish as to believe it could be different? He thinks of the many times he has imagined the reunion with his family: the tears and recrimination, the eventual forgiveness. *You're an idiot, Otto.* He will finish his beer, return to his hotel. And in the morning, he will get in the van and drive home.

The young people prepare to leave, setting bills on the table, sliding cellphones and wallets back into purses and pockets. The blond woman says something quietly to the others, then comes to his table and sits in front of him.

"My parents divorced when I was eight," she says. "My dad moved away, down to Texas, and I never saw him again. I heard he remarried a few times, had more kids. He never sent even a birthday card. Two years ago, I heard he died. He was driving his truck and slammed into a tree. He was drunk." She pauses, twisting a ring around her index finger. When she looks up, her wide eyes hold traces of grief. "I would give anything just to see him again. If he suddenly appeared on my doorstep, I'd know he hadn't forgotten me. He'd taken an effort to contact me, let me know he still cared, even if it was too late. And if he stayed around, kept in contact—well, I guess I'd try. It would be hard, but it's better than what I have now." She waits a moment, then stands. Otto reaches across the table, touches her wrist in gratitude.

Twelve

RUBY IS FLOATING, her arms wide, the skin of her face pressed back until it feels as though it has been peeled from her skull. It's her birthday, and she has called in sick to work, not caring if they don't believe her story of a migraine. The material of the instructor's flight suit flutters against her cheeks. He pulls the ripcord; the upward pull of the parachute as it opens sends a jolt through her body, and then she is vertical again, the world between her feet—the houses, trees, and roads—mere microdots. And then there's this, a single moment of clarity: *what the hell were you thinking?*

Closer now. The jump master flares hard, and they slow. The ground rushes up, feet hit and tangle, but then it's done. Ruby can't catch her breath.

"How was that?" he asks.

"I want to do it again." And again, and again. A flush of contentment warms her arms and legs, her cheeks. The instructor laughs.

"That's what everyone says."

AT ELEVEN, Ruby had a gangly boyfriend named Peter who had wispy brown hair and blue eyes. He had a pool and tiny hard lips: if she held her two fingers together and kissed them it felt no different. She liked to ride on the handlebars of his bicycle, feeling the wind erase the heat of the summer sun. In the winter he wasn't much use.

At Angela's, they tried on hats in her room, preening in front of the mirror, or practised making up their faces with lipstick and eye shadow stolen (*borrowed*) from Angela's mother. Sometimes they still played with dolls, but now, instead of walking each other down the aisle, Barbie and Ken got naked and were twisted into various positions as the two girls giggled furiously, their faces turning red, whispering the word *sex* in horrified tones.

"What happened to your dad?" Angela once asked. She held a bowl of raspberries in her lap, took one now and popped it into her mouth. Ruby loved Angela's house, loved the way it looked so small from the front, a house of surprises. The back dropped down over the ravine; a long staircase wound its way down to the road. Trees and brush grew on either side, as if you were in the middle of a forest instead of the city. From here, they could walk to the park or the river, where Lenore took them all on Sundays for picnics.

"He ran away," Ruby said, cautious now, treading unfamiliar territory. She had never spoken of her father to anyone, not even Gavin (who was too small to remember, in any case), or her mother. But at night she dreamed of him, remembered the way he talked, smiled, and held her hand, remembered the pale blue eyes and fair eyelashes.

"Why did he run away?"

Angela's parents were divorced; her father had moved away overseas, and she only saw him only once every few months. She spoke of him with a casualness that Ruby couldn't understand. To treat your absent father with so much disdain or carelessness! If Ruby's father were still around, Ruby would love him so much that he would never leave again.

"There was a fire in our house," she said. "We think he started the fire, and then he ran away." She waited for Angela's laugh, her mockery, but her friend opened her mouth in a small oval of awe.

"Did it burn up?"

"The house? No. Not really."

"Oh." Angela considered. "Is he ever coming back?"

The question brought her near tears. She bit her lip hard, a trick she once learned, and shook her head.

"I don't think so," she whispered.

"I miss my dad too," Angela said, her lip trembling. She let out a sigh, dramatic and exaggerated, then smiled at Ruby. "I think we were meant to be friends forever."

RUBY OPENS SOME WINE and waits for Angela, for the raving and dismantling of a marriage, the dissection of all that's gone wrong. And Ruby will smile and nod sympathetically, will bring their friendship back to where it belongs. She won't throw away more than twenty years.

"Wait till I tell you what I did today," she says breathlessly, but Angela is in a foul mood, throwing her purse down on the couch, ripping open a bag of potato chips, and attacking the wine with such vigour that she smears lipstick along the side of the glass.

"Fuck him," she says. Her fingertips shine with salt.

"Right."

"I can't say I'm surprised," Angela says. "About his leaving, I mean. It's not like we had the greatest marriage going." And yes, here it comes, a litany of complaint. But instead, Angela sighs. "I thought I could make it work. I can't believe he just left like that. It's humiliating."

She wraps both hands around her wineglass, head down, shoulders pulled in. For the first time that Ruby can remember, Angela looks fragile.

"I'm sure it wasn't an easy decision for him," Ruby says.

Angela snorts. "Oh yes, his biggest fan comes to his defence."

"That's not fair, Angela."

"Oh, come on, Ruby, it's so obvious. You've had a thing for Duncan for years. *Everyone* has noticed." She stops, presses a hand to the side of her head. "I'm sorry. I shouldn't have said that."

"No, you shouldn't have." Ruby walks to the kitchen for more wine, brings the bottle back with her, and places it on the coffee table. Before pouring some into her glass, she hesitates, then gestures with the bottle questioningly. Angela nods, but the mood has shifted. Ruby is defensive, her shoulders and neck tense. Angela looks brittle, hard, the makeup on her face caking in the corners of her mouth. Ruby thinks of Duncan's lips, moistened with wine, and jerks her eyes back to Angela. *No, you won't.* The afternoon's clarity begins to slip.

"Are you really going to keep Bram from him?"

As soon as she asks the question, she realizes her mistake. Angela lifts her head. Dark rings of makeup have smeared below her eyes.

"You've talked to him? When?"

Ruby bites down on a piece of skin on her lip. *Fuck.*

"He came by the night he told you he was leaving," she admits. What else can she say?

"Interesting." The room shrinks, becomes stifling.

"It's not what you think," Ruby says, but then she makes her second mistake: she looks away from Angela. It's exactly what Angela thinks.

"Isn't it?"

"No."

Angela reaches into her purse and pulls out a travel-sized packet of Kleenex. She unfolds and folds the small rectangle before wiping her eyes. *What did you think, Ruby? Did you think you could hide it from her forever?* Ruby crosses her arms in front of her chest, holds on tightly to stop the trembling. Her neck and shoulders ache.

"I'm sorry, Angela."

"You have some kind of self-destructive gene when it comes to men. You're all screwed up, Ruby. Mr. Todd was a long time ago."

"It doesn't have anything to do with that."

"Yes it does. You don't know what you want, you never have. You've been chasing your father ever since he left. And now you're mirroring your mother, carrying a torch for someone else's husband. It's pathetic." She spits out the word, her mouth settling into a flat line, the corners of her lips angling downward.

"You leave my mother out of this. She's done nothing wrong. Nothing!"

Angela picks up her purse, heads towards the front door. "Stay away from my husband, please." Ruby feels dizzy, sways slightly on her heels. Sour liquid burns a path up from her stomach and into the back of her throat.

"I can't," she says.

Angela stops, her back to Ruby, her shoulder blades standing out clearly in the halter top she wears, her thinness only accentuating what Ruby has always thought of as her *regality*. Her copper hair is twisted up in a messy bun on the back of her head, and small silver pendants dangle from her ears. She turns slowly.

"What do you mean, you can't?" Ruby doesn't say anything, her skin suddenly dry, tight, as if it would crack and slip down over her face. Angela keeps her face still, blank, but her eyes are too bright, and she blinks fast.

"No," she says, shaking her head. "Oh, no." Her hands shake when she reaches out for the doorknob. She turns once again. "How can you do this to me? I've been there for you through *everything*. We've been friends forever." Her voice is tight, choked with anger, nearly a whimper. There's a long silence as Angela waits. Ruby doesn't know what to say, how to address the sucking emptiness in her chest or the pain she has inflicted.

"You want him?" Angela asked. "Here's the reality of life with Duncan: I worked my ass off so that he could play all day and still have his music on the weekends. So that nothing changed in his world, even though Bram changed everything in mine. Working part-time at that bar, playing his damn gigs on the weekend. God forbid I ask him to stop or get a real job, something that pays the bills. God forbid. I even got a nanny for him." Her face is contorted. "I never get a break, Ruby. Never. I'm working or taking care of Bram or Duncan. And he has the gall to say that I've changed. 'You're not the same person anymore,' he said. 'We never talk anymore.' Well, no shit! I had to change. He sure wasn't going to. What the hell was there to talk about?"

And then she's gone, heading down the street that almost shimmers with the heat rising from the pavement. Ruby watches her from the porch, but Angela doesn't look back.

Ruby cleans up the apartment by rote, clearing the glasses from the coffee table and rinsing them in the sink. Without taking off her clothes, she slides the pocket doors of her room shut and turns out the light. In the darkness, anything seems possible. *Chasing your father. Ridiculous.*

RUBY'S FIRST SERIOUS BOYFRIEND had long stringy hair and no ass to speak of: his pants always lay flat against the back of his thighs, and nothing shifted up or down when he walked. She was mad about him, the way you could be completely mad at the age of fifteen. He wore Obsession cologne, deejayed at a local all-ages club, and wrote poetry. Ruby took these poems home and pasted them on the walls of her room, read them over the phone to her girlfriends, and they said, *How sensitive!* She put the posters for his dances on her wall, too, his name at the bottom. As if he were famous. When her mother raised her eyebrows or rolled her eyes, Ruby was hurt and defensive. *He's a poet!* she cried. *He feels things!*

He felt them, all right. They lay in his bed and made out, letting their hands roam, breathing heavily, lips and tongues swollen. But there were barriers, No Trespassing signs. There were many firsts with him, but not that, not yet. Everything was later analyzed with friends. *Should I do it?* He was older and therefore cool, an expert in the ways of the world. Every word that came from his mouth, those wide lips that felt so good over Ruby's, was the ultimate truth. This was what she thought.

This was what she felt: she waited, trying to breathe, for those moments with him in his bed, his room, or just with him, smelling him, feeling his hair under her palms. She thought she was in love, thought they would probably get married and have a couple of kids, that he would write poetry and use her as his muse. They would be happy forever, smelling of Obsession and sleeping together on crumpled sheets.

He gave her the first drag off a cigarette, the first toke off a joint, and he laughed with his friends when her lungs seized up and made her cough and choke. At his dances, she and Angela and a bunch of other girls danced and danced, lost control, and let go. They were only fifteen; they didn't care what they looked like or what they were wearing, at least Ruby didn't. Maybe they wore lipstick and a bit of eyeliner. They had their youth, pink cheeks, and smooth skin. And they danced, little drops of sweat dampening their hair and above their lips. Boys came in from the parking lot, where they had been secretly drinking beer in their cars and flicking beer caps out the windows. They leaned against the wall, eyeing the girls and making whispered comments to one another, cackling and nudging one another's ribs with their elbows.

One night, another girl stood next to Ruby's boyfriend behind the table (*Ruby's* spot, her place, her right). She had that look of sophistication: long sleek hair, tall black boots, charcoal eye shadow. Ruby pushed her way through darkened bodies, the beat from the music hitting her collarbones and sinking all the way down her thighs. By the time she found her boyfriend, his mouth and her mouth (that other girl's) were meshed together. The other girl laughed at something he said, and he turned with confidence, saw Ruby, and didn't have the grace to look ashamed. He only half smiled and shrugged, as if to say, *It was worth a shot.* And Ruby felt a sinking in her body, a devastation. She was nothing, only two legs with a hole in between. A target, a bull's eye painted red with blood. For a split second, she was filled with a horrible rage against him (*how dare he?*) before she directed it against herself, and that was the worst thing of all.

Outside, she cried on Angela's shoulder, leaning against a parked car. When she got home, she ripped the posters and the poetry from the wall, tore them into pieces, and shoved them into the garbage. Her mother heard, listened quietly, then put her arms around Ruby's shoulders and said the worst thing she could have said, not realizing the words would burn into Ruby forever.

"That's what boys are like," she said.

Her mother rose to open the window in Ruby's room, struggling a little with the metal latch. She wore her yellow housecoat, the one that wrapped tightly around her waist and had buttons down to her ankles. There was a quiet sadness in the angle of her mother's head as she turned to look at her daughter.

"Just remember who you are," her mother said. "Don't ever lose yourself."

Ruby puzzled over these words, her eyes lifted to search the ceiling as if for answers.

"What about you?" she asked, picking at the comforter with her fingers, not looking her mother in the face as she waited for the answer. What she meant was *Haven't you lost yourself?* The Wednesday dinners. The details: the way Barrett smiled at her mother, the way her mother's fingers lingered on his arm. For eight years, the same routine. *Isn't he married, Mom?*

"What do you mean?"

"I mean ... Barrett," she said. "How do you ... doesn't it bother you? How can you share him?"

She held her breath. You just didn't ask Lenore questions like this, not outright, without warning. Her mother took a long time to answer, and for a moment, Ruby feared she would just ignore the question and withdraw, as she usually did to avoid a confrontation. But then Lenore shook her head, let her hand rest on Ruby's leg.

"Do you remember a few years ago, when I said that Barrett was away?" Barrett was always away at conferences. Once he went to

Paris to work for a few months with the man who trained him, her mother said.

"Yes."

"He wasn't. We'd had an argument. A fight, really."

Ruby tried to imagine her mother fighting, but couldn't. She refused to raise her voice; her face would pale and she would simply turn away. *I won't fight with you*, she would say. *Talk to me when you're feeling better.* They grew up believing their mother to be too fragile for harsh words, as if she would break into a million pieces.

"What did you fight about?"

"About Rena, about us. I decided I wasn't happy with the way things were. I didn't see him for a while."

"And then you changed your mind."

"Yes." She looked at Ruby. "You won't understand, but Barrett was the first person who wanted to take care of me, instead of the other way around. And I know it seems strange to you, but I couldn't imagine my life without him." Her smile then was sad, wistful.

"You have your whole life ahead of you," she told Ruby. "Don't let one boy ruin it for you. He's worse than nothing for making you feel the way you do right now."

Ruby lay back on her pillow and stared at the ceiling after her mother left, her chest split open, mangled.

THUNDER OUTSIDE. The clouds have been gathering all day, knitting together in angry grey wads. As she walks into her living room, it begins to pour. She imagines roots digging in deeply to drink and opens the windows so that the sound of the storm comes in. These are the nights for reflection, for poets, she thinks, for open notebooks and the scratch of pen against paper.

Instead, she takes the subway across town and then walks south. The rain is sluicing down, biting against her skin, but she drinks it in, each hard drop a punishment. She presses her face to the window. He is behind the bar, idly wiping down a glass with a dishcloth. The place is nearly empty, only a few grizzled regulars perched like hunchbacks on the swivelling stools. He sees her at once. She smiles, waves, then begins to run down the street away from the bar, runs until her legs protest and tremble, not stopping until she hits the lights. And then she closes her eyes and waits. *If he hasn't followed me, I'll let it go. I'll walk away, and I'll be fine.*

"Ruby!" She turns. His mouth works, but he says nothing more, just stands, hands loose by his sides, his own chest heaving from the effort of the chase. She sees him naked again, stripped bare. *I'm in love with you. I've been in love with you since I met you.*

Fuck it.

She walks towards him with purpose. His face changes, broadens and lightens, and then his arms are around her again. Here, here. Yes. Damn the people who stare, damn the cars in the street, the shrill horns. He kisses her. And kisses. And pulls her into a doorway and continues. It has never been like this.

THEY HAVE SPILLED RED WINE on the sheets, and the stain spreads from the middle outward, like blood. Their clothes lie mingled on the floor where they were tossed the day before, barely put on again. Duncan likes to be naked, likes to walk around her apartment and stand in front of the uncovered front window, daring those on the outside to look in. Most of all, he likes the sense of freedom it gives him, swaying in the breeze like that. *Angela hated it*, he starts to say, but Ruby presses her fingers against his lips, silencing him.

She is more modest at first, clutching the sheet or a T-shirt in front of her, covering her ass with her hands. But in the end, what does it matter? He has seen her at her most intimate, has peered into her soul and sliced her open. Or so she feels. It terrifies her, this vulnerability. Now that she has found this, she is sure it will be taken away, and the guilt hides, lethal, just beneath the surface.

She lies crushed against his furry chest.

"What are you thinking?" he asks. She turns to face him, her nose pressed against his, smiles. She won't say. Can't.

"Mmm," she says instead. "Yummy." *I think I'm so in love with you. I think this is what I've been waiting for. Everyone said it didn't exist, but it does, it really does. And I think I have to end it soon, because of Angela, because of our history and old loyalties. And she can never, ever know.*

He laughs, slides his hand down her thigh. "Sex maniac." And that too. Under the kitchen table—vegetables in the wok fried crispy black and had to be chipped off with a knife—in the hallway, the shower. Belt unbuckled on the front porch before she managed to get the key in the lock. It was so very good.

"Happy belated birthday," he says.

Thirteen

GAVIN WATCHED RUBY paint her toenails. She was seventeen and gangly, her legs thin and knees bony and protruding. A thin silver anklet drooped over her left heel as she propped her foot on the ottoman.

"Stop staring," she muttered, without looking away from her toes. When she was in a bad mood like this, Gavin liked to stare as much as possible. He liked to see how far he could push her before she exploded.

"There's nothing else to do," he said. It was true. Later tonight he was meeting a bunch of friends at the park, where maybe he would get stoned and make out with Sara Green. For now, there was nothing, and worse, there was no air conditioning in the apartment. Lenore set up a standing fan in the corner of the living room and shut the windows against a heat so heavy that it hung in his mouth, cottony and dry.

Gavin parked himself in front of the fan and spread his arms wide, letting the air cool the back of his neck.

"Get out of the fan," Ruby snapped. When Gavin was eight, he peered through a crack in Ruby's bedroom door, watched her staring at herself in the full-length mirror that leaned against one wall. She was naked. She raised her arms, began a kind of chicken thrust.

I must, I must, I must increase my bust.
The bigger the better, they fit in my sweater,
I must increase my bust.

He backed away, squeezing his burning eyes shut, and tripped. But later, when the horror of her nakedness had faded, he realized he had found a new way to torment her.

He pumped his arms once, twice. "I must, I must—" he began.

"Shut up." The joke was too old; she didn't blush anymore, didn't even pause in her nail-painting. But then she did look up with a shadowy smile. She looked him up and down, slowly, taking in his faded Jim Morrison T-shirt, his ragged jean shorts, the sneakers on his feet that stank so badly in the summertime that he couldn't take them off in front of other people, and Lenore made him leave them on the balcony to air out overnight.

"You're starting to look like Barrett," she said. "You kind of act like him too." A long pause. Then, "Maybe he's your real dad." He nearly fell backwards against the fan. She must have been saving it for just the right time. She smirked.

"Ha, ha," he said.

"No, I mean it." She tilted her head to the side, as if she had given it great thought.

Logically, he knew it couldn't be true. Illogically, something stirred in his chest, a flutter. *How do I look like him?* No, he wouldn't ask, would not give her the victory.

He flapped his arms, waved each hand under an armpit.

"Hope I don't stink too much," he said. He turned and put his lips close to the fan. "*Luke, I am your father*," he intoned, listening to the vibrations, the way the fan distorted his voice. The smell of her nail polish drifted across the room.

You look like him. Tall skinny Barrett, with his wilful hair and an expensive watch around his left wrist, a sick wife in that big house of his. Gavin knew where Barrett lived: he spotted his car one day and followed him on his bike, tires silent when he turned onto his street, the bumpy feel of those cobblestones. He waited across the street on the sidewalk, but Barrett never noticed him.

He flicked his eyes in Ruby's direction, keeping his lids partially lowered so she wouldn't catch him staring. She had finished with her toes and had moved on to her fingernails, her posture giving nothing away, unaware (or perhaps keenly aware) of the avalanche she had triggered inside him.

"WHAT COLOUR ARE YOUR EYES?" Across the dinner table, Ruby hid a smile behind her hand. Barrett took off his glasses, leaned in close until Gavin saw the pores of his skin.

"Hazel," Barrett said.

No one asked why Gavin needed to know. His mother's eyes were green. He began to make a list and hid it in his Grade 9 math book.

You act like him. In the garage of his house, Barrett built miniatures, or so he told them.

"I have a whole studio set up," he said.

"Miniatures of what?" Ruby asked.

"People. Houses. That kind of thing."

"Dolls? You make dolls and dollhouses?" Gavin bit his cheeks to stop from grinning.

"Sort of." He cocked an eyebrow, lips curving up in a sardonic smile. (Barrett had a dimple in his left cheek, Gavin noted on his list. You could see it only when he smiled or laughed, but it was there.)

"Dolls," Ruby said. He looked at her then, his eyes behind his glasses magnified.

"I make things that are important to me," he said.

Gavin didn't have any hobbies, unless you counted smoking pot and trying to feel up Sara Green. Every morning during the school year, he woke with the best intentions. Maybe that day, a teacher would say something that would spark an interest or plant a seed of fascination that would make him listen, really listen, like the smart girls in the front rows who took notes in girlish, curving letters, pausing only to shake a wrist or flick back a strand of hair. The girls who were beginning to look at him with their own version of interest. But by lunchtime, his best intentions had morphed into a complicated system of deciding which class to skip, and where he could score some pot or a few smokes for the afternoon. *Move along. Nothing to see here, folks.* Late at night, Ruby and Lenore pulled out books or watched television; Gavin retreated into his bedroom and played music on the stereo until someone yelled for him to turn it down. He had an entire wall of music, cassettes fitted into wooden slots, albums below his desk in special cubes that Barrett had given him one year for Christmas or his birthday. Sometimes he would put on an album and pull the others out one by one as he listened, fanning them on the floor or reading the liner notes yet again: The Clash, the Pixies, the Ramones; older stuff like Simon and Garfunkel, The Beatles, The Rolling Stones.

Most of the albums were gifts from Barrett, as was the stereo. He was a doctor and made tons of money, judging by the grand house nestled in the tree-lined, curving street. Gavin, on his bike, surveyed the signs of casual affluence: the woman raking leaves in a cashmere sweater, the collar of a white blouse peeking over its neck; the men in suits sliding from leather car seats, the doors closing behind them with a muted click; two speed walkers chatting as they passed, arms pumping, trim and neat with their blond hair pulled back, baseball caps on their heads, tanned skin and diamond earrings the size of a penny. And there was Barrett, rumpled slacks and shirt untucked, his hair a tufted halo, driving glasses sliding down his nose as he searched in his pocket for his house keys and waved absentmindedly to his neighbour.

Look at me. See me.

He rode home to the apartment, which bore signs of the seventies: an old brown couch, fraying at the bottom; a teak coffee table and two matching side tables stained with overlapping rings; weird chairs covered in vinyl with footrests that flipped back and forth; and beds that squeaked and cringed when you sat on them.

"She wanted to keep all our old furniture," Ruby said.

"Why?"

"Don't you get it? She's a kept woman, Gavin. We're a kept family. Barrett pays for everything."

"So?"

"So maybe she can't ask for all new stuff too, on top of everything else."

"But she works." On Tuesdays, she led a reading group for kids at the library. On Thursdays and Fridays, she worked in a small jewellery store.

"Oh, Gavin." Ruby rolled her eyes and sighed, as if Gavin's education in all things worldly rested on her fifteen-year-old shoulders. "She works to keep busy, not to make money, dumb-dumb. She doesn't want all that time to really think about things."

"How do you know?"

"I know," she said, "because I'm a woman too."

RUBY FOUND HIS LIST on one of her laundry days. They took turns doing the laundry. *It teaches you real-life skills*, Lenore said. The washing machines were in the basement of the apartment complex, in a dim and damp room. *It's only three floors down*, Lenore said, but that was easy for her to say. She didn't have to trudge up and down those stairs with basket after basket of clothes.

The day that Ruby found the list was hot, the air sticky with impending rain. Gavin slung a leg over an armchair, listened to his skin squeak against the orange vinyl, and slid the patio doors open farther with his toe. Sometimes he would sit for long periods just to peel his skin off slowly, inch by inch, to see how much it hurt.

She must have knocked his math book from the table where he kept the list. Or maybe she wondered why a math book would be sitting on his desk in the middle of the summer and flipped through it nosily, suspecting that something would be hidden between the pages. In any case, Gavin heard a burst of laughter from his room. Before he could unpeel himself from the chair, she came down the hall, the list balanced on top of the dirty laundry.

Barrett	*Me*
Eyes: hazel	Eyes: green
Dimples	No dimples
Tall	Tall?
Smart	Maybe?
Has hobbies	No hobbies
Preppy style	Rebel style

"Rebel style?" she asked, her chest hitching. "*Rebel?*"

"Maybe it's true," he said. "Maybe Barrett is my dad."

She stopped laughing and put down the laundry basket, tugging at her cut-off jean shorts, a pair of men's boxer shorts peeking below the hem. She spent hours with her clothes, ripping apart jeans and shorts, inserting panels of material, arranging her Ralph Lauren shirts carefully on padded hangers. Before leaving the house, she tried on a multitude of outfits, posing this way and that.

Why do you care so much what other people think?

I don't. I'm trying to decide what I want.

Her hair had grown long over the summer and now brushed her collarbones.

"I was just bugging you. He's not your dad."

"Maybe he is."

"No. You just want him to be."

"I just want to know."

"Why? What difference does it make?" But of course it made all the difference.

"I'm going to ask Mom," he said.

Ruby's eyes widened before she looked away. In this family, you didn't ask questions outright like that. Usually, you just tried to find out the answer yourself, like when Gavin wanted to know more about sex. He never even thought about asking Lenore, not because she was a prude, but because he didn't want to startle her.

At night he punched his pillow into a ball, turned it upside down, aiming for a cool, dry spot. Gavin wanted the kind of dad that other kids had, someone always there, someone to offer you a taste of beer straight from the bottle, someone to laugh when you chipped your tooth on that bottle. Gavin wanted someone to see every day, so that he could imagine himself in thirty years, a mirror of the future. He wanted to see him so much that he could take him for granted, could slam doors, mutter about him, and wish he never existed. Ruby was right, in a way: he did not have a father at all.

"How come Barrett only comes over once a week?" he asked Lenore the next morning, milk dripping from his lips as he spoke, his bowl of cereal held under his chin. He never took them to the water park or beach or a hockey game, never hung out in a backyard tossing a ball or mowing the lawn.

"You know why," she said.

Ruby looked up from the book she had been reading.

"How can you be happy with that?" she asked. Lenore paused at the question, her hand up around her neck, tugging and twisting (which always meant nervousness or insecurity).

"I wouldn't say *happy*."

"He's never going to leave her."

"I'm not going to have this conversation with you."

"But why?"

"It's really none of your business. It's enough for you to know that Barrett and I have come to an agreement, and we're both content with that for now."

"I'm not content," Gavin said. Lenore's eyebrows rose, and Ruby dropped her book. He never fought with his mother. Ruby tried to fight with her, but Lenore had a way of disappearing before your eyes, of shrinking until she was five centimetres tall, and you fell silent, amazed by the spectacle. And then she just turned away, and you realized you had lost. There were no fights with Lenore.

She studied them.

"You know nothing about it," she said. "You think you have it all figured out, don't you? I'm telling you right now that you'd be surprised. Barrett is a good man, better than most, I'd say. He's done so much for us, and he treats everyone with respect. Think what you want, but what I'm telling you is true."

"Is he my real father?"

Gavin hadn't expected the question to come out like that. He heard Ruby's short inhalation and imagined her wide eyes, her shock, but he didn't look away from his mother's face, her eyes, waiting for her reaction. She pressed her lips together hard but didn't answer.

"I've never seen a picture of my dad," he said. "Show me. Just one."

He was trembling, and his knees ached. *How dare you!* But Lenore blinked a few times, shook her head a little, and left the room. He turned his head. Ruby's mouth hung open.

"Oh, Gavin," she said. "You shouldn't have asked."

Later that night, he knocked on his mother's bedroom door. He had slept in her bed until he was eight or nine and began to feel embarrassed by her bare knees beneath her nightgown and the smell of her breath in the morning. But he missed those nights when he could just curl against her and imagine he was invincible.

"Come in." She was reading, her pillows propped against the wall behind her, sheet pulled up over her lap. He loved to see her like this, her hair spilling down over her shoulders instead of pinned back the way she wore it to work. She looked younger, her skin softer.

"I'm sorry," he said. He didn't have to say any more. She nodded, and he pulled the door closed again.

MELANIE IS IN THE HOUSE, the bandages gone but railroad tracks (red and black) criss-crossing her face in raw lines. For a moment Gavin doesn't say anything. He slips off his shoes, arranges them neatly into the closet (as she likes), and closes the door quietly. The ceramic tiles under his feet are cold; she has turned up the air conditioning (as she likes). She sits still on the leather couch in front of the television, the remote in her hand, back straight and stiff, but he can see her eyes darting about.

"What are you doing here?" he asks.

"I live here." She keeps her voice level, a monotone, and doesn't look in his direction. He sighs, continues past the living room into the kitchen. The fridge is bare, save a few bottles of beer, a single, wretched lime that has been cut into quarters, and a bag of cheese curds. He pulls out the cheese and a beer. When he turns around, she is standing in the doorway, her arms folded sternly across her chest. Her face looks so wounded that he almost winces.

"Your face," he says. She unfolds her arms and raises a hand to hover over her cheek. "Does it hurt?"

"They gave me some pills," she says. And yes, that would explain the glaze to her eyes, the slightly dazed, unfocused expression. "My parents dropped me off. I can't drive yet."

"I can drive you home later," he offers, wondering how long she is staying and why she has come, but she doesn't fall for the trick.

"Have you packed up your stuff yet?" she asks. He shakes his head. He has boxes stacked and ready to go, and a suitcase borrowed from Lenore for his clothes.

"It won't take me long," he says. Nearly everything in the house belongs to Melanie: the furniture, decorations, books. Aside from his record collection and all his CDs, Gavin brought a single box with him, along with his clothes. Melanie helped him donate the rest to charity before the wedding. Mismatched plates and chipped mugs weren't exactly her style.

"Did you find a place to stay?"

"At my mom's."

She smirks. "Running home to Mommy?"

"What's the difference?" he asks. "Me staying with my mother, and you living here in a house your parents bought for you? It's the same thing."

"Except I'm not almost thirty-five."

"I'm not almost thirty-five either. I'm only thirty-two, for your information." The back of his neck feels hot. He takes a swig of beer, relishing the way it fizzes on its way down his throat. He belches just to watch her grimace.

"You'll be thirty-three in a couple of months."

"Is that why you're here right now?" he asks. "To try to pick a fight? Because I'm not interested. I've had enough of that."

"So have I."

There were times when they first married when he would be caught suddenly by his reality—cornered and captured, unable to move, his bare feet planted here in a single shaft of sunlight falling on the ceramic tiles. God, it seems repetitious. He rolls his eyes and leaves her standing there in the kitchen. She doesn't follow.

IT DOESN'T TAKE HIM LONG, as expected. He zips up his suitcase and surveys the three boxes he has managed to fill with crap, mostly papers and pens from the spare room they have made into an office, his toiletries, and some music magazines. His album collection is still taped and secure in a box; he had never unpacked it after the wedding, after the move. Melanie made him get rid of his old stereo, replacing it with some fancy high-tech model that played only CDs. There is another box, somewhere, of old tapes from the eighties, many of their cases broken or missing.

From the master bedroom window, he stares out at the churned-up, dried-out muck in the backyard. Even with a lawn, maybe a fence to separate their yard from the others, this place would seem like a prison to him. The sameness of it all—the neighbours waving in their chinos and striped golf shirts, flashing white-veneer smiles, the SUVs and minivans parked in front of double garages—makes him twitchy, as if he has just quit smoking or stopped taking some kind of feel-good medication.

Downstairs, there is no sign of Melanie, but Gavin can still smell her perfume and knows she's around, lying in wait. He expects to find her curled up in a corner, her eyes red rimmed and weepy, but she's in the kitchen, boiling up a pot of spaghetti, her skin moist from condensation.

"How can you cook in this heat?"

She shrugs. "I felt like pasta," she says, raising one bare leg to scratch idly at the other. The simple sight of that bare sole—pale in contrast to the tanned skin of the top of her foot and her toes—turns him on, but he shakes his head and looks away. *Don't fall into that trap, Gavin!*

"Well, I've packed up my stuff," he says. "You can drive me to my mom's after dinner, if you want, and them I'm out of here."

Her shoulders hunch forward. She turns off the stove, moves the pot of spaghetti to a back burner, and takes a bottle of white wine from the fridge. Her movements are slow and sure, her small hands perfectly manicured and adept as she twists and pulls and pours herself a glass.

"I'm staying tonight," she says, her bottom lip pushed out in stubborn defiance. "And I'm not driving you anywhere. I told you. I can't drive right now." She lifts her chin. *She's daring me.*

"Why?"

"Pardon?"

"It just seems odd to me that you're back already as if nothing happened," he says. "You only left a week ago. Did your life flash before your eyes when you had your accident?" It's difficult to keep the sarcasm from his voice. The look she flashes is reproachful, hurt. She picks up her wineglass and turns away.

He follows her to the backyard, watches her settle into the lawn chair, her back to him. The light is fading, but there's no privacy here, no trees for shelter, nowhere to hide. Around them, the sounds of summer in the suburbs: the low murmur of voices, children laughing, a shout from the street, the scrape of hockey sticks on pavement. The clouds above them have darkened and clustered together in angry knots. Someone close has a pool; Gavin can almost smell the chlorine.

A swath of Melanie's hair hangs over the edge of the lawn chair, smooth and unruffled by the heat. This is all they have done so far: set up four chairs in forest green, a matching umbrella, and glass-topped table. Sometimes she lights candles out here, sits close to the flames, her skin glowing and pupils wide, as if drugged.

"You probably shouldn't be drinking," he says. She ignores him.

Gavin takes his pack of cigarettes from the pocket of his shorts, slides one out, and flicks his lighter. She turns at the sound. Once upon a time, she liked the taste of ashes in her mouth, but he quit a year ago, before the wedding. She shakes her head.

"I can't believe you started again," she says. "After all you went through to quit." She sounds more sad than angry, disappointed but not surprised. He shrugs, fighting the momentary surge of guilt (*she's right, you know she's right*). She looks away, stares across the empty yard into nothingness.

"It's going to rain," he says.

Looking at the back of her neck, the way her arms bend sharply, he is overcome by a weariness he has never before felt, his muscles suddenly loose and weak. He drags a chair next to her and sits, resting his forearms on his knees, blowing smoke from his cigarette away from her face. She doesn't say anything, but seems to relax, her finger-tips losing their white grip on the edge of her wineglass, a smear of lip gloss left behind on the rim.

"I promised my parents I'd try to sort things out with you," she says.

"Your parents? But they hate me."

"They're not big fans of divorce," she says.

"Neither am I," he says. "But I think it's okay to admit we made a mistake." She leans forward, her head bent, and begins to cry, her hair falling into her face. He resists an urge to comfort, to push the blond strands behind her ears, away from the tears. He can't comfort her anymore.

"I didn't want to make this kind of mistake."

"You think I did? You don't think I'm disappointed too?"

"I don't know"

"Well, I am."

"Why did you marry me?" she asks.

Now it's his turn to look across the yard and blink slowly.

"I don't know," he says. "Maybe because there was no one to tell me not to get married."

"That's not much of an answer."

"I think it is."

She snuffles beside him, places a tentative hand on his shoulder. "Melanie."

She lifts her face expectantly, and he waits, his throat closing up in dread of what needs to be said.

"I can't," he says finally. Wet smears on her cheeks. She nods.

IN THE MORNING, his chest feels bruised. In the bathroom, he brushes his teeth and runs wet fingers through his hair to wake himself up. He slept on the futon in the spare room, tossing and turning, trying to find a comfortable place amid the lumps, listening to the rain and thunder, jumping at cracks of lightning. All night he saw her face, marred and scarred by disappointment.

Remnants of Melanie's breakfast in the kitchen: crusts on a plate of crumbs, lukewarm coffee in the pot. He is pouring himself a second cup before he notices the note on the kitchen table. "We didn't make a mistake. You did." The anger seeps through, the period at the end of the second spare sentence made with such force that there is a small tear in the paper. He imagines her fury, her gritted teeth and fingers pressing down on the pen. He doesn't have to look out the window to know that she has taken her car and disappeared.

After a shower, he carries his suitcase and few boxes to the front door, and calls a cab to take him to the bus station. Time to go home. He takes a last look around the house, noticing certain things—the framed wedding picture on the entertainment unit above the TV, the knickknacks placed so carefully here and there—as if for the first time. How much attention did he pay to Melanie, to this house, or this marriage? Poor Melanie. She never had a chance.

At the station, he loads his possessions into the belly of the bus, takes a seat at the back, and leans against the window, arms folded across his chest. Drops of rain snake down the glass, and cold air blows from the vents against his knee. Someone has left a portion of a newspaper on the seat beside him. He flips through it without interest. Lenore meets him at the bus station.

"The prodigal son," she says, eyeing the suitcase and boxes he loads into the trunk and backseat of the car.

"Very funny," Gavin says, putting his arm around her. "Temporary."

"Until you get your own place, you mean?" She pokes him in the ribs to take away the sting of her words.

Gavin frowns. "That's what I meant," he says.

She insists on driving. "Ruby's coming at around four," she says.

"I'm so glad it's raining."

"She's thirty-six. You kids are getting too old on me."

"I hope it pours. Thunder and lightning."

"Are you all right?"

"I'm fine. Tired." Gavin closes his eyes and leans his head back against the headrest, conscious again of the knots and kinks in his neck from his restless night. Lenore has the softest bed and smoothest sheets in her house.

She pulls into the driveway, parks the car near the old carriage house. As he hears the solid click of the door closing, Gavin realizes how much this place has come to feel like home despite the fact that he has never actually lived here. When Lenore first moved in, Gavin was still toiling away at his useless history degree, and Ruby was in her apartment downtown.

"Pick a guest room," Lenore says. "Ruby will be here soon. I was planning to have dinner outside, but with the rain, I guess we're stuck."

"That'll be fine," he says. "It doesn't matter." She disappears upstairs. He watches the confident way she walks, her back straight and head held high.

GAVIN PLACED HIS PALM flat on the heavy oak door and gave a small push, looking over his shoulder at Ruby. The air inside the room was heavy and thick with sunless age, and the hairs on his arms prickled. There was her bed, neatly made with hospital corners, the top of the white duvet folded back, throw pillows in shades of blue. And there was her bedside table, still with an empty glass, a framed picture of a young couple on their wedding day, an old lamp layered in dust, and a box of tissues. A chair in the corner held a folded blanket and what looked like a robe, and a book was splayed open on the chair's velvety cushion. Beside him, Ruby shuddered.

"It's like a tomb in here," she whispered.

"I know," he said, glancing at her out of the corner of his eye, wanting to snicker, but somehow unable to manage it, his throat too dry.

"Yes, a tomb."

They both turned, though they knew immediately they had been caught. Barrett stood in the doorway, his arms crossed, the skin of his face settling down into sad folds.

"Rena's room," he said. "I don't want it disturbed. Not yet."

Rena died last year. Gavin saw a picture of her once. A newspaper shot from a gala, and there they were, the happy couple. Barrett wore a tuxedo and smiled wanly. Beside him a small woman, fragile, her head held up by a neck that seemed much too thin. She held on to her husband's arm with a bony hand.

One Wednesday, Barrett didn't come by. Rena had died.

"It wasn't entirely unexpected," Lenore said, "but Barrett is devastated, of course." Gavin studied his mother, wondering how she could speak so casually of Barrett's feelings for another woman (his *wife*). And Ruby never understood how her mother could have put up with the arrangement for all these years.

"How can she let him take advantage of her like that?" she raged.

But Barrett had held his grief for more than a year, kept the door to what had become her room closed against intruders and change. They didn't see him for more than a month after Rena's death, and when he came back, the way he walked—a little stooped, bowed—aged him.

Now his spine relaxed as he leaned against the doorframe.

"Sorry, Barrett," Gavin said. Lenore had asked them to respect the rules of the house. *I've only just moved in*, she said. *I still feel like a guest*.

Barrett stuffed his hands in his pockets and gave a slight nod.

"I just don't want you to think …" he started, then stopped, his lips parted, caught grasping for words. "It has nothing to do with your mother," he tried again.

"No, it certainly doesn't," Ruby said.

"Never mind," Gavin said. "It's none of our business."

Barrett's mouth moved up and down. Gavin could tell that he wanted to say more, wanted to make them understand, but didn't know how. Finally, he just gave a half shrug and smiled lamely.

"How do you think this makes my mother feel?" Ruby asked. His smile disappeared. A week later, Rena's bedroom was torn inside out to become a study for Barrett, the dust of her fingerprints erased from the flat surfaces and windowpanes.

GAVIN OPENS BARRETT'S study door with a gentle nudge. The stack of papers rises up on the corner of his desk beside the new computer, neater now than when he had last seen it, and complete with a cover page. Gavin walks closer. "The Pattern of Life," she has called it. He lifts the cover, skims the first sentence—"I was alone for the first time in my life when I met Otto Sinclair ..."—before putting the pages back and patting the sides to even it out, feeling guilty.

Fourteen

LENORE FOUND THE RHYTHM of steady work comforting. Every morning, she pulled on her stockings and slid her feet into the low-heeled pumps, pinned back her hair, and dabbed on lipstick with her fingertip, facing her reflection in a small, hand-held mirror. Her mother-in-law left the house early. Lenore waited until the footsteps above faded before heading upstairs for her breakfast of black coffee and toast smeared with marmalade.

The children were usually awake when she left to catch the bus, looking forlorn and tousled, the smell of sleep still clinging to their skin and pillow lines traced on their cheeks. Otto liked the routine, at first, reverting back to the young man he was when they first married. He showered and shaved, whistled as he dressed in clean shirts and shorts, his arms, legs, and neck growing steadily darker as the summer wore on. But maybe there was one too many startled housewife: *You stay home with the children while your wife works?* And then maybe a quick laugh to cover up the shock, the smallest hint of mirth, insinuation. Or this is what Lenore imagined. It wasn't that uncommon in the seventies, but in this neighbourhood people clung to tradition.

Something had pulled apart between them, the fabric torn. Otto didn't talk to her anymore, not the way he used to, holding her hand and tracing the lines gently, tickling, with his finger. But just because he didn't speak of it didn't mean that nothing had changed.

He began to watch the way she smoothed her hair and applied her lipstick, his eyes slightly narrowed in concentration.

"What?" she asked the first few times she caught him staring, ready to laugh, but he just shook his head or shrugged as if it didn't matter.

She left behind the crowded space of her family, traded it in for the hectic pace of the clinic, the rattle of trays in the cafeteria. Here, her heels clattered against a hard floor and her stockings rubbed in whispers. She sat behind the desk arranging everything neatly, filing patient folders in the grey cabinets that lined the wall behind her. She admired Dr. Barrett, in the way you admired someone who walked with confidence and had the aura of success, but her admiration was strengthened by what she remembered of their first meeting in the hospital, three years ago—his ghostly fingerprints fading from the nursery glass. And already something more.

He used a small room at the end of the hallway as an office. Behind the desk piled high with assorted papers, a bulletin board hung heavy with pictures of grinning children, overlapping thank-you cards, notes, and drawings. Here, the graceful handwriting: "We are so grateful. Thank you many times over. You have changed our lives." Infants with cleft lip and palate, toddlers with tumours, bulbous noses, or eyes blind with lumpy mountains of flesh. She tried not to stare at them when they arrived for appointments with black eyes, white bandages, distorted faces, and wired jaws. Or afterwards, the angry scars covered by newly grown hair. She learned to look at the mothers and fathers and smile without sympathy, learned to imitate the bustling Mrs. Fielding.

"Don't look at them with pity," she said. "They're the same inside as everyone else. And we're here to make their lives easier."

There were three other plastic surgeons in the clinic, all of them courteous, taking charts from Lenore with a smile. She kept a coffee pot filled and fresh on a shelf behind her desk, colour-coded patient files, a large appointment book open and completed in tight, cramped letters and numbers, her finger tracing available spots as she answered the phone, over and over again. She would never admit—at least not in those early days—that everything stopped when Dr. Barrett came into the room.

Once she brought him coffee and found his office empty. As she set down the cup and saucer (black, one sugar), she studied the photograph of the woman in the frame propped up and angled on the corner of his desk. She was petite, pretty, with rounded cheeks and a long, slim neck, tight fistfuls of curls framing her face.

"My wife," a voice said from the doorway. Lenore looked up, startled.

"I'm sorry, Dr. Barrett," she said, blushing and nearly trembling with misplaced guilt.

"Lenore." His serious tone stopped her cold, as if he had reached out and gripped her arm. "Stop calling me Dr. Barrett," he said, letting a smile slip out. "Or I'll start calling you Mrs. Sinclair."

She couldn't bring herself to call him Lloyd, but the thought of *Mrs. Sinclair* (Elsa?) sneaking into this life was unsettling, and she enjoyed the way he said her name. So he became, simply, *Barrett*, which he seemed to enjoy, and it suited him well.

RUBY PICKED SPLINTERS from the old picnic table and lined them up on the vinyl tablecloth, pressing on them until her skin showed the indentations.

"Go on," Lenore said, her hand against Ruby's back, feeling the knobs of her spine against her palm. Ruby swung her legs, pausing to examine a scab on her left knee, then propelled herself forward across the yard, walking fast to get away from Gavin, who followed eagerly.

Lenore propped her elbow on the table and leaned into it. Otto was still eating, crunching through salted cucumbers and corn on the cob, his fingers shiny with butter. They hardly spoke these days, not in the way she always imagined husbands and wives spoke to one another. Now they surrounded themselves with the lives of their children and looked away too quickly, too often.

"When are you quitting your job?" he asked suddenly, scraping his fork across the plate, smearing potato salad.

"I didn't know I was," Lenore said. Otto looked up then, wiped his mouth on a napkin, and crumpled it in his hand. His eyebrows rose; he shrugged and began to clear up dishes.

"When are you getting a job?" she asked. He ignored her.

Lenore called the children and led them inside, a curtain in an upstairs window fluttering just as she looked up. Otto had invited Elsa to join them once, but she had declined, choosing instead her strange solitude. But always, in the backyard, the sense of eyes behind the windows, a curious watching.

In the basement, the children cleaned their feet in the kitchen sink using dish soap, first Ruby, then Gavin, who liked to inspect each bubble before it burst on his skin. Otto was supposed to bathe them each afternoon before Elsa came home, but it was obvious from the line of clean skin around their ankles and the ring of dirt left behind in the sink that he forgot.

She read them stories in their bedroom. Ruby pulled her feet under the hem of her nightgown and chewed on a strand of her hair. She was six. Gavin lay back against his pillow, fighting sleep, his eyes drooping and then snapping open. When she leaned forward to kiss him good night, he gripped her in an unexpectedly strong hug.

"I miss you," he said. She pressed her nose into his scalp, blinking fast to keep the sudden tears away.

"I miss you both, too," she said.

Otto was still in the backyard, drinking a beer. She stood behind him, willing him to look over his shoulder and grin crookedly, wanted him to touch the back of her neck and whisper, *I miss you too*. That would be enough.

He looked over his shoulder and gazed through her, face expressionless and eyes blank. He lifted the beer bottle by the neck and tilted his head back as he drank. *Barrett would use a glass*. The comparison came out of nowhere, surprising and sudden. She blushed, her fingertips tingling.

That night, Barrett reached out to her in a dream, slid one hand up her thigh, and she woke sweating, the sheets twisted around her legs. She steadied herself by the sound of Otto's snores as he lay on his back, one hand behind his head, the other open, relaxed, on his chest. How long had it been since they touched? Long enough. She could reach over and take him in her hand now, could force the silence and awkwardness away. But she couldn't. She turned onto her side instead.

THAT'S ALL IT TOOK, a single dream. Otto watched more closely now, uncertain as she smiled and kissed his cheek quickly, impersonally, her heels clattering on the basement stairs in her haste to leave the house. How she liked to be behind her desk in time to see Barrett arrive and catch his first smile. Everything he did now was tinged with promise, sexuality, his voice low as he murmured instructions or requests, his breath (she imagined) hot against the back of her neck, his hand only centimetres from hers on the desk. His skin was darker than hers, brown bristly hair curling below the rolled-up shirtsleeves. She could hardly bear to look at him, unable to tear her eyes away from his lips, the smooth lines of his neck, the way his hair arched up in front at the end of the day, as if pushed upward by an invisible hand.

In August, he disappeared on holidays for two weeks. When he came back into the office, his skin was darkly tanned, and he smelled like lotion.

"Have fun?" she asked.

"We rented a place in Cape Cod," he said. "Have you ever been down there?"

Lenore thought of the trips she had taken: once to Niagara Falls (high school), and her honeymoon in Mexico. She shook her head.

"Oh, you should," Barrett urged. "Rent a cottage right on the beach. Makes you forget about your worries."

"As if I could," she said, then smiled to show she was joking, to say that sure, they could afford a Cape Cod vacation. She remembered her honeymoon, the sand caught between her toes and the delicious feel of the sun on her skin in the early afternoon. Remembered napping while white towels dried on their balcony in the breeze. She must have smiled wistfully then, because Barrett angled his head to the side and studied her closely.

"One day," he said.

"One day," she agreed.

ON SATURDAY MORNINGS, Elsa came downstairs to do her laundry. She came down early, at six, wearing slippers and a robe, her hair covered by a light blue kerchief. Often, when she came down, Otto and the children were still asleep, but she made no apologies for the hour or the noise she made: SLAM! The basket of clothes on the floor. BANG! The lid of the washer. It was her house, after all. She never looked down the hall at the sleepers, but the light spilled down, illuminating her bulky form, the steady way she went about her work. Routine. Lenore was always awake; beside her, Otto's breathing caught and halted, then resumed a false rhythm. This too, was routine. Like her, he pretended. When Elsa climbed back upstairs, the washer shook and rattled, moving across the floor bit by bit, and the smell of detergent filled the apartment. *Someday I'll look back and laugh at all this.*

IN EARLY SEPTEMBER, everything changed. Ruby started school. She had a new skirt and blouse, socks that were too warm to wear, but had to be worn precisely because they *were* new, and a fresh pack of pencil crayons. At breakfast on the first day, she removed and sniffed each one before placing them all back in their box, folding the lid closed carefully, reverently. Before she left for work, Lenore pressed a kiss on the top of Ruby's head and wrapped her in a tight hug. Otto would walk her to school. Sometimes guilt came hard and fast, gripping her by the throat. She watched her kids sleep, cheeks flushed and hands open and relaxed on the sheets, and she counted their breaths. But someone in the family had to miss their day-to-day lives.

Barrett wasn't at work that day, but the phone was ringing as she placed her purse on the desk and hung up her sweater.

"Lenore," he said before his voice caught, and he paused, clearing his throat. Lenore twisted the phone cord around her index finger, tighter and tighter, then released it, watching the pale bands of indented skin fill with pink.

"My wife is ill," he said after a moment. "Cancel all my appointments today." And that was it.

He showed up the next day, looking wan. He smiled briefly, nodded, and disappeared into his office, emerging only to escort patients down the hall, his smile forced, hair flat against his skull. By noon, her skin itched beneath her stockings, and the silence behind his closed door irritated her.

In the cafeteria, she ladled mushroom soup into a bowl, stacked two packets of saltines onto a small plate, and carried it back upstairs and down the hall to his office, ignoring the curious expression on Mrs. Fielding's face.

She knocked tentatively, then did it again. She was about to leave when she heard the smallest of sounds and pushed the door open. He stood with his back to her, staring out a tiny square of a window that looked out at the red brick wall of an extension built onto the hospital back in the fifties.

"I brought you some lunch." She placed the tray on his desk. He didn't move. She wasn't sure what to do and just stood helplessly, uncomfortable and awkward, unsure if she had crossed a line somewhere. Without turning around, he spoke, his face reflected in the small frame of the window.

"Thank you, Lenore."

He swivelled abruptly, his face so open and grieving that she sucked in her breath. Pressing fingers to his temple, he lowered himself into the chair behind his desk and leaned back.

"Sometimes work is the only thing that keeps me going." There was nothing to say to that, so she did what she thought was good enough: she nodded.

He laughed, not kindly. "Yes, you understand? Or yes, you agree?"

"I suppose both."

"Work is the only thing that keeps you going?"

"And my children."

"Right, your children. I don't have any," he said. "I never will."

"Never is a long time." How could she say such a thing? She remembered the scene in the hospital, the way he flattened his palms against the glass. *We can't have any children.* She felt the heat in her face, and her hands trembled.

"I'm sorry," she said.

He nodded, turned his face away to gaze out the window again. "Tell me, Lenore. Why aren't you home with them, instead of here with me?"

The question sat between them uneasily. Again her face felt hot. She resisted the urge to twist her hands or blink, simply left his office wearing a stiff smile. Back behind her desk, she rubbed her knuckles against the wooden edge until they bruised.

"Lenore."

He tugged at his tie. "I'm sorry," he said. And then he touched her, his hand on her shoulder, pressing too hard.

"I CALLED YOU TODAY at lunch," Otto said.

"I went out for lunch."

"Really." A hard edge in his voice warned her. He chewed too quickly, forcing the food into his mouth with determination, his jaw set. Twin spots of colour traced the edges of his cheekbones.

"Did your boss take you out?"

"Yes, as a matter of fact, he did."

"Tell me what you and your doctor could possibly talk about." It was a slap in the face, as if Barrett couldn't possibly find Lenore interesting. She set down her fork.

"Pardon?"

His touch, pressing down. *Come for a walk?*

"Well, tell me, Lenore. Is it your impressive intelligence, your interest in politics? Or does he just like your legs?" He wasn't looking at her.

"Stop it, Otto. You don't know what you're talking about." It was hard to ignore the sting of his words, the implication: *What could a man like Barrett possibly see in you?*

THEY WALKED AROUND THE CORNER to a small parkette with benches and trees and a small flock of pigeons. Lenore smoothed her skirt before sitting, grateful for the shade. Barrett sat silently beside her, his shirt sleeves rolled up, eyes hidden by sunglasses. He kept his sideburns neat, not wild and travelling like Otto.

"So what do you think?" Barrett asked.

"About what?"

"What's his story?" He gestured with his chin. Across the street, an old man sat at a bus stop. "What do you think he's waiting for?"

"The bus?" Lenore tried to laugh, but Barrett didn't smile, and she turned back to the old man, nervous now, as if this were some kind of test. He wore a plaid button-down shirt, suspenders, blue work pants that looked like polyester, and thick-soled orthotic shoes. His pants must have been too short because Lenore could see a patch of pale skin between the hem and the tops of his socks. One of his shoes had come untied. She imagined from where she sat that his socks didn't match.

"Senile?" she guessed. His skin looked dry, tired, but maybe that was the sun burning down from above, making him squint. His spotted, veiny hands moved on his lap, twisting a gold wedding band around and around his finger.

"Look at his face," Barrett said. "His eyes. There's pain—can you see it?"

She couldn't, not from here. She lifted a hand to her eyes, as if that would help.

"He comes here every morning and waits," Barrett said. "He was married for sixty years. For the last ten years, his wife has taken his hand and shown him the way to the washroom, the bedroom, and the kitchen. She's helped him turn on the television and radio, brushed his teeth and hair, and read his favourite novels out loud. She went out for groceries by bus, took her little wire cart and blue hat, which he loves and which she wears just for him. That's their house behind him. He's waiting for her to come home." He glanced sideways. "She died two weeks ago."

Lenore's breath caught. Yes, she imagined she saw it, his grief, the way his eyes probably watered. She wanted to reach out and place her hand over Barrett's then, not in a sexual way, but in understanding. Before she could move, a bus approached; the old man stood, shaking his legs one by one to loosen material caught around his hips, and boarded. He made his way slowly up the aisle. Beside her, Barrett's shoulders shook with laughter.

"You believed me," he said.

"So what am I talking about?" Otto asked.

"You're being ridiculous." Lenore rose from the picnic table, her skin suddenly grimy from the day's heat. "Barrett is my boss, but that doesn't mean we can't be friends, does it?"

"I don't know, does it?" He looked at her closely then, and Lenore saw the worry creeping around the corners of his eyes, the way his mouth sloped down. She kissed him on the forehead to reassure him, but it was too swift and automatic.

"WHEN RENA AND I GOT MARRIED, she was pregnant. Everyone knew, but didn't say anything. She lost the baby. We were both devastated, but in a way, it was for the best, we thought. I was just about to start medical school. So we were sad, but we went on with things and put off having kids for a few years. We tried again when I specialized. She lost that baby too. Funny things started happening: her hand went numb for a week, then a leg. At first, we thought it was her job. She drew pictures for a clothing catalogue. Bad posture, maybe. Or sewing, hunched over like that. She sewed a lot back then. She would bring home these awful gowns and tear them apart for the fabric. Raw silk, embroidered lace. She would make something entirely new, and everyone wanted to know where ..." He paused, his eyes looking past Lenore, unfocused and distant. *Does he know he's still talking to me?* She should have stopped him, told him that it was none of her business, that his confessions were making her nervous. But at the same time, his revelations—his *intimacy*—was somehow thrilling.

"The symptoms got worse. A lot of little things that all seemed to add up. We found out about the M.S. when she was thirty. There was one more baby after that," he said. "We really thought this one would stick." He swallowed, turned his face to the side momentarily. "Anyway, after that, the doctors told her she shouldn't try again, that it was too hard for her physically."

"I'm sorry, Barrett."

"This is the life we have. She's not always sick, but we never know when to expect an attack, and she's never the same after one."

"It must be difficult," she said, but that was so inadequate.

"It's ironic," he said. "I've spent my life studying, working so that I could put people back together again. But I can't fix her."

Lenore looked down at her lap, at the hands she found there, as if they were detached, belonging to someone else. Something inside shifted.

"I'm working for you instead of staying home with my children because my husband ..." She stopped, unsure of how to say what she wanted to say without disparaging Otto. Then decided she didn't care. "We lost our apartment, we have no money. We live in the basement of his mother's house, and he takes care of the children." Now he would know her shame. She lifted her chin.

"He's living my dream life," Barrett said. He tried to smile. "Want to trade?"

WE'RE JUST FRIENDS. She wiped her palm across the steamed-up mirror. Her mouth appeared, a cheekbone, two eyes, deep and wondering. Elsa was at church—thank God for routines. She unwrapped the worn towel, hung it neatly on its hook. Like everything else in this house, each towel had its proper place. Elsa didn't like disorder. Lenore tried to understand, tried to see it from her perspective, imagined herself sitting down to a cup of tea with her mother-in-law, as if they were friends. She wondered what kind of woman Elsa had been when her husband was alive, though from the little Otto had said of his childhood, not much had changed. But that kind of grief (*suicide*) would leave its mark.

She dressed quickly. The temperature outside had fallen in the last few days, but the heat wasn't on in the house, not yet. *Too expensive*, Elsa said. Lenore had no choice in the matter, in any case, since they weren't contributing much to household expenses. And yes, she was grateful they had a free place to stay, but at night Ruby told her she was cold, and pulled the comforter up to her chin reproachfully.

THE WIND PUSHED dried shells of leaves, then snow, across the sidewalks and down into gutters. It was too cold for lunches on park benches. Instead, they ate in a diner with Formica booths and red vinyl. He listened to her stories without comment or platitudes. He knew that sometimes you just carried on.

"Tell me about your sister."

"Helen? She's a few years older. We're not as close now; I don't know why. When we were little, we did everything together." At twelve, Helen had straight hair that hung nearly to her belly button. "We shared a bedroom." They lived in a two-bedroom bungalow. There was never a lot of money, but there was enough to get by, and then some. "My father owned a clothing shop for men in the east end, came home at six-thirty every night, Sundays off. My mother died when I was eighteen in a streetcar accident. She was crossing the street. The driver didn't see her, or maybe his foot slipped on the brake."

Barrett made a sound—sympathy, perhaps, or just a sound of listening. At her mother's funeral, Helen stood beside her in sunglasses, a belted black coat, hair cut short and teased at the crown. She had just married Sal the year before. *You can come live with us*, she whispered. Lenore stared down at the coffin, dry-eyed, skin so tight that it felt as though it might crack.

"I stayed to take care of my father. He never got over her death, seemed to sink down inside himself. I stayed with him until he died. Ten years. Otto was the first man I ever dated."

"I swore I'd always take care of my mother," he said. "We owe our first allegiance to our parents." Barrett too was an orphan: his father died years ago, his mother only recently.

"Yes."

"She was the one who wanted me to go to med school. I always did well in school, liked science, math. And so I thought, why not?"

"And you married Rena."

"Those were tough days. I was in school, she was working as an illustrator for catalogues. We didn't have any money. My mother had a small apartment uptown. We didn't buy the house until I finished my plastics training."

"What about the children?" His face changed, lengthened. He thought she meant the miscarriages. "The clinic," she said. "Working with children."

"Ah, Tessier," he said. "He was a physician from France. He lectured all over North America. You have to understand that no one was doing then what we're doing now—changing the skeleton of the face. Kids with facial deformities were sometimes institutionalized. Imagine that." Dr. Tessier moved bones, repositioned eyes. "I went to hear him speak. His pictures were incredible." Lenore knew; she had seen the images, before and after, remarkable transformations. "I shadowed him for three months in France, came back just last year, and began to practise his techniques."

The waitress brought coffee. Barrett checked his watch.

"Have to get back," he said.

"Barrett..." She touched his wrist. "You have children. I see them in the clinic every day. Those are your kids. You make them whole again."

His smile began slowly.

A MISTAKE, meeting him at the mall that Christmas. Ruby's face darkened when she spotted Barrett, elegant and handsome in his slacks, pristine shirt, and sweater. They ate lunch in a real restaurant, and she tried not to flinch when his skin brushed hers. They were balanced on the edge of something, and they both knew it. That night she couldn't sleep, thinking of what had changed, how important he had become to her, so suddenly.

She peered into the mirror again and let her hair down, tugging the damp strands to release the knots. *We're not having an affair.*

"Lenore." A light knock on the door.

"I'll be right out." She waited for him to leave, pressing her palms against the porcelain sink. She heard instead an exhalation or sigh, the creak of a single floorboard. Otto had tried to make love to her last night, but she had pushed him away, affronted and saddened by his breath on her mouth, the awkward forced casualness of his leg, heavy across her thigh. This morning, she watched him sleep, taking in the hairs in his nostrils, the movement of his eyes beneath the lids.

He didn't smile when she opened the door, simply stood against the wall, head back, resigned.

"What's the matter?" The question felt forced; her throat tightened in rebellion. She did not want to offer the opening, did not want to discuss it at all. *What isn't the matter?* Her marriage was slipping loose, bit by bit. He must have felt it more deeply.

He stared for so long in silence. Her hands drifted up to her hair, smoothing and patting, then travelled down to her collar and cuffs, fiddling until he spoke.

"Tell me," he said finally.

"Tell you what?" *We're just friends. We're not having an affair.*

"Lenore …" He broke off, squinting as if guarding against a bright light. She looked away.

"I don't know how to fix us," she said. She kept her voice quiet, low, didn't want the children to hear by mistake.

"I know where to start," he said. "I think you need to quit your job."

She couldn't stop it: her head snapped up, eyes wide, cheeks flushed. He nodded slightly.

"After Christmas," he said. "In January. A fresh start for all of us. I'll get a job again. We'll find a place of our own."

"No." She brushed past him but stopped at the bottom of the stairs. Otto stood rooted where she had left him.

"Please." His eyes—dull, hooded. *Oh, Otto.* An image came to mind: Ruby, hurtling through space to wrap her arms around his legs, sun falling on tanned arms, the utter joy as she tilted back her head.

"Okay," she said. "Fine. A fresh start." Yes. Better to cut it off now, whatever had started. And with the decision came a certain relief.

THREE DAYS BEFORE CHRISTMAS, Barrett slid a small square box across the table at lunch and folded his hands in front of him. Lenore couldn't breathe.

"What's this?"

He shrugged but looked pleased with himself.

"Merry Christmas," he said. "Just a little something."

The box, wrapped in green and red, grew larger on the table, radiated a glow. She couldn't take her eyes off it, but her arms and shoulders were stiff, as if made of metal.

"I can't," she said. He frowned.

"It's nothing, Lenore. Not what you think."

And now she felt foolish, and her fingers trembled as she pulled the gift towards her and slowly began to unwrap it.

"Oh." A bracelet, thin and delicate.

"Do you like it?"

"Of course," Lenore said. It was light and slithered over her fingers. "But I can't, Barrett. Otto—"

"You can wear it at the office," he said. "I just wanted you to have something nice."

She hadn't told him yet that she was leaving, hadn't been able to bring herself to say the words, but now it couldn't wait.

"Barrett, I'm leaving in January." At first he thought she was joking and looked confused.

"Because of the bracelet?"

"No." She touched the gold circle again, smiled. "This means a lot to me." She swallowed as he took the bracelet from her and wrapped it around her wrist, the gold like a kiss against her skin. "Otto's tired of playing housewife." She tried to laugh, but couldn't quite make it work. When he saw that she was serious, his face closed up, and he leaned back in the booth, impassive.

"That's terrible news," he said. "I'll be sad to see you go." He checked his watch, signalled for the waitress.

"Barrett?"

"I have to get back to the office," he said. "Please finish." He gestured to her coffee, laid bills down on the table. "Please."

"Barrett."

But he was gone, without a look back. She had lost him, then. And even though it was expected and decided, she slumped forward, her chest against the edge of the table, hurting.

She drank the rest of her coffee, licking sugar from her lips as she stared out the window and imagined herself back in the apartment, day after day. She left her coat open on the way back to the clinic, not caring as the wind rushed down her neck, her scarf coiled around the same wrist bearing the bracelet, its velvet box nestled inside her coat pocket. She sat woodenly at her desk until the phone rang.

"Please come to my office," Barrett said.

He half rose when she entered. She closed the door and locked it, walked towards him and put her hands on his cheeks. He grasped her wrists, pulled her down onto his lap, and kissed her.

She let it go on and on, her eyes closed, dizzy, but when he stopped, she stood, smoothed her skirt.

"I have to leave now," she said, keeping her gaze averted, afraid to look at him and see what she was feeling reflected in his eyes. She swallowed twice past the solid mass lodged in her throat. "I won't be back."

She took a last look around the empty waiting room, twisting her scarf around her neck, and buttoning her winter coat, fingers trembling and eyes heavy with the burden of tears kept at bay. But out on the sidewalk, out in the cold wind, she let them drop down over her cheeks and didn't bother to wipe them away.

Fifteen

KIDS ARE ADJUSTABLE, PLIABLE. They adapt, at least on the surface. Ruby had always been a quiet child, but here in this house she seemed to have shrunk in her skin, down and away from everyone else.

"If we stay here much longer, she'll just disappear." This is what her mother said once late at night, assuming that Ruby was asleep behind the wall. Other things she heard when everyone else slept: the startling roar of the furnace coming to life, the soft snores that Gavin made in his sleep, the creak of bedsprings as she rolled over in the night. Her bed (their bed; she still shared with Gavin, though her mother said it was only for now, only temporary) was too old, and the smell of must rose up with every twist and turn.

Her dad was supposed to be working but couldn't find a job. She knew this made her mother unhappy by the thin flat line of her lips and the way her father avoided looking at her. In the summer, Ruby and Gavin played a lot with their dad, amazed and delighted to find him at home day after day. Dad let them do things that Mom never did. With Dad, they never had to wear shoes inside or outside, and grass stuck to the bottom of her feet and smeared onto her sheets at night. When school started in September, she set off through the doors with a sense of loss, a space between her shoulder blades itching under the sun.

She was in Grade 2 this year. Her teacher was Miss Mackle, who dotted her ears with dangling bright fish and wore a brown-and-yellow bracelet on her left wrist. The bracelet jingled when she moved and bent over desks, the scent of light perfume drifting down in a cloud. On Valentine's Day, Miss Mackle gave everyone a big red heart decorated with a doily and "BE MINE" written on the front in magic marker. Ruby left it by mistake on Grandma's dining room table, and when she came back up to get it, Grandma told her it was gone, thrown in the garbage, then stood impassively while Ruby cried and cried. *She's so mean*, she told her mother, her face buried in her pillow, the soft touch of her mother's hand on the back of her neck. Her mother didn't say anything, but later, Ruby caught a certain look thrown in her father's direction, a narrowing of her mother's eyes that meant business. At night, their voices came through the walls, low and angry, between the sudden roars of the furnace.

In April, her father still wasn't working, and Grandma decided it was time for weekly piano lessons in the dark front room of the house. Grandma lifted the cover, touched the keys reverently, and let Ruby press down on them to test their weight, watching with a tight smile. Grandma didn't smile much, not that Ruby had seen, but they didn't come up here often, as if they weren't family at all. *As if we're her tenants*, Ruby's mother complained, to which her father replied, *We are*. Only on Sundays did they all sit down together for dinner in the dining room. On Saturday nights, Ruby's mother listened at the foot of the stairs, her head cocked, before tugging Ruby and Gavin up to the second floor for their bath. Listened to make sure Grandma had climbed safely to the third floor where she slept.

Ruby looked forward to her lessons at first, mostly because Grandma smiled when she touched the piano, her face crinkling and becoming soft and pink. She thought they would be friends now, that they would laugh and share knowing looks over Sunday dinner, and the strange anger that seemed to hover over everyone in the house would shrink and finally disappear. She perched on the hard bench, her legs bent and dangling, hands hovering, wrists relaxed as Grandma taught. No matter what she did, her skin always sweated, her fingers slipping and sliding and leaving marks until Grandma came with a rag and wiped down the keys, muttering to herself. It was the first sign.

"Your father took lessons for a while," Grandma told her. Ruby straightened her back when she heard this; she wanted to be just like him. But then she looked over her shoulder and saw Grandma shaking her head. "He was terrible," she said. "We just gave up." At the mention of *we*, Ruby glanced at the wedding portrait on top of the piano, where all the photographs were displayed in thick, heavy frames of pewter and silver. Her grandfather had died a long, long time ago, though no one talked about how he died or mentioned him at all. In the wedding picture, Grandpa stood just behind Grandma, his hand resting on her shoulder, both faces serious, cheeks smooth and round. It was hard to imagine Grandma married and young like that, like her mother and father. Something in her grandfather's eyes told her that he wasn't always so solemn, that sometimes he liked to laugh and play and joke, and Ruby wished he were still here.

"Pay attention!"

Ruby fumbled over the keys, her fingers refusing to march in time up and down the scale, but jerking along, awkward and stiff. The more she concentrated, the higher her shoulders rose. She held her breath, and her muscles clenched tighter and tighter so that when Grandma began to hit the legs of the bench with a cane, it was almost painful, and she jumped.

There weren't any photographs anywhere else in the house, at least not that Ruby had seen. Here was her father when he was eight or nine, wearing ridiculous shorts with suspenders and knee socks, his blond hair cut short. And one of her grandmother in long braids before she was married. If she liked Grandma more, this would be her favourite photograph of all because of the sly expression she wore.

Ruby struggled to keep up, her legs shaking with each strike of the cane. Grandma sweated, her hair slick with it and dark patches spreading under her arms and showing through her housedress. When Ruby slid from the bench, she expected to find a stain where she sat, but nothing showed, no sign of the last half-hour. She walked on weak legs downstairs, keeping her face stoic and tight, only bursting into tears when she was safe in the apartment.

"This can't go on," her mother said. "No more lessons." Ruby's heart smashed against her chest until she felt faint. Her father nodded.

One afternoon, she came home from school to find her father surrounded by long pieces of wood and the smell of pine and something burning still lingering in the air.

"I'm building us our very own bathroom," he told her. Gavin hopped eagerly around his legs, hammering on walls with plastic tools. Ruby thought her mother would be excited, but when she came home, she let the grocery bags slip from her arms. Vegetables spilled across the kitchen floor, and something wet and vinegary soaked through the brown paper.

"Are you kidding me?"

"I thought you'd be happy!"

"Happy? This was supposed to be temporary, Otto. How about our own apartment? Never mind a fucking bathroom."

She whirled around then, blushing, a hand slapped across her mouth. Ruby's chest rose and then stopped, and she couldn't breathe. She tried again, but no air came through, and she began to panic, her legs and arms flapping until she collapsed on the floor and everything turned black.

When she opened her eyes again, her head was in her mother's lap, and her father held Gavin in his arms, worried. Her mother had been crying.

"We're sorry, Ruby," her mother said, pulling her up and kissing her over and over again across the cheeks and forehead. "We're so sorry."

LENORE HAS MADE A CAKE, vanilla and lemon. Ruby's favourite. Round, ringed with candles.

"Not thirty-six," her mother says. "Maybe twenty-nine." They laugh, but Barrett's absence—his empty chair, the tablecloth pristine and smooth—is more noticeable around the dining table. Even Lenore, who surely must be accustomed to the new silence in the house, seems to pause, her hand playing with the skin of her throat.

"Happy birthday." Gavin raises his glass.

"Thank you."

They have always been a silent family, intent on chewing, swallowing, immersed in thought. Gavin and Ruby came every Sunday, and Barrett always had questions, probing the mundane details of their lives.

How's Frank, Ruby?

His mouth twitched, stumbled over the name of her imaginary man. Sometimes she wondered what he knew, and how.

He's fine.

How piercing his eyes. But he never let on, turned his attention instead to Lenore or Gavin, a metaphorical wink for Ruby, as if they shared a secret, and he would never tell.

Lenore arranges gifts on the table by Ruby's plate, touching two small boxes on top.

"Barrett bought these for you before ..." She stops, looks away.

"I'll open them first, then." Her fingers pull at the wrappings. Silver links with a single heart fall from the blue Tiffany box. She clasps it around her wrist, holds it up for them to admire.

"I love it."

"Open the next."

Ruby turns to the anonymous white box, longer than the first, stares at the silver barrettes nestled in white cotton.

"He had them engraved."

Yes. On one: *Roo*. The other: *Bee*.

"He bought these himself?" But she doesn't need to ask. A pale beach, white rickety fence partially swallowed by dunes. Ruby's arms freshly tanned, shoulders burnt and smarting, the hair on her legs blond from the sun. She sat with her knees pulled up, sand creeping under the edges of her bathing suit. Gavin and her mother played at the water's edge, her mother in a wide-brimmed hat, Gavin nearly naked, his shorts slipping down his bum to show untainted skin. Ruby dug her toes in deep as her hair blew across her face, dipped into her mouth.

Barrett sat down beside her. She didn't know this man, in his shorts and bare feet. She turned her head to give him a look, then focused on the water again.

Do you know what Ruby stands for?

She shifted, sliding her arms down her legs to play with the sand. *No.* She kept her head bent, but looked at him curiously out of the corners of her eyes.

Let me show you. Before she could say anything, he was heading towards the water, his feet leaving prints on the hard-packed sand near the shore. She stood, balanced on one leg, wiped her palms on her thighs, squinting. He stopped and waited. If he had smiled or beckoned, she would have made a point of ignoring him, of turning her back or crouching in the sand. But he just stood and waited, so she followed.

Here.

He poked a long finger into the sand and drew. *Part kangaroo. And part bee.* A wave washed up, licking the edges of the curving letters.

"Try them on," Gavin says.

"No." She puts the barrettes back in their box, replaces the lid. The walls are caving in. Over the past few days, the utter *uselessness* of it all has come in a rush, deadening her arms and legs with a superficial weight of fatigue. She just wants to give up, give in, bury her head beneath the pillow in her room and slam the pocket doors into complete darkness.

"Why not?"

"Just leave it, Gavin."

Lenore rises abruptly, her chair wobbling on its legs before righting itself. She carries her plate into the kitchen. Gavin sits back, his eyes dark tunnels.

"You never gave him a chance."

"Like you did?"

"I loved him." She sees the effort it costs him to say it like that: the muscles of his face pull and pull, his mouth sliding down.

"I loved him too." The words sound weak.

"Right. You're carrying on like nothing happened, like he was nothing to us."

"That's not fair."

"You went back to work the day after the funeral."

"I had a meeting, Gavin. I know you wouldn't understand, not with your incredible work ethic, but there were things I had to do—"

"Oh, save it." He waves his hand. "He never measured up, never fitted into the space you left for someone who was never coming back." The ashes in the ink, the smell of burnt matches, her fingers stained black with newsprint.

"He was a substitute," Ruby says. "He was never there, Gavin."

"Because you wouldn't let him."

"He was never there *physically*. How can you think that's a father?"

Gavin used to be skinny when he was a child, his spine knobby, his legs twig-like. *Grasshopper*, they used to tease. *Play us a song, grasshopper. Rub your legs together*. His back now spreads wide against his chair, a fleshy, doughy mass.

"He was my only option," he says.

Ruby looks at the half-eaten cake, white icing smeared on the edge of her plate. Her fork scrapes. *Happy Birthday to me.*

Lenore appears in the doorway, her arm braced against the frame.

"I want to show you something," she says. "Both of you."

LENORE TOUCHES HER COLLAR, opens the gatehouse that Barrett transformed into a workshop back in the eighties, even before Rena died. Ruby knew he made miniatures, of course. They all knew, had been inside the shop a number of times over the years, brief moments of half interest (at least on Ruby's part). Here he had installed long tables on two walls and rows of shelving above, to hold his supplies in their carefully labelled cardboard boxes. Ruby looks at them now, taking stock of the dolls, miniature trees and bushes, the paintbrushes and poster paint, modelling clay, shoeboxes of glues and putty, scraps of paper and wood. He had standing lights in the corner, used portable heaters in the winter, wore gloves with the fingers cut out when the snow piled up and brushed through the crack between the two heavy doors.

"He worked on this one for about two years," Lenore says, standing back so they can see, her face flushed, anxious for a reaction.

"It's the house," Gavin says, bending forward to take a better look.

"It's a wedding," Ruby says quietly. It is the house, in stunning detail, but out back by the ravine, a bride walks down a makeshift aisle while guests watch from white wooden chairs decked out with long ribbons.

"A wedding?"

"Mine." Her throat tight, Ruby leans forward. There's no doubt it's her, or is supposed to be: the doll's hair has been cut across her forehead and is held back by tiny barrettes, and freckles dot the bridge of her nose.

"It's how he imagined your wedding," Lenore says. Her voice is hesitant, and she keeps her distance, as if she's afraid she will intrude by coming closer or by saying too much.

"He's walking me down the aisle."

"Of course."

"Where am I?" Gavin asks. Ruby puts a finger on the head of a male doll sitting in the front row.

"Look," she says, "you have a baby." And, yes, a woman next to the Gavin figure holds an infant wrapped in blue. Gavin's face puckers and darkens. He turns away.

Ruby takes it all in. The gown, the lawn with tulips lining the makeshift walkway. The groom waiting under a trellis, his face blank and nondescript. She pokes again, knocks him over (*who are you?*), then glances back to see if Lenore has noticed.

Lenore is looking instead at Gavin, her brows knitted together in worry.

"Let's go inside then," she says.

A strange numbness spreads over Ruby's body. All this time she thought she was fatherless, and all along, he was right here, gently pulling a wedding veil down over her face and tucking her arm into his, confident in her ability to fix her life, figure out what she wanted, and how to get it.

Barrett, Barrett! Often he didn't hear the first time she called his name. He was too engrossed, his attention focused on what lay on the table before him, the sleeves of his sweater or shirt rolled up, his hands casting shadows on the small figures. Why had she never noticed how important it was to him?

She turns to say something, anything, but Lenore and Gavin are huddled by the edge of the dollhouse. Gavin's arms are folded across his chest, and he has straightened his spine so that he's taller and looks down on his mother.

"He spent hours out here," Lenore says defensively.

"Playing with dolls?"

She blushes. *Score one for Gavin.* But it's hard to stay mad at Lenore. Her face crumples inward, innocent and lost.

"Mom," Gavin says, more gently now. "I know what you're trying to say. But Barrett could have spent more time in the real world. With us, rather than playing out his fantasy of what his family should be." He looks over at Ruby, maybe hoping for a nod or some kind of agreement, but Ruby can't, not now.

"I knew you wouldn't understand." Lenore's voice breaks, and Ruby looks more closely. Her mother rarely cries or loses her composure, at least not around other people.

Lenore looks down, her fingers caressing the models, one by one. "Family was everything to him."

No one speaks for a long minute. A rush of cool, rain-soaked air meets heat still trapped in the corners of the garage, a stifling pressure that makes her legs and arms rubbery, heavy.

"I'm going inside," Ruby says finally. When they don't answer, she walks ahead, down the long driveway, her feet tapping against the interlocking brick. As she opens the door, a welcome coolness embraces her, but there's something else, a familiar sound that stops her cold. She reverses herself, heads back towards the garage, towards Lenore and Gavin, who look up in surprise as she returns.

"Is there anyone else in the house?" she asks.

Lenore shakes her head, raising her eyebrows, and Ruby's heart thuds against her rib cage, her face hot.

"Are you sure?"

"Of course," Lenore says. "Why?"

And now she's shaking, her hands clutching at nothing, opening and closing on air.

"Ruby, what's wrong?"

Her mind fastens on the image of a man with stringy hair, a man in a white-and-orange VW van. If she walked around the block now, would she see the van parked beside the curb? Someone's down there, buried deep in the bowels of the old house.

"I heard a toilet flush," Ruby says quietly. "In the basement."

GAVIN BRAVELY GOES FIRST, though the look on his face suggests he might be more comfortable trailing the women. They brandish knives carefully chosen from Lenore's wooden block in the kitchen. Ruby follows Gavin, her body protecting her mother's. Of all of them, Lenore looks the calmest, the least alarmed.

"Probably nothing," she whispers. "Old plumbing."

They reach the bottom of the stairs and the smell of mould, damp, and concrete. Exposed beams and complicated masses of wiring hang above their heads.

"Hello?" Gavin calls. He clears his throat to get rid of the tremor, then tries again. "We know there's someone down here. Come on out!" He looks over his shoulder for Lenore's approval. Ruby hides her smile. Gavin has watched too many bad movies with blustery, macho heroes. Did he expect to see them cowering at the foot of the staircase? Lenore's holding her knife loosely by her thigh in one hand and running a finger along the top of the washing machine, checking for dust.

"I told you," she says. "No one's here."

And then there's a noise from the furnace room, a strangled sound somewhere between a cough and a sneeze. Lenore stops, her feet taking her backwards, fist tightening on the knife handle. Ruby tries to swallow, her tongue scraping against a mouth and throat suddenly parched. Gavin pales, takes a deep breath. They move forward.

Inside the furnace room, Gavin flips on the light. Ruby looks around, but there's nothing out of place.

"I don't—" she begins to say, but Gavin places his finger over his lips and gestures with his head towards a small space that used to be occupied by an oil tank, a long narrow corridor of drywall and concrete. And there, at the edge, she can see a small piece of material protruding, checkered orange fleece. A sleeping bag.

Suddenly, it's no longer a joke. Before she can react, Gavin disappears into the space. A cry of surprise, another shout: "Stay where you are!" Lenore grabs Ruby.

"Call the police," Gavin says from behind the wall.

"No," says another voice. Lenore's fingers briefly tighten on Ruby's arm, but then she lets go and moves in the direction of the voices.

"Mom, stay here."

She ignores Ruby.

"Bring him out, Gavin."

A scuffling movement, and then Gavin emerges, knife poised, with a small balding man in his sixties. He seems more fearful than dangerous, but his face relaxes when he sees Lenore. He nearly smiles.

"Hello, Lenore."

Lenore's face freezes, pale marble etched with blue along her temple. For a moment nothing happens, and then her legs buckle, and she sinks to the floor.

"Mom!" All three of them reach for her. Gavin pushes the man back, his hands under Lenore's arms, Ruby cradling her head.

"I'm fine. I'm fine. Please."

Lenore sits up, then stands, one hand grasping her neck, one holding on to Gavin's arm.

"My God," she whispers.

"I'm sorry," the man says. He has backed up against the wall. "This isn't the way I planned things."

"Who are you?" Gavin asks, tightening his grip on the knife and bringing it into the man's view once more. Before he can say anything, Lenore pushes Gavin's arm down.

"No," she says. "This is your father."

The blank face in Ruby's memories fills in with his watery blue eyes, thinning grey hair, his square jaw. He looks like an older, shorter version of Gavin, down to the sloping, rounded shoulders and the way he holds his head slightly tilted as he looks at them curiously.

"Please don't call the police," Otto says.

Gavin's mouth hangs slightly open, the knife dropping to hang beside his leg.

"This is him?" he asks Lenore. She nods.

"How have you been?" Otto asks. It's ridiculous, really. Ruby stands beside Lenore, still shaky and pale.

"What are you doing here?" Ruby asks. "Whose sleeping bag is that? Were you *sleeping* here?" Ruby takes in his rumpled, stained khakis, the Hush Puppies on his feet, the cheap white T-shirt. "How long have you been here?"

"In the city?"

"In this house."

He considers. "Two weeks."

"Oh, my God."

"You bastard." They all turn. Lenore takes a step forward, another, her cheeks flushed now. "My house. *Mine.*" She flies at him, slapping his arms, his chest, while Ruby and Gavin stare, dumbfounded. Not Lenore, calm, cool, and at peace with her history. Otto raises his arms to shield himself from her blows but makes no effort to stop her.

"Mom." Gavin pulls her back. "Mom, stop." Finally she does, leaning back against Gavin.

"You made your choice," she says. "You have no right to be here."

"I'm sorry."

"What do you want, Otto?" Ruby takes care to use his first name. It's easier that way to face the sudden onslaught of memories. Her throat feels thick and uncomfortable. *What do you imagine a seven-year-old thinks when her father disappears?*

Otto takes a deep breath. Ruby notices that his hands, slender, aged, and dainty (*I have his hands*), are trembling, and he hides them in the pocket of his dirty khakis. His eyes are the palest blue and shimmer; it takes a moment before she realizes that he might be crying.

"I came for you," he says. He turns to Gavin. "And you." And then Lenore: "You."

"Why are you really here?" Gavin asks.

"I told you."

"Is it the money? You heard that Barrett died and now you want to manipulate her again?"

"I never manipulated her."

"Sure."

"You know nothing about it." Otto's eyes flash in anger. "I came because I left you all with nothing, the way my father left me with nothing, and I wanted to tell you how sorry I am. I didn't want you to think that I didn't love you. Because I did. I do. I think about you almost every day."

A new memory, undated, unfolds. In the backyard of her grandmother's house, there was a single, dead tree in one corner. It used to bloom with pink-and-white flowers, according to her grandmother (and the neighbour, an old man in a white tank top and grey slacks held up by suspenders, nodded in agreement, said how beautiful it was), but now it was just a bunch of twisted, gnarled branches, and a thick, knotted trunk. This spring, her father brought her to the tree and pointed out a single green sprout at the base of the trunk. *See?* he said. *Everything is reborn.*

The sprout was now sixty centimetres high, bearing leaves of its own. Ruby sat in the lawn chair beside her father, here at the back of the yard, trying to watch it grow. They both had bare feet. Ruby marvelled at the difference in their legs: hers so slender, brown, and smooth; her father's hairy, knobby, and pale, with a line halfway up his leg from his tight socks. Dark hairs sprouted from his big toes. Ruby liked to press her foot against his, measuring; she liked the feel of his skin against hers.

He was drinking a beer tonight straight from the bottle, while Ruby sipped from a blue plastic cup of Kool-Aid, her lips and tongue stained dark pink. Her grandmother didn't like to see Ruby's father drink, but tonight she was across the street playing cards with some of her friends, a group of old-smelling women who had permed hair and wrinkled mouths. Her mother was inside giving Gavin a bath. Ruby savoured this moment alone with her dad. Soon Gavin would come running out in his truck pyjamas, hair slicked behind his ears, and he would ruin the quiet with shrieks and laughter and sloppy good-night kisses.

Her father looked over at her and smiled. He wore Ruby's favourite pair of shorts—orange and brown, with a wide belt buckle—and a brown, collared T-shirt. His sideburns were furry, overgrown. Ruby's mother used to trim them, along with his hair, but she hadn't offered to do this in a long time, as if she didn't care anymore.

"Want to hear a secret?" her father asked. Ruby nodded, her face open and bright. Her father leaned in so close that his lips touched the folded skin at the top of her ear lightly, and she shivered and giggled. He waited for her squirming to stop, waited until she forced her legs to still by placing her hands palm down on the tops of her knees. His voice was low, serious now, though she had expected teasing.

"You are my life," he said in her ear, and then pulled back, watching her face. She wasn't sure exactly what he meant, but she liked the way he looked, and the smell of his cologne had rubbed off from his cheek to hers, so she smiled. He took her hand and wrapped his fingers around hers, brought her fist to his chest, and knocked twice over his heart.

"Here," he said. "No matter where I am or what I'm doing, you'll always be tucked in here. I want you to remember that."

Don't cry, Ruby, don't cry. The memory fades.

"So there it is, for whatever it's worth," Otto says. "I felt like I didn't have a choice. That moment—when I started the fire, when I ran ..."

But Ruby shakes her head, her shoulders and chest aching with a great weight.

"If you'll just listen—"

"Why should I listen?" She is nearly taller than he is. Why did he seem so much bigger in her memories? "You could have written. You could have called. So why now, after all these years, should I care about you? You think you can bring back the lost years?" She meets his eyes, pale and watery, holds his gaze without flinching. He doesn't move but releases a long, slow sigh.

"You're right," he says. "I can't take those years back. I can't undo what I've done. I'm a failure."

No one says anything. He takes gulping breaths.

"I've failed at everything I've ever tried." He looks at each of them in long turn. "I thought this was the right thing to do, coming back here. To let you know it wasn't any of your fault." His gaze rests on

Ruby, slides to Lenore. "It wasn't your fault," he says again, this time more softly.

Ruby breathes in the smell of mould, aware that she's shrinking, becoming that little girl on the piano bench, dust dancing in the sunlight, fingertips slick against silky keys.

Sixteen

A TYPICAL SUNDAY DINNER: a table set meticulously with his mother's wedding china, but paper napkins folded and arranged just so on the table. His mother at the opposite end, glaring while Ruby licked her fingertips, tore bits of napkin, and pasted them on the table. Gavin, only three, rolled peas along his tray before squashing them flat. Elsa reached out, slapped Ruby's hand hard.

"Don't!" she said.

The colour rose in Lenore's cheeks; she looked at him to set things right. He said nothing, pushed overcooked meatloaf into his mashed potatoes. *You sad spineless fool.* His wife slid back her chair, the legs scraping against the worn wood, and came around the table to comfort the child, pressing her palm against the skin of Ruby's cheek until she quieted.

"I'm sorry," Elsa said. "I shouldn't have done that."

"No, you shouldn't have."

That night in bed, blankets gathered around her body, Lenore rolled over once and turned her back without saying good-night.

Yes, that was the beginning. How many dreams had he ruined? He lay in bed and listened to his mother's footsteps above.

Better find another job.

Yes, Mother.

What does it look like, a grown man and his family living under his mother's roof?

Yes, I know.

But she didn't say any of it. He saw it in her expression, the way she held her head when she looked at him, the disappointment creeping into her eyes, though she remained silent. He slept in his bedroom until his twenties, but his mother kept the room as it was: the single bed that groaned and moved a centimetre or so across the floor every time he turned over, the dresser and mirror (the right knob on the bottom drawer pulled off and then lost years ago), the wooden chair in the corner of the room by the window, and the rag rug woven by his mother still on the floor by the side of the bed. There weren't any pennants or trophies; Otto was never that kind of student.

"You'll never meet a nice girl if you keep living here," Elsa had said before he moved into the basement. But that wasn't the problem. Otto met plenty of them. Unlike men, who were repelled or confused by Otto's softness, women always liked him, were drawn to his blond, wavy hair and slender hands, his pale blue eyes. They took him back to their apartments and made love to him on beds that smelled of perfume and independence, and Otto came home to his mother's house, vaguely dissatisfied, every time.

Please. A single word from Lenore at night. It used to mean something else, that word, used to be cried out in a moment of twisted, sweaty sheets, her hair spread out on the pillow like feathers, her tongue darting out to taste the groove in his chin. But that was before he lost his job, before they moved in with his mother. The house would swallow them whole or break them into sharp splinters. And the harder the pressure fell, the more paralyzed he became, until the newspaper ads tentatively circled and then scratched out mocked him from where they were stacked in a corner of their bedroom.

He promised he would find a job, but instead he built a bathroom in the basement apartment. It was the only way he knew to ignore the grinding sensation deep in his chest when he thought of his wife and that Barrett. He didn't know for sure that she'd had an affair, but he suspected she had come close. And now he had spared himself the humiliation of watching her preen in the mirror every morning before she left for work, her cheeks flushed with what he imagined to be anticipation. Almost out of spite, he refused to find work, as if berating her for what she had done. He watched her face drop and redden, watched the way the muscles in her cheek tensed and clenched.

In the silence of night, as she slept with the sheet twined around her body, he often thought of how far they had strayed from the early days, when the simple blush of colour on her cheeks (the glossy curve of hair against her neck) was enough. Worse, he could not imagine how to bring it back, and he lacked the energy to try. Instead, he built his bathroom, taking refuge in the smell of lumber, his hand wrapped around beams of solid wood, or cutting pipes, brushing his forehead with the back of his arm to wipe away sweat and grime. An honest man's work, satisfying and mind-numbing.

Snow climbed up against the small windows, blocking all the light and burying them within the apartment. He worked while Lenore cleaned, cooked, or read a book on the couch, her legs pulled up underneath her like a young girl, eyes glazed and finger hooked in the corner of her mouth. She read mostly magazines, but sometimes romance novels, those cheap ones they sold at the drugstore, a blanket pulled over her shoulders for warmth. He stole glances at her while she read, seeing then what she was when they married. Her concentration and absorption shrank the worry from her face, loosened her skin. She didn't move, save the rise and fall of her chest as she breathed. The way she looked then would stop him so completely that he'd forget his petulant anger. She would look up into his open face and smile in return, just for a moment, before the familiar tension crept back and hardened her mouth.

Did you sleep with him, Lenore? Did you?

He abandoned the bathroom project in the New Year, got a temporary job selling knives door to door. But it was too time-consuming without a car; he wasted hours riding the bus and streetcar, his knives wrapped in cloth and nestled in velvet in a briefcase on his lap. He looked down at his pants, noticed the way the fabric was beginning to shine at the knees, and felt a headache pressing against his temples. And when he came home, he stared with dismay at the dismantled room in the back, the bare beams and small mounds of wood shavings, the exposed pipes and fittings.

One night, Gavin stepped on a nail and bled across the linoleum.

"When are you going to finish this?" Lenore demanded.

"When I have time." He turned away. There was always time, at least in Otto's life. He quit the knife-selling job and told Lenore he had been fired to save himself endless explanations. In the morning, he flipped through the newspaper, half-heartedly circling potential employment ads, wrote down numbers he would never call. He had nothing to wear to an interview, in any case; his shirts were stained yellow under the arms and some were torn through at the elbow. There wasn't any money for new clothes—at least, that's what he told himself.

And, in fact, there wasn't much money at all. By the time Ruby finished school for the year, Otto had grown a beard and put on ten pounds, and their savings had run out.

"You'll have to ask your mother for money," Lenore said. This time, she turned away first and didn't look him in the eye.

THE MORNING AFTER his father died, Otto woke to a sound he hadn't heard before. His legs were heavy, solid lumps sunk into the mattress, the sheet tangled and pushed around his ankles in the humid morning at the end of August. He was eleven years old. He lay still, frozen and disoriented, until it dawned on him what it was: the sound of his mother crying in the next room. She cried low, her breath hitching.

He listened for a while before guilt got the better of him, and then swung his legs out of bed, planted bare feet on the rag rug. His mother made all the rugs in the house, twisting and pulling leftover material, careless of colour or pattern, and then scattered them across the worn wood floors in every room. Once a week she gathered them up in her basket and beat them outside. She had sewn a small number on the underside of each rug so that she knew exactly where they belonged. Otto's rug was number fourteen.

He was seven when she took him to the doctor with her worries. Otto sat on the examining table, his hands in his lap, and listened as she detailed his problems with reading and writing, his inability to concentrate. A fan on the corner of the desk blew against his bare knees.

"I've seen many boys like this before," the doctor said, ignoring Otto. "You need to be strong, set guidelines and schedules. Rein him in."

His mother looked unsure. "There's nothing wrong with him? With his eyes or ... with his *mind*?"

"Nothing a bit of discipline won't cure, Mrs. Sinclair. He just needs to learn how to pay attention. I suggest a strict routine so he knows what's expected. Get him up at the same time every morning, meals on schedule. After school, you sit him down with his books. No playing outside until he's done his homework. You can't let him run wild. This type of boy will drive you crazy if you do. What's his father like? Easily distracted? Can't sit still?"

Elsa nodded.

"You see? It's in the genes. You need to correct the lazy tendencies now. And don't coddle him at all. You'll turn him into a sissy."

On the way home on the streetcar, he let his leg brush her skirt. She rested her hand on his knee and kept it there for the remainder of the trip. He always remembered the pressure of her hand that day, the way it pressed sadly into his soft flesh.

She must have stayed up late that night. The next morning, she had a list, sat him down at the dining room table after school.

"This is how it will be now," she said. Every moment of his day planned. He rose, slept, and ate on schedule. After school, she marched him up to his room and arranged his homework on the desk, steadying him against the back of the hard chair until he stopped squirming. In the summer, he had chores and assignments. She brought home books from the library she thought he should read and asked for book reports after supper, while the sounds of normal play came through the open windows—a bicycle bell, laughter, a basketball against the sidewalk.

She let him out of the house for one hour in the morning, and one in the afternoon. He joined groups of children, usually boys, as they built tree forts in backyards, always feeling like an outsider. They wondered what he did with the rest of his day, but he couldn't tell them, knew instinctively that their faces would twist in pity or worse. After a while, he stopped looking for others and spent his free time wandering down the street with a stick in his hand, poking at ants and beetles in hedges or gardens, his head down and cap pulled low.

For a long time he thought he was being punished for some unmentionable sin or grave error, and he couldn't understand what he had done. When his mother came in to kiss him good-night, he watched her face carefully, wondering if she had stopped loving him.

Now he counted the steps to her room, peeked inside. She faced the window, her hands braced on the sill for support, shoulders slumped forward and down. He noted the same blouse she wore yesterday, tucked sloppily into the waistband of her skirt. He had never seen her feet before, not bare and naked as they were now, one arched and flipped sideways so that he could see even from here the rough, flaky skin of her heel.

Maybe his hand knocked against the doorframe by accident, or maybe he inhaled too loudly, for she turned to look at him, face stripped and pale. He almost didn't recognize her. He expected an explosion of anger at the sudden intrusion, but her mouth pulled down and swelled with a sob.

"Otto," she said, beckoning with one hand.

Had she ever held him like that before? Both hands pressed against his back with an urgency he did not understand, his face against her neck. The smell of her crept up his nose and slid down the back of his throat, and her blood pulsed against his cheek. *Mama*.

Her embrace lasted for a minute, no more. When she pulled back, she had composed herself, straightened her lips, and relaxed her brows into a sterner, more familiar face. He bathed and dressed, and by the time he came downstairs, she had erased all signs of her mourning, save the black dress she wore.

ON THE PIANO, Elsa kept a photograph of her wedding day, Otto's father fresh, unsullied, his mother's skin creamy and paler than his father's. Otto stood here in the dusty living room of his childhood and remembered the lessons he so hated. And now Ruby had taken his place, her palms sweating as Elsa barked out instructions using a cane to set the rhythm, smacking it against the piano bench so that Ruby's legs trembled on each beat. Yes, he remembered his turn at the piano well, the way the sweat trickled down into his ears in the summer because his mother refused to open the windows or let in any light for fear it would distract him from the task at hand. *Concentrate!* A walking stick marking the time in sharp stabs on the edge of the bench.

His father put an end to it when Otto was eight, broke the walking stick into pieces and burned them in the fireplace. *No more piano*, he said, placing a heavy palm on the top of Otto's head. Too bad he wasn't more like his father, too bad he couldn't stand up to his mother, tear the cane from her hand, watch the colour mottle her face, and match her glare with his own. He should never have agreed to those lessons, not for Ruby, but the way his mother asked, the corners of her mouth turned up in pleasure at the thought of it—well, he had taken so much from her already.

"Otto?"

He turned, and there she was, framed in the doorway, her hair pulled back into the knot she always wore, the aging body concealed by one of those blooming, shapeless dresses she always wore. Standing there in the fading light like that, he was suddenly struck by her haggard appearance, the flesh sinking from her bones. *Thin, so thin now.* Was she ill? Her face flooded with hope at the sight of him, and guilt stabbed sharply under his skin. A wondrous understanding, one that straightened his spine: *she needs me.* His lips parted, his mouth as dry as if he had swallowed the dust that swarmed thickly in this room. The structure of their relationship had shifted. This small, thin woman, the way she looked at him with hesitation.

"I couldn't ask her," he told Lenore later.

"Why not?"

"I'm going to get a job," he said. "I'll fix this."

"Oh, Otto." Lenore looked down, but not before he saw the tears and the expression of utter defeat.

When she woke him the next morning, she was dressed neatly in a skirt and silk blouse, a bracelet he had never seen before wrapped daintily around her wrist.

"I'm going out," she said. "Get up. The kids need you." And before he could shake off the sleep, before he could protest or at least interrogate, she was gone. The smell of perfume lingered.

Gavin clung to his leg.

"Peanut budder!"

Ruby waited at the breakfast table, her hands folded in front of her, serious.

"Where did Mommy go?"

"I don't know," Otto said.

"Is she coming home?"

"Of course she's coming home." He busied himself smearing peanut butter and jam onto two slices of bread. Ruby frowned when he slid the plate in front of her, looked up at him, and tilted her head to the side.

"When's Mommy coming home?"

He was certain she would be home by noon, then again by dinner. Ruby was distraught at bedtime.

"She's gone!"

He did his best to reassure her, wondering how it was that she knew so much.

"Don't look so sad, sweetheart," he said. "She'll be home soon. Mommy would never leave you."

He left her awake with Gavin, closed the door on her worried face, and sat at the kitchen table to wait. When the light faded from the one small window, he didn't turn on a light but still sat, hands clenched around his knees. At midnight, he slumped forward, head in hands, with the certainty that he had lost her. *You're such a failure.* He didn't know despair could hurt so much.

He fell asleep eventually in their bed, pressing his face into her pillow to force the guilt and pain to the surface, smelling her and imagining her body curled up beside him, her dark hair dishevelled and caught in her mouth. He forced himself to walk through the days without her, saw Ruby's grief, Gavin's bewilderment. What would he tell them? They would go places as a family of three, and everywhere, other women would shake their heads sadly, with pity, or perhaps admiration. *He's a devoted father*, they would say. *His wife just up and left!* they would whisper to one another in horrified indignation. His mother would welcome them upstairs, give them comfortable rooms on the second floor, would let down her guard, and accept their need for her and hers for them. Under the blanket, Otto's legs shifted, bent, and relaxed.

In the morning, he kept the kids busy with fingerpaints, and then took them to the park. Gavin shrieked and dug in the sand, but Ruby perched on top of the jungle gym and refused to move, her long skinny legs dangling and kicking at the bars while she stared at him from beneath her hat. She was so precious, those freckles and tanned shoulders, her face like Lenore's.

"Is Mommy coming home today?" she asked. Otto swallowed a pocket of air, his stomach burning.

"Maybe," he said, and she turned her face away, her mouth puckered and quivering.

Lenore was waiting for them in the kitchen when they returned, freshly showered, her hair still wet, her hand wrapped around a steaming mug. Without makeup, she looked vulnerable and young. The smell of coffee filled the small kitchen. Ruby buried her face in her mother's neck, her breath coming in short gasps. Lenore stroked her back, bent to whisper in her ear. Gavin dumped a sandy shoe in her lap, and she smiled, ran her hand through his blond curls, but she kept her eyes focused on Otto.

Otto just watched, surprised by the disappointment he felt to see her here, surprised by his lack of relief.

"We thought you left," he said, his voice flat. She didn't answer, but pushed a slip of paper across the table towards him.

"What's this?"

"It's a cheque." She disentangled Gavin's arms from around her neck. Ruby leaned against her.

"You're not leaving again, are you, Mommy?"

"No, sweetheart, I would never leave you. Never." Lenore kissed her on the forehead. Satisfied, Ruby headed to her bedroom and began talking to her dolls in singsong. Lenore sat patiently, looking at Otto.

"I know it's a cheque," he said tersely. "What's it for?"

"We needed money." She lifted her chin as if daring him to respond. Otto looked down at the cheque again, the amount, and the signature: "Lloyd Barrett." Lenore wore a small smile now, or maybe a smirk, the corners of her mouth turning up slightly as she watched him, waiting for his response. And it seemed to Otto that she had done this on purpose to inflict the most hurt. It was her way of telling him where she spent the night, her way of belittling him. *You can't take care of our family, so I found someone who can*, the patronizing smile seemed to say.

"You tell me what else I was supposed to do," she said. "Tell me. We have no money, Otto. No money for groceries or clothes for the kids. You can't ask your mother for money because of damn pride. What about us, Otto? Where does that leave us?"

She was right, of course, but Otto could think of nothing but the image of his wife with that man last night, bare legs and arched necks.

"Where did you sleep last night?" he asked.

"In a hotel."

"A hotel? And who paid for that?" She didn't need to answer. Who else would pay?

"So did he give you the cheque after you slept with him, or before?"

"Stop it, Otto."

"Because if it was after, you're a prostitute. A whore." The colour rose quickly in her face. The chair scraped back, and his cheek stung from her slap.

"Mama?"

Ruby, standing uncertainly in the kitchen, her eyes round saucers, fingers twisting her lower lip. Lenore's hand flew to her throat.

"Sweetheart, let's do something fun today." She took Ruby's hand and led her from the room.

"Are you going to leave me?" he asked her back. She shot him a look.

Not now, Otto.

OTTO COUGHS. It's dusty in Barrett's basement, the cement hard under the soles of his shoes. He would not have thought such a grand house could be so ordinary.

Lenore, my first love, you're still beautiful and radiant. She has aged, of course (haven't they all?), but she has kept her elegance within the lines of her pale, ghostly face. His shoulder still aches from one of her blows; he underestimated her strength. After her flurry of rage, she has remained silent, watchful.

Look at his children, grown into adults with separate lives and worries. Ruby looks like her mother but has Otto's freckled skin and impression of fragility. And Gavin, just a baby with a slight lisp and a favourite blanket, dirty and ragged from trailing on the ground. He sucked on it in his sleep. Gavin is impenetrable with his stone face. Of all of them, Ruby carries the worst of the pain. She had invested more of herself than Gavin did; she had more to lose.

Otto's eyes prickle, and it's hard to breathe again.

IMAGES HAUNTED HIM. A hotel room, dimly lit by moonlight, skin against glowing white sheets, Lenore's mouth on that man's body. Barrett's dirty money, his signature an arrogant scrawl. Otto paced the apartment, his face tight, hot around the eyes. In the damp room, a tap dripped incessantly in the kitchen. Too many things: the tiles peeling from a corner of the backsplash above the sink, the smell of mould, the rust around the elements of the small stove, the creaking springs of the sofa bed, and the way its fabric left curling remnants on sweaty skin. Down the hall beside the washer and dryer, the unfinished bathroom, with the walls marked up by Otto's hand, sawdust and shavings in the corners, and scattered nails and splinters. He never finished projects when he was a boy either. He also couldn't swim, and his pale skin was dotted with freckles. *Imperfect, imperfect, imperfect.*

He walked upstairs, through his mother's kitchen, into the living room, where the photograph of his dead father stared out at him. Otto had nightmares for a month after the suicide in which his father sprawled dramatically on the couch, one arm and leg dangling, his face tilted up with an expression of horror, mouth open in an imagined scream. But of course it wasn't like that; his father went to bed as usual and just didn't wake up in the morning. His mother found the empty bottle of pills in the garbage can and a glass of whisky smeared with messy fingerprints on his bedside table.

Your father is dead.

Just like that, that's how she said it. There was no sparing him. Elsa believed in both brevity and bluntness. *Tell it like it is*, she always said. *No point in sugar-coating the truth.* She said it so plainly that Otto had trouble matching the meaning of her words to her face.

You might as well know now that he killed himself with pills. He left us on purpose, Otto. Later he would attempt to understand the immediate anger that must have shaped her words, but then, at eleven years old, he felt the truth slice him in half. That afternoon, he went down to the lake with a group of neighbourhood kids. They weren't friends—he barely knew them—but Otto was always invited at the urging of their mothers. Women liked Otto when he was young; he was so quiet and thin, a jangle of elbows and knees, with that translucent skin, those round eyes and loose blond curls. He must have seemed fragile.

He just wanted to stay in his room, bury himself under the covers, or stare at the ceiling. His skin hurt to touch. His mother made him go. *Nothing you can do here,* she said. *Best to keep yourself occupied.* He didn't argue, never did. Mrs. Rhodes from across the street drove them, gloves on her hands, even in this heat. He sat in the back with four other boys, all of them crammed in and overlapping. He leaned his head against the window, watched without seeing anything, remembered his father's playful smiles, a warm hand on his shoulder.

At the lake, Mrs. Rhodes looked over the seat at him, frowning.

"Are you all right, Otto?"

There was drool on his chin. The other kids had already slammed the doors and raced down to the beach, towels flapping behind them, sand kicked up under bare feet.

"I'm fine."

Her face wore the worried expression that adult faces always wore when they looked at Otto.

"Is everything okay at home?"

Did the neighbours like Elsa? She always held herself apart from them, never cared to join them for tea or socials, never baked a cake or sent Otto to school with a platter of cookies. It's not that she was unfriendly, exactly; she just couldn't be bothered, and it showed.

"Everything's fine."

Why did he lie? He spread his towel out on the sand and hunched forward, arms around his knees, pictured Mrs. Rhodes knocking on

Elsa's door, beginning to awkwardly dance around the subject of Otto and his strange behaviour in the car. Elsa, in her black dress, would say it as plainly as she did that morning, though she would never speak of suicide to anyone else: *His father's dead. Died in the night. Otto will be fine in time. We just have to carry on.*

"Otto?"

Cindy Cooper, from down the street. She must have come in another car, or maybe she took the streetcar with her friend Roberta. Strands of white-blond hair blew back from her suntanned face, brushed against perfectly round and smooth shoulders. She had always been nice to him, her smiles never false. Is that why he told her suddenly and began to cry, his face pressing in shame against his knees? Sand scraped between his toes as her hand came down against the back of his head, her throat clicking with comforting noises. He loved her then, though later he would be too embarrassed to look her in the face again.

Otto placed his father's photograph back on the piano, blinking, his cheeks wet. He had not been to a funeral since, could not bear the memories that the smell of all those flowers brought back. It was only too easy to blame his mother. Why else would his father kill himself? Why else would he leave no note, nothing to let Otto rest or give him any sense of understanding? He shuddered, imagined the nerves under his skin shredded like fine strands of sinew. The silence of this great dusty room bore down and tunnelled through his ears.

The summer he was thirteen, Elsa went to work as an operator for the telephone company, reluctantly setting him free during the day. No more schedules or studying. *Free.*

"I'm trusting you," she said. She set a list of books in front of him. "I think you should read these over the summer." And gave him a hard look.

He made an effort, bringing the books home from the library and placing them on the desk in his room, even flipping through the first and laying it face-down, pages creased to make it seem more convincing. The summer stretched before him, long and unfettered. He ate sandwiches thick with peanut butter and jelly, left the dishes in the sink and crumbs on the sofa, built houses of cards, rode his bicycle downtown, stopping in front of construction sites for as long as he wanted, dozed in the backyard with his shirt off, and learned to use the hammer and nails he found among his father's things, buried in a box in the basement.

The other boys in the neighbourhood took no notice of him until Elsa put up the flag in the front window. He knelt in his driveway, fixing the chain on his bicycle, when he found himself surrounded by four older boys. He looked at them blankly. They said nothing for a moment until one of them nudged another. The boy thrust out his chin, holding tight to the handlebars of his own bicycle.

"Are you a Nazi?" he asked.

"What?" He first heard the word by chance when he was six, in a conversation between his mother and father. *Treating them as if they were Nazis*, his mother muttered as he came into the room. She stopped at the sight of him and pressed her lips together. At bedtime, he repeated the word out loud. *What does it mean?* he asked. His father arranged the blankets around Otto, taking his time to answer. For half an hour, he talked, explaining it all carefully so that Otto understood.

"My father said you must be Nazis," the boy repeated.

"My mother says your mother should go back to Germany if she loves it so much," another said, to vigorous nodding. The tallest of the group leaned in close enough for Otto to see the flecks of golden brown in his eyes.

"I'm Jewish," the boy said. The others fell silent, waiting.

"Good for you," Otto said. The boy reached out and pushed him. Otto fell back against his bike, sending it clattering onto its side.

"This is your first warning," he said. "Take down that flag or go back where you came from."

EVERY MORNING, Otto pulled the flag from the window and put it back carefully before his mother's return in the late afternoon. For a few days, he kept to the house and yard, but boredom drove him farther afield later in the week. He wheeled his bicycle around the side of the house, peering cautiously left and right. The street drowsed in the midday sun, the leaves on the trees limp and still. His bike chain clanked in the silence. Only when he hit the main street—the busy sounds of the city reassuring—did his heart slow. He lingered in shops, pored over comic books, and stuffed penny candy into his pockets.

He was nearly home when he heard them behind him, a silent force of four. They pulled up beside him on their bikes and kept pace. He pedalled faster. There, just ahead, his house. And, to his horror, he saw the flag, pinned again in the front window, though he remembered—or thought he did—taking it down that morning and draping it across the back of the sofa.

His hand slipped from the handlebar as he veered left onto his driveway, and he fell. *They'll get me now!* He ran for the front door, stumbled again as he climbed the stairs. The doorknob refused to turn at first, and he looked over his shoulder. The boys had not moved. They watched him with blank faces, their shoulders relaxed, backs rounded as they slumped on their bikes. One of them—the tall one—seemed to be smiling.

Inside the house, he pressed his forehead against the door for a moment, taking deep breaths, and turned to find his mother staring at him.

"Did you take down my flag again?" she asked. He exhaled.

"No," he said.

THE PIANO LESSONS resumed.

"Do it for your father," Elsa said. She worked an early shift now, returning at three and leading him to the bench by four for an hour. She sat by his side in a hard-backed dining room chair.

"Stop," she said, and leaned forward to riffle through the pages of music. He turned his face to the side and saw the faces of four boys pressed against the window. His mother followed his gaze, and the heads disappeared.

"You should tell your friends to come back later," she said.

"They're not my friends."

"Then ignore them."

He tried, but his neck felt stiff, the muscles of his shoulders sore. Through the open window, he heard rustling, a low laugh.

"Concentrate," Elsa said. "Ignore them."

His fingers slid on the keys. *One, and two, and three, and four.* A new walking stick from the garden, stripped of bark and twisted, hit the legs of the bench. The notes of a chord jarred, his pinky misplaced. His mother corrected his fingers.

"Again," she said. As he pressed down, he heard a sound, a soft knocking, and looked towards the window again to see an image crudely stuck to the glass with bubble gum. *Swastika.* He cried out, fingers pressed to his hot cheeks and dragging downward, as if drawing trenches in sand. Elsa stood still, skin mottled, before taking up her walking stick and sending it sharply against the window, once, twice, shattered glass falling in sharp patterns around her house slippers.

"You little bastards!" she screamed out the window, but they were gone, leaving in their wake only shrieks of derision. Otto shrank on the piano bench. He squeezed his eyes shut, covered his ears with his hands, and hunched over the keys, his shame and humiliation complete.

Elsa surveyed him. "I'll fix the window," she said. The feel of her tentative hand on his shoulder made him shudder, and he slapped it away without thinking. She grabbed his shoulders turned him back to the piano, forcing his fingers onto the keys, pressing down as he resisted. *No, no, no!* His ankle caught the edge of the keyboard as he arched backward, and the top of his head crashed into her chin. She let go, brought her hand to her mouth. He felt a slow, grim satisfaction to see blood on her fingers.

"You will sit here for the rest of the day," she said. She turned him once more to the piano, the old faces staring down at him from their heavy frames. The black notes on the music sheets blurred, swooped from side to side, wet and magnified.

He sat for four hours. When his tears dried, he rested his head in his arms, impressions of the keys on his skin like teeth. Around him, the room darkened as the sun descended, and shadows sprung up in the corners. He could hear his mother, the whisper of her dress, dishes rattling in the kitchen. The intensity of his hatred at that moment left him paralyzed, even as every part of him ached to move. She came and stood in the doorway, silent. He didn't look at her.

"Otto, go to bed," she said finally, before disappearing upstairs. Still he sat on, waiting for the sounds of water upstairs, the slow footsteps that stopped on the landing for a while. He imagined he could hear her breathing, pictured her in the upstairs gloom, her robe pulled tightly around her nightgown.

"Otto?" When he didn't answer, she seemed to sigh. A door closed upstairs. He sank to the floor, his body a curve on his mother's rag rug beneath the bench.

ELSA USED TO POLISH the piano every day, her hand lingering on the photographs, the keys. When Otto was five, he found her dusting cloth where it had fallen from the broom closet and held it to his nose, inhaling the lemony scent of the oil she used. His mother found him in the corner nearly smothered, the edges of blue flannel peeking out between his fingers. Now he traced patterns in the fine layer of dust that had accumulated. Elsa was letting things go.

They never spoke of the flag incident. The knotted rug left marks in his calves as he slept, and he woke to find his mother above him, her face obscured by sunlight and dreams of his father. He stumbled when he rose, swayed unsteadily until she grasped his arm. He looked away from the worry and—what? fear?—nestled in the creases around her eyes, the downward slope of her mouth.

The four boys ignored him for the rest of the summer. His heart skidded when he saw them pass on their bicycles or walking in a loose group, swinging sticks and kicking stones down the gutter, but they barely glanced at him, as if they had lost interest, the shattered glass and Elsa's raw curse a grand, satisfying finale. In September, he started high school with resignation, intimidated by the sheer size of the building, the decibel level in the crammed hallways, everyone bigger, stronger, and louder than he could ever be. He thought maybe he could survive if he kept his head low and stuck to himself, but by the end of that first day, it was there, drawn on the front of his locker. Sounds around him swelled, then hushed. He imagined students clustered in tight huddles, whispering and pointing, but didn't turn his head. Instead, he waited, waited as the hall cleared of moving bodies, waited still as doors closed and he stood alone in silence, then fell against his locker, beating his fists against the metal door. He rubbed at the swastika frantically until only a faint outline remained and his fingers were blackened and shining, the colour of lead. He turned and walked down the hallway, his sneakers squeaking in the emptiness. As he pushed open the heavy front doors of the school, a blast of sunlight and cool September breeze made him pause, but only for a moment. *You've ruined me.*

The room shrank until just the piano remained. Poor Ruby, with her trembling hands and tear-stained face. He should never have allowed his mother near his children, not like that. He slammed his palms on the keys, the harsh discord lingering in the empty room. *End it, you coward.*

He dragged the rug out, laid it carefully on top of the bench, and pushed it forward so that it slid under the keyboard. The match scraped and flared. The flames caught in the cotton, curved around the bench, and reached towards the keys. She would return to a smouldering heap, the destruction of bad memory.

Barrett's cheque lay on the kitchen table in the apartment. He stuffed it in his wallet, packed a small bag with his toothbrush, a change of clothes, and surveyed the room until the smell of smoke drifted down the stairs. In the living room, the fire had bridged the gap between piano and drapes. Otto's throat closed in panic.

"I TRIED TO PUT IT OUT," he says. "I couldn't find an extinguisher, so I brought buckets of water into the living room." Flaming polyester snowflakes fell onto the sofa, the chair, a rug under the coffee table. The stench of burning plastic seared his eyes and mouth.

"It happened so fast."

"Why didn't you go for help?" Gavin asks.

"I did."

He called the fire department from a pay phone, then cashed Barrett's cheque and took a bus out of the city, heading west.

"And then you ran."

"Yes."

At night, he slept in motels, tossing on uncomfortable beds, pushing down covers that felt damp with grime. He watched television with the sound off, drinking beer and eating potato chips while the crumbs fell around him, and the ache for his children spread across his chest.

"I didn't know what to do."

But he did, clearly and with certainty. It hit him one day in the gloom of the motel room. *They're better off without me*. He could only return in shame, but his disappearance—his complete absence—would set them free. In time, they would think of him with sorrow, perhaps regret. He could never undo his past, but he could make sure he didn't drag them down with his future. Shifting images from the soundless television patterned his legs on the bed.

He discovered his monstrous mistake in the form of a single sentence under the headline "MAN WANTED FOR QUESTIONING IN LOCAL ARSON CASE," a sentence that would torment him for nearly thirty years: "Homeowner Elsa Sinclair died in her third-floor bedroom."

Relief slid into terror. As usual, Otto had fucked up. That his act was unplanned, rather than premeditated, offered little comfort. *Empty, I thought the house was empty*. He imagined that she didn't suffer; it was the only thing he could do.

They have fallen silent, all of them. Even Ruby has lost her hard edges and seems to have softened. Her mouth relaxes into a small frown.

"I never meant to hurt anyone," he says. Those staring faces, betrayed, weary. For a moment no one speaks. Ruby bends her head, looks away.

"I never even knew what you looked like," Gavin says.

"I'm sorry." There's nothing else Otto can say. His knees pop as he stands. He would like to hug his children just once before he leaves; the ache to touch them is so strong that he puts his hands in his pockets to keep them still. Gavin would probably hit him. And then he remembers, holds up a finger: *Wait*. Returns to the space behind the wall and emerges with the crumpled page.

"The morning of the fire, do you remember what we did together?" He looks at Ruby first, then Gavin. Of course they don't remember. He shakes his head, shows them. The paint has dried and cracked, flakes falling like snow as he lifts the paper. Two sets of handprints in red and blue amid a swirling mass of colour, saturated and thick.

"You were covered, both of you." He smiles. He had stripped Gavin down to his Underoos in his mother's kitchen, and Ruby had gone to work, drawing a happy face in the middle of his chest. Gavin pressed his hands in the paint and touched his cheeks, his eyelashes dripping green and yellow.

"I took this with me when I left," he says. The paint was still wet; he had held on to a corner and let it drip down onto the sidewalk. On the bus and later that night, in the cheap motel, his hand covered both sets of prints as he imagined tucking them into bed.

Ruby bolts from the furnace room. Her feet clatter up the stairs. Gavin takes Otto's arm, not roughly.

"I think you should go," he says.

Seventeen

GAVIN FITS THE LAST of his boxes into the trunk of Lenore's car and slams down the lid. *You don't have to leave*, she said, but he does. He had taken Otto's arm and led him outside, the skin yielding under his fingers like warm dough.

"This is me." They stopped in front of an orange camper van. Otto turned to face him, apprehensive.

"You must hate me."

"I don't know you."

Looking at Otto, Gavin saw into the future, or what could be the future. He could be the man in plaid pants and dark-framed glasses lighting a fire in his mother's home, weighed down by his failures. A drowning, sucking existence. *No.*

"Now what?" Otto asked.

"I guess you go back to where you came from. And we go on with our lives."

"That's it?"

"What else do you expect?"

"I don't know."

The rain had stopped. The back of his shirt stuck between his shoulder blades, and a single line of sweat trickled down to his belt.

Otto opened the door of his van, standing aside as stinking hot air escaped. He rummaged through a mess on the passenger seat until he found a piece of paper, a gas receipt. Another bit of rustling, and he emerged triumphantly with a pen. He scribbled, handed Gavin the paper.

"My address and telephone number," he said. "I know I've missed out on everything. And I know you're probably confused about how you really feel. But I see me in you, and I'd like to try again."

"I'm not confused," Gavin said, clenching his fist so that the paper crumpled, dug into the crease between his thumb and forefinger.

Otto climbed into the driver's seat and shifted, his pale eyes searching Gavin's face.

"I've given you nothing," he said. "I'm sorry."

He started the van, and Gavin stepped back to let him shut the door. He stood on the sidewalk long after his father had driven off, hands in his pockets.

HE HAS RENTED AN APARTMENT downtown, close to Ruby. She's there now, in fact, arranging his furniture and organizing his things. Gavin suspects she is more excited about his new place than he is, especially now that she has so much free time. The apartment is small, a studio on the third floor of an old house, but he has a wooden deck off his kitchen, and sunlight pours in throughout the afternoon.

"So? All set?" Lenore comes towards him, smiling, trim and neat in her thick cream sweater and dark wool pants. He smiles in return, nods. She has come through everything unscathed, he thinks, that one moment of lost composure in the basement erased. He wondered if she'd ever imagined the reunion in her head late at night or when she woke, disoriented, the moon casting shadows in the dark corners of her room.

He walks down the driveway, his feet kicking leaves to the side of the house. The door to Barrett's studio is half-open, and he can't resist. Already the room has the feel of a time capsule, the air still, dry, and silent. He looks again at the wedding scene, his fingers unconsciously twisting his bottom lip. When he first saw it, he felt a rush of disappointment. Barrett didn't know him at all. *I don't want a child.* But now he looks more closely, sees that the Gavin in the scene is different—much older, for one thing, with hair greying along the temples and tiny lines spreading from the corners of his eyes. And the woman beside Gavin, the one holding the child, is not Melanie. She is older too, with dark hair. Gavin wears a suit, looks confident, as if he has finally found his place.

His shoulders relax, and his head bends of its own accord, drawing his gaze away from the wedding itself. Here is a dance floor and tables, each with a small flower arrangement and place cards. And there, a table with albums and speakers for the deejay. The chair behind the table is empty, pulled out as if the deejay has just left and will soon return. Gavin picks up the tiny card resting next to the equipment, and a flash of bright light nearly blinds him. "DJ Gavin," the card reads. He waits out a sudden wave of dizziness, a sense of awakening blooming, spreading out along the surface of his skin until his hands tingle. Maybe Barrett knew him better than he thought.

LENORE HAS GIVEN THEM a box of photographs. In Gavin's new apartment, they take them out one by one.

"You look like him," Ruby says.

"So do you." She wrinkles her forehead.

"I suppose. Funny how small he seemed."

"And old."

"Did you remember him at all when you saw him?"

Gavin shrugs, rises to fetch a beer from his fridge.

"I don't think I really remember him," he says. "But there was something. He seemed familiar. If I saw him on the street and didn't know who he was, I'd probably look twice, trying to figure out where I'd met him before."

"Here." Ruby hands him a photograph. In it, Otto grins as Gavin sits on his lap and reaches up to pull on his sideburn.

"He's so young," Gavin says. It could be Gavin now, today: the same grin, the same pale blue eyes crinkling upward.

"He looks happy." She studies the photograph, then throws it back in the box. "Did he write to you?" she asks.

"Yes."

"Me too." For a moment they just look at each other.

"To hell with him," Ruby says, but her voice sounds weak, unsure.

"To hell with him," he agrees.

She picks up another photograph showing Otto on all fours in the yard, Ruby hanging on to his neck, Gavin curled on his side in shorts and bare feet. They face the camera, caught in laughter. Otto's eyes shine.

"He looks happy," Ruby says.

"We all do."

"That's something, at least. Isn't it?"

He has always cursed Ruby for the memories she carries, the memories he is missing. But for once he is glad he can't know the depth of her loss.

"Yes," he says. "That's something."

Eighteen

RUBY WAKES, REACHES UP in a long, luxurious stretch. She stares for a minute into the darkness, fingertips resting lightly above her head before sliding the pocket doors open. Her arms and legs feel loose as she walks in her pyjamas into the kitchen and begins making coffee. Mornings are her favourite part of the day now that she's unemployed.

It is ironic, though. Last weekend she sat with Gavin on his wooden deck and drank mulled wine that she made in his small kitchen.

"It's about time you had your own place," she teased, but she is proud of him, in a way. He even looked better, the slight paunch gone, his face more confident, somehow.

"So they gave you your own show?"

"Once a week," he said. "I have to go through orientation and training, but it looks pretty simple. They liked my ideas."

"Retrospectives?"

"I pick one band each week, go into the history and all that, dig up old interviews."

He kicked out his legs, leaned back in one of the folding camp chairs he had arranged out there.

"What did Mom say about you going back to school?"

"She was sort of doubtful." He smiled again, raised his voice in mimicry. *"Are you sure, Gavin? Radio broadcasting? This is what you want?"*

"Well, who can blame her?" She paused, smiled. "I'm proud of you," she said. "And here I thought you'd end up like Cousin George, living with Mom until you were old and grey."

"At least George knows what he wants to do," Gavin said. "At least he's happy."

"Okay."

"It's kind of funny," he said. "I've finally decided what to do, and now you're the one who's lost."

"I'm not lost," she said, lifting her mug and taking a small sip, licking away the sweetness on her upper lip. "I like to think of it as a temporary stop."

"What will you do?"

She was quiet, looking out over the still yard, the bare trees arching into the darkening sky. There was a chill, a forewarning of the coming frost.

"I'm going skydiving."

SHE TAKES HER COFFEE to the front porch and settles into the great chair she bought recently, the striped green cushions thick and springlike, full of hope. Wrapped in her duvet, winter boots on her feet, she lets the steam from her coffee warm her nose before taking a sip. Rust-coloured leaves scuttle and scrape along the sidewalks and slide into the gutters in the early November morning. She thinks of nothing but the way the air holds an edge of frost. When she finishes her first mug, she goes back inside for a refill and a shower.

I'm taking some time to figure out what I want to do with my life. Lenore had simply nodded, as if she expected Ruby to do something like this all along. It felt strange, at first, this freedom, and she did feel a little lost. She tried scheduling herself into a routine, as though she ought to make use of all her time, but now she just does as she pleases and lets herself relax. She has enough money saved up to last at least a year, though she hopes it won't take that long.

What are you good at, Ruby? What do you enjoy doing?

She doesn't know, not yet.

The mail drops into the shared front hall with a thud. Ruby sorts through the envelopes, setting aside small piles for each apartment. In her stack, there is a letter from Otto. She doesn't need to open it to know what it says: a running commentary of his life and what he's doing. *I'm sorry, please forgive me.* Never written, but there, between the lines. Since he left in August, there have been three letters, and she is still not sure how she feels about them. She has not responded, but she also has not thrown them out. Instead, she keeps the letters on the shelf above her computer, folded neatly in their opened envelopes so that she can reseal them at any time, if she wants.

Funny, over the years Otto emerged in her memories as a much bigger man. In person, he was small—a little on the short side, and slender. Looking at him in that basement, his hands in his pockets and tear stains on his cheeks, she felt an instant of relief. *I matter. He came back.*

AFTER HER FATHER LEFT, Ruby walked to clear her head. Her street twisted and turned as it wound its way south. She walked in the shade of overgrown trees—maples and oaks—that towered over the sidewalks. She had always liked this walk, though in the heat it wasn't as pleasant as usual. No breeze blew to brush the sweat from her forehead. By the time she hit the end of the street, her feet were sweating, her toes sliding in her flip-flops.

In the courtyard of an apartment complex, a fountain beckoned, the water pooling in the concrete basin too inviting to resist. Her feet almost sighed as she dipped them into the coolness. *Oh God, thank you. Thank you for inventing fountains.* On a bench across from her, a little boy, maybe five or six, stared. He looked up at the woman beside him—a grandmother, perhaps—hopefully, with longing, then back to Ruby. The woman kept reading her tattered paperback. He kicked a plastic toy on a string that lay on its side by his feet. Ruby couldn't tell from where she sat what it was, but she could see that it was well used, scuffed on the sides, and much too babyish for a boy his age. She took in his small shirt, the shorts that seemed too wide and cinched with a belt at the waist, the cheap sandals on his feet, the way his hair hung too long at the sides and into his eyes. And there they sat, the two of them, the boy swinging his legs, the woman unaware, engrossed in her book.

Ruby wanted to splash her, shake her, drag her from the bench and show her the boy's neglect, but of course she knew nothing about the situation, did she? Maybe they were waiting for someone, maybe his mother or father was about to arrive. Maybe the day was just about to start for him, for them. She pulled her feet from the fountain, slipped her shoes back on, and smiled at the boy, but as she walked away, her throat felt too thick, and it hurt to swallow. *Bram.* She couldn't come in the middle, wouldn't do that to him.

She met him at a bar downtown. He looked rather hopeful when she walked through the door but greeted her cautiously. They didn't touch. Ruby sat down beside him, unsure of how to begin, how to say what needed to be said. She could have done this by email, perhaps, or even telephone, but that would be cowardly. Looking at him now, though, was difficult. His T-shirt hugged his chest, and his eyes behind his glasses seemed too large and deep, too full of thinking and feeling.

"My father ran away when I was seven," she said. She didn't look at him, rested her elbows on the bar, fingers tracing the wet rings left by the bottoms of glasses, poking in scattered cigarette ashes and torn bits of coasters shredded from nerves or habit. "He set fire to the house. I've never been able to remember that day. Or maybe I just didn't want to."

They could smell the fire before they saw it. By the time they reached the house, firefighters were already there, two trucks and an ambulance, a crowd of people standing on the sidewalk, staring. Some held their hands to their mouths. Her mother tugged them along quickly (*oh my God, oh my God*), Gavin squealing to see the fire trucks. The smoke got in her mouth, her hair; she tasted it in her sleep later. Through the back of the open ambulance doors, she could see a stretcher, a covered form. Covered with what? Maybe a sheet, maybe a black bag—possibly she has invented those details. The stretcher stood alone, as if no one cared.

"Where's Daddy?"

Her mother began to cry. One of the neighbours came forward, put her arm around Lenore's shoulder. A policeman approached them.

"We need to ask you some questions."

Someone pulled Ruby and Gavin away. Ruby stared at the smoking house, the main floor charred and crusted. *The piano room.*

Lenore took them to her friend's apartment downtown, where the three of them slept together on a pull-out couch. That night, her mother spoke with her friend on the balcony about what she would do, the patio doors open a crack, so Ruby heard their low tones. She rose from the lumpy bed and peeked through the curtains, saw her mother's head fall forward into her hands. Ruby crept back into bed.

"But you weren't there," Duncan said.

"No. Only my grandmother."

"Who you hated."

"I was only seven. I didn't know *hate*. I only saw what he wanted me to see. What he wanted all of us to see."

"It's not your fault that he left."

"No. You'd have to be pretty shitty to make your dad burn down your house." Duncan laughed, his arm brushing hers. She pulled away, but had to smile. She loved the way his face seemed to widen and lighten when he laughed.

"I didn't blame myself," she said. "But it changed me forever, didn't it?"

"Did it?"

"I thought for a long time that I was angry at him. That he was a terrible person for leaving, that we were better off without him. Enraged. I held on to that anger for a long time."

"I understand."

"I don't think you do. I wasn't angry—I was devastated. I lost one of the most important people in my life, and I thought he didn't care at all. When someone dies, you grieve, but in the end it's okay, because you know the person who died had no choice. He had a choice. His leaving hurt like nothing else."

This wasn't working, this conversation. It had no beginning and no end.

"You're the only person I've ever really talked to about him," she said. "You and Angela." *There, bring it back to the point, Ruby.*

He examined his hands, long fingers splayed.

"She called me," he said quietly. "She told me to stay away from you, that if anything ever happened, she'd never forgive either of us."

Ruby blinked, her muscles melting, bones shifting, giving way. This was a defining moment, she knew. The back of her neck prickled with awareness. She exhaled, her lips numb.

"When I was seventeen, there was this man." *Chasing your father.* She studied her hands, fought the urge to bite the flesh between her thumb and forefinger. Mr. Todd was the father of one of her friends. Tall, dignified, a top criminal lawyer in the city. His daughter Sylvia ran with a different crowd, a bit harder around the edges, and was a year older. *The Richies*, she and Angela called them. The kids with parents who were always away, big parties in grand houses, kids with bags of pot hidden in their rooms and empty cases of beer in the trunk of their cars. Sylvia wasn't her friend, exactly; she sat, perfumed and dimpled, at the back of her French class wearing Polo turtlenecks and Bass Weejun shoes.

"You're good at this stuff," she said to Ruby. "How would you like to make some money?"

She wanted Ruby to write her independent study for her. "I was thinking of doing something on French cheese. You'd have to do all the work, and I'll give the presentation." And so Ruby did. She researched and wrote a paper, then arranged a sampling of cheese on a small tray for the class. The night before the presentation, Ruby walked to Sylvia's house with a handful of cue cards. She meant to drop them off, but Mr. Todd answered the door and pulled it wide.

"You're helping Sylvia with her presentation. Come in and have dinner with us."

Curiosity propelled her through the golden lobby with its grand arching entry, the chandelier suspended and lit with tiny orbs of light above them.

"Hi." Sylvia gave her a look to mean, *Don't say anything*. Her mother, thin and immaculate, sat at the head of the table, lipstick bleeding into her lip lines. Fine china, roast duck, new potatoes crumbly on the edges, and steamed asparagus. Ruby dug her toes into the plush carpet, straightened her spine, and ate awkwardly with her left hand. Mr. Todd asked her too many questions. His sleeves were rolled up on his arms, exposing thick forearms, muscled and hard, bristling with dark hairs. Sylvia said nothing. Halfway through dinner, Mrs. Todd laid her knife and fork neatly across her plate and lit a cigarette. She blew smoke out of the corner of her mouth, watching her family finish their meals. Mr. Todd made himself a drink.

Ruby followed Sylvia up the wide staircase to her room, handed over the cards. Downstairs, Mr. Todd waited, car keys in his hand. He waved off her protests.

"It's dark," he said. "You can't just walk."

Ruby stopped in the telling, settled her twisting hands firmly on the bar. "It wasn't far," she said. "The drive. But he took a shortcut and got lost. We wound up down by the river."

How did we get here? He laughed, his breath sweet with alcohol. *I'll just turn around.* He put a hand on her knee, just below the hem of her jean skirt, fingers against bare flesh, and stopped the car. He stared straight ahead, his fingers roving up and down along her thigh. And she didn't stop him.

"I don't know why," Ruby said. "I think I wanted to see what would happen. I wasn't scared, not like that."

You're a good-looking girl, he said. There was something alluring about him: the scent of power and money, his strength and assurance. He watched her with a half smile, then pulled her onto his lap, sucked on her mouth, and unbuckled his pants. The strap of Ruby's tank top fell down, and his thumb came up to caress the exposed skin. He bucked against her hip.

When he dropped her off at the apartment, she walked inside backwards to hide the stain on her skirt, and went to bed thinking of the way he wiped his fingers on a fast-food napkin he found in the glove compartment. The next day in French class, Sylvia pressed a twenty-dollar bill into her hand without a word.

"Christ, Ruby." Duncan hunched forward. "He violated you."

"I let him."

"You were a child."

"I went back to the house later." A week, maybe more. "I don't know what I expected." She imagined his hand reaching out to grip her wrist, urgent. She wore pants, a belt, just in case.

"What happened?"

"He wasn't home." His wife answered the door, her hair pulled back, stretching the skin of her face, earrings catching in the light and drooping down, too heavy for her fragile earlobes. Her smile genuine, unaware. Ruby's face burned with shame.

"I never went back." No. In her dreams, he never kissed her, but took her bottom lip in his mouth, as if swallowing her whole. The match struck, caught.

Usually they were married, always older. But it wasn't affection she sought, or even sex. The illicit thrill drew her, the dance of words, gestures, before anything happened. The knowledge that she could have such power over them, and the allure of aged confidence.

"It's almost like a sickness," she told Duncan. "I'd see an older man on the street—well-dressed, broad shoulders—and I'd follow him. I'd have to make him look at me, notice me. I'd brush past him, touch his sleeve, his back." She always focused on their mouths, their hands. "I had a trick, you know. I'd get them to look at me and I'd sort of smile, shy, look down slanted, then back." Their smiles always widened. "Or I'd pretend to be lost, helpless. That worked too." There were so many ways to rope them in. And then what?

"What were you looking for?"

"You tell me."

She wishes now she smoked so that she had the luxury of pretense, of inhaling and exhaling through a cloud of silence.

"That's a terrible story," Duncan said.

"Only Angela knows." She watched Duncan's face shift. The muscles of his jaw clenched, unclenched, as he looked away.

"You already knew."

"She told me a long time ago," he said. "I'm sorry."

She sighed, long and slow. She would never be able to start anew with him, never be able to peel back the layers, one by one. He already knew her life, but not from her. "It's too complicated," she said. "Too messy in the middle, Duncan."

"I'm not sure I understand."

"It's supposed to be simple. And this … us …" She rose, hooked her bag over her shoulder. "I just wanted to tell you in person. It's not easy for me. I just can't. I won't." There was much more that she wanted to say; she wanted to sit down beside him again and place her hand on the back of his, wanted to feel the blood pulsing beneath his skin. But it had to be enough.

IF THIS WERE A MOVIE, the instructor would be young, dashing, with a grin of straight white teeth, maybe some dimples. There would be a single knowing moment when their eyes met, an epiphany. But her instructor today is straggly and tall, his teeth crooked and stained. He has a crust of sleep in the corner of an eye.

She spends four hours in the morning watching videos, studying photos, and listening to the crusty-eyed man talk about the difference between good and bad chutes. After lunch, she hangs in a harness for practice, signs a waiver, and puts on her jumpsuit, parachute, and helmet. In the gutted Cessna, the other jumpers are quiet, stilled by the thought of what lies ahead. For Ruby, the calm has returned, white noise rushing through her ears.

The jumpmaster waves his arm. *You! Your turn.* She steps out onto the wing of the plane, hanging on to the doorframe with one hand. There is no epiphany, but there is one moment of suspended waiting. And then she lets go.

Nineteen

LENORE CLIMBED THE STAIRS to the main floor after she put the children to bed for a nap, called the woman's name and waited, listening to the shuffles upstairs.

"Yes?" Her voice sounded unsure, as if she thought a stranger had come to the door and simply walked inside.

"It's Lenore, Elsa."

The woman's head appeared at the top of the stairs, her hair dishevelled, face pale and rumpled with sleep.

"Something wrong?" she asked.

"I was wondering …" Here Lenore faltered, started again. "Would you like a cup of tea?"

"I don't think so."

Elsa's rudeness was startling.

"I mean with me. Have a cup of tea with me." When the other woman didn't respond, she added, "I need to talk to you. We need money. We have nothing left, Elsa."

She came down the stairs slowly in her robe, staring at Lenore, her hand on the banister. Lenore noticed that she had rough hands,

hands that were used to working, unlike her own smooth, white skin. She stood where she was, waiting. Elsa cinched her robe around her waist. The material bloomed around her shoulders, hung loosely down her arms.

"I'm not feeling well," she said. She looked ill, the skin of her face dry and chalky, her lips cracked. "I was sleeping."

"I'm sorry. I could come back—"

"I know what you think of me," Elsa said.

"I don't think anything," Lenore said.

Elsa studied her for a moment, then nodded. "Kettle's on the stove. I'll go change."

By the time she came back down, dressed in one of her shapeless, functional dresses, Lenore had found the china and brewed a pot of tea. She brought everything on a tray into the living room, settled herself on the sofa. She wore shorts, and her thighs stuck to the plastic cover in the heat. Elsa sat opposite her in a gold tapestry wingback chair, her hands folded primly in her lap.

"I should have warned you," she said.

"Pardon?"

"My son. I should have warned you away." Elsa looked away, lifted her cup to her lips, blowing to cool the tea before taking a tentative sip. "You wouldn't have listened to me, in any case."

"I'm sorry. This is awkward."

"You think I'm a monster."

"I don't think—"

"Yes. I see it in the way you look at me." She rose, selected a record from the cabinet, then lifted the lid of the stereo, her movements slow, unsteady. She winced.

"Are you all right?" Lenore half rose to take the woman's arm, but Elsa waved her away, settled into a chair amid the sound of strings and violins, the high notes of an oboe. Elsa seemed to be waiting for something, her head slightly cocked, her eyes focused on Lenore.

"When I was a young girl, my father had a record player. A phonograph, they called it back then. The most wonderful sounds it played. Classical music, you know, composers, not this rock and roll you have now. Bach, Handel, Mendelssohn, Wagner. German music. When you listened, you could imagine so many things, lives, tragedies. Every evening, I'd lie on the floor of the living room and just listen. I had hopes for my life, back then."

On the piano, there was a picture of Elsa in sepia, taken when she was a teenager. Blond braids, impish smile—mischievous, alive. Lenore planted this Elsa of the past on a floor in a room lit by oil, Elsa in a dress with a white collar, one arm flung up on the sofa cushions as she listened to the phonograph, her face rapt.

"My father died just before the second war. My mother sold the phonograph. She said she never wanted to listen to his music again. He died on the floor of our bakery. My mother sold that, too."

Lenore watched Elsa's face, noticing the deep grooves curving down from her wide nose, her skin beginning to deflate and sink. She was only in her fifties, but life had been hard for her.

"Otto's father was a little scattered. Had trouble keeping his attention on any one thing. But he was handsome, back then. When we first met, I told him about my father, about his love of music, and the way I would listen to the records at home. And you know what he did? He bought me a record player, one of those ones with the handle you had to wind. I barely knew him, and he wanted to give me that. Can you imagine?"

And then he died, Lenore thought. She knew little about Otto's father, save the dry facts of his suicide: the date, the method used. Otto never spoke of him or the impression his death must have made.

"You don't know who I am. You've never come upstairs to talk to me. You sit across the table from me on Sundays and don't even look in my direction."

"You've made it clear how you feel about us," Lenore said.

"You know nothing about how I feel," she said. "You only know what Otto has told you. And you believed him." Elsa sat for a moment without speaking, her spine straight, hands in her lap cradling the teacup. "I would have liked to know you," she said, her voice soft.

"It's not too late," Lenore said. "We could start over."

"It's too late." She seemed on the verge of saying more, her eyes open, imploring, before a shutter came down. *Oh, Elsa, if only you let the cracks show.*

"He can't read, did he tell you that?"

"Otto?"

"Not very well. And don't ask him to write anything. He can't do that well either." Lenore remembered how long it took him to read the newspaper, his face creased in concentration, his lips moving soundlessly.

"All his life, he's struggled. I don't know where it comes from. His father wasn't like that, exactly, but he had strange habits. Things got into his head and he couldn't seem to shake them. He'd get worked up about the smallest things. Spent hours at night writing letters raging about this and that, problems with the city, society. Sent them in to the papers, but they were never published. I read some of them, and they made no sense. Just rambled on and on."

"I'm not sure—"

"But Otto … he was never normal, not even when he was three years old. Never had any friends, never paid attention in school. No question of university. I was so worried. 'It's in the genes' the doctor said."

"I'm not comfortable talking about Otto this way."

"It's who he is," Elsa said. "You can't change it. I did what everyone told me to do. Before he married you, I told him to think seriously, to make sure it was what he wanted. How could he support you, have a family? He couldn't even take care of himself. I told him so. He didn't listen. He cut me out of his life completely."

Don't you think you should call your mother, Otto? Doesn't she want to meet the children?

"I knew he'd come back. 'Temporary,' he said. 'We'll live in the basement. I'll keep them out of your way.' He typed up a list of rules for you all to follow. And I knew you'd come up those stairs one day for my help."

"The basement was Otto's idea?"

"Yes."

"I thought—"

"You thought it was my idea, putting you down there like mice? No."

Elsa's voice betrayed nothing, no hint of triumph or rancour. Lenore felt sick. She bent forward, head between her knees until Elsa put a hand on her shoulder. Lenore looked up.

"My mother wanted me to come live in Germany after Otto's father died, to be with her. I couldn't do it to Otto. Too many changes all at once. She died last week." She reached into a pocket, pulled out a tattered, folded piece of paper. "I keep reading this over and over again, to see if I read it wrong the first ten times." Her laugh caught on the upswing. Elsa swallowed, her mouth trembling.

"I'm so sorry."

"I couldn't have any more children after Otto," she said. "I started bleeding, and they had to …" She made a sawing motion over her belly. "He's all I have left in this world. If you think I don't care about him or his family, you're wrong. He told me to stay away from you. In my own house!" She sat back, her face contorted in a grimace, her left arm held slightly aloft.

"Are you all right?"

Elsa shook her head, leaned back carefully in her chair. "You can't push him too hard," she said. "But you can't let him run free, either. You have to find the right balance."

SHE DIDN'T REMEMBER what she did with the first part of the day after she left Otto in the basement with the children, the day before the fire. Perhaps she sat on the bench where she and Barrett used to lunch, her fingers idly twirling her bracelet, the soft, light touch of gold encircling her wrist offering up a kind of hope. Or maybe she wandered down the streets, listening to the click of her heels against the sidewalk. It was hot, she remembers; she could not have moved too quickly or too much, for fear of sweat and stains.

She circled a few job ads in the paper, but couldn't bring herself to make the calls, seized by a paralyzing sense of despair, even rage. So many moments of happiness now sullied. Ruby's birth, for example: Otto's tears, his arms trembling as he reached for the baby, unwrapped the swaddling blankets and counted her toes, one by one. They exchanged a glance then, a look of pride and exhilaration. *Look what we made!* By the time Gavin appeared, they were a little crumpled around the edges, less fresh, but still there was the surge of happiness to watch both children sleeping, skin plump and flushed, eyelids fluttering. Otto once sat on the floor of their room for more than an hour, listening to them breathe. Somehow, they had lost sight of each other, become consumed by ordinary details.

But he's changed, Lenore. A mean, insistent voice. Everyone changed in life, in love, but Otto couldn't seem to find his voice in his mother's house. It was as if he were crushed beneath her heavy, invisible thumb, but the Elsa she encountered was different—less threatening, somehow shrunken—than the almost mythical woman in Otto's memories.

She ate lunch in a diner downtown, sitting by the window in a booth, listening to the hum of conversation around her. The waitress smiled, tilting her head to the side, and studied Lenore, as if wondering what she was doing here by herself. Maybe she saw the way her mouth curved down, or the heaviness of her eyelids. Lenore twisted her wedding band around her finger, then pulled it off and slipped it into her purse. Without the ring, her finger felt strange, too light and naked. Around her other wrist, the bracelet, shining in the light, her hands unbalanced.

After lunch, she walked through the downtown streets, watching other people: businessmen in suits and hats, smartly dressed secretaries, mothers pushing babies in prams. One woman approached slowly, a toddler taking wobbly, crab-like steps beside her. Lenore smiled. She should be so content.

She wound up at the clinic in the late afternoon, as she had known she would. The new secretary—young, fresh, with curling blond hair bouncing against the tops of her narrow shoulders—was packing up for the day and looked up in surprise to see Lenore.

"The clinic is closed," she said, her mouth setting in a firm line. Her eyebrows were plucked bare and pencilled back in, and Lenore could see a layer of powder on her cheeks and under her jaw. She pictured the girl peering into her mirror every morning, the routine and details as she drew in her brows, patted the powder, blinking and applying her mascara to make her blue eyes seem wider. She probably lived with her parents and would work until she was married, just like Lenore. But then she saw a glint of gold, a wedding band on the slim finger, and felt a pang of envy. The girl's husband would be young, dark against her blond, and supportive of his wife's independence. Two young people with a future.

Before she could ask after him, Barrett came down the corridor, lab coat gone, shirt sleeves rolled up to his elbows. Was he happy to see her? He stopped, his breath catching in his chest, and his eyes seemed to darken in anger. The pretty secretary opened her appointment book and flipped through the pages in confusion. Barrett stopped her, his hand briefly touching the back of hers.

"Mrs. Sinclair used to work for me," he said. "We have a few things to discuss. You don't need to stay."

The secretary looked from his face to hers, trying to fit the pieces together. Lenore kept her face still, disinterested. *Professional.*

"There's been a problem with her final paycheque," he added. "Damn hospital administration." He sighed, his eyebrows knitted in a show of annoyance. This seemed to appease the girl. She rose, pulling down her skirt, and nodded at Lenore.

When the door closed, Lenore said nothing but pressed her fingertips on the desk hard enough to blanch the skin. She had bitten her nails throughout the afternoon, unconsciously, and the skin around her thumb looked nibbled. She turned her face away from the sight. Barrett said nothing, and she was sure he was angry with her for coming here, but then she felt his hand on her shoulder, and she began to shake.

"What's wrong?" His voice was gentle, his eyes kind and soft. She wanted to weep, grasp him by the collar, and press her nose against the dip in his neck between the collarbones.

"Lenore." Suddenly his hands were in her hair, pulling at the pins until the knot she created so carefully unwound, hair trailing down to cover him, hands on her neck, near her ears, lips, mouth.

"Lenore."

She closed her eyes and imagined a different world, only for a moment. He took her to a hotel with a marble lobby and uniformed bellhops, clasped her hands demurely as he registered them as man and wife. His hand on her elbow as they rode up the elevator burned her flesh. Did she think of what she was about to do? No, she only saw him, the softness of his eyes and the crisp whiteness of the sheets folded back on the bed, then nothing, nothing.

He ordered dinner that arrived in silver serving platters—steak and lobster tails, garlic asparagus and new potatoes. It had no taste. Her robe fell open as she ate, and she let him push it down over her shoulders again. He didn't mention the months of absence, and she didn't talk about the times she had thought of him late at night, her back turned to Otto as he slept. *If only, if only.*

They sat on the balcony with glasses of wine. He looked older to her, the lines around the corners of his eyes more prominent.

"I'm leaving Otto," she said simply, and the lines on his face deepened. She looked down, felt the thickness of the white robe. When he remained silent, she swallowed awkwardly. Her fingers were long, bony, and the sight of her thin wrists growing out of the wide sleeves of the robe—the desperation she felt—was too much. She shuddered once, and then her shoulders caved forward as she cried.

And yes, there was a single moment when he did nothing, a single gap of uncertainty and fear, before he moved and pulled her against his chest. He held tight until she stopped, then released her, set her back on the sofa, and handed her a tissue.

"I'm sorry," she said, but he shook his head.

"Don't," he said.

"It's impossible." She looked down again, her next words too full of shame for eye contact. "I came to ask for my job back. We're broke. He hasn't had a job in months, and all our money is gone." Her chest was tight, waiting, waiting for what seemed like ages. How embarrassing to tell him about Otto and their problems, how shameful to say *we're broke*. Why wouldn't he speak? And then finally he did.

"I can't, Lenore." Now he was the one to look away. "I can't."

In the silence, she struggled to compose herself. *Of course.* She lifted her chin, turned her face to the side so she didn't have to look at him, or what she imagined must be a glance of anguished pity.

"Where does Rena think you are tonight?"

His mouth tightened as he looked at her reproachfully. He had never lied to her, not once, never promised anything.

"I told her I'm having dinner and drinks with some colleagues," he said.

"Does she know, do you think?"

He shook his head. "I don't think so."

"She'll know."

Barrett looked out over the city, brought his glass to his mouth. His legs stretched out in front of him, long and thin.

"Yes," he said. "But we'll never talk about it."

"I shouldn't have come," she said. "This shouldn't have happened." Had she known it would be like this? The night was so quiet, the balconies on either side empty. Only a black, starless sky, the city lights.

"I'm not leaving him for you," she said. "I'm leaving him for us. Me, the children." She wanted to make sure he understood, or maybe she wanted to convince herself.

"I know."

"Barrett?" He turned his head expectantly.

"Was all this ... just a game? Does it mean nothing?"

"How can you say that?"

She pounded her thigh repeatedly, unconsciously, until she winced in awareness.

"It just seems that I shouldn't have bothered."

He moved quickly, grasped her wrist.

"Don't," he said. "Not like that." He held on, his fingers searing.

"Don't you understand?" he asked. "I can't see you every day again. I just can't. It would tear me apart."

"I have to go," she said. She needed to find a job, a place to sleep for the night. She couldn't go back to the house, not with Otto there, not yet. Tomorrow she would feel better, her head clearer and heart less tangled.

Barrett shook his head. "Stay here tonight."

"I need to find a job," she said. "And a place to stay. My kids … I need …" An ache welled up through the crack in her voice, stopping her. *The children.*

"Listen to me." He took her hands. "I never lied to you. I'll never leave Rena, I'll never tell her about us. But this isn't a game. You mean everything to me." And then: "I'll always take care of you."

She can't remember if she cried again; probably she did. And probably he held her in his lap and took her inside, cradling his arms around her, gentle, protective. He left her lying naked in bed, the sheets crumpled and tangled around her waist. She rose when the door closed behind him and ran a bath, sinking down into the warmth and letting her arms rest on the sides of the tub. And then she slept deeply.

In the morning, she wasn't lost anymore, and her head had cleared. She would leave Otto and start life again with the children, but first she would find a job, and then a place for them. Small steps that filled her with optimism.

Only as she was dressing again did she notice the cheque on the bedside table, signed for an extraordinary amount, the short note—"Do with this as you will"—clipped to the front.

Lenore stomps snow from her boots, closes the doors of the studio, and flicks on the light. She comes here every day, as a sort of meditation, a remembrance. She stands in front of the tableau Barrett made, taking it all in yet again: Ruby's wedding, Gavin's child, Lenore smiling, smiling from the front row. Her hair is pulled back, and she wears a silk dress in rose. How many times has she sat in front of this house after his death? Too many to count. The more she looks, the more details she finds extraordinary.

Away from the wedding crowd, the interior of the house has been inhabited. In her bedroom, the covers are folded back, and a book lies face down on the sheets with a pair of reading glasses on the cover. He has patted down two indentations on the bed, a place for two bodies to rest, and placed a set of blue-and-white fingertip-length pyjamas on the bed, his slippers peeking out from beneath the bedskirt.

When she first moved into the big house a year after Rena's death, they stayed in the master bedroom together. Lenore found it awkward sharing a bed with someone after years spent alone, each snore or rustling of the sheets from his side startling her awake. More than that, the history of that room disturbed her, as if the ghost of Rena still lurked in the corner. In the morning, he rose on one elbow to peer down at her.

"You hate sleeping in here," he said. *I hate this house*, she wanted to say. Because there were two ghosts. The healthy Rena, who ripped out the sagging wooden steps in front and replaced the ugly tiled floor with hardwood, who turned the patchy grass into a garden, pushing through the earth with young, feeling hands—before the numbness took hold—until her fingers were filthy. That version of Rena still slept with Barrett in the master bedroom and cooked for dinner parties of ten, and Lenore could feel her watching in the living spaces of the house. And then the other Rena, hidden away in her room on the main floor of the house when it became too difficult for her to navigate the stairs. Her presence was less formidable, but full of reproach.

And Barrett knew. He could never sell, he told her, and she tried to respect the request of a dying woman. *I promised her*, he said. It was ridiculous to be jealous of a dead wife, and she had become adept at stifling the first signs of resentment.

At dinner one night, too much wine loosened a flood of bitterness.

"I'll never be the first anything for you," she said. "I'll always be stepping on her memory." His astonishment gave way to genuine remorse.

"I'm so sorry," he said.

"I think I'd feel more comfortable with my own room."

And she was. Even after he turned Rena's bedroom on the first floor into a study and hired decorators to refurbish the master, Lenore stayed in the guest room next to his, appreciating the sense of ownership it afforded: her antique armoire with shelves of scented clothes, her window into the yard, her duvet and—importantly—a door that she could close.

Oh, Barrett. She pulls cold hands up into the sleeves of her sweater. Christmas this year will be difficult, but she will try her best, with a real tree and the decorations she keeps in her basement. They will eat a turkey dinner with mashed potatoes and stuffing, and the kids will try to convince her to sell the house and move into something smaller. She will laugh and wave her hand at them, but she will think about it. And maybe one day when she's ready, when the spring has come and the sun burns off the frost and cold of hibernation, she will decide to clear out her memories.

JUST AFTER THE FIRE, he rented a cottage with whitewashed boards right on the beach in Cape Cod. He flew them all down and stayed next door, for the sake of the children.

"I told Rena I had a conference," he said. But she hadn't asked. They spent the days on the beach, growing browner and trying to heal. Barrett mostly kept out of the way, but brought them lobster, mussels, and corn for dinner. In the evenings, when the children were in bed, he sat with Lenore on the beach in front of the cottages, legs drawn up and arms clasped around his knees. His feet were bare. She stretched out her tanned legs, gently touched a foot to his. She listened to the ocean, let the sand climb between her toes. Once she leaned into him, laid her head against his shoulder, and he pulled his fingers through her hair. That night, after he had returned to his own cottage, she lay on her bed and cried, wishing that things were different. She cried for an hour, and when she finished, she blew her nose in the darkness and patted her swollen eyes with a damp cloth. When the kids woke in the morning, they found her smiling at the table, breakfast on the stove. She never let them see her pain.

FOR NEARLY THIRTY YEARS she willed serenity into her face. But seeing Otto there with that familiar expression, his casual manner (*How are you?*), as if they were mere acquaintances passing in the street, left her suddenly broken. All this time she thought she had made peace with the past, but she had merely buried the truth, which was this: Otto enraged her. Not for leaving her stranded with two young children, not for years of absence and silence, but for the naked desperation on his face in that corner of the basement. And later, in the restaurant where they agreed to meet, the stiff way he stood, the smell of his soap and cologne, the effort he had made for her. She wanted to weep with the hopelessness of it all.

Back in the house, she takes her manuscript from a shelf in the study and carries it into the living room, sinks down in Barrett's big chair. And she reads, the pages fanning out on the floor beside her. The sunshine dims, disappears, and she reads on by lamplight. The last page drops. She sits for a moment, palms turned up on her lap, no will or thought, letting relief take hold. For all this time, she had been worried that Barrett was merely an afterthought, a substitute for what she had not acknowledged but had stuffed in the bottom of a box and piled high with photographs and written words. But it was Otto who filled a gap, Otto who was the square peg. *I never expected anything from you*, she told him, but that wasn't true.

"How's he doing?" Helen whispered. Their father had pushed back his chair after dinner and headed down the hallway to the bathroom, a newspaper under his arm. Lenore shrugged, rose to clear the plates, forks, and knives sliding into puddles of gravy. A lone pea fell to the floor. Helen picked it up and followed her into the kitchen.

"Let me help." Sal was at home. *The flu*, Helen said, but Lenore knew he just didn't want to come.

She set up the dish rack, placed a folded tea towel on the counter for the glasses.

"I'll wash," she said. She wore her mother's rubber gloves, despite the hole in the right thumb, the jagged tear in the palm of the left. She had been gone for four years. Lenore dipped the cloth into soapy water, worked the inside of a glass, washing up the sides and down around the base. The water was almost too hot. Strands of hair that had escaped her loose knot curled along her neck.

"What are you going to do?" Helen kept her voice low. "You're twenty-two. You should find someone, get married, have babies."

Lenore bit her tongue. She passed Helen the glass, took up a second.

"He needs me," she said finally.

"It's not like he's an invalid," Helen said. "He can take care of himself."

Under the water in the sink, Lenore's fingers seemed to float in the rubber gloves. She held her hands still for a moment.

"You could at least get a job, start saving some money. Just in case."

"I'll think about it."

"I know you think you owe it to him, but you have a right to your own life," Helen said. She shook out the drying towel, reached for the second glass. It slipped from her fingers, bounced on the linoleum, and rolled. Lenore moved to pick it up, but Helen touched her arm.

"Don't give your life to him like Mom did."

Long after Helen left, Lenore turned off the stereo, watching the record slow to a stop.

Don't leave me, Lenore. Her father slurred his words. She covered him with a blanket, removed his shoes. *You'll take care of me, won't you?* And he had reached out, grasped her wrist, and held on tightly.

SHE CARRIES THE PAGES back into the study, arranges them in the paper box on Barrett's desk. *Alone again.* For the first time, her solitude doesn't signify someone else's choice. She takes a last look around Barrett's study, then slowly—purposefully—closes the door.

Twenty

THE VAN SHUDDERS and breaks down about four hours from home. Cursing, Otto stands on the side of the highway, waiting for the tow truck to arrive. Dark clouds cluster together in the open expanse of sky. Out here it's drier and windier than in the city. Tires crunch against the gravel, and he turns to see a police car slowing to a halt. One officer emerges, hitches up his pants, and ambles towards him.

"Trouble?"

Otto forces a smile, shakes his head.

"Car broke down," he says. "I'm just waiting for the tow truck." The officer nods. Otto's neck and shoulders tense, and perhaps he stands defensively, or looks guilty, because the officer takes out a notebook.

"What's your name, sir?"

"My name?"

Otto can't remember. Everything is blank, his mouth dry. The officer frowns.

"Yes. You have a name. What is it?"

Otto shakes his head, panic setting in. The memories are too fresh and crowd his mind until nothing else exists. For twenty-eight years, he has been someone else, and now he can't remember who that person is.

"Licence and registration, please."

Of course. His hand is slick with perspiration. He opens the door of the van, finds his wallet.

"My name is Ray Parker," Otto says. The officer studies the cards, takes them back to his cruiser without a word, leaving Otto by the side of the road. He tries to relax. The tow truck arrives, and the driver flicks his headlights on and off once. The officer gets back out of his car, holds up a hand to the tow truck. He approaches Otto, leans down, and passes back the cards.

"You have a nice day," he says.

"Thank you, Officer. Same to you."

He waits until the cruiser pulls out and passes before lowering his head to touch his steering wheel.

LENORE MET HIM at a restaurant before he left the city. He arrived first in a new shirt and pair of slacks from Sears, requested a table facing the large window so that he could prepare himself. He saw her hesitate in front of the restaurant, her body still among a moving, heaving crowd of busy shoppers and pedestrians, her hand at her throat in a gesture of uncertainty he well remembered. The rain had finally stopped, water pooling in dips and crevices along the sidewalks. She saw him then through the window, and her face cleared of expression. The hand at her throat wafted down in a gentle wave before resting, briefly, on the glass.

He rose as she came towards his table, wanting to brush her cheek with his but holding back.

"Thank you for meeting with me."

"I'm not eating," Lenore said. "I'm not staying."

"You're angry."

She made a sound—a snort, a puff of air through her lips.

"I'm just tired," she said. "What do you want, Otto?"

He wasn't sure. When the waiter brought their drinks, he attempted a smile, lifted his glass. "To old times," he said. Lenore didn't move. His arm sank.

"You've had a good life, despite me."

She sighed. "I don't want to do this."

"You've had a good life," he persisted. "Better than you would have had if I'd stayed."

"You're a coward." Her quiet voice held a sharp edge. "You left me with no choice. Your children grew up without a father. You think I preferred it that way?"

"I think you preferred Lloyd Barrett."

"Jesus, Otto." They both looked away. Lenore picked up the menu, threw it back on the table. "I never said a word against you all these years. Don't put the blame on my shoulders. You left gaps in their lives that couldn't be filled. I tried my best, but Barrett was no substitute, and that wasn't his fault or mine."

Otto took a breath, exhaled, willing his hands to steady. "Let's start again," he said.

"Do you have any idea what happens to a family when someone just disappears like that?"

"As a matter of fact, I do," he said.

"Yes, you do," she said slowly. "And now you come back as if everything can be forgiven."

"I didn't expect forgiveness," he said. "I might have hoped. Isn't it better that I tried?"

"I just don't understand what you expect."

"I don't expect *anything*." He slammed his hand flat onto the tabletop. Her wine rose up to the edge of her glass and threatened to spill on the white tablecloth. And now he *did* know why he had asked her to meet with him one last time: he wanted her to understand.

"You think I don't know what I did to my kids, to you? That I don't think about it all the time?" He leaned forward, his voice lowering. "It would have been easier for me to stay away forever, to keep pretending to be someone else. But I wanted to give the kids something, let them know that what I did had nothing to do with them. That leaving them was my biggest regret."

"And what's your smallest regret? Me?" She pulled at her throat, leaving mottled skin, pink and pale.

"I'll never regret you," he said. He tried to take her hand then, but she refused. "I know I messed things up. But, Lenore, it's not like you were completely innocent. You were having an affair, remember."

"I remember."

"It was just one more thing on top of all the other things." Otto raised his glass to drink, his lips clamping down. He forced himself to swallow, the glass nearly sliding from his fingers before he settled it back onto the table. "I'm sorry if I made you feel unloved," he said. He looked away in the silence that followed.

"I knew you loved me," Lenore said finally. "But sometimes that's not enough, the knowing."

"I'm sorry."

Lenore leaned forward, elbows on the table. Around her wrist, the gold bracelet that seemed familiar, her fingers slender, delicate as she grasped the stem of her wineglass.

"Me too," she said.

Restaurant sounds rose in detail: the clinking of cutlery against plates, the low murmurs of voices. Someone's cellphone rang, and patrons a few tables over burst into laughter.

"My mother was terrified that I'd be just like my father. I've always blamed her for what happened, but it's *me*. She could never win with me, and neither could you. I didn't know who I was or what I wanted, and I could never figure it out." He crossed his legs, knocking his knee against the underside of the table in the process. He steadied his glass.

"You see?" He tried to smile. "No matter what I do, something goes wrong. You spend enough time thinking you're a failure, and you start to believe it. When you found me in the basement—that wasn't supposed to happen. I was staying at a hotel. I went to a bar near the house, and at the end of the night, I realized I'd left my wallet at your place. Two waiters from the restaurant drove me home." And then, too drunk to contemplate flagging a taxi, he had unrolled the sleeping bag once more.

"I've had a lot of time to think about things," he said. "And you know what? I think my mother tried her best with what she had. And she died because of me. I'll never forgive myself for that."

"It must have been hard for her after your father died."

"And for me."

"Yes." Lenore studied him. "Your mother was very sick, did you know that?"

"No."

"They did an autopsy. She had advanced breast cancer. It had spread to her lymph nodes and her bones."

"My God." Maybe he hadn't killed her at all; maybe she was dead already. How immense the relief to know he wasn't a murderer, even inadvertently. But Lenore shook her head.

"She died of smoke inhalation," she said. "But, Otto, she died a better death than she would have." Grateful for the kindness in her voice, he reached across the table and placed his hand close to hers, wanting to feel her touch. She didn't move.

"When I went out west, I had no illusions," he said. "I knew I would fail at everything I tried. But it's funny. I did well. I liked my job. I reinvented myself." Lenore watched him carefully. "Maybe it was the lack of expectations."

"Or your freedom," Lenore said. "I never placed too many expectations on you."

"You didn't have to. It was all there in that house, the history."

She drank the last of her wine, began searching in her purse for her wallet.

"No, please," Otto said. "I'll take care of it."

Lenore inclined her head, a slight nod. "Thank you." Still she sat, her purse balanced on her lap, a light cardigan slung across her shoulders. "I'm glad you came out here."

"You are?"

"Closure," she said.

IN HIS APARTMENT, Otto sits on his couch in the silent room with a college recreation guide open in front of him and wonders what he could do. He needs a hobby to fill the blank spaces of his days, the waiting hours between work and sleep that have begun to torment him. He lost his job at Belco, of course, his boss nearly apoplectic with rage when Otto finally called to tell him that Ray Parker was dead. He now works for the city picking up trash on the streets and in the parks. It doesn't sound very noble, but it's fitting, he thinks, and somewhat satisfying.

After flipping through the pages, he pushes the guide away and writes letters to Ruby and Gavin instead, gripping the pen with a closed fist, just as he used to when he was a child. Letters they will no doubt throw in the garbage without reading, but the act of putting pen to paper comforts him, no matter how much he still struggles. He writes to them not as children, but as the adults they have become in his absence.

AT FOURTEEN OR FIFTEEN, he told her he wouldn't go to church with her anymore. The pastor with his dome-like head, his sharp chin and small eyes, the smell of the church, of bodies too close together, the way his mother sang with open mouth, her inward breaths too loud, gasping as if in rapture—he hated it all and told her so. He didn't think he believed in God, in any case. None of them had, before his father died, and now his mother read the Bible on Sundays and sometimes closed her eyes in prayer before dinner.

He braced himself for her astonished rage, but she seemed unsurprised. Perhaps she was swayed by his arguments, his earnestness, or perhaps she just didn't care anymore. It seemed to him that she looked at him differently now, as if he somehow deserved her respect.

By the time he was sixteen, she never asked him about school anymore or pressed him to read her list of library books, but she watched him cautiously, almost fearfully. His resentment—that quiet, simmering sensation that gnawed in the pit of his stomach—grew into something like anger. At twenty, he watched a plumber solder pipes and learned to install cabinets and put up wood panelling. Then he moved into his new basement apartment in the bowels of the house. He came up for dinner promptly at six-thirty, and kept his dirty laundry in a basket beside the washing machine, unsorted, so that she had no reason to come into his space looking for it. Since he had never had to think about his life or what to do with it, he worked in short stints at a variety of jobs, and came away with the impression that all work was unrewarding.

And that was her crime, then: she let him be. Because his mother was right about him, in the end. For all these years, he blamed her for what he did. Later, surrounded by his family in their cramped apartment, a few years at the insurance company under his belt, he held everything against her. He thought he had escaped. When he moved his family back into her house, he asked for her forgiveness, but he never gave his, and he planted his rage inside Lenore's head.

But this—*this* was reality: he sat across from her on the plastic-covered sofa in the sticky heat of late afternoon, the sweat trickling down the back of his neck, and took in the smell of those rooms, the darkness, and he saw that he would never leave. He would fold.

ONE AFTERNOON, he takes out his toolbox. The heavy frame lies on his bed, the fingerpainted paper back in place against the glass. *What a wonderful way to remember your grandchildren!* the woman in the framing store had exclaimed. *My children*, he should have said. Now he carries the frame into the living room, rummages around for a nail, a hammer. Finally, he has done the right thing. He no longer wakes in the night with a sinking, sucking sensation in his chest. The emptiness has been replaced: in the absence of regret, a sort of peace. He centres the picture above the sofa and stands back to admire his handiwork. One day they will come to visit, they will see the picture, and understand. He is sure of it.

Twenty-One

ELSA SMELLED SMOKE. She tried to turn over in bed, the covers caught and twisted around her waist. The skin stretched under her left arm, an agony of knife against flesh. Pain in her back, spreading between her shoulder blades, burrowing deep. She had left it too long and was past the point of a cure, she knew with certainty. Also known: if she looked in the mirror now, if she stood naked before herself, she would see nothing out of the ordinary. How could the body hide such destruction? But there, along the curve of her breast, the tumour swelled.

Oh, Elsa, the end is near.

She wasn't foolish enough to believe it a coincidence, simply an unfortunate turn of events. She was meant to die, and who was she to mess with God's design?

The smell of smoke drifted upward, the smallest trace. Perhaps she had left the stove on after her tea. It was difficult to remember. She had missed the last three days of work, slept instead, eating little, barely emerging from the fog of sleep to recognize her room, the walls painted blue as she requested. *Haven't you always wanted a room up here?* Otto asked. To get her away from the children, from his wife, so that she wouldn't taint them all. They crept around the house like criminals, using the washroom on the sly. She could smell them in her living room, saw their fingerprints in the dust on the piano, the pictures moved.

Let me teach your girl piano. Will you at least let me do that?

That small bowed head, slender neck, and her faltering fingers on the keys reminded her of Otto at that age. *Concentrate!* The chain must be broken. When the girl crumpled into tears, sobbing, Elsa fled the living room, climbed heavily up to her room, and cried herself, alone on the edge of her bed.

She pushed back the covers, swung her legs out of bed with effort. She pulled on a bathrobe over her loose dress. She bought them bigger now, or maybe her body was shrinking. She couldn't bear the touch of fabric against her chest, her arm, but she was always cold, even in the heat of the summer.

The stairs leading to her room were narrow and steep. She grasped the railing, each step draining, painful. On the second floor, she stopped and peered over the landing, saw the smoke curling up the stairwell. She put her arm over her mouth and nose, breathing through her sleeve.

I love you, she said that day on the telephone, but he had already hung up. She stood clutching the receiver for a moment, then raised it as high as she could above her head, and sent it crashing down on the table, again and again, before she crumpled.

THE SUNLIGHT POURED THROUGH the open window above his desk. He had cleared a space framed by books, pens and pencils, a ruler. She stood behind him for minutes before he noticed her presence. He glanced over his shoulder, fearful but somehow defiant, a house of cards on the desk in front of him.

"What are you doing?" He said nothing, brought his hands to his lap and bowed his head. Elsa fought the urge to crush the cards, sweep them to the floor, and instead sat on his bed. Outside, she could hear the sounds of children laughing.

"I only want the best for you," she said. "Do you understand that?" He nodded but kept his gaze averted. She rose and walked towards the desk, hating the way he shrank from her approach. She placed her hand on his shoulder.

"Do you?" He looked up, his face so like his father's, and nodded again.

"Why aren't you studying?"

"I'm not any good at it."

"You could be, if you tried harder. Remember what the doctor said?" His small face creased.

"I do try," he said. He looked so miserable, hunched over and small.

"You want to play outside instead?"

His face brightened. He nodded again, this time eagerly.

"Go, then. Before I change my mind." He jumped up, his chair scraping against the hardwood, and kissed her neck.

"Thank you, Mama!"

She watched him go with a smile. *The doctor was wrong.*

Two days later, she woke to Thomas in bed, eyes half open, his body rigid and cold, and a great fear swept over her. *It's in the genes.*

WHEN OTTO WAS FIFTEEN, she found him slumped over his desk, an elaborate tower of cards in front of him, sets of squares. Beside him, a nearly empty bottle of sleeping pills, hers, the ones the doctor prescribed after Thomas' death. The pills left her dreamless, her limbs weighted. She hid them at the back of the medicine cabinet. She preferred to face her grief, the sharp blade of it in the middle of the night while she slept alone.

Otto could not tell her how many he had taken. His eyes were half closed, slits of blue, his speech mumbled and slippery, the words sliding into each other, unrecognizable.

Don't you do this to me!
He fell forward, heavy.
In the hospital, she sat by his bed among all the whiteness. When he woke, she wept, her body caved inward, clutching at the sheets, his still legs and arms.
"I just wanted to know how he felt before he died," Otto said. He turned to face her, eyes blank.

ELSA LAY ON THE SECOND-FLOOR LANDING, frozen by inertia. She was aware all too well that suicide affected the living more than the dead, but who would mourn her death? She was too tired. Taking your own life was a sin, but she knew who waited for her in hell. And then a movement below her: Otto running, his back to her, out the front door, white paper spread out like a fan behind him.

She rose unsteadily. The air would be clearer in her room, and she would have more time. She climbed the stairs one by one. Her chest ached, the pain in her back insistent. From her bedside table she took her Bible, her favourite photograph of Thomas holding Otto as a baby. Thomas looked unsure but pleased, both eyes nearly straight behind his glasses as he smiled for the camera. Elsa eased herself onto the bed, the Bible on her right side, the picture propped on her chest. She wished she could rewind the film, step backwards through time, and make it all right. She would like to iron out the wrinkles: that first meeting with the doctor, the schedules, those boys at the window. Otto through high school, the way his shoulders sank lower and lower, the fearful way he clutched his books to his chest, like a girl. She had not known what to say, how to ask, but she would be better the second time around.

Tell me, she would say, and he would, the words pouring out in relief.

OTTO AT AGE ONE, naked but for a diaper, toddled across the floor with lurching, drunken steps. He sat and picked up a small cardboard box, a folded piece of paper in his other hand. Elsa hugged her knees to her chest. In the hospital after he was born, she began to bleed. *We almost lost you*, Thomas said, stroking her cheek. This baby would be the first and last, the only.

Otto fitted the small rectangle through the flaps of the box and removed his hand, looking surprised to find the paper still clutched in his fingers.

"You have to let go," Elsa told him. She guided his hand back into the box, unfurled his fingers, and shook the paper free.

I'm sorry, Thomas.

Don't.

The nurse brought the baby, swaddled and layered, and placed him in Elsa's arms. She held him on her chest, undone by his soft, animal snuffling, his mouth opening and closing against her neck. Thomas sat on the bed and leaned into her, his hand over hers on Otto's back.

He's perfect, he whispered.

Otto looked up, his bottom lip pushed out in a concentrated pout, then down at the box again, turning it over in his hands as if to find a better angle, a more promising entry. For maybe twenty minutes he sat, sunlight catching on the tips of his eyelashes. Elsa watched, engrossed by the dimples in his cheeks, the arch of a neck that still seemed too thin for his heavy head. And then, triumph: his hand emerged empty. He shook the box until the paper fell out and looked up at Elsa with momentous baby pride.

"Well done," she said. "You did it!"

She gathered him up, drowning in soft, pliant skin, and kissed him in the crook of his arm, pressed his fingertips to her lips. "There's no stopping you now," she said. He touched her face and smiled.

Acknowledgments

Enormous thanks to the many people who offered encouragement and advice during the writing of this book: my wonderful agent, Helen Heller, who always says the right thing and works tirelessly on my behalf; my editor, Laura Shin, for making the editing process so painless; Alison Reid and Jonathan Webb for fixing my mistakes; and everyone else at Penguin Canada for wrapping my pages in such a beautiful package. I was lucky to have a group of intelligent, perceptive readers for an early draft of *Absent*. Thanks to Caleigh Askew Clubine, Arwen Sheldon Hunter, Trudi Hickson O'Malley, and Samantha Smeaton for their honesty and wit.

I am grateful to the experts: Dr. Ronald Zuker at the Hospital for Sick Children in Toronto, who answered my questions about craniofacial abnormalities and made me aware of the real Canadian pioneer in craniofacial reconstruction, Dr. Ian Munro; Dr. Antoine Abugaber at Bayer Inc. and Dr. Mark Freedman at the University of Ottawa for help with medical details; and to Paula Taillefer for her account of living with multiple sclerosis. Thanks also to Lisa Burgis for taking the time to look up old cases for me, and Kristin Carlson, for the question about cards.

Portions of this book were written with the financial support of the Ontario Arts Council, for which I am indebted.

Finally, acknowledgment must be made to the members of my secret society for their continued support, suggestions, and gossip. You know who you are, and I'll never tell.